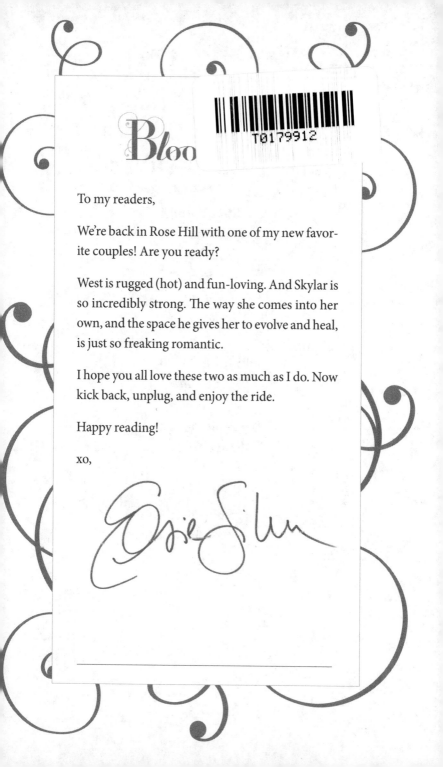

Bloo

To my readers,

We're back in Rose Hill with one of my new favorite couples! Are you ready?

West is rugged (hot) and fun-loving. And Skylar is so incredibly strong. The way she comes into her own, and the space he gives her to evolve and heal, is just so freaking romantic.

I hope you all love these two as much as I do. Now kick back, unplug, and enjoy the ride.

Happy reading!

xo,

ALSO BY ELSIE SILVER

Chestnut Springs
Flawless
Heartless
Powerless
Reckless
Hopeless

Gold Rush Ranch
Off to the Races
A Photo Finish
The Front Runner
A False Start

Rose Hill
Wild Love
Wild Eyes

WILD EYES

ELSIE SILVER

Bloom *books*

Published by Bloom Books, an imprint of Sourcebooks
P.O. Box 4410, Naperville, Illinois 60567–4410
(630) 961-3900
sourcebooks.com

Cataloging-in-Publication data is on file with the Library of Congress.

Printed and bound in Canada.
MBP 10 9 8 7 6 5 4 3 2

For all the ones who have felt crippled by the opinions of others. I hope you learn to love what you're doing so completely that all those critical voices cease to matter. And until then, remember that thriving is winning. Go forth and thrive.

THE ELSIE SILVER UNIVERSE

BRITISH COLUMBIA

ALBERTA

SASKATCHEWAN

Vancouver Island

Ruby Creek

Emerald Lake

Blisswater Springs

Rose Hill

Chestnut Springs

Edmonton

Calgary

READER NOTE

This book contains references to childhood psychological abuse and trauma. Substance abuse and death by overdose are mentioned on the page. It is my hope that I've handled these subjects with the care and attention that they deserve.

CHAPTER 1

West

THE SUN IS SHINING, THE LAKE IS SPARKLING, AND THERE'S another fucking tourist on the side of the road trying to get a selfie with a bear.

Not just any bear either. A *grizzly*.

"You have to be kidding me," I mutter as I press gently on the brakes of my pickup truck and shake my head. I don't have a clear shot of the woman, but I see skin-tight jeans, a crop top, and a waterfall of loose bronze waves spilling down her back in shiny ripples.

While the bear forages in the ditch behind her, she lifts one hand, gesturing to it wildly as she talks at the phone held up in front of her.

I pull over in front of her Tesla. Because of course she drives a Tesla. And she has to be a good thirty feet away from it, like she's slowly edged herself closer to the animal.

When I finally roll to a stop, I watch in pure,

dumbfounded shock for a moment. During the summer months in Rose Hill, you see this city-folk stupidity, and it never fails to blow my mind. It's like people go from having "see a bear" on their bucket list to "get killed by a bear" on their bucket list.

I press the button to lower my window because I don't want to startle the animal, and I also don't particularly want to get out of my truck. I enjoy living, and my days of testing those limits are—mostly—behind me.

So using the calmest voice I can muster, I say, "Ma'am."

But she continues talking to the camera, clearly recording herself without a care in the world. "It was just a casual drive down a scenic backroad when—bam!—the most beautiful bear saunters down into this ditch behind me."

"Ma'am!" I lean against my door and wave my arm to catch her eye. Maybe my unwelcome voice in her video will snap her out of it.

And it does. She spins on me with furrowed brows, fiery eyes, and a face I'd know anywhere.

A face most of the world would know anywhere.

Yes, country music superstar Skylar Stone is mean-mugging me for interrupting her video. For a moment, I'm starstruck. At a loss for words. I suspect I know what brings her to town, but I don't bother with small talk at a time like this. I don't want to be known as the guy who stood by while a hungry grizzly devoured a beloved starlet.

"What?" she asks, arms held wide, like she's not standing with her back to an unpredictable apex predator. "I'm going to have to rerecord this for my socials now."

"That's a goddamn grizzly bear. You need to get back in your car," I hiss, hiking a thumb over my shoulder toward her car.

She shakes her head and continues glaring. "You know what I'm fucking sick of?"

"Is it living?" I bite out as instinct takes over and I step out of my truck. As much as I'd like to slam the door, I leave it open to avoid making more noise. "Because that's what it looks like right now."

She scoffs. "No. But I am fucking sick of people telling me what to do."

Her piercing gaze rakes down my faded black jeans, the ones caught on the ridge of my scuffed charcoal Blundstones, before perusing back up to my plain white T-shirt. Her eyes hover over the hole near the neckline and a small wrinkle crops up on her dainty nose, as though she's found proof that I'm not worthy of giving her advice.

I approach with caution, craning my neck to glance down the slope, where the telltale brown grizzly hump peeks out above the shrubs. I can hear its deep, satisfied grunts as it forages, likely ripping berries off a bush as an appetizer before it comes up and tears the limbs off our bodies for the main course.

"I relate. I really do. But this may not be the hill to die on right now. Literally and figuratively. If we survive this, I will drive you to a zoo and film your social media content for you. And I hate social media, but I don't break promises."

She follows my gaze and then lifts her chin to face me head-on. Plush, heart-shaped lips purse tightly and hazel eyes narrow at me like missiles ready to launch. She hides her phone by crossing her tan arms.

Pure sass.

She reminds me of my six-year-old daughter, Emmy. Something that's only emphasized when she stomps one foot. The difference is, I'd have picked Emmy up like a football under one arm and gotten the hell outta here a solid sixty seconds ago.

"It's eating. It doesn't even know I'm here. And I've never seen a bear in person." She whines the last part, like I'm the bad guy ruining all her fun.

My jaw drops as I look this woman over. She's got diamond studs the size of ripe blueberries in her ears. They're so big that if she were anyone else, I'd think they were fake. "Listen, I get it. There aren't bears in the city. It's an experience. But that"—I point at the bear—"is not Winnie the Pooh."

Her expression is strained as she glances longingly back at the ditch. It's as though she sees my logic but so badly wishes she didn't.

I keep going because it seems like the children's fiction reference really hit home. "Eeyore isn't trapped in a well. Piglet isn't off finding him a pot of honey. Just…pretend I'm Owl, and I'm giving you really wise advice right now."

"But…there are babies." She all but coos the word *babies*, saying it with extra emphasis, like it should make this entire thing endearing. Like it makes her irrational behavior more logical somehow.

But anyone who knows about bears knows that things

just got so much worse. I edge closer to the ditch, as though needing to see them with my own eyes to confirm just how bad this situation is. I crane my neck, and sure enough... there they are. Two.

"Please," I say, trying a less forceful approach while also filling my voice with as much pleading as I can muster. With one arm held out, I fold my fingers over my palm repeatedly, gesturing her forward like I might a skittish horse. As a horse trainer, I've got lots of experience with those. All bluster— until they're not.

She must pick up on the urgent tone in my voice because her shoulders fall, and she swallows heavily as her eyes dart back and forth between mine, seeming to weigh whether I'm trustworthy.

Finally, I get a nod and a tentative step away from the deep ditch. A heavy, relieved breath rushes from my lungs as she moves toward me.

But that relief is short-lived because, as soon as she moves away, the bear follows her as though attached to an invisible leash.

I can't blame it.

She's alluring. There's something about her that makes it hard to peel my eyes away. You can see it onscreen. Hear it on the radio. And it's even more pronounced in person.

"Okay, doll."

"Don't *doll* me—"

"You need to shut up," I blurt out, keeping my voice as even as possible. My gaze moves beyond her to the massive bear emerging from the slope, four-inch-long nails clacking as it takes its first steps onto the asphalt. The sound freezes Skylar in her tracks. "Walk toward me slowly. Do not run. Do not look behind you. Stay calm."

She blinks hard and fast. I can see she wants to tell me to go fuck myself, but she has some survival instinct underneath all that attitude because she follows my instructions.

The bear lets out a loud huff, and Skylar stutter-steps, wide eyes latching onto mine for dear life. I nod and gesture with my hand again. As though I can do a single fucking thing for her right now other than get her close enough to dive through the open door of my truck.

She continues walking, but her steps increase ever so slightly in speed. Her breathing turns ragged. I start to edge back toward my truck, hoping she'll follow.

"Good girl. You're doing so well." Any other time, I'd laugh at myself for talking to this woman like a horse. But in this moment, my skin hums with tension and my muscles coil as though ready to spring into action.

She nods, then peeks over her shoulder and makes a small squealing noise as if she's just realized the massive size of the bear following her.

But that noise was not the right one to make. Because the grizzly notices it and is suddenly more interested than it was. The bear stops and rears up onto its hind legs.

The sound it makes now is more of a bark, followed by a sniff and an interested head tilt.

A show of curiosity, not aggression.

Not yet anyway.

"Oh god, oh god, oh god," she whispers, her voice coming up choked and tearful.

With one hand outstretched, I summon all the calm within me. "Whatever you do, don't r—"

Before I can say the word *run*, she fucking sprints toward me. And against what would be most people's better judgment, I leap into action without thinking.

I head straight toward her.

And the bear.

The bear that is now pawing at the road like it's ready to charge. It takes a few powerful leaps forward before drawing back.

Now in defensive mode, I do the only thing I can think of. The instant I reach Skylar, my fingers wrap around her bicep, and I curl one arm around the back of her head before tossing us to the ground. My tall body covers her smaller one like a shield.

She squirms against me. "What are you—"

I cut her off by clamping a palm over her mouth, propping myself up on my opposite arm, and shaking my head. "Stop. Please stop. I need you to be quiet and still. And the bear will probably go away."

She nods subtly. Enough so that I can remove my hand and cage the entire top of her head in with my forearms.

Her terrified golden eyes search mine again and I can smell something sweet on her breath as she pants nervously into the air between us. Tangerine and sugar.

"Can we make it to your truck?"

I can barely hear her over the sound of my heart pounding

9

in my ears. "We're not close enough and I don't like our odds of outrunning a grizzly."

"Okay." She licks her lips nervously and I watch a stray tear leak out of one eye. It rolls down over her temple before trailing toward her ear. I trace the wet path with my gaze before meeting hers and giving her my full attention, conveying an outward sense of calm that doesn't necessarily match the way I'm feeling inside.

More tears leak out as we stare at each other.

"I'm sorry." Her choked sob hits me hard in the chest.

I can hear the bear huffing as it draws within mere feet of us. I swear the ground trembles beneath the weight of its steps. Lighter footsteps thump from lower down in the ditch. And I assume those are the cubs.

My thumb rubs soft, slow circles over the crown of her head. "It's okay. You're okay. We're just gonna be quiet together and then everything is going to be okay." I whisper the words to her, but I say them for myself.

She blinks in recognition, and I blink back. Then I distract myself by counting the swirling hues of her irises. Brown, gold, green, and a delicate gray woven between them. Minimum four colors.

And even covered in a sheen of tears, they glow.

I'm not sure I've ever gotten this lost in a perfect stranger's eyes.

"Tell me it's going to be okay again." The words are a breath, weaving into the hush of her long exhale. Even this close, I barely hear them.

The tips of our noses brush as my face slants down over

hers. My lips move silently against the skin on her cheek as I mouth the words, *It's going to be okay.*

I've done a lot of wild shit in my day. Done a few things that I'm surprised to have survived, if I'm being honest. But in those moments, I'd always been alone. There's something about lying this damn close to another person, knowing she could be the last thing I see, that makes everything around us stand still.

Shit, maybe I'm just getting old and sentimental.

Then I feel the hot, damp breath of the grizzly as it sniffs the back of my neck. An eerie sense of calm settles over me, even though it shouldn't. I'm calmer than I have any right to be. It's as though my body knows that giving into my own rising anxiety won't help.

Because while I may have seen my fair share of bears growing up in Rose Hill, I have yet to feel one breathing down my neck. To be frank, it's an experience I could have done without.

But there's no time for me to wallow in my anxiety. I have to remain composed for Skylar. So I keep my eyes locked on hers, willing her to stay still and in the moment with me even though she's clearly so far out of her element that she's on another planet.

Her lips part, and her breaths come fast and frantic. She clamps her eyes shut. I can smell the bear, so I'm sure she can too.

All sweat and musk and old gym shoes. It's overpowering. It's a combination I'll never forget.

The sun beats down on my back, and the heat of the

bear's enormous body beside me makes the moment down-right stifling. I rest my forehead against hers and try to regulate her breathing with my own.

Three seconds in.

Three seconds out.

Soon, the heat feels more bearable. The heart-pounding clatter of nails aren't as loud. The stench, less overpowering. The rustling from the ditch dissipates, and I assume the cubs have followed mom away too.

Skylar squirms a little and peeks up at me from beneath her thick lashes. "Did you see the babies? They're so cute."

I roll my forehead against hers as I stifle a laugh, wondering how I constantly end up in the orbit of women who are this atrocious at following simple instructions—even when their lives depend on it. "Let's stay quiet" is all I respond with.

I'm not sure how long we lie on the ground breathing in and out together. Five minutes? Ten minutes? Long enough that her knuckles must be cramping from clutching at my shirt. Her entire body is still trembling uncontrollably, so I smooth my hand over her hair to ease her shaking.

Logically, I know the bear has moved on, but I still feel like I could glance up and come face-to-face with it.

So I stay in place, stroking this woman's head and trying to get my bearings before I make a move to stand up.

To lighten the moment, I blurt out the first thing that comes to mind. "I saw the results of a survey recently that said six percent of Americans think they could beat a grizzly bear in hand-to-hand combat."

"What?" The question is breathless and hushed, but the expression on her face is pure disbelief.

"I know. Can you believe that?"

She stares at me like she's wondering if I'm for real right now. "Hand-to-hand combat?"

I nod down at her before peeking up over the top of her head.

No bear.

I push up onto my knees and twist to look back over my shoulder.

No bear.

I flop back onto my haunches and run my palms over my close-cut hair as I take in a full three-sixty view of our spot on the backroad.

No bear.

Just bluebird skies and warm yellow sunshine.

It's with a ragged sigh that I finally glance back down… to see I'm straddling Skylar Stone.

My eyes catch on the graceful line of her collarbone, the swell of her breasts pressed high over the neckline of her shirt. I close my eyes and shake my head, but no—she's still there. Under me.

With one hand, she wipes at her eyes but makes no move to escape me. She lies flopped on the road looking beautiful, and stunned, and completely exhausted. Her teeth strum at her bottom lip as though she's thinking hard. And she doesn't let go of my shirt. Her arm is straight, and her knuckles are still white as she grips the cotton.

Finally, a giddy laugh shakes her shoulders. "When they say six percent, though…it's probably more."

I sigh, and then I laugh with her. "Yeah, you gotta rule out children and the elderly."

Her pointer finger taps at my thigh. "And women."

"What?"

She rolls her eyes at me now. "Only a man would think he can fight a grizzly bear with his bare hands."

"Rich coming from the woman who just tried to take her photo with one."

"It was a video!"

I push to stand on wobbly legs and reach a hand down to pull her up. With a grin, I say, "Right. For your socials. That makes it *so* much better."

Her eyes slice to my hand, but all traces of earlier humor have been erased. Tensions are already running high, and now she's annoyed.

"Don't judge me. You don't even know what I was doing."

"Okay, what were you doing?"

Her chin lifts. "Creating relatable content."

"To be decided. I'll have to search up the percentage of Americans who have been charged by a grizzly in their lifetime."

She pauses for a beat, as though shocked by my off-handed joke, then she grits out, "You don't know me well enough to mock me." A frustrated growl rumbles in her throat as she claps her palm against mine aggressively.

With one firm tug, I haul her up. She's lighter than I expected, though, and I pull too hard, which throws her off balance.

Her free hand lands on my chest to steady herself, the

tips of her fingers awfully close to that hole in my shirt. She stares for a beat and pulls away abruptly, like she's been burned.

I may not know her, but I know her face has been splashed all over the headlines lately for freezing up in front of the camera.

Today, though? Her words seem to flow just fine.

"It was all going great until you showed up acting like fucking Crocodile Dundee crossed with...with..." She waves a hand over me as she struggles to find the right insult. "With Superman or something."

I lift a hand and scrub it over my chin. "It's the strong jawline, isn't it?"

"No, it's the obnoxious hero complex."

I snort and cross my arms, regarding her with amusement. I always perceived her as this sweet southern-belle type. All airy laughter and good gollys rather than curse words and cutting one-liners.

I wasn't looking close enough. Because she is none of those things.

"And the"—she waves a hand over my body—"the know-it-all smugness."

Now I'm full-on grinning. "We both know I saved your ass. Just say thank you."

She shakes her head as she crouches to pick up her phone. "I would have. But now you're demanding it of me, and that makes it feel forced and insincere. And I'm so sick of everyone treating me like I owe them something." She brushes at her jeans, agitation lining every movement as she tries and fails to get all the gravel and dust off her body while muttering, "Skylar, do this. Skylar, do that. Skylar, smile and wave. Skylar, say thank you."

With a tired sigh, she stops and looks up. "You know what? I'm sorry. I'm having a bad month. You don't deserve this shit. I've put you through enough today. Thank you for being willing to die for me. That's new and unexpected and something I'll have to process with my therapist at a later date."

I quirk a brow at her confession. She's still trembling, so I try to draw the conversation out. Give her a second to catch her breath. "A bad month?"

A forced smile touches her lips, but then it falters as she kicks at a stone near her sandal-clad foot. "Actually, more like a bad year."

"I've had those before," I reply, watching her carefully. I can't help but wonder what's got a woman who seems so strong acting like she can't meet my eyes.

She redirects the conversation with phoney brightness. "Right, so anyway, I need to find Wild Rose Records. It's a little boutique recording studio. Brand-new. Maybe you know the owner? Ford Grant? I took a scenic route and got lost. These roads aren't even marked, and there's no reception. And I thought it would make me feel alive to just like… hit the open road. Ya know?"

I scoff good-naturedly as I turn to walk back toward my truck. When I grip the still-open door, I glance over my shoulder at her. She looks beautiful, and confused, and totally forlorn.

And I'm not the least put off by her outburst. In fact, I like that she came back from that terrifying moment all feisty.

"Nothing quite like a near-death experience to make us feel alive, am I right?" I haul myself up into the truck. "Follow me, and I'll take you to Ford Grant."

Skylar walks my way with surprise painted on her face. "You know him?"

I turn the key in the ignition right as she approaches my open window. "You could say that."

Her brows knit together and she seems nervous as she tucks her hair behind her ears. For the first time today, she looks beaten down.

"I'm sorry. I'm just overwhelmed by…by everything. That was fucking terrifying, and I don't know how to thank you. I don't think anyone has ever been willing to lay their life on the line for me."

She says it so offhandedly. It catches me off guard.

What a damn shame.

The thought pops up in my head instantly. What a shame to be an adult and not have felt that kind of loyalty. To be as beloved as Skylar Stone is and still not feel it.

When she peeks up at me from beneath her thick lashes, I offer her a reassuring wink. "You can thank me by not apologizing anymore. Then you can get in your car and follow me."

She nods, teeth digging into that distractingly full bottom lip once again. "I don't even know your name."

"Weston Belmont. Rose Hill's very own

Super-Crocodile-Dundee-Man at your service," I reply with a dramatic salute.

She rolls her eyes, and a ghost of a smile touches her lips. I tap my hand on the outside of my truck as I roll forward.

I'm happy to have saved her life, but I've still got four horses to work today, a farm with chores that never seem to end, and two little kids who need their dad. I have to get going.

No matter how tempting it is to stick around and chat.

"Wait! Don't you want to know my name?" she calls as I pull away slowly, giving her time to hop in her Tesla and trail behind. I don't respond because I know who she is. I've been a closet Skylar Stone fan for years.

But I don't want to make her uncomfortable, so I don't say that. Plus, there will be plenty of opportunities for conversation.

Because if she's heading to Wild Rose Records…we're about to be neighbors.

CHAPTER 2

Skylar

I HAVE A THING FOR HANDS. I WON'T EVEN DENY IT.

Men's hands, specifically. The way the tendons on top flex and ripple when they strum at a guitar. The way they use up the entire length of a microphone handle. The way they can be warm and gentle on my skin.

I've dated famous people. Artists and musicians. Handsome men, influential men. And yet, I've never found myself as obsessed with a man's hands as I am with the ones wrapped around the steering wheel of the truck ahead of me.

The steel grip on my bicep as he threw us to the ground.

The scratch of his callouses against my skin as he told me it would all be okay.

The tattoos on his knuckles that I stared at every time he scrubbed his beard.

I can hear my dad in my head, clear as day, warning me away from a man like Weston. He'd be overly concerned about the person I'm dating tarnishing my pristine *America's sweetheart* reputation.

Respectable men don't get tattoos a shirt can't hide.

But what about heroic ones? Ones with dusty blond hair and muscles that make their shirt look just a little too tight through the shoulders.

Weston Belmont saved me from a grizzly bear. Saved me from myself, really. From my own naiveté.

A smarter girl would be captivated by his bravery, or his deep voice, or his quippy one-liners.

Not me. I'm following him down a backcountry road in the middle of the Canadian wilderness, daydreaming about his big fucking hands. I make a mental note to follow up with my therapist about this too. I have to be diagnosable. It has to be a coping mechanism of some sort.

Do daddy issues give you a hand kink?

I scoff at myself before muttering, "God, Skylar. You really need a people detox."

And it's true.

Or at least that's what I told everyone when I packed up and left. Some might say that fleeing Los Angeles is running from my problems. Others might think it's rude to show up unannounced for an unconfirmed job.

Me? I'm calling it fleeing the world's most humiliating breakup.

I'm calling it desperation.

But I also have a plan. One I have kept secret from my parents, who work as my managers, as well as my agent, who is mostly just their paid puppet.

I'm going to record my own album. And I'm not going to tell a single soul about it. I don't want their input. I don't want their opinions. This project will be by me, for me.

I am desperate for a fresh start. Desperate for a change of scenery. Desperate to escape the chokehold my life has on me.

And I mean a *literal* chokehold.

One where my throat goes so tight that every word fails me. Put a mic in my face, turn a camera on me, or trot me out in front of an audience, and your girl goes blank. All I can do is blink and giggle. My mouth goes dry, and I do my absolute best "bimbo impression," as a recent headline called it.

I'm not even sure if they're wrong anymore.

My most recent speechless moment came as I tearfully left a restaurant after enduring the aforementioned breakup. I walked out into a sea of questions.

"Skylar, what's wrong?"

"Skylar, did something happen with you and Andrew?"

Something.

I scoff again in the quiet car. It was something all right. Something I can't confess out loud.

I've always prided myself on being an honest person, but what if everything about me is fake? The world thinks they know me, but they've been spoon-fed a lie.

I've been spoon-fed a lie.

My life has been turned upside down, and I don't have a single soul to talk to about it. The truth is just too humiliating to acknowledge.

I definitely can't go public with it. Not yet anyway. The

press would eat me alive. The fans would either pity me or mock me—neither of which I want.

It's funny how I can be surrounded by so many people who profess to love me and still feel so utterly alone.

So my new move is staring into a camera blankly, feeling like my lungs are full of concrete and my throat is swollen shut. The only thing more difficult than finding the right words to say is catching my breath.

Yes, a girl who has performed in front of millions of people, who sings and dances and says all the right things, now shuts down in front of cameras.

My jaw clenches as I physically brace to endure the mental beating I'm about to give myself, but the pickup carrying the man with the nice hands signals, prompting me to do the same. He turns at a weather-stained wooden gate that opens onto a freshly paved driveway, and I follow his lead.

A thick frame of emerald pine trees entirely blocks the property beyond, and without even thinking about it, I press the button to roll down my window, letting the fresh country air into my car—into my system.

"Too slow!" Cherry squawks from her cage on the backseat. This bird loves car rides.

"It's a driveway, Cherry. I have to go slow, you rebel."

"Too slow!"

I chuckle and crane my neck to see where we're headed, pushing away the anxiety cropping up. Where would Cherry have ended up if a grizzly had eaten me on the side of a back-road? Another humane society? A zoo? One of my parents, who would have marched her out before the press like a commemorative spectacle?

All the options are truly too awful to contemplate, though I already know they'll keep me up when I'm lying in bed tonight. As sad as it sounds, Cherry, the sassy African grey parrot with a penchant for swearing, might be my only friend in the whole damn world.

The driveway weaves and turns, and there's something cozy about the press of trees and the scent of soil and crushed pine needles wafting through the window. I suck in a deep breath and feel incrementally better.

So I keep doing it.

Three seconds in.

Three seconds out.

An image—clear as day—of Weston's sky-blue eyes boring into mine as we breathed together on the asphalt flashes through my head. I wanted to clamp my eyes shut and hide until that moment of terror was over, but I couldn't look away.

He'd trapped me. But being trapped in his gaze soothed me in a completely unfamiliar way.

"Too slow!" Cherry bitches some more, drawing me out of my head just as the trees dissipate.

I gasp as the landscape filters in before me.

Ford's emails prepared me for a picturesque setting, but this is surreal.

The property is set on a gentle slope. Straight ahead is the main building with its wraparound deck and freestanding copper mailbox that matches the copper roof. Although the siding looks like old barn wood that's been preserved, there's something grand about the place. It's rugged but elevated.

Above that, it's trees, rocks, and deadly cliffs, all topped off by the bluest sky. No haze, no pollution—just pure, unfiltered blue. Like Weston's eyes.

But it's the view of the lake beyond that truly enchants me. It's downright breathtaking. So still that it makes me feel like I could walk across it. Or skate—if I knew how. The water appears navy, transitioning to a teal hue where the sun sparkles against the surface.

Next to the big truck, I jam my car into park and flop back against my seat to soak in the surroundings.

It feels totally unique. There's no sterile polish or obnoxious white pillars. No fountains or valets. In fact, there are no people as far as the eye can see. My body relaxes as that realization hits.

Until Weston Belmont pops up out of nowhere and startles the shit out of me.

I must have zoned out and missed him rounding my vehicle, because his big, manly hands are here, propped above my window as he peers down at me. "You gonna just sit here all day?" he asks, right as Cherry squawks, "Go away!"

His head swivels sharply to eye her up—black beak and bluish-gray feathers with a splash of red at her tail. "What is that?"

"You mean, *who* is that? She's my parrot. Cherry."

He blinks twice before blurting, "She's rude."

I can't help but laugh. "You have no idea."

"She's rude," Cherry adds in a mocking voice that has me pressing my lips together and wincing.

"Sorry. She has an extensive vocabulary, and her shit-talk is legendary."

All the man does is stare at my bird with a furrowed brow before shaking his head. Then his hand taps on the roof of my car as he draws away. "Right. Well, the office is in there." He hikes a thumb over his shoulder. "I can introduce you if you'd like. Otherwise, I'll be on my way."

"Go away!" Cherry says. Again.

I grimace as I open my door and step out. Weston doesn't move back. He stays exactly where he is, towering over me. Filling out his T-shirt in a way that artsy city boys just…*don't*. My eyes catch on the hole in the fabric on his left pectoral again and the glow of golden skin beneath. The golden skin of a man who spends his time outdoors with no shirt on.

I come from the land of pale skin and spray tans, so there's something mesmerizing about what might be beneath the cotton material. I sweep away the urge to wiggle a finger through the opening to find out for sure.

But men—especially men who catch my eye like this one—are the last thing I need in my life right now. I swallow and take a new vow of celibacy because dick will not help my predicament.

Then I peek up into his bright blue irises. They're so electric that if he weren't standing before me, I'd scoff and make a dismissive comment about how anyone can have eyes that color with Photoshop. Everything can be altered to look a certain way. Nothing is real.

But his eyes are.

He is.

I clear my throat, realizing I've been gawking for too long. "Well, I wouldn't put it like Cherry. But truth be told, you've done more than enough for me today." I smile softly, watching him regard me with a level of intensity that makes me squirm. "And this is something I need to do on my own," I add quickly, nodding more for my benefit than for his.

The man's gaze drops to my mouth, and I roll my lips together.

"I—"

"*Go away!*" My fucking bird cuts me off. I love Cherry, but goddamn. Some days…

Some days, she is a possessive little hag.

And I'm not so sure I want him to go away.

Weston smiles, eyes still on my mouth, as he makes a light clucking noise. "All right, Cherry. I hear ya. I'm leaving, I'm leaving." He steps back, hands held up in surrender.

I almost want to hug him before he walks away, and I've never considered myself a hugger. Physical affection isn't something I grew up with, at least not behind closed doors. In public, my parents never hesitated to throw an arm over my shoulder or offer me a hug when the cameras were rolling. Affection was for show.

"Should we shake hands or something? What's the protocol when someone uses his body as a shield for you in an almost bear attack?"

"Nah, you already said thank you. You don't owe me anything. I did it because I wanted to."

I blink a few times at that.

You don't owe me anything.

It's a basic sentiment, yet it catches me off guard. I've lived a life of constantly owing someone something. Tit for tat. My attention in exchange for a favor. Constantly caught in the middle of warring sides and having to smile my way to the top.

I'm so sick of smiling.

"I'll see you 'round!" He waves and offers me a wink before turning away and gifting me with a view of his firm ass.

Maybe I should have offered ass-grabs as a thank-you.

As I brush the thought away with a chiding shake of my head, I hear him mutter to himself from the other side of his truck, "Fuckin' Tesla and a talking bird."

It makes me smile. A genuine smile. But only for a beat because I turn away and suck in a deep breath, preparing myself to face Ford Grant.

The man is in for a bit of a surprise.

Yes, we have spoken about working together.

No, I did not tell him I was coming.

"Guard the car, Cherry." I check to make sure the air conditioning is on before slamming the door and steeling my spine as I make my way up the front walkway. There's no doorbell, which makes perfect sense for the place. Instead, there's an ornate door knocker shaped like a bear with a ring held in its mouth. I chuckle—bears are my theme for the day—and knock.

Within seconds, a feminine voice calls, "Coming!" from inside.

The door swings open and I'm face-to-face with a

blue-eyed woman. She takes one look at me and her jaw slowly falls open.

"Oh my god. *Hi.*"

"Hi," I say back, my voice low as I glance at the ground, feeling a blush rise to my cheeks.

"Who is it?" a man's voice asks.

The blond woman ignores the question and sticks her hand out to me. "I'm Rosalie, the business manager here at Wild Rose Records. It's so nice to meet you."

I shake her hand, a little taken aback by her firm grip. "Hi, Rosalie. I'm Skylar."

She grins, pumping my hand with vigor. "Hell yeah you are."

"Rosie," the man's voice calls, closer now than before. "I know you get off on annoying me, but—" Ford Grant rounds the corner and draws up short when he sees me. His dad is a famous rockstar, the guitarist from Full Stop, and the resemblance is clear as day.

His copper-brown hair is artfully mussed, and he's tall and fit-looking—he could easily pass for a model. Ford would blend in well where I come from. But I hate where I come from, so I find myself noting that he lacks the heavy muscle of the man who brought me here.

He's dressed casually, but it's an expensive sort of casual. There are no holes in his shirt, no scuffs on his boots. He has polish, and for the first time in my life, I find myself indifferent to it.

"Skylar?" His voice is absolutely brimming with confusion.

I hold my hands up beside my head with a shrug and deliver a simple, "Surprise?"

"I'll say!" Rosalie adds, clearly amused by the entire situation.

Ford strides closer and lays a possessive hand on her lower back as he steps in beside her. She peeks up at him, her lips quirk to one side, and the interaction is so chock-full of genuine affection and respect that I feel like a voyeur.

I glance away, twisting my hands together. "I'm sorry. I know this was unexpected. I just…I needed to get away. Needed to work on something fresh. Any chance we could start early?" I pour all the positivity and enthusiasm I can muster into that last sentence and hope it will be enough. I'm definitely feeling short on positivity and enthusiasm lately.

Ford's thick brows furrow as he peers down at me. I don't *think* he's mad, but there's an imposing aura about him.

Rosalie shoves an elbow into his ribs. "You're doing the resting prick face. Stop it."

He slices her an annoyed glare before turning his attention back on me. "Sorry, I was thinking. The reason I haven't gotten you out here yet is that the cottages aren't ready to go, and neither is the recording studio. They're being framed in, and I don't have—"

"I'll wait. I'll stay anywhere. Pitch me a tent. I don't care." What I'm not short on is determination.

He looks me up and down now, and a flicker of compassion appears on his handsome face. No doubt he heard the desperation in my voice. And he's probably pitying me after all the brutal headlines lately. "Why don't you come in and we'll see what we can work out? There are only a couple of hotels in town, and I doubt they have availability for a longer stay in the middle of the tourist season."

Rosalie wrinkles her nose and says "tourists" like it's a dirty word. "Good news is they only flock here for July and August. Come on." She ushers me inside. "Let's get you sorted."

"Thank you." I practically sigh the words as I hit her with a grateful smile and follow Ford into the office space.

The building is just as beautiful on the inside—fresh and rustic all at once. Wood beams line the vaulted ceiling, complemented by wide wooden floorboards with a strange mess of paint on them that matches the muted blue on the walls. There are two desks, set apart but facing each other, as well as a cozy sitting area with massive couches and a vinyl library that resembles a record store.

But the sliding glass doors facing the lake steal the show, adding a modern touch to the barnlike space. They open onto a sprawling deck surrounded by lush gardens and topped with wicker furniture.

"I'll buy a bed and just stay here," I blurt to a chorus of chuckles. "This place is incredible."

"Glad you like it," Ford says as he leans back against a desk and crosses his arms.

I glance at him, and it's like I can see his brain working behind those green eyes. He bleeds intelligence—and it's the intimidating kind.

Rosalie bumps her shoulder against mine. "Sorry," she whispers, like she's read my mind. "He's not really the warm and fuzzy type."

I shoot her a smile. "That's okay, I'll take not warm and fuzzy over fake any day."

She claps her hands once like she's amused. "Well, the two of you should get along famously."

As she stands, hands on her hips, looking back and forth between Ford and me, I find myself extra thankful for her presence. Without her, this might have been even more awkward.

"Ford, what's going on upstairs?" she asks.

"I'm just weighing options."

"You look like you're plotting a murder."

His eyes narrow at Rosalie, and I don't know what they are to each other, but it's abundantly clear they're more than just coworkers. Their tension is off the charts. I feel like I'm intruding just by standing in their presence.

He waves her off. "No, I'll save that for when Skylar wants to tell me who she's running from."

I start, but Rosalie just snorts at his observation. "He's extremely protective of the people around him," she whispers to me. "Borderline vengeful, really."

"You could stay at our house until one of the cottages is ready," he muses, scrubbing at his stubble and staring at the floor. "Do you need time to work on songs? We could start hammering out some details. Maybe we can meet on Monday and work on a timeline. Work out out a bit of a plan?"

Stay at their house?

"Oh, I would never impose like that," I say. Inside, I'm floored that this person I barely know would offer me a room in his house. I don't want to be indebted to him beyond allowing me to crash here early. "But a meeting on Monday sounds perfect."

"I don't think the office would work since Rosie and I…"

Is he for real? What's next? Is he going to give me the shirt off his back?

"That part about living in the office was a joke," I say. "A compliment."

I'm suddenly feeling the weight of my imposition, realizing what a tremendous burden it must be for them to have me show up here unannounced. I should have thought before I jumped.

My actions were self-centered. Self-serving. Everyone has bad breakups.

"You know what? I'll head back. I'm so sorry. This was… beyond desperate." I start to spiral. My breathing quickens as the walls tilt closer, and I press a hand to my chest and cover with a nervous laugh. "Just plain rude."

It's the gentle way the woman beside me cups my elbow and steps in front of me that takes some of the weight away. "Hey, don't stress about it. We're laid-back out here." She peeks over her shoulder at Ford before adding, "And I know a place you can stay. My brother has a bunkhouse."

"Rosie, that place is a dump."

She doesn't bother looking back at Ford this time, choosing to roll her eyes at me instead.

"I know you just rolled your eyes," he bites out, but he's smirking.

She clamps her lips together to cover a giggle, then forges

ahead. "He's right. It's not fancy. But it's only one property over, and it's private. And my brother won't mind. He's busy with his work and his kids and his stupid bowling team. You'll hardly see him—unless you want to. Then he'd happily be your friend. Making friends is his special talent."

Ford snorts at that statement, shaking his head with an amused twist to his mouth.

"Private sounds wonderful. I'm a little sick of people right now. And I don't need fancy," I say with forced enthusiasm.

But the truth is, I know nothing other than fancy.

I've been famous my entire life. Have lived lavishly my entire life. Have been *performing* my entire life.

It's time I take a break from performing.

Not fancy may be exactly what I need.

CHAPTER 3

Skylar

When Rosalie said "not fancy," she wasn't kidding. And by bunkhouse, she literally meant bunk beds.

It's stark white and super small. The narrow deck, which overlooks the lake, has a weatherworn rocking chair propped in the corner.

Earlier, I watched Rosalie casually dust the cobwebs from it with her bare hands. She didn't seem concerned, but as we stand side by side in the musty bunkhouse, I can't stop wondering if she's going to wash them.

"So, when I stayed in here, I slept on the bottom bunk and used the top bunk as my closet, basically."

I nod along, like this seems normal to me. It's not. I might sing about country living, but I am a spoiled city girl through and through. I don't think I've *ever* seen anything like this before.

But I refuse to act like that's the case. This is me being the cool, new, low-maintenance version of myself.

Not-fancy Skylar.

"Over on this counter is a hot plate, toaster oven, and kettle. That's the fridge"—she points to a short white box in the corner—"but there's no freezer. My brother will definitely share his with you. His kids are obsessed with freezies, so hopefully there's room somewhere around their piles of sugary frozen goods. The bathroom is through that door at the back. There's only a shower."

I try not to wince. Baths are my favorite.

She stops her tour and nibbles nervously at her lip. "I should also tell you that my pet mouse, Scotty, lives here. He's harmless. Sweet, really. If you could drop him some crumbs once a day, it will keep me from having to come do it myself."

"Your pet...mouse?"

"Pfft." She waves off my question. "You won't even notice him. But I am rather attached, so please don't tell my brother. He'll set a trap and I'll never forgive him."

I don't know what to say to that, so I go for being relatable. "Oh yeah, I've got a pet bird. So that's cool." I nod as I speak while mentally convincing myself that I really won't even notice her *pet mouse*.

She chuckles good-naturedly and tucks strands of dirty blond hair behind her ears as she peeks at me. "Cute. Will this be okay? I'll get fresh bedding from the house for you. Oh, and a Wild Rose Records sweatsuit. It's pink. You'll love it."

"Yeah." I nod and force myself to look certain. Based on the way Rosalie's nose wrinkles, I must not nail the look. "That's perfect. I love it."

Fake it till you make it, as they say.

Her eyes search mine. I don't think she's buying what I'm selling. At all.

"Once you're settled in, we could…I don't know…grab a drink or do something fun? I promised my friend Tabby a night out, but I've been so busy with the studio that I've let it slide. I need to touch base with her. You could join us."

I blink.

"Like, when you aren't feeling peopled out. No pressure. Ball is in your court."

No pressure. Those two words make me blink harder. They hit me in the heart. I feel like I could crumble under the weight of the pressure in my life. The expectations.

What would it be like to go for a drink with someone for fun? Not because it would be beneficial to be seen with them or because of the status that comes with being associated with them.

All I can do is nod and choke out, "Thanks, I'd like that."

A wide, genuine smile spreads across her face. "Great! Now let's find the man of the house and let him know there's a guest staying at his hotel."

With that, she strides out of the bunkhouse and into the sun like none of this is out of the ordinary.

Me? I feel like I've crash-landed on another planet. And we all know the appropriate response when you crash-land on an alien planet is to act like a local.

My phone dings and I pull it from my purse. Another Google alert. A brand-new mention of my freshly minted ex out at Nobu with some hot model. The headline reads

"Skylar Scorned" and my stomach sinks and my throat goes tight.

I don't want to care.

So I shove my phone back in my bag, tip my nose up, and follow Rosalie out into the warm summer day—checking on Cherry, who is comfortably dozing in the air-conditioned car—and up a dirt path that leads to a slightly older-looking farmhouse. The sight instantly soothes my nerves.

It exudes the lived-in cozy that I've only seen in movies.

My steps slow as I take in the white-painted wood and the exposed redbrick chimney that has mortar squishing out from between each block. Charming rust-colored shingles cover the roof.

This place looks like a proper childhood home, or at least what I always imagined one to be like. The wraparound deck has patio furniture dispersed on every side and children's toys tossed in for good measure—a bike, a skateboard, a bottle of bubbles, there's even a plastic tea set sitting on top of a small table. Beside the house, there's a gigantic elm tree, its branches holding a rope swing swaying gently in the summer heat.

I itch to sit on it.

"Follow this way." Rosie waves me ahead, and with a quick smile, I spring into motion and hustle through the yard to her side. There's no paved road or perfectly spaced stepping stones. We go straight across the yard and past the house.

The air smells like freshly cut grass and wet rocks from the lake, but the farther we press into the property, the more it smells…worse.

I wrinkle my nose. "What is that *smell*?"

Rosalie snorts right as a barn and other outbuildings come into view. "Horses. My brother is a professional trainer. Runs his business out of the barn here. You get used to the smell. I actually like it. You'll get there eventually."

My eyes bug out at her, and she laughs. *I like her*. This girl who touches cobwebs with her bare hands, feeds a wild mouse, and likes the smell of horse manure.

"Ah! There he is," she says. "The man of the hour."

And yup.

There. He. Is.

"West!"

Weston Belmont stands shirtless, his back to us, next to a horse that is tied to a fence. He's hosing it off, making its bright reddish coat turn dark and slick.

And I instantly know why his skin looked so tan through that tiny hole in his shirt.

"Rosie Posie, now's not a good time." He barely reacts. Stays turned away, all his muscles rippling and bunching as he reaches up to carefully wet the horse's mane.

Beyond him is a white and red barn that matches the house. Then there are pastures and paddocks and more buildings that I have no clue about.

"Need to get this girl all cooled down and still somehow make it to two different summer camps if I plan to pick the hooligans up on time."

"I can always go get them."

He shoots his sister a surprised look from over his shoulder, blue eyes flashing in the sun. And suddenly I can see the resemblance clear as day. How did I not take one glance at this woman and wonder if they were related?

His eyes slice to mine and then back to his sister again. "You're gonna let Emmy in your car?"

Rosalie shrugs. "Nah, she's feral. I'm gonna strap her to the roof."

He laughs, and the deep, warm sound reminds me of lying beneath his body on that hot asphalt roadway.

"But first, I need to introduce you to someone. She's going to stay in your bunkhouse until Ford and I can get one of the guesthouses up and running."

I wince inwardly. She's not asking him. She's telling him.

He crouches to wet the horse's stomach, and from his side profile, I can see he's grinning as the water sprays him back and glistens on his golden skin.

Even as the spray of water leaves wet spots on his jeans.

"Bird girl. Didn't expect to see you again so soon."

Rosalie's head whips in my direction, her brows knitting together as confusion paints her pretty features. "*Bird girl?*"

Lord help me. "I'm not *bird girl.*"

He stands and turns to face us, hitting me with the full impact of his physique. It's *absurd.* My facial muscles get an extra workout as they struggle to keep my jaw from dropping open.

With a teasing grin, he lifts one arm and wipes it across his forehead, which does nothing but make his abs look more defined.

"Bear girl?" he tries again, with a cocky lift to one eyebrow. "You like that one better?"

His sister is *very* interested now. She nudges me and says, "*Bear* girl?"

All I do is glare at Weston, and all he does is smirk back.

"So…" Rosie's head flips between us. "The two of you have met? That's what I'm taking away from this? West, this is Skylar. Skylar Stone, you know—"

"Oh yeah. I know." The Adonis in front of us turns to crank the water tap. It squeaks as he does, and the horse's head flips in his direction. Without a second thought, his hand reaches out to stroke her neck with a soothing "Easy, girl."

I'm not proud of the way that simple sentence makes my body clench.

All that goes away when he recounts our bear story. "Skylar here was trying to make friends with Winnie the Pooh on the side of the highway earlier today. I had to stop and help her, so she didn't get turned into a snack." He wipes his hands on his jeans as he chuckles. "Was actually a pretty close call."

"I didn't know that it would notice me!"

Rosalie seems alarmed. "What kind of bear?"

"Grizzly," Weston provides dryly, entirely ignoring my explanation.

Her expression is full-on horrified now. "Oh my god, Skylar. Honey, *no*."

I gaze at her, hoping to prove I'm not a total idiot. I didn't mean to be stupid. The photo opportunity was just too good to pass up. I wanted to post something *real* on my social media. Connect with my fans after the mess I've been lately. Prove I can still form full sentences. "He's forgetting there were babies."

"That doesn't make it better." Rosalie's eyes go bigger, and Weston laughs behind her.

"It's not funny," I snap at him. Recently, too many people have had too many things to say about my intelligence, and even though this could be a charming moment, the mockery smarts.

He must hear the frustration in my voice because he stops instantly. Though I'm not sure the way he's looking at me now is any better. His gaze is too heavy, and his jaw altogether too square when he swallows deeply.

"Right." Rosalie claps her hands again, startling me out of my stupor. "Well, leave it to West to jump headfirst into a situation with a grizzly." She points at him. Then winks. "I'll leave that out the next time I talk to Mom and Dad, but only if you say yes to Skylar staying at the bunkhouse."

He grunts at that, but he's still staring at me like I'm a puzzle he's trying to figure out.

"I don't want to impose on Weston—"

"Please, no one calls him Weston. And while we're at it, call me Rosie."

"Okay, well, I don't want you to blackmail someone into helping me, and I don't want to impose on West—"

"Take the bunkhouse. It's no imposition. No one is getting blackmailed here. It's more that Rosie shit-talks just as well as your bird. I'm not worried about her threat."

"See?" Rosie says brightly. "Told you it would be fine."

I force a smile. *Fine.* Yeah, it'll be fine. That's what I keep telling myself.

"Just make sure you give her some privacy, yeah?" Rosie tells her brother.

She gets an eye roll in return. "Please, you know I barely have time to keep up with my kids."

"Okay, great. I was going to grab bedding for Skylar, but can you do that for me? I'll get Emmy and Oliver."

West nods at his sister. "Thanks."

"It's great to have you here, Skylar. I promise this will just be a placeholder until we can get you set up somewhere else."

"No, it's perfect, really," I lie as I smile and shake her hand once more. I'm so good at this. *Too* good at this.

I should be, considering my entire life has been built on lying to people.

When I turn back to West and meet his eyes, it feels an awful lot like he sees right through the charade.

And I can't have that.

CHAPTER 4

West

SKYLAR IS STANDING IN FRONT OF ME A LOT SOONER THAN I expected. Sure, I knew we'd cross paths, but I didn't imagine we'd be sharing my property.

Judging by the defiant glint in her eye and the proud lift to her chin, she didn't expect it either.

Hell, she might not even like it.

"Just give me a sec to get some of the water off her, and I'll help you out."

"Great," she says, her voice a little icier than earlier.

With a shake of my head, I turn and pick up the sweat scraper to remove any excess liquid from the filly. I lead her back to her pasture and Skylar follows, propping herself against the fence with a curious expression on her face.

The minute I remove her halter, the horse drops and rolls in the dirt.

I smile, but Skylar's gasp draws away my attention. She

looks on with a hand thrown daintily over her chest as the horse wiggles and slathers her wet coat in dust and dirt.

"You *just* bathed her."

"Oh shit, right. One sec, I'll tell her she shouldn't have done that." I turn back to the filly. "Hey, Meli. Don't get dirty, ok—"

"All right, I get it. You don't need to mock me." She's back to having that sour expression on her face.

"I'm not mocking you. I'm cracking a joke. Plus, there's no stopping it. I'll be back out here tomorrow to brush her clean. And if she's too warm after working, then I'll hose her down. Rinse, repeat. It's like I'm her bitch, if you think about it."

I can see Skylar working that out in her head. "Don't you get annoyed? You just spent all that time making her clean."

Now I'm the one quirking my head and looking confused. "No. I spent all that time making her feel good. Cooling her down. She's a horse, doing horse things. See how happy she is?" I glance at the filly, who is grunting and rolling.

Meli makes it all the way over again before clumsily pushing to stand. Once upright, she shakes her entire body, but the dirt still clings to her as she wanders over, eyeing Skylar inquisitively. Skylar stays frozen in place, and I wonder how she ever thought she could get close to a bear when a horse is clearly making her nervous.

However, she braves her discomfort and reaches out tentatively, letting Meli's nostrils flare over her flat palm as the filly sniffs. Seconds later, Meli bobs her head, knickers, and wanders away, all calm and content, before stuffing her face into the hay I stocked in her feeder.

"See? She's so happy. How could I begrudge her that?"

Skylar is laser-focused on the horse. "But is there a way to keep them clean?"

"I mean, sure. I could keep them indoors with a sheet all the time and muck their stalls multiple times a day. Keep 'em locked up. But that's not the life these horses are meant to live. These aren't show horses—the odd one might be down the line. These are working horses, young horses. They're lucky they get brushed at all. I do it because I like the process and I know it feels good for them. We build trust this way, and I don't care if they make a mess of it later. Can't hold their nature against them."

"Huh" is the only thing she says as she continues staring at Meli. Like what I've just said confuses her on a deeper level.

A ringing from her purse makes her jump and she's immediately diving for it, scrambling to find her phone in what appears to be some sort of bottomless bag. When she pulls it out, her brow furrows, her eyes water, and her jaw tics.

Then she presses the button on the side to silence it and I watch her face transform into this fake mask of serenity. It's too practiced. Honestly, it's a little creepy. It makes me question every photo and interview I've ever seen of this woman.

"You can pet her while she eats if you want. She's a sweet girl. I'll go grab the bedding set and be right back."

She nods but doesn't give me her attention. Instead, she

approaches the horse again with caution, and I decide to give her a moment to herself.

I dart into the house and don't bother taking my shoes off. The floors are a fucking mess from the kids being here all week anyway. I'll do a deep clean when they leave for their mom's place this weekend. I rush upstairs, tug open the closet, and grab the red-and-white gingham set that Rosie used when she crashed in the bunkhouse. It looks like a picnic blanket turned into a bedspread.

As I'm stomping back down the stairs, I stop at the landing and glance out the window. Skylar has gone right up to the fence where Meli is eating and is reaching out for the horse's forehead like she's about to touch a hot stove or something. Her purse is dropped at her feet and she seems almost relaxed.

I swear, if I made a loud noise, she'd jump straight out of her skin. The girl is stressed. Anxious. It keeps me from outwardly fan-girling over her. I think if I did, she'd bolt. So I keep my slack-jawed expressions locked up real tight.

It also didn't occur to me that Skylar may not have spent time around horses. I just…assumed. Country music star and all that. It just seems like it fits her whole persona.

But based on the way her stiff, flat palm taps the star in the middle of Meli's forehead, I realize I was sorely mistaken.

So I stand and watch. Her taps evolve into rubs as Meli continues happily munching on her hay. Soon, Skylar's dainty fingers weave themselves into her forelock, and she combs it out carefully.

When she's done pampering Meli, she reaches into her

pocket and lifts her phone. She fluffs her hair, makes some weird duck pout with her face, and switches from vulnerable young woman to confident bombshell in the blink of an eye.

She talks into her phone while Meli munches behind her. With her perfectly combed-out forelock. Like that somehow made her more presentable. The recording doesn't last long, and as soon as she puts the phone down, her entire body sags. Then she stares at the phone, most likely watching the video back, and her face falls.

I shake my head.

And not because I'm mad, but because I'm sad. I just witnessed a tender moment evaporate behind a shiny veneer. I watched vulnerable Skylar morph into starlet Skylar. And on the other side of that recording was an empty version of the girl whose eyes flashed with so much life on that back road.

Another shake of my head has me jogging down the stairs and back outside to the paddock. "You done with whatever it is you're doing?" I ask, noting the way she's still frowning at her screen.

"I just…I need to do another take. I don't like this one. I look gross, and I've sweat all my makeup off. I need a filter."

My eyes race over the woman before me. She looks like a lot of things to me, but gross isn't one of them. "A what?"

She finally glances up at me. "You know, a filter. For my face."

My head tilts as I work out what the hell this girl could be talking about. She has the kind of face people would show their plastic surgeon as inspiration.

"What's wrong with your face?"

She sighs heavily and turns her attention back to her phone. "Apparently, I'm looking old."

"Old? How old are you?"

"Twenty-six."

"Yeah, fair. That is super old," I reply solemnly.

She hits me with a scowl.

"Who said that?"

A sullen shrug precedes her response. "Some article. Something about me looking older."

"I hate to alarm you, but that is actually what happens as you age."

She laughs, but it's not a happy laugh.

"If you want my advice...ignore that shit. Don't even read it."

"Easier said than done." Her words are soft and lined with embarrassment.

My chest feels tight, and I don't know what to say. I'm already terrified to be raising a little girl, let alone a little girl in a world where she might feel like she looks old in her mid-twenties.

Before I can get my words together, she perks up and lands a jab. "Now that I think of it, I don't actually want you to give me advice. And you don't get to call me *super old* with fine lines like that. You need a filter too." She waves a finger over my face, but it's playful.

I chuckle and tip my head in amusement. I shouldn't have considered this girl down for the count because she just came back swinging.

"Come on, fancy face." I tilt my head in the direction

of the bunkhouse. "Let's get you set up. You can come do your photo shoot with Meli and beat yourself up about your accelerated aging anytime. I think you've done enough of that for one day, though."

"Did you just call me fancy face?"

I shrug and turn to walk away. "You didn't like 'doll' or 'bird girl.' And your complete lack of any fine lines is pretty fancy."

I can hear her soft footsteps as she follows. "Maybe I don't like 'fancy face' either."

"Well, it's a lot better than 'old face.'"

This time when she laughs, it's a happy laugh.

And somehow that feels like a win.

When we get to the bunkhouse and I see angelic Skylar Stone standing in the hovel that she's about to call home, I try not to cringe.

Instead, I blink at her. Big diamond earrings. Perfectly white teeth. Manicured nails. She could not be more out of place than she is in the bunkhouse.

I drop the bedding onto the mattress, and she shocks me by asking, "What do I do with these?"

"You…make the bed?"

A jittery laugh falls from her lips as she tucks her hair behind one ear. It's a nervous tell. It's the same as when a horse flicks their ear, rolls their eye to the side. I'm especially attuned to these things. Spend all day watching for signs of discomfort in animals who don't talk, and you can't help but notice them in humans too.

"Yeah, totally. I'll figure it out."

I blink again. "Are you telling me you don't know how to make a bed?"

She scoffs. Rolls her eyes. Tucks the other side of her hair behind her other ear. "How hard can it be?"

I blurt out the first thing that crosses my mind. "How are you twenty-six and you don't know how to make a bed?"

I know it wasn't the right thing to say by the way her eyes flash. Any comment—joking or otherwise—about her capabilities is a pinch point that sets her off.

"I've been polished, propped up, and trotted out like America's favorite show pony my entire life. I was a child star who lived on the road. I didn't get to go to school. I didn't learn how to make a bed. I never *needed* to. No one ever told me to. It was always just done. But you know what? I'm not dumb. I'll figure it out without your"—her hands fly up and make angry air quotes—"big manly bed-making help."

"Skylar, I didn't mean—"

She flicks a dismissive hand at me and refuses to meet my eyes. "There's a YouTube tutorial for everything. You can go. Thank you for all you did today." She pauses, gaze fixed on the red-and-white sheets as her teeth strum violently at her bottom lip. "It might may not seem like it, but I really appreciate your help."

There's something deeply earnest in her words, and it keeps me from saying anything more. Instead, I honor her wishes and back away slowly.

"You need anything, knock on the door. Anytime. I'm just up the hill, all right?"

Her head bobs delicately as a tear tumbles from her lower

lashes and lands right on the apple of her perfectly bronzed cheek.

She swipes it away as quickly as it falls.

I want to walk back in and hug her. But I don't. I'm well acquainted with the fight-or-flight response. Right now, this girl looks ready to pack up and fly away. Which I can't stand because I get the sense she needs this place right now.

And for some inexplicable reason, I don't want her to leave.

CHAPTER 5

Skylar

"This place is a dump," I mumble as I do some semblance of unpacking.

"*This place is a dump!*" Cherry calls out from where she's perched on my shoulder, making me wonder if she's the one with legendary shit-talk or if I'm the problem.

I attempt to shift my way of thinking. "This place is charming."

Cherry makes no such attempt. "*This place is a dump!*"

My phone rings, and when I pick it up to check it, I'm not at all surprised to see that it's my dad. My "Dad-ager," as we've jokingly referred to him my entire life since he's practically managed everything about my existence. My career. My money.

My relationships.

I click the call off again. Not ready to speak to him. I know he'll gaslight me and make me question everything I think I know about myself. And my agent, Jerry, will support him quietly by giving me jobs or advice that meet my dad's goals.

The text messages that continue to pile up tell me as much.

Dad: You can take time away. But you're overreacting by refusing to talk to us. This kind of erratic behavior just gives the press more fuel to call you crazy.

Jerry: I'm going to release a statement saying that you're hard at work in the recording studio. Be back by next week and I can get you seen out at Nobu with someone even hotter than Andrew.

I scoff. *Back by next week my ass.*

Now that I've left, there's this little part of me that doesn't want to go back at all. Ever. The constant exercise, primping, practice…it all exhausts me. Sure, it makes my performances better for the fans—and I do love my fans. But I miss just singing. For fun. In the shower. In the car. As I tidy my house. I've lost the simple pleasure of those moments.

Music used to bring me joy; it used to put a skip in my step. But now I dread it. I dread stepping out onto the stage. And even a sea of happy faces and young girls singing my songs back to me doesn't make a dent in my melancholy.

My gut drops as I drive. The realization that my parents have managed to ruin my one passion in life makes my stomach turn and my blood boil.

I've been furious with them for weeks, but yesterday's

humiliation was the final straw. Thinking about it makes me sick, so I don't. I focus on settling in and instead get lost thinking about tattooed hands and golden skin.

Unpacking goes quickly as my mind drifts and soon I find myself wanting to wander down to the lake. I place Cherry back in her cage with a fresh dish of food and then leave the bunkhouse without a backward glance. I don't tell anyone where I'm going, and there's no deadline on when I need to return. No obligations.

There's something about having nowhere to be and no one to impress that is profoundly freeing. I might even sit by the water all night and sleep under the stars.

I'm not sure yet. All I know is the world is my oyster in a way it never has been.

I scramble down the short drop from grass to lake in the least ladylike fashion anyone could ever muster. I'm like Bambi on ice, all limbs as I tumble down onto the pebbled shoreline.

There's a massive tree straddling the lake's edge, held strong by thick roots on one side that grip into the soil behind it. The other side's roots go straight out before dropping a good three feet at a gnarled right angle into the rocks and silt lining the shore.

My palm lands on one of the roots. It's smooth, weathered—no bark remains. But there's beauty in it—the streaks of distinct colors, the distress marks that tell a story.

Fine lines. The term pops up in my head and makes me smile as I admire the wood. I feel connected to this tree in a way. The tides have tried to wash it away, but it's here. Still standing.

As I take another step to see the tree from the front, I freeze in my tracks. Wedged between two of the huge roots, seated on a log, is a boy with a book on his lap. I've always liked children, been drawn to their honesty and simplicity, but I'm not familiar enough with them to know how old he might be.

Old enough to be reading. Young enough to be all knobby knees and missing teeth.

He stares at me with wide, alarmed eyes. Blue eyes. I'm not making the same mistake twice. This kid has West stamped all over him.

"Hi. I'm Skylar. Sorry to interrupt you. I just wanted to see the lake."

The boy doesn't say anything, but his eyes go from startled to studious. I don't want to make him uncomfortable, so I keep talking.

"I don't think I've ever seen a place like this. I'm sure it's not that impressive to you, being that you live here—or so I assume. But it's…" I pause and hold a hand over my brow as I turn in place to take it all in. "It's so peaceful. I can see why you'd read down here."

I peek at the boy, and he gives me a soft smile just as "Whose Bed Have Your Boots Been Under" by Shania Twain blasts from farther up the hill. A classic, really.

The boy rolls his eyes, and I can't help but laugh.

"Is that your dad?"

He shakes his head, still with an amused twist to his mouth.

"Sister?"

Now a nod.

I smile to myself as I turn and stare back out over the water and imagine what it must be like to grow up in a home on a huge chunk of land. Where your aunt picks you up from summer camp and your dad lets you blast music for fun.

Only now, face-to-face with his child, does it really hit me that West—the West I've been eye-fucking all day like a hungry little ho—is a *dad*. And he didn't make them on his own, which means I've been salivating all over a married man.

Under the self-loathing heading in my brain, I add *another* tally mark and vow to knock that shit off.

It keeps things far simpler. I'm in no position to be lusting after some manly man. Not when I'm not staying here long-term. And not when I don't trust a single person.

I'd be a goddamn nightmare in a relationship right now.

Yes, this is much, *much* better. It'll keep me focused on my career. It'll keep me focused on figuring out my shit, rather than looking for validation anywhere I can find it.

I, Skylar Stone, need to learn to love myself.

And right now, I don't.

But I do love the view.

The water twinkles and the bugs dip down on top of it, dotting the surface with tiny ripples. The sun is lower in the sky, more golden orange than the blinding lemon color it was earlier.

I feel warm to my bones.

"I'm actually staying in your bunkhouse for a while. I hope that's okay with you. Your dad seemed to think it would be fine. So no stranger danger here—Oh!" I exclaim as a large bird torpedoes toward the lake headfirst. It hits with a loud slap, submerging itself for only a moment before surfacing with a shiny, wriggling fish. Then it ascends, back into the sky, heading toward the nearest treetop. "Fuck, that was incredible."

The kid laughs in that manic way children do when an adult swears in front of them. I should feel bad, but there's something mature about this boy that makes me feel like he can handle it.

"I have no idea what kind of bird that was, but it was cool. I love birds. Imagine being able to fly and just see it all?" I sigh. "That's how I usually trick my brain into falling back asleep when I wake up at night. I take a bird's-eye view cruise over all the places I've been in the world. And I've been a lot of places."

But none of them have grabbed me by the throat quite like this one.

"Sorry, what's your name?" I ask without glancing back at the boy.

He clears his throat, like there might be something stuck in it, then his voice comes. It's quiet and surprisingly sweet. "Oliver."

"Do you mind if I stay here, Oliver? I'd like to sit and watch the world go by for a while."

I peek back at him now, wanting to make sure he's not just saying yes to be polite, but he's already shifted over on the log. He pats the spot he opened up for me. A genuine grin takes over my face—it pops up out of nowhere—and I close the space that separates us, plunking down beside him.

It feels cozy with the water lapping toward our feet and the roots of the tree curled around us.

"It's nice to meet you, Oliver," I say in a hushed tone.

He doesn't respond, but I see him smile down at the page of the book he's back to reading.

So I sit with him. This boy I barely know. In a setting that is all new. In a silence that is companionable.

And I can't remember the last time I felt so at peace.

I don't know how long we sit on our log. Long enough that the sun drops even lower over the mountains on the opposite side of the lake and the smell of grilled meat wafts down to the shore.

My stomach rumbles, and I realize I'm going to need to get some sort of groceries to cook. Truth be told, the list of things I can cook is pretty limited. I could eat out, but most people aren't as cool as Oliver, and I don't feel like being gawked at or asked to sign autographs.

I'm making a mental list of the groceries I'll need to get for a box of mac 'n' cheese when I hear heavy footfalls running toward us. Within a moment, a tiny girl is airborne as she takes a flying leap from the yard down to the water's edge.

"Time's up, nerd," she huffs as she lands on the rocks, catching herself easily. Then she's upright and spins on the spot with one hand already propped on her hip.

Her eyes are blue, but where Oliver's hair is a dusty, light brown, hers is a strawberry blond that reminds me of my favorite rose-gold bracelet.

"Oh. My. God." Her dainty jaw drops open and her lightly freckled cheeks glow a bright pink. "Are you Skylar Stone?"

She shrieks the question so loud that I can't help but wince. When I glance at Oliver, he rolls his eyes.

They're cute. *Really* cute.

"Are you the girl who has been blasting Shania for the past hour?"

She grins, and her eyes twinkle. "Yes. But next time, I'm blasting your music."

Wow, that sounds like fucking torture.

I don't say it out loud, but the idea of sitting around listening to my songs makes my skin crawl.

"I could choreograph you a dance," she adds matter-of-factly.

"Yeah?"

"I'll come up with one and show you. If you like it, we'll need to negotiate a price. I don't work for free."

Oliver groans like he's embarrassed, but I can't help the grin that curves my lips. She's so…*confident*. I wonder what it must feel like to be that sure of yourself, to have that much faith in your own capabilities. To know your time and work have value at such a young age.

I wish I'd been that aware. I might be in a different position than I am right now.

Don't worry about it, doll. I'll take care of everything.

My dad's voice filters into my head as the flash of a contract being shoved in front of me appears in my mind. That nickname that seemed sweet for so long but now just oozes condescension.

I'd been a doll to him. Prop me up. Make me sing. Collect your paycheck.

If I'd been even a fraction as shrewd as this girl, I might have taken a glance at that paperwork, even asked a few questions.

But no. I trusted him. Implicitly.

And that blind trust fucked me.

With a shake of my head, I turn my attention back to the girl. "What's your name?"

"I'm Emmy. I'm six." She sticks her hand out to shake mine and includes her age like she's very proud of it. "And that's my brother, Oliver. He's eight."

I take her small, sticky hand and think back to Rosie mentioning the pile of freezies. "Pleasure to meet you, Emmy," I say, infusing as much enthusiasm into my voice as I can. "I already met Oliver. He was kind enough to let me sit in his spot with him."

Her brows scrunch as she watches her brother, who pushes to standing and flips his book shut. "You already met him?"

She seems confused by my story, and I tilt my head with a slow nod. "Yeah. He introduced himself."

Her eyes flare, and her small, Chiclet-like teeth light up her entire face. Then she punches him in the shoulder—lovingly but still rather forcefully. "Oh, hell yeah, Ollie."

I don't know what the exchange means, but Oliver's cheeks go a dark red and he becomes fixated on the rocks beneath his feet.

Before I can ask anything, Skylar slips her sticky hand into mine. "Come. You're having dinner with us. My dad makes the *best* burgers."

"Oh, no. I really couldn't. I don't want to interfere with your family time. I bet you and your parents have plans."

Emmy scoffs and tugs me toward a narrow path I missed when I off-roaded down the drop. Her tight grip makes me feel like I'm being taken in for questioning. "Please, it's just Dad. And he won't mind."

My inner nosy bitch pops up out of nowhere. "What about your mom?"

Emmy shrugs casually. "Dunno. I bet she and Brandon are at their house eating something really healthy."

My confusion only builds.

"Who's Brandon?"

I let her lead me up onto the grass and can hear Oliver's footsteps behind me. Her brother can't get a word in edge-wise, not with Emmy talking a mile a minute.

"Our stepdad." I stutter-step, and Emmy yanks on my arm, pulling me forward. "Hurry up, I'm *starving*."

My feet move forward, but my mind is spinning. *Stepdad.* As in…divorced?

I know it's not my business, but it gets me wondering all the same. It makes me want details.

Details I have no business asking about.

Most of the questions that spring to my mind are easy

enough to push away. I'm a twenty-six-year-old woman. Just because my parents' recent divorce blindsided me doesn't mean I need to quiz a little kid about her experience with it.

In fact, she is handling it a lot better than I am. Then again, her parents are no doubt better people than mine.

Which, to be fair, is not that hard to achieve.

What is hard, though, is keeping myself from wondering just how single Weston Belmont might be.

CHAPTER 6

West

I FLIP THE BURGERS AND LEAN BACK A LITTLE TO INSPECT MY handiwork, only to be interrupted by a shrill, excited, "Dad! Guess what!"

I sigh and let my eyes flutter shut.

Emmy.

Emmy is the apple of my eye. My little mini-me. But she is also the primary source of my exhaustion. A tiny tornado. Short in stature but full up on attitude and zest for life.

She never stops.

Talking, moving, watching, questioning.

She's smart, brash, and downright hilarious. I wouldn't have her any other way. And if anyone ever tries to put out her fire or make her feel like she's somehow too much, I'll break their face.

But goddamn.

Emmy *exhausts* me.

Some days I text my parents a simple *I'm sorry* because I know she's exactly how I was as a kid. Even though they've loved me through it all, I now know the depth of their exhaustion with me and my antics.

"What's up, girlfrieeend?" I call over my shoulder, doing my best and most dramatic Valley-girl impression. Something that never fails to make both of my kids laugh.

And they do laugh. Emmy. Oliver.

And someone else I don't immediately recognize.

As I'm turning with a pair of tongs in one hand, I place the laugh. A little smoky, a little restrained, like she's holding herself back because a loud laugh might not be ladylike.

Skylar.

Skylar, who is holding my daughter's hand.

Skylar, who takes one glance at my apron, lets her eyes go wide, and slaps her free hand over her mouth.

I glance down and realize I'm wearing the "This Guy Rubs His Own Meat" apron that Rosie got for me last Christmas.

Joke goes right over the kids' heads.

But not Skylar's.

Inwardly, I cringe. Outwardly, I roll with it.

I toss her a wink and smirk. "Sorry, if I'd known we were expecting company, I'd have worn my classy apron."

She quirks a brow at me, all attitude as her hip pops out and her arms cross beneath her breasts. It props them up in a way that I shouldn't notice.

But I do, so I force my eyes not to linger for too long.

"And what does your classy apron look like?" she asks.

I click my tongue against the roof of my mouth with an amused tilt of my head. "Well, my classy one makes me look like I have a beer belly and super hairy chest."

Skylar watches me while my kids smile broadly, their eyes bouncing between us. "Does that mean you don't naturally have a beer belly and a hairy chest?" Immediately following that wisecrack, her lips pop open and her jaw drops wide. It's as though she can't believe what just came out of her mouth.

Emmy and Oliver cover her shock by bursting into peals of laughter. Luckily, they don't get the innuendo yet, but time's ticking on being granted that kind of grace.

"I'm pretty sure you got a good, long look earlier today," I volley back, seeing her cheeks flush pink even as her eyes roll.

Just as I'm about to keep going with a teasing response about being willing to show her again if she can't remember, Emmy pipes up.

Because *of course* she pipes up. Emmy always pipes up. And Emmy, for all of her jokes, loves to skewer her dad.

"He doesn't have a beer belly. *Yet.* But I bet it's coming because he does drink beer. And he already has a hairy chest."

I feign outrage with an audible gasp as I hold my metal tongs out to the side and stare at my daughter accusingly. "Emmy, I do *not* have a hairy chest."

She snorts, her cheeks all rosy, her hair wild and messy across her forehead. My daughter acts half-feral, and that's one thing I love best about her. She doesn't give a flying fuck how she's perceived. She is genuine through and through.

Except when she's fucking with me and trying to pull a fast one. Then she's a little fibber.

Oliver stifles a quiet chuckle behind her, his palm cast tightly over his mouth as though he'd betray himself somehow if someone who isn't family heard him laughing.

"Yes you do, Dad," Emmy insists. "It just doesn't look that way because you shave it."

This kid.

Now it's Skylar's turn to burst out laughing. I shake my head, watching Emmy's expression go from amused to pissed-off in one breath.

"Dad, you told me that lying is bad, so don't be a liar. Everyone knows you have a hairy chest and that you shave it. I saw you doing it in the shower once."

"Yes, Emmeline. Everyone knows because you're shouting about it at the top of your lungs and because you come barging in there uninvited to talk my ear off more often than you should."

Oliver laughs so hard, his hand moves up over his eyes as though he can't bear the crushing weight of my humiliation.

I turn to Skylar to explain. "I really only shave it sometimes. Not always."

She has tears of amusement gathering in her eyes that she wipes away frantically.

"It's okay, Emmy." Skylar struggles to catch her breath in an attempt to cover for me. And it's the least she can do after I saved her from a grizzly bear. "It's okay," Skylar repeats breathlessly. "I shave in the shower too. Most adults do. Totally normal."

Emmy turns, scrutinizing her like she's not sure if Skylar's telling the truth or if this is an adult plot to fool her. "Your chest? Prove it."

I suppose we all get a turn to burst out laughing tonight, and this is mine.

Skylar's hazel eyes go wider than they did when a bear was charging us. Oliver falls to the ground dramatically, now lying flat on his back on the grass, covering his face with both hands.

If Skylar weren't here right now, I know he'd say *Just leave me here to die. That's it. I'm done.* Melodrama is his current go-to reaction because he's getting to that age where everything embarrasses him.

I opt to save Ollie from his embarrassment and Skylar from having to "prove" that she has hair on her chest by rerouting this utterly out-of-pocket conversation.

"Well, Skylar, now that you've met the whole ragtag crew, can I interest you in a burger tonight?"

Skylar's lips roll together, eyes still dancing with delight as she peers around the space. Emmy is giving us what most people would call a dirty look, and Oliver is still flat on his back.

Her lips continue moving, and I find myself distracted by them.

Doesn't matter that my kids are here.

Doesn't matter that she and I seem to be a little hot and cold.

Something about the ridiculousness of the moment makes everything else around us evaporate, and all I can think about is how close my lips came to hers on that road today.

I also can't get over how Skylar Stone is absolutely nothing like I expected in person.

"No," she says. "I wouldn't want to inconvenience you during family time. I've taken quite enough of your time for one day."

Emmy glances between us, never missing a beat. "Wait a second, you two have met?"

"Earlier," I reply simply as my daughter props her hands on her hips. At least she missed the part earlier about Skylar seeing me shirtless.

"You met Skylar Stone today, and you didn't even tell me about it?" She gives me a deadly glare.

I know Emmy is a fan—hell, so am I—but we don't need to run around making the poor woman feel like she's a sideshow attraction. Rosie told me she needed space, and that's what I intend to give her.

Which is why I throw my sister straight under the bus.

"Auntie Rosie met her too. Did she mention it when she picked you up?" I swear I can hear Emmy's teeth grinding as she processes what I've told her. "Not everything is your business, Emmy-Lou."

"Dad, if I didn't love you so much, I'd be real mad at you right now."

Based on the way her ears have gone red, I'd say she is, in fact, real mad at me.

"Well, Emmy baby, it's a good thing that you love me so much, then." I wink at my daughter, and it instantly diffuses the situation. Her pudgy cheeks squish up into perfectly round apples as she rolls her eyes.

Quick to anger and quick to let go. Can't say the kid didn't get my temper.

"Skylar, I haven't made proper introductions yet. This pint-sized barrel of attitude and oversharing is my daughter, Emmeline, but she'll shank you if you don't call her Emmy—"

"I would never shank Skylar Stone," she mumbles as I forge ahead.

"And that boy lying on the grass in a pile of embarrassment is my son, Oliver. Or Ollie. Call him what you want—he won't shank you."

"Yeah," Emmy says, as though it's her job to answer for everybody. "She knows. She met Oliver down by the lake. He *introduced himself.*"

That gives me pause. I try to hide how much my daughter's words have affected me as I glance between Skylar and Oliver, who has now edged two fingers open to peek at me through the space between them.

He introduced himself.

Truth be told, I'm floored.

Skylar forges on like there's nothing unusual about that. "Yeah, he was reading by the lake, and I needed some peace and quiet. It was a beautiful view, and he let me sit on the log with him. I watched the birds and the sky, and he read his book…" She trails off, eyeing me carefully, most likely reading my shock as disapproval. "I hope that's okay. I didn't mean to overstep. I just…"

She turns to glance down at Oliver with an affectionate grin. "You're good company, you know? It was exactly what I needed."

I'm trying not to make a big deal about this, so I stare

down at the grill and gather my thoughts. Over the last few years, I've learned that making a big deal out of Oliver's selective mutism serves zero purpose other than embarrassing him and making him quieter.

So instead of disclosing that Oliver never speaks to anyone other than immediate family and friends who might as well be family, I carry on like there is nothing out of the ordinary about what Skylar just said.

"Well, that's great. I'm glad you guys got the chance to meet, and I'm glad my boy was such a gentleman and shared his bench with you."

"But, Dad, don't you—" Emmy starts, and I cut her off with a serious look. It's not one I give her often. I'm not known to be an especially great disciplinarian, but this is a moment where we need to just change the subject and not make him talking a whole *thing*.

I just have to pray she picks up what I'm putting down. Boundaries aren't her strong suit, but she's pretty intuitive. "Emmy, can you please run inside and get Skylar a drink?" I turn to our guest. "Skylar, what do you want? Beer to help with a matching beer belly? Or I've got wine, soda, juice. Really, whatever you want, I've got it."

"What about me? Can I have whatever I want?" Emmy, again. Jumping right into the fray.

"Oh em gee, girlfriend," I whine, leaning again into my favorite Valley-girl voice that elicits a giggle from Emmy. "You get water because you already had a freezie."

Skylar chuckles softly, and Emmy grabs her hand, hauling her into the house with a disappointed growl.

I turn to watch them walk away, and when they get close to the door, Skylar glances back at me over her shoulder. Her shiny bronze hair falls loose around her shoulders. My eyes catch on her hazel ones for a moment, and she seems uncertain. Like she doesn't know what to make of today's developments. I mean... Why would she?

The girl has to be entirely out of her element. She's gone from world tours and selling out stadiums to getting hauled into an old farmhouse by a sticky-handed hellion.

Her lashes flutter down over my apron once more before her lips press into a flat line to cover a smile. She shakes her head slightly and follows my daughter into our house.

"Dad?" Ollie says to me, finally pushing up onto his elbows. His sandy-blond hair and his bright blue eyes feel a bit like looking straight into a mirror of myself at his age.

"Hell yeah, girlfriend. What's up?" I continue in that voice and his eyes take an exasperated tour around their sockets. "If I'm annoying you now, just imagine how much you'll hate me when you're a teenager. I'm going to have to learn how to play it cool by then. Or do you already think I'm pretty cool?"

He ignores my line of questioning altogether and jumps in with, "You can't leave her alone with Emmy."

"And why not?" I ask as I lift the edge of a burger to check the sear.

"Because Emmy is absolutely obsessed and totally over-bearing and is going to make her not want to be here. She was talking about choreographing her a dance and then charging her for it like she's some sort of entrepreneur."

I stop and stare at my son. When he does talk, he sounds like he's twenty and has been to Harvard. Must be the absurd reading level his teachers keep telling us about. "Your vocabulary never fails to impress me. But your sister shouldn't work for free. Child labor is a crime, you know."

"Dad, I'm serious."

"Okay, okay. So you *do* want her to be here?"

He shrugs and tips his head back, looking up at the darkening sky. "I guess so. Yeah, she's… Well, you know I'm not into her music, but I like *her*. She seems nice, right?"

I study him. I don't know what went on between the two of them down at that lake, but there must have been something. Ollie is shy and reserved and slow to trust, but there's something about Skylar that's speaking to him.

There's something about her that speaks to me too.

"I'm surprised, that's all. You're usually not a big fan of strangers."

His eyes are downcast as he kicks at the ground. "Haven't met anyone before who can't talk, even when they want to sometimes."

Realization dawns on me. Skylar's recent freeze-ups on camera have received a lot of attention in the press. Most people see a young woman embarrassing herself publicly.

But Ollie sees someone like him.

"Dad," he starts up again. "Please don't let Emmy ruin this."

I scoff, not wanting him to be too hard on his little sister. "Ollie, I'm not gonna let her ruin this. But your sister's got a lot more charm than you think. That girl could sell a hamburger to a vegan."

72

He quirks a brow at me. "Are you done being wise now? Can you please go save Skylar from Emmy?"

I point my tongs at him. "Mouthy little shit."

Then I oblige him. I place the utensil down and jog toward the house, hearing my son mumble to my back, "More like she'd hold a vegan down and force-feed them a burger."

I can't help but chuckle at his remark as I approach the front door. It's wide-open, so I step inside and opt to watch for a moment.

Just to make sure Emmy isn't force-feeding her anything after all.

Perched on a worn wooden stool at the butcher block countertop, Skylar watches while Emmy plays bartender with a can of locally made cider.

"No, fancy girls don't drink out of cans, Skylar," Emmy argues. "What about a champagne glass? I think Dad has one back here somewhere."

"Maybe I don't want to be a fancy girl anymore," Skylar responds.

She says it in a joking manner, but something about the sentiment hits me in the chest. Something about the way she got all defensive when I made the jibe about the bedsheets.

It's become abundantly clear there's a lot more to Skylar Stone than just a pretty face.

She's a girl on the run—I know that much just from watching and listening—but what I'm realizing is that she might be on the run from herself.

Emmy ignores Skylar's reply, refusing to accept the fact

that she'd drink out of a can. And I smile to myself, because now that I think of it…this is actually a little like force-feeding someone.

My daughter crawls up onto the countertop, the picture of independence as she reaches into the cupboard.

She hasn't noticed me standing at the door, and I suppose that's why she starts shit-talking me. "My dad always tells me not to do this, but you know what? He doesn't know every-thing, and I can handle my business. He's always all"—she drops her voice in a mocking imitation—"*Emmy, you need to be careful.* But you know what? I've heard stories about my dad from when *he* was a kid. And it doesn't sound like he was careful. So, like, what does he know?"

She cuts off when the tips of her fingers bump against the glass, but instead of getting a grip, she ends up pulling it closer and it tumbles from the cupboard. It lands on the countertop before bouncing once and shattering everywhere.

Hundreds of tiny, sharp pieces of glass litter the kitchen in an instant.

"Yeah, all good points," I pipe up as Skylar lets out a sharp gasp. "You really showed me. What do I know, right?"

Emmy freezes, mouth popped open, as I push my propped shoulder off the doorframe and let out a smug chuckle. "Emmy baby, this is exactly why I tell you not to do that. Not because I'm being a buzzkill. Just stay right where you are."

My daughter's eyes are wide as I move toward her, but it's Skylar's reaction that hits me in the gut. She has one hand flat against her chest, and she's staring at me like she's afraid of me.

My brow rumples as I take her in. "Hey, it's okay. Everything's fine." I take on the softest tone I can so as not to startle anybody. "It's not a big deal, it's just a glass. Not even crystal, because we're not that fancy. Perfectly replaceable. Most importantly, is everyone all right?"

I walk through the kitchen until I reach my daughter and scoop her up off the countertop.

Glass crunches beneath my boots as I carry her to the back door. Then I swat her playfully on the butt. "Back outside, where animals like you belong. And can you please go ask your brother to turn the barbecue off?"

She nods as she says, "I'm sorry, Daddy."

I almost laugh. She only pulls out the *daddy* card when she's in trouble or wants something.

"You better be," I fire back with a wink. She grins at me, and I shoo her outside. "Quick, before the burgers burn."

When I turn, Skylar is still staring at me. Her face is devoid of any color. I quirk my head at her, attempting to figure out why this grown woman looks so traumatized over a broken glass. "Skylar, are you okay?"

She nods woodenly. "Yeah. Yeah." Her voice comes out creaky.

"Want me to carry you out of here too?" I ask, hoping to lighten the mood.

Her responding laugh is thin. "No." She glances around her. She left her shoes at the front door. "No, I'm okay." She says the words but still makes no move to get up. Crossing a room littered in glass shards with bare feet will be a challenge.

"I'm sorry. I shouldn't have let her do that. I was

enjoying watching her climb and listening to her talk. She's funny."

I nod. "Yeah, she's funny all right."

Skylar swallows and lowers her gaze to her hands, fiddling with her fingers like she's been sent to the principal's office. "Please don't be mad at her."

My head tilts. "Why would I be mad at her? It's just glass. I'll clean it up. No big deal. She's a little kid. Little kids make mistakes." Skylar nods but doesn't glance up at me. "Shit, adults make mistakes too. God knows I have."

"Same," she whispers.

And I can't fucking stand how sad she looks.

"Okay, that's it, fancy face." I take two long steps toward her, and her chin shoots up, eyes widening when she realizes I've closed the distance between us.

"What are you—"

I cut her off when I reach for her. I barely know this woman, and I don't know what I'm doing. But have I ever really known what I'm doing? I've spent my entire life ruled by impulses and instincts. So why would I stop now?

She squeals when my arms slide beneath her knees and around her waist, but she doesn't pull away. Instead, her arms reach up and circle my neck as I straighten my legs to stand.

"West!"

"What?"

"Put me down!"

"No. I don't think I will. That's too much sad face for one day."

A disbelieving laugh lurches from her throat as she tips her face up to stare at me.

Meeting her eyes feels like it might be too personal, so I choose to whisper gruffly against her ear, "And I won't stand for it."

She shivers and presses closer as I fold her against my chest and forge ahead, over the sea of glass. I march outside to the sound of Skylar's shocked giggles, Emmy's loud bark of laughter, and my son's embarrassed groan.

I feel her fingers grip the back of my neck and the rush of her breath against my throat, but I don't put her down, not even when she gasps as I take the few steps off the deck.

Only when my boots hit the grass do I finally let her go.

Her bare feet land lightly on the ground, and her hands stay linked behind my neck for a beat before she slides them down over my shoulders.

Over the sounds of my kids' laughter, I hear her softly say, "Thank you," as her fingers rap against my chest.

It pulls my eyes down, her nails trailing against the apron where it says, This Guy Rubs His Own Meat.

A shy smile touches her lips. Her soft fucking lips.

And I have to draw away. Because this apron is feeling just a little too apt for the moment and what I'll no doubt be doing later.

CHAPTER 7

Skylar

Back in the bunkhouse, I pull up a YouTube video on how to make a bed.

Fuck Weston Belmont and his thick thighs and his cocky smirk for implying that I wouldn't be able to do it on my own.

I'm a grown-ass woman. I'm perfectly capable of making a bed. I've just never had to, and there's no time like the present.

I decide learning how to do things I've never done before is part of my fresh start.

As my mom would have said with a smug smile on her face, "Living like the other half."

Turns out, making a bed is simple. I speed through it, and truth be told, as soon as I take a look at the sheets, what I need to do becomes apparent.

It's simple enough that my mind wanders as I complete the task.

I find myself thinking about dinner tonight. About watching West's kids and the way they interact with him. About the cozy feeling of sitting outside under the patio lanterns strung above the front porch. The table we gathered around reminded me of a classic diner table, with red vinyl on top and a metal trim wrapped around the edges. The spots where the screws attached to it showed slight signs of rust.

There were six chairs at the table, and not a single one of them matched. The same could be said for the plates, cups, and cutlery. And even though there was no fine china or crystal as far as the eye could see, I've never been invited to sit at a more charming table.

I don't think I've ever spent time around children as relaxed and playful as Emmy and Oliver. And I don't think I've ever seen a more hands-on dad in action than when I sat there watching West.

As the night wore on, I retreated into my head. I couldn't help it. Watching them together felt like watching something that wasn't meant for me. It felt foreign and inspiring and special.

Seeing them was a punch to the gut that I didn't see coming. It was the family life I never realized I missed out on until I watched it play out right in front of me.

There was laughter and good-natured teasing, not a single mention of business, or money, or upcoming events. They didn't engage in mean gossip about people who weren't present. They just…talked about their day.

West didn't criticize the way they sat or the way they

held their cutlery—or lack thereof. He didn't make a big deal about the ketchup all over Emmy's face or say anything to embarrass her about the broken glass from before dinner.

Who knew a broken champagne flute could trigger me the way it did?

It dredged up a matching memory. Except it didn't match at all.

My memory involved being forced to pick pieces of similarly broken glass off the floor with my bare hands. Apologizing profusely and trying not to bleed on the marble—thus creating more mess—while my dad screamed at me about needing to be less clumsy if I was ever going to be presentable in public.

When he got mad like that, his face would turn red like a tomato and his jowls would shake. I'd feel the spittle fly from his mouth and splatter against my face. For years after that one mistake, my mom would crack offhanded jokes about how I could dance so gracefully onstage but had a bad case of butterfingers around the house.

They never laid a hand on me in their mission to mold me into the perfect doll.

But they scarred me all the same.

My heart sank to my feet the moment Emmy fumbled, and the sound of shattering glass tossed me violently back into my own strained childhood.

I don't know what I was expecting, but it wasn't West's calm, kind words or the complete absence of anger in his response.

His first concern was for his daughter.

His second concern was for me.

The importance of the glassware didn't even factor into his reaction. I braced myself for the shouting. I was prepared to be berated so that Emmy would be spared. I was ready for the loud bark, the condemnation, the underhanded insults that were subtle as a child but became more obvious to me as I grew older.

But none of it ever came.

In fact, the entire thing ended in laughter as West carried me out into the yard and acted as though he'd just rescued me from a burning building.

He'll never know, but in that moment, he healed me.

Just a little bit.

A knock jolts me from my walk down depressing memory lane as I toss the pillow covered in the checkerboard case onto the bed.

I pause for a moment, not sure about how safe it is to answer the door at night in an unfamiliar town. With my luck, there will be a cougar at the door.

Whoever it is knocks again, so I pad cautiously across the hardwood floors and pull back the floral curtain to peek outside.

I smile as I take in the small figure standing at the door. She's bouncing on the spot and twiddling her fingers, a ball of vibrating excitement. I'm not sure if she's supposed to be out and about after dark, but I figure it's better for her to be safe in the bunkhouse than wandering the property.

So I twist the lock and unlatch the chain before pulling the door open and looking down into the eyes of little Emmy Belmont.

"Emmy?" I say, using her name as a question.

"Hi!" The words practically burst from her mouth. "I was hoping you would still be up."

"Yep, I'm still up. Is there something I can help you with?" I glance down at my watch and see that it's 9 p.m. "I feel like it's probably time for you to be in bed."

She dismisses that with a casual wave. "Oh, nah. It's the weekend. I don't have anything to do tomorrow." She taps a finger against her chin. "Actually, tomorrow is Saturday and I do have a soccer game before I go back to my mom's house."

"A soccer game? So you should definitely get a good night's sleep."

"Yeah, but I'm the best on the team. Even if I'm tired, I'll be better than everyone else."

I chuckle, amused by her confidence. Once again, I wish I had even an ounce of Emmy's carefree surety in myself.

But I don't.

Instead, I'm a bundle of anxiety, riddled by second-guessing. I'm a woman driven by a bone-deep, simmering anger, who predicts disappointment at every turn.

I'm fucking Eeyore but make him famous. Saggy shoulders but never forgetting to put that bow on his tail.

I need to learn how to channel my inner Emmy. A little bit of her would be good for me.

I smile at her. "I have no doubt you are."

"You should come watch," she says so simply. Like we haven't just met today. Like there's nothing she requires of me other than to come watch her play soccer.

"You came here to invite me to your soccer game?"

I feel like, within twenty-four hours, I've become quite the interloper in the Belmont family activities.

"Yes."

"Sounds like fun. We'll see how tomorrow goes," I say.

She shrugs, satisfied with my noncommittal answer, and barges straight past me into the bunkhouse like she owns the place.

"So what are you up to? Are you watching something? Are you doing something?"

I follow her in, glancing around the small space, not really sure what there is to do or how I'm going to pass several weeks in this setting. Probably walking up and down the hill obsessively to stay thin so the tabloids won't say anything about my weight when I inevitably have to face the paparazzi in the city again.

"I was just making my bed. I don't know what I'm gonna do."

"Take a hike!" Cherry squawks at the little girl, and I grimace. Bitching at West is one thing, but at Emmy, it's just too far.

"Cherry, watch your mouth, young lady," I snipe back at the parrot.

Emmy approaches the cage eagerly, hands clasped behind her back like she knows better than to reach for her. "I would take a hike, but it's too dark. Maybe tomorrow."

Cherry blinks at her, like Emmy's enthusiasm throws her off as much as it does me.

"Cool bird," she announces, spinning back my way.

Cherry blinks again, and I bite down on a smile.

"Are you gonna write some music? Maybe if you wrote some music, I could choreograph the dance for you."

"I don't know. I've never written my own music."

Her eyes bulge now, and I force my features into a happy expression. "Really?"

"Really," I say, trying to brush past the embarrassment I feel about this subject.

She sits on my bed and smooths her hands over the top of it. "Why not?"

I lean back against the counter and watch as she glances thoughtfully around the space. It gives me a moment to figure out what to tell her. *Because I'm not that talented and everything about my public persona is carefully crafted to make you think I'm a lot cooler than I am* probably isn't the answer she's after.

"There are a lot of gifted songwriters who help me with that" is what I settle on.

"I think you should try it," the girl responds with a firm nod.

"I've never done it before."

"Why not? Have you ever tried?"

"A couple of times. It was fun but not good enough to record."

"So someone told you no, and you stopped trying?"

I groan, staring up at the ceiling. I didn't expect an interrogation from a six-year-old to hit this hard. "Yeah, I guess that's what I'm saying."

As if she's disappointed in me, she makes a low grumbling noise, crosses her arms, and looks me dead in the eye.

"My dad always tells me that no means to try harder. So, if I say, 'Dad, can I have a freezie?' and he says, 'No,' I just try harder. I'm working on a pony now. He keeps saying no, but I'm not giving up."

I can't help but laugh. She really is a spitfire. "Does it work?"

Her head wobbles back and forth and a troublemaking little smirk touches her lips. "Sometimes. And sometimes I sneak a freezie and don't tell him about it. But the times it works make all the other times worth it."

Her philosophy is so simple. So elementary in its logic. Yet it only drives home what a pushover I've been. How I've never pressed back, questioned, or raised any complaints. I've been obedient beyond compare.

And this is where it's gotten me.

Facing crippling anxiety and alienated from my family. Or, well, what I thought was my family.

"I'm going to take this advice into consideration, Emmy. I think you might be onto something."

She smiles and kicks her feet, which don't quite reach the floor from where she's sitting. I strum at my bottom lip, not sure what to talk to her about now.

"Does your dad know you're here?" I ask.

Her tongue pops into her cheek as though she's weighing her answer. "He told me not to bother you, and I decided to try harder."

"Does that mean you snuck out?"

"I don't feel like I'm bothering you. Am I?"

I swallow a chuckle. I'm not oblivious to the fact that

she's smart enough to work her way around admitting she snuck out. I'm treading on dangerous ground right now. I don't want to undermine her father, but she also truly isn't bothering me.

"No, Emmy, you're not bothering me. But from only knowing you and your dad for a day, I can tell he loves you very much. And if he can't find you or is wondering where you are, he's going to get worried."

She heaves out a breath. "No, he'll ask Oliver first."

"Oh, you told Oliver you were coming here?"

"Yeah, he told me not to do it. He said I was gonna scare you away."

I tilt my head at that. "Scare me away?"

"Yeah, he told me that I'll annoy you, and you won't want to stay with us anymore."

"Emmy, you are not annoying me, and you will not make me leave. Truth be told…" I say sadly, not able to even look the girl in the eye as I admit to it, "truth be told, I don't have anywhere to go."

She nods as though she understands what could be going on in my life. "Oliver likes you, you know," she says.

"That's good. I like Oliver too."

"I mean, he has terrible taste in music, which means he listens to the same stuff that Uncle Ford does. But he likes you. He never talks to anybody, and he talked to you."

That stops me in my tracks. "What do you mean by he never talks to anybody?"

"I mean, he doesn't talk to anyone other than me and Dad and Mom. And Brandon sometimes. Ford, Rosie, Cora…"

She lists off only enough names to fit on both hands, and I'm stunned into silence.

It's not as though Oliver and I had some big conversation, but he did offer his name. I never thought about the fact that he was quiet. I'm used to people being struck silent by my presence, or fumbling around me, or just generally treating me like I'm something special, which only makes me uncomfortable.

Oliver's reaction was comforting. And so was his dad's.

West hasn't even mentioned recognizing who I am, though I know he does, and that's why I feel relaxed here. Even if I'm staying in a tiny dump with a mouse for a roommate.

"Well, he only told me his name, but I didn't know that. And it doesn't matter to me. That's his business."

"Yeah." She nods. "Dad tells me all the time that I shouldn't tell people about it, but Oliver does like you. He told me so. So just…maybe he'll talk to you. I think that would be nice for him. So just don't give up on him yet."

I feel my cheeks heat. It's such a profound request from someone so small—someone I don't even know. I'm not used to these kinds of expectations.

Human expectations.

There's no financial gain. There's no priority placement in a magazine. There's no clout to be gained. It's just a little boy's heart and a little girl who's looking out for her brother. It warms me to see how much they love each other.

Has anyone ever gone to bat for me the way Emmy does for her brother? Just over something that makes me happy? Just over something that I want for myself?

I don't think they have.

And it makes me feel more appreciative of these two kids I just met. It makes me want to know them better. And since I intend to spend at least a couple of months here, they don't need to worry about me leaving. There's time. There's time for all of us to get to know each other.

And there's time to see if Oliver feels inclined to talk more.

"You don't need to worry about that, Emmy. I've got no plans to leave. If anything, I'll be moving next door into one of the guesthouses, but we'll still be close, and I'll still be around. I don't know anybody here, so you'll likely catch me wandering aimlessly, trying to figure out the purpose of my life and how I ended up where I am and what I even want to do with myself."

I realize I've blurted out more than I should to a six-year-old, and her wide eyes tell the tale. So I scoff and wave a hand. "Ignore me. I'm just rambling. How about we get you back up to the house, so you don't get in any more trouble?"

She hops off my bed, and I take in the perfect french braid in her damp hair. It's pulled tight but not too tight, all artfully twisted down the back of her scalp into a rope that lands between her shoulder blades, topped off with a silk tie.

I can't help but wonder if West braided his little girl's hair himself. The thought of his big, gentle hands twisting strands of hair together with such care makes my chest pinch uncharacteristically.

It makes me wonder what else those hands could do.

It makes me annoyed at myself for continuing to think about him in that way.

I push my wandering thoughts away and walk to the house, hand in hand with Emmy. She doesn't say a word, and I suspect that means she might be tired. When we round the corner out of the trees, West is standing at the front door, shoulder propped against the frame as though he knew we'd be coming.

He's wearing boxers and absolutely nothing else.

Contrasted with his close-cropped, sandy-colored hair, his beard seems thicker than it did earlier today. Like it's grown right before my eyes.

Warm light shines from behind him, illuminating every plane and dip on his chiseled body. What jeans hid before is now barely left to the imagination. Thickly muscled thighs. A body dusted with a masculine spread of hair.

He looks comforting and intimidating all at once. I wonder if he'd be gentle or rough. Or the perfect blend of both.

And then I hate myself for wondering about these things. *Again*.

I straighten when I see his jaw pop and his eyes laser in on his daughter.

"Emmeline Belmont, where have you been?" His voice is deep but not loud, yet I flinch.

I never realized how much my parents yelled at me until I moved out on my own and found my house to be incredibly quiet. I never realized how traumatizing it was for me. When I got in trouble, there were no soft tones or asking if I was okay. One wrong step and voices got loud. Words became vicious.

And when I got in trouble, it wasn't for sneaking out. It was for not giving the right answer in an interview or for eating so much that my dress didn't fit the way they wanted it to.

No, when I got in trouble, it was merely for being human in a way that may or may not have affected my parents' paycheck. The one I've been handing over to them for years because I trusted them implicitly.

And they fucked me over.

There is absolutely nothing similar about the way West says his daughter's name and the way my dad would scream mine at me. There's no berating her, no intimidation, there's no cowering.

And it stops me in my tracks.

"Sorry, Dad," she says immediately.

I don't want to get her into any more trouble, so I add, "She just came for a quick talk. I walked her back almost immediately."

West's irises become a shade closer to midnight blue in the dark. Navy like the blanket of the sky above us. I could wrap myself in that blue and maybe finally feel some peace.

Emmy turns pleading eyes on her dad. "I only snuck out to tell her she can't leave because Oliver likes her, and he talked to her, and Oliver never likes or talks to anyone."

West stares at his daughter, eyes keen, but she trusts him enough that she holds his gaze. They have a stare off of sorts, but it's not an intimidating one. It's as though they're having a conversation, a silent one that only they can understand.

It's touching.

Eventually, he sucks in a deep breath and lets it out with a heavy sigh as he scrubs one hand over his close-cut hair. "Emmy baby, we really got to talk again about minding your own business. You know that, girl?"

She nods and gives him a solemn, "Okay, we can talk about it. But I don't think I'll ever be able to mind my business if it means lying because you told me I can't lie, and all I did was tell Skylar the truth."

Just like his daughter, West pushes his tongue into his cheek as he stares down at her, and I choke back a laugh. I don't know Emmy well, but I'm getting the feeling that she's a bit of a challenge. A test for his patience. Regardless, the way he looks at her tells me he loves every minute of it.

"This is true, Emmy. You shouldn't lie, but you also can't be sneaking around the property after dark when I think you're in bed."

He turns his attention back to me. I can see the apology on his face. Which is funny because I am also feeling apologetic standing on his front step. Again.

"Emmy, get your ass in bed," he grumbles, gently gesturing her inside while ruffling her hair. "We'll talk about this tomorrow."

She scampers past him, but after taking a few steps, she turns and gives me a full grin, displaying all her Chiclet teeth and the twinkle in her troublemaking eyes.

West must realize that he can't hear her footsteps because he swiftly turns and catches her giving me that look. "Get gone, kid." He raises his voice, but his tone is all exasperation and playfulness.

She laughs and barrels up the stairs as he groans and turns his attention back to me.

"Got your hands full with that one," I say with a chuckle.

He scrubs a hand over his face. I can hear the bristles of his beard against his palm, and it draws my attention to his full lips. Shapelier than any man has the right to have. People would pay good money for lips like his. My brain is a horny little slut today, and she wonders what it would feel like to have those lips on my body.

I'm jolted back to the present as he grumbles, "Don't I fucking know it. Love her to bits, but good lord, that girl will be the death of me."

"Well, she didn't bother me at all, but maybe…" I bite down on my lip, hard enough that it could leave a dent. "Maybe we should exchange numbers? Just in case she finds herself at my place again? Then I could drop you a line, so you don't worry."

He studies me, keen blue irises bouncing between my eyes as though he's searching for more answers. As though he's searching for a clue. I hope he can't tell I was thinking about his lips. Suddenly, I feel like I have my innermost thoughts written on my forehead in blocky capital letters for him to read.

"Yeah, sure, that seems like a smart idea," he answers, but he doesn't look into my eyes when he says it. Instead, his gaze drops to my lips, and I can't help but turn my attention back to his.

His tongue darts out over the full bottom one, and I drink him in from top to bottom. Chiseled pecs to his narrow waist and that delicious V shape that makes me want to run my tongue over his hips. I glance quickly over the bulge in his tight boxers, trying not to be too obvious before I make my way down. His legs, his calves, his feet—everything about Weston Belmont is so goddamn masculine I can hardly stand it.

"You done gawking? Or should I flex while I wait for you to pull that phone out and take my number?"

I start. And then I turn red.

God, I'm embarrassing.

"Yeah, sorry. I lost my train of thought there for a second."

Now it's his turn to bite down on his bottom lip, his cheeks pinching up in a knowing smirk. "Yeah, that train was a runaway all right."

"I have no idea what you mean. I was only checking to see if you have razor burn from shaving your chest," I say as I scramble to reach for the phone in my back pocket.

Google alerts and angry texts litter the screen. My anxiety surges. There's a grainy photo of me talking to an airline agent at the airport with the headline, *Skylar Stone throws fit to sit in first class.* "Fucking assholes," I mutter.

"What's wrong?"

I smile blandly. "Headline. Apparently politely asking if there were any upgrades for my flight here is throwing a fit." I roll my eyes. Trying to act more unaffected than I feel.

I swipe past, vowing not to read the whole thing until I'm in bed. I swipe through the screens, mumbling, "For the record, I sat in economy. Middle seat. Not a single fucking complaint," as I pull up a new contact. I type his name in without glancing back up, though I can see his amused smirk from the corner of my eye.

He's distracting.

"Okay, I'm ready for the number."

With a deep chuckle, he recites it to me, and my fingers tap across the screen.

"Great, well, great." I turn quickly to walk away. "See you tomorrow." I wave nervously over my shoulder, hating myself for checking him out so blatantly.

He doesn't take a hint, and he doesn't lay off.

"Hey, fancy face!" he shouts. "You can take a photo of me like this for my contact card if you want!"

But I don't turn back to take a photo.

Instead, I hustle faster, to get away from West and his chiseled fucking *everything* before that horny little slut in my head turns around and takes him up on his offer.

CHAPTER 8

Skylar

IT'S THE PROSPECT OF BEING CHEWED ON BY A MOUSE WHILE I sleep that keeps me from drifting off.

Cherry suffers from no such concerns. Her cage is in the corner and she's dead quiet, but I swear I can hear her breathing.

In fact, I can hear far too much.

Where I'm used to a white noise machine or traffic or the footsteps of somebody walking down a hotel hallway, everything in the bunkhouse is silent. And when things get too quiet, all I'm left with are the thoughts in my head. To be frank, I'm not in the mood to sit with those lately.

No, when I sit in the quiet for too long with only myself for company, my constant companions turn out to be regret, fear, and resentment.

Not wanting to face those feelings, I get out of bed. It's warm but not stifling. As soon as the sun dropped behind the mountains, the temperature dipped. So I reach onto the top bunk, tug down my thick-knit cream duster cardigan, and wrap it around myself. It covers the matching Calvin Klein sleep set I got from a shoot I did not so long ago.

The size of my suitcase and the amount of shit I brought with me barely fits on the single bed up top. I considered sleeping up there to be farther from the floor, but the lower bed is at least six inches wider and is still most likely the smallest bed I've slept in since I had a crib.

I've decided this experience is good for me. That I could stand to build a little character.

With that in mind, I toe on a pair of slides I left near the front door and head out onto the quiet, rural property. To my right is the lake. Lights from the houses on the other side twinkle in the night against the black silhouette of the mountains. Their peaks stand out against the indigo of the cloudless sky.

The milky stars above blanket the valley in a way I've never seen. Sure, I've seen stars, but not this many, not in so many sizes and intensities.

Some are so bright that I wonder if they're planets. Others are more subdued. Some are so faint I have to squint to see them. I'm sure those are the ones I wouldn't see in the city at all.

Nickers and whinnies filtering down from the stables draw my attention to the left. The sounds remind me of the sweet noises Meli made after covering herself in dirt today.

I can see the path that winds through the trees, leading me back up in that direction. I check my watch and decide

11 p.m. is late enough that I won't be doing anyone any harm if I visit the horses. To watch them, listen—acquaint myself with the smell.

Seeing Meli eat earlier today soothed me. I don't know if it was her warm breath against my hand, or the deep, rolling chewing noise that her teeth made on the dried grass, or the way her big, kind eyes peered at me from beneath those thick lashes. The way she looked at me was different somehow, like she expected nothing more than pets and food. She didn't give a shit about my video or my filter either. Meli just noted my presence and went back to eating like I was no big deal.

Having spent my entire life being told I'm a big deal and that everything I do is a big deal, there was something comforting about the way I was of such little consequence to her.

The feel of constant pressure has finally hit a boiling point. I don't want people to be impressed by me. I just want to *be*.

Be myself. *Finally*.

My feet carry me up to the barn, and when I clear the thick copse of trees, I see warm light spilling out from between the barn doors. It shines over the sand ring, toward where I stand. Like a yellow brick road pulling me in.

Before I know it, I'm right up to the edge of the barn, where the dirt road meets the concrete alleyway. Cautiously, I wrap my fingers around the edge of the aluminum sliding door and crane my neck to peer inside the barn.

From within, I hear faint footsteps and rolling rubber wheels. And when I get a good angle, I see West.

He's wearing the same jeans from earlier, the same shirt

with a hole, the same pair of worn slip-on boots. I bet people would pay to have them distressed in that exact way. He's humming a song beneath his breath and doling out hay to each horse.

I watch him for a moment, trying to place the song.

But then he sings. No, he *belts* it out and does a little two-step with a thin piece of hay.

"*Chasin' that high! Feelin' so alive! Every day with you feels like another golden prize.*"

I recognize the song now…because it's one of mine. Watching him strut down the alleyway, singing one of my songs in that deep voice, makes me giggle.

I don't mean to.

I didn't want to get caught.

Nevertheless, here I am.

West freezes and doesn't bother turning to face me. He drops his chin, dimples denting his cheeks as he stares down at his feet. "Fancy face, are you spying on me?"

I didn't go looking for him, but I found him all the same. *Again.*

The two of us, drawn to each other like moths to a flame.

Maybe it's just today. Or maybe there's something in the air. Maybe there's a cosmic force in the stars I was just staring at that makes it so we're constantly thrust into each other's paths. Whatever it is, there's an uncanny vibe about the whole thing. Serendipitous even.

With a smile, I say, "Yes, I came up here to spy on you because I could hear you belting out my song all the way from the bunkhouse."

He chuckles now and turns his chin over his shoulder to glare at me. "You're full of shit. I was not *belting*. And even if I was, there's no point in being embarrassed—we both know I sound good. And we both know you just came up for the show."

I scoff and roll my eyes. But the apples of my cheeks hurt from the pressure of my smile.

West turns to face me. He has a welcoming quality about him and doesn't make me feel like I've crossed some boundary or overstayed my welcome. "You were probably hoping I didn't have my shirt on again. So you could check the quality of my shave, *of course*."

I waggle a finger over the length of his body as I take a cautious step into the barn. "Never mind your shirt. It's your jeans that are distracting."

My sandals slide across the concrete as an expression of mock outrage morphs his features. "Skylar Stone, are you checking out my ass?"

I lick my lips quickly.

Are we flirting?

It feels like we're flirting.

And I don't have the good sense to put a stop to it.

"No. It's your thighs."

He peers down at where his muscular thighs do indeed fill out his jeans. "What about my thighs?"

I hold my hands up and make a squeezing motion with both. "They're meaty."

Now his jaw truly drops open. I might have caught him off guard with that one.

"Did you just motion squeezing my thighs?"

I shrug and twirl a piece of my hair around my finger as I search for something interesting to stare at. "More of a grope. And don't judge me. City boys don't have thighs like that."

He barks out a laugh now, propping those distracting hands on his hips. "No, I suppose not. City boys don't spend all day riding horses. I don't believe you weren't checking out my ass, though. I have a great ass."

I shrug, still refusing to turn my head in his direction. Or to admit that I definitely was checking out his ass. And it definitely is great. "The right jeans can make any ass look good."

I peek at him as one of his cheeks hikes up. The dimple there is borderline blinding. "Should I take them off so you can test that theory?"

I laugh, shaking my head and scooping my hair behind my ears. My ears that are suddenly warm from his blatant flirtation.

It's freeing to exchange these quips with West. I don't know if it's because my parents wouldn't approve of him or that I feel safe with him. It strikes me that even if I said the things I'm thinking, he'd roll with the punches and not get weird about it.

It's like breaking the rules and knowing there will be no repercussions.

But as fun as this is, guys like West and girls like me don't work. Not in the long run anyway.

"Well, am I losing the pants so you can keep gawking at me like a piece of meat? Or are you gonna get your fine ass in here and help me?"

I blink. "Help you?"

He shrugs. "Yeah, you can toss hay. It's night check."

"Toss hay?" I ask, not familiar with the term. "Is that what it's called when you hold it in your arms and do a two-step?"

He chuckles roughly and shakes his head. "Yeah, you can do the tango with it first if that's more your speed. But this thing here is a square bale." He points at the rectangular bundle of hay in the wheelbarrow. "And if you do this"— West runs his hand over the prickly green hay and digs his fingers in where there appears to be a slight gap—"you can just pull it open right here." He lifts a thin square piece of hay off the end of the bale that somehow sticks together. "And this right here is a flake." He does a dramatic pirouette with the flake in his hands and hits me with a wink before heaving it into the feeder attached to the stall beside him.

I press my lips together, to keep from bursting out laughing. "You're ridiculous."

"Thank you," he replies casually before continuing with his tutorial. "After you toss it, you pop your head into the stall to make sure our horse is safe and sound and happy. Not cast up against the side or in distress or anything. And then you move on to the next one."

"You want me to pick up the hay?"

He peers down at himself, realizing that he's covered in dust and bits of the green feed. Between his thumb and forefinger, he pinches the fabric of his T-shirt, shakes it out a little, and wipes it off before looking back at me. "Yeah, see? Now I'm clean. *Magic*."

I glance at the hay and must make a face because West adds, "Might do you good to get dirty. Don't worry, even covered in hay, you'll still be fancy with your diamond earrings."

Without thinking, I reach up and feel the studs in my ears.

Andrew bought them for me for my birthday and I haven't taken them out since. The reminder has my skin itching and my throat feeling tight.

Suddenly, I want them off my body. Urgently. They feel dirty. They make *me* feel dirty.

I don't want to be the girl who wears two-carat diamond studs. I'd rather be the girl who tosses hay without worrying about getting dust on her clothes.

West watches me with an indent between his brows as I tug the earrings out of my ears and shove them in the pocket of my sweater.

"I…was joking. You didn't need to take them off."

"No, I forgot I was wearing them." I press the pad of my finger into the pointed bar of one earring. It hurts. It feels good. "Actually, do you want them?" I pull my hand back out and hold my palm up to him. "You can have them."

West blanches. "What?"

It's an impulsive offer and I know it. But I feel all tangled and torn. I don't trust myself right now—hell, I don't even know myself right now.

"I don't know. I heard feeding horses is expensive. Or you can buy a pony for Emmy? Here, have them." I shake my hand gently in his direction, and he eyes me like I've lost my mind.

After a beat, he takes a few tentative steps forward,

leaving the wheelbarrow behind him. He curls his fingers around mine, forcing my palm closed and encasing the diamond studs in our hands. His voice is so sure, so kind, it almost makes me want to weep.

"Why don't you sleep on that one? If you want to donate them to a good cause in a few days' time, I'll help you pick one out."

The warmth of his touch seeps into my bones, and his eyes search mine in a way that's full of questions. Questions he doesn't ask. Instead, he steps away, taking the heat of his nearness with him.

It makes me want to follow him. It makes me want to chase that warmth, that comfort I feel when I'm close to him.

But I shimmy my shoulders and stand up tall before shoving the diamonds back into my pocket. Then I clear my throat and look him square in the eye. "Okay, I'm ready to toss some flakes. Let's do this."

He watches me for a moment, assessing me. I fear he's going to ask one of those questions swirling in his irises. I swear I can see it sitting there on the tip of his tongue.

I'm no open book, but it seems as though all West needs to do is look at the cover to know something's wrong. He sees past all the vibrant colors, all the shiny foiling. It's like no matter how pretty the cover is, he knows that if he opened the book, the pages would be blank.

I can't fool him. He sees right through me.

I realize I'm holding my breath when he finally points to one side and says, "You take left." Then his opposite hand points the other way. "I take right."

We spend the next several minutes working our way down the long concrete alleyway, pulling the flakes from the wheelbarrow and checking on each horse. The hay is prickly against my skin. It leaves me feeling itchy and like I can't escape the dust that permeates my clothes or gets caught on my cardigan. Regardless, the sweet smell of the grass does something good to my nervous system—calms it.

We work in a companionable silence for the next ten minutes. Our soundtrack is the horses' content huffing as their teeth grind on the hay and the wheelbarrow's low hum as West rolls it farther down the alleyway.

When we get to the far side of the barn, I glance up at him, thinking he'll dismiss me now that we've completed the task.

But he surprises me.

"Wanna do the outdoor paddocks with me too?" he asks with a quirk of his head.

The relief I feel is instant. Sharp. I'm thrilled he doesn't seem in a rush to get rid of me. I'm relieved that I'm not an annoyance to him—a liability.

Otherwise, surely, he would tell me to go to bed. But he didn't. So I press my lips together and nod, following him out into the dark on the opposite side of the barn.

Somehow, being in his company out in the open air, under the milky sky, feels more oppressive than in the barn. Once again, I'm struck by the feeling of everything here being way too fucking quiet.

I feel the inexplicable need to say something, to soften the tension between us, to end the silence.

As our feet thud against the dirt path that runs between the paddocks, I'm just desperate enough that I blurt out, "My ex-boyfriend gave me those earrings."

West pauses and then continues walking.

He doesn't turn to stare at me, so I forge ahead. "Or, well, I thought he was my boyfriend. And, actually, now that I say it out loud, I *think* he bought me those earrings. But it's possible he didn't."

West carefully pulls a flake of hay and tosses it into the feeder at the paddock beside him. He's not dancing now.

"What do you mean? Did he steal them?"

I laugh softly at that. "This story would be a lot more interesting if he did."

I don't know how West does it, but he has a way of taking a fragile moment and injecting humor into it. "No, I don't think he stole them. I don't even think he picked them out."

"So he had a friend do it? An assistant?"

The laugh that erupts from my throat now is not amused. It's dry and painful, and it hurts my lungs as it rips itself from them. "I don't know if you could consider him and my dad friends. More like partners in crime? Contractually tied? I'm not entirely sure what the word would be for your dad paying another musician to be your boyfriend."

West stops and stares at me now. "Come again?"

"Yeah, funny story, right? The kicker is, I had no idea."

"That's not funny, Skylar. What the fuck?"

"It's funny but not *ha-ha funny*, right? Welcome to the world of Skylar Stone."

West is stock-still, except for the tic in his jaw.

"Not the America's sweetheart story the world likes to think it is, huh? I've been dolled up and traipsed around and shined to the perfect luster to appeal to the consumer since I was a child. That was a weird awakening to have at twenty-six."

I gaze up at the stars, a dry hum in my throat. "Everything that you thought was real is"—I wave a hand at the sky with a resigned sigh—"*poof*...not. You only figure it out when you sit down to lunch with your boyfriend and he opens with, 'Sorry, Sky, haven't received a payment from your dad lately, so I'd say the jig is up.'"

I laugh at my awkward monologue, but it's uncomfortable. And West doesn't laugh along with me.

He stands at attention. His eyes narrow as he regards me, like I might turn and flee or break down or...I don't even know. Melt at his feet? I feel like I could explode. Yet saying it out loud, telling someone who doesn't know me from Adam, relieves the smallest amount of pressure.

It makes me feel just a bit more comfortable in my body.

"What. The. Fuck." West bites out the words and they drip with fury. His head is shaking and his fists are flexing. He puffs up just a little bit and it makes him seem bigger and more imposing than ever before.

"Hilariously, I'm not even sad about the breakup. We were never close. It was very transactional. But I *am* humiliated by it."

He looks like he could kill someone for doing this to me. A comforting heat suffuses my bones. No one has ever been incensed by the things that have been done to me. And I've been subjected to some wild shit.

It makes me feel like I'm standing here staring at him with hearts in my eyes. It inspires an instant and irrational sort of loyalty. A little part of me at the back of my head knows it's tragic to feel this impressed by simple human kindness.

And yet, here I am. Slack-jawed over it.

West steps closer, knees bumping against the edge of the wheelbarrow that separates us, dipping his head to meet my eyes. "Skylar? Why? Why the fuck would your dad do that to you?" His rage mingles with genuine confusion.

"Because..." I glance away, teeth biting at my bottom lip. "Because marketing Skylar Stone in love with everyone's favorite heartthrob crooner, Andrew McCann, makes sense. It's easier than marketing the girl with no personality and a dependency on Auto-Tune, who can't keep a man. It's more palatable. I'll give him that. Welcome to Hollywood," I add with a sad, sarcastic smile.

West rounds the wheelbarrow and eats up the space between us, heating the surrounding air with the intensity of his stare. He's too big, too nice. He's too fucking *much*.

I shift my gaze to the blackness of the trees that line the property.

"Skylar, what are you looking at?" His voice rolls over my skin, coaxing me back toward him.

I swallow and dig in, too embarrassed to meet West's eye. "I think I saw something in the trees."

"Was it your ability to lie fleeing the premises?"

Fucking intuitive motherfucker. I suck in a sharp breath through my nostrils, the scent of pine cooling me from the inside.

"I'm not a good liar, okay? I don't even want to be. But I've been unknowingly living a lie for…" I swallow. I can't say *my entire life* out loud. That's too heavy. Too real. "For years" is what I settle on. "*I* am a lie."

"Hey." His harsh voice lashes through the night air. I start, and he reaches for my chin, showing zero hesitation to touch me. "Look at me, Skylar."

I tip my nose higher but shake my head subtly. I don't want to look at him.

His fingers tighten, and he turns my face to him anyway. Then his eyes are on me. Seeking. Searching. It feels like he's digging right under my skin. "Nothing about that story is palatable."

I clamp my teeth and stare back up at him defiantly.

His hand moves, giving me a soft shake. "And you are not a lie. You are brimming with personality and humor and important things to say. And your relationship status just might be the least interesting thing about you. I've known you for one day, and I already know that."

"What's the most interesting thing about me?" I whisper, feeling the pads of his fingers firm against my jawbones as I speak.

He smirks, and his eyes drop to my mouth. "The way you lick your lips when you stare at my thighs." I huff out a laugh. "You look like you should carry a Chihuahua in your purse, but instead you have a bird that swears like a sailor."

Cherry. That makes me smile.

Then, I watch his expression turn more thoughtful as he quietly adds, "And the way you inspired a little boy who never talks to anyone to introduce himself to you. That's something special."

The urge to touch him overwhelms me. The tip of my pointer finger finds that hole in his tee and trails a circle on his bare skin. His rough hand lands at my waist. Gripping me. Making me wish not so many layers of clothing separated the feel of his fingers on my skin.

My heart pounds in my ears. And maybe it's because I can't hear myself think over the beat of that drum. Or maybe it's that I don't think at all.

But in one sweeping motion, I push up onto my toes, press a hand against West Belmont's chest…and kiss him.

I hear his surprised intake of air and feel the barbs of his stubble against my cheek. He doesn't kiss me back, though. Even when I move my lips against his…*again.*

He doesn't press his body against mine. Instead, he holds my hips, keeping me a respectable distance away from him. When I try to push closer, the right angle of his arm holds me at bay.

It has me drawing back.

My first reaction is confusion. People always want this from me. Men are always pleasant to me with this kind of payoff.

I don't think I've *ever* been turned down.

The fact that West is standing stiff as a board, borderline pushing me away, has alarm bells sounding in my head.

It has reality creeping in—the nickers of horses, the smell of hay, the weight of several carats of diamonds in my pocket.

"I'm sorry," I gasp before I flip a hand up over my lips, replaying the weight and heat of his kiss.

When I finally brave a look up at West, he has a soft smile on his face. And a slightly sad glint in his eye.

I see it.

Pity.

And that douses the flames I felt just moments ago.

He pities me. How could he not? I spilled my guts to him and kissed him. Latched on to him like he could be a comfort blanket for me.

A comfort blanket with big fucking hands and the world's roundest ass.

And now I'd like to dig myself a hole in this dirt path, crawl in, and die.

"Don't be sorry." He gently strokes my cheek, lifts a piece of my hair, and stares at it like it means something, then tucks it carefully behind my ear. "You have nothing to be sorry for."

I vigorously shake my head as I step back from his touch. "I shouldn't have kissed you. You were just being nice, and I don't what…well…we…we're…"

"Friends?" he offers tentatively as I take a second step back.

Internally, I sag.

Friends.

I'm short on friends. But my stomach doesn't flip when friends look at me. I don't push closer and hope my friends will slide their tongues into my mouth. I don't itch to feel my friends' hands on my bare skin.

But still, I'm not in a position to turn down a friend. Especially a man as deeply *good* as West. So I force a bright expression onto my face.

And with the most practiced smile I can muster, I repeat the word back to him. "Friends."

It feels like acid on my tongue. But West seems relieved.

So I tell myself I kind of like the taste.

Another day. Another lie.

CHAPTER 9

West

OKAY, SO SKYLAR STONE KISSED ME.

I don't think she meant anything by it.

It was a momentary lapse of judgment, obviously.

Because although I have no doubt that I'm perfectly kissable, that one felt more like a girl seeking comfort and not really knowing what she was after. It seemed like a moment I shouldn't take advantage of, though I'd be lying if I said I didn't think about it for a beat.

I barely know Skylar, but I do know she's been hurt. She's low on friends and even lower on trust. And what kind of pig would I be if I took advantage of that after listening to her spill her guts in the most heartbreaking and infuriating fashion?

But none of that prevented me from staying up, laid out flat on my back, staring at my ceiling while replaying the kiss in my mind.

WILD EYES

The only thing that distracts me from the kiss is the story about her ex. And her parents. And what royal assholes they all sound like.

I have staff to do morning chores now, but my body still wakes me up at the crack of dawn on the best days. The morning light has been shining through my useless curtains for some time now, and I know I need to get moving, but I'm trapped in my head.

Thinking.

And no one has ever accused me of being a big thinker.

But I can't let this one go. Can't stop wondering how her parents could have put her through what they did.

My parents have come through for me at every turn. Even when I was at my wildest—at my worst—they bailed me out. They may not have always liked me, but they've always loved me, no matter what.

I strive to be that type of parent. It's never occurred to me that anyone would strive to be any other type of parent. I feel naive for the first time in a long-ass time.

It's a stark reminder that Skylar and I come from two different walks of life.

What's more troubling is I sense she gave me the vaguely summarized version of her family history. I didn't miss the way she froze in the kitchen when that glass broke. Which means it's gotta be worse than what she let out. It's none of my business to ask her more, but it doesn't keep me from wondering.

I've never been especially good at doing what I'm supposed to anyhow.

That's why I'm still lying here with a light sheet over my legs, mulling over the few pieces of her puzzle she handed to me.

In a matter of one day, my image of her and what's going on in her life has taken shape. She's like a new problem horse at the barn. I assess them just as carefully and get a read before I do any hands-on work.

Not that Skylar is a horse.

And I don't think she needs any hands-on work. If anything, she needs space. A friend. And if I'm known for anything, it's making friends with absolutely anyone.

I, Weston Belmont, am the world's best friend.

And the world's worst enemy. I'm the guy who lets fists fly if the situation warrants it, but I've mostly outgrown that phase in my life. Now I'm the life of the party. The social calendar planner. I'm the guy that brings grown men together to bowl on Thursday nights for Dads' Night Out.

So if Skylar Stone is here to stay and she needs a friend, who better to take her under their wing than me?

I could *easily* be Skylar's friend. Sometimes friends accidentally kiss. Sometimes friends get accidental raging hardons thinking about said kiss. *Totally normal.*

Yeah, I've got this in the fucking bag.

"Dad!" Emmy's shout precedes the heavy thumping of her elephant-like footfalls blasting down the hall to my room. Her peach-toned hair flies in a wild mane behind her as she takes a running leap onto my bed and lands on all fours like the animal she is. "What time is soccer again?"

With a groan, I reach for the bedside table while she snuggles into my side. I ignore the pang in my chest when I realize she doesn't fit quite like she used to. She's growing too damn fast. I'd like to shrink her, freeze her at about four years old, when her voice still sounded all sugary and she followed me everywhere.

My arms tighten around her as I search for the phone that I know is there somewhere. When my fingers wrap around it, my eyes widen. I've been lying here for a lot longer than I thought.

Thinking. Obsessing. Planning.

"Shit. We've got forty-five minutes before we need to be at the field with the rest of your ragtag team."

"Five more minutes," she mumbles, nuzzling her face into my ribs. And how the hell am I supposed to say no to that? Soon, she'll want nothing to do with me. Soon, I'll get eye rolls and scoffs and doors slammed in my face.

So I turn and tug her against me, taking five more minutes to snuggle with my baby girl.

I don't open my eyes, but I smile when I feel Ollie's quiet presence as he crawls in on the other side and presses his back against mine. I can hear the soft flick of the pages in his book as he turns them.

It's the coziest moment. Ruined only by the fact that I can't stop thinking about Skylar. Wondering if she got any moments like this with her parents.

As if this morning wasn't hectic enough, two messages come in back-to-back. Both my assistant coaches are bailing on me at the last minute.

ELSIE SILVER

Which means it's just me and fifteen girls at a chaotic kids' soccer game.

Just me to do subs.

Just me to switch pinnies.

Just me to retie laces that come undone at a rate that downright defies the odds.

Knowing other people's kids are relying on me to make this experience a good one weighs on me. Which is why it only takes me a couple of minutes to realize what I need is a *friend* to help me out this morning.

And I have a brand-new friend, one who owes me for saving her from a grizzly.

So, with my coffee in hand, I head out the front door while Emmy and Oliver bustle around the house getting ready.

"If you're not ready to go in five, I'm leaving without you, and you can walk into town," I call before letting the screen door slam behind me.

"Really nice, Dad!" Oliver shouts back at me. And I can't bring myself to chide him. If he wants to yell, I'll just be grateful he's talking.

I hustle across the yard to get to the bunkhouse, hoping I can talk Skylar into this. The prospect of doing it on my own makes me want to throw my hot coffee in my face. And the prospect of doing it with her feels much better.

I'm not above holding a favor over Skylar's head to get her to help me. It's for the children. Plus, after watching her with my kids' last night, I think it might be good for her.

The aromatic press of warm, dry pine needles eases, and the

clearing toward the lake opens before me. I spent my entire life here, and the view still brings me up short some days. There's something magical about Rose Hill. Something that stops you in your tracks. Forces you to take in the view, even for just a beat.

And that's all the time I have this morning, so I soak in the lake and mountains quickly before forging ahead. I take the dirt path down to the house that loosely matches the main one. The white shiplap siding appears more weather-worn than ever, and the red tin roof has gradually trended toward more of a chalky pink hue.

On the small wraparound porch, I find Skylar sitting in the old rocking chair, wrapped in a Navajo blanket, with her fucking bird on her shoulder. She's staring out over the water, rocking gently and looking alarmingly at peace.

Before I can make my presence known, Cherry announces me by shouting, "*Go away!*"

Skylar jumps and turns to face me. She's pulled up her caramel-colored hair with a big black claw clip and her face is scrubbed clean of the makeup she had on yesterday. I can tell because the dark circles under her eyes are on full display.

She looks beautiful and forlorn all at once.

Not that I would tell her that.

I may be single, but it's not because I make a habit of putting my foot in my mouth around women.

It's because I can't quite bring myself to settle down. Don't especially want to bring someone new into the fold with my kids either.

"I think your bird hates me," I joke, trying to ease the tension from last night's moment of insanity.

The expression of surprise fades from her face, but it's replaced by the two splotches of pink that match the roof taking up residence on her cheeks.

Mission not accomplished.

She can't even meet my eyes. Instead, from the corner of her eye, she peeks at the gray parrot and smiles softly. "I think she really only likes me."

The parrot rubs the top of its head against Skylar's pink cheek, bunting against her lovingly as though that might help erase the blush.

"Clearly," I reply dryly.

"I rescued her from a shelter. She wasn't well taken care of. I was there to do a commercial and something about her just spoke to me."

"Did she literally tell you to go away?"

Skylar chuckles now. "She didn't talk then."

"She, uh"—I flick a hand toward the bird—"have her wings clipped?"

"They used to be. I never could bring myself to do it to her, though. They've grown back now. Physically, she can fly, but she never does."

Her eyes meet mine now, the confidence she oozed yesterday absent this morning. She looks small and vulnerable wrapped in the blanket. "Sometimes I sit outside with her and will her to just try, you know? I want her to know she can. But I'm scared she won't come back."

I shrug. "Maybe she knows she can fly but doesn't want to leave?"

Skylar blinks like I just said something she hadn't

considered. She moves her gaze back to Cherry, and her eyes go a little glassy as she reaches up to stroke the bird's back.

She looks *sad* and I can't fucking handle sad. So I spit out what I came here to ask. "Remember that time I saved your life?" Because who knows? Maybe watching a bunch of hooligans run back and forth across a field will make her less sad.

She snorts and hits me with a droll expression. "I have officially erased all of yesterday from my memory. So…no. That doesn't ring a bell."

I react with a dramatic gasp and throw an offended hand over my chest. "Oh my god. You erased our kiss? How *could* you?"

Her heart-shaped lips pop open, as though she can't believe I'd dare to bring *that* up.

"Want me to tell you about it so you can commit it to memory?"

A dry laugh lurches from her chest. "No. God. Please don't."

"Oh, come on. I'm a great kisser. Everyone says so. Trust me. You won't want to forget it."

She shakes her head at me, but now her eyes twinkle with amusement rather than unshed tears. "It felt like kissing a corpse. You didn't even move."

"So, this might come as a surprise to you, but *you* kissed *me*. I was in shock. Cut me some slack."

"West!" She drops her head back and stares up at the pale blue morning sky.

"Dragged me outside and practically mauled me. Like a bear."

Her shoulders shake as a silent laugh racks her body.

"And being the gentleman that I am, I took one for the team. Then you just shoved your tongue down my throat and preyed on all this—" I gesture over myself like I'm a prize you can win on a game show.

Skylar wheezes a hollow threat. "I'm going to kill you."

But it's Cherry who scares me with her echo. "*Kill you. Kill you.*"

That's what sends us both into a fit of giggles.

Her murderous bird and all the diffused tension.

She wipes tears from the corners of her eyes, and while I think they may have originated as sad, they spill from her eyes as tears of laughter.

I must be a simple guy to please because knowing I helped change them gives me pleasure. It fills me with pride and satisfaction.

"So, about that favor?"

"What is it?" she asks, straightening and trying to gather her wits.

"Everyone bailed on me, and I need help with coaching Emmy's soccer game in"—I tug my phone from my back pocket and check the time—"ten minutes."

"I'm…" She hesitates. "Not a soccer coach."

"No shit. But guess what?" I lift my coffee mug in her direction. "Me fucking neither."

"I—"

"Do you know how to tie shoelaces?"

Her brow furrows, and now she's back to looking offended.

"Jesus, Skylar, it was a joke, not an insult. I know you can tie shoelaces. Let's go." I turn and wave her along. The blanket rustles as she moves it.

"But I need some time to get ready. I haven't washed my face or put on my makeup—"

"I don't care. We've got a game to get to. Let's go, Coach Plain Face!"

Skylar responds with a disbelieving laugh. I get the sense no one has ribbed this girl in her entire life. She's in for a rude awakening, being friends with me.

The door to the bunkhouse creaks open and Cherry squawks, "*Kill you!*" one last time.

"I dare you, Cherry," I shout back, hearing Skylar's soft laughter and the *thunk* of the door as she shuts it behind her.

Then, "Hey! Wait up, Coach Thick Thighs! I need a ride."

And all I do is groan and slow my steps, because despite my best intentions and internal pep talk, my head is way down in the gutter where Coach Plain Face is concerned.

CHAPTER 10

Skylar

THIRTY UNBLINKING EYES STARE AT ME.

Wide, shiny, unblinking eyes.

West is talking, but not a single girl on his team is paying attention, because Skylar Stone is standing beside him. It would seem that even without makeup on, they all recognize me.

My first inclination is to freeze up. Look for an escape route. Flee.

I'm like a deer in the headlights over a mob of six-year-olds.

West bumps me with his elbow as he introduces me, and the brief touch drags me out of my head. I peek over my shoulder to see Oliver sitting at the top of the bleachers. He's got a book in his hands, but he's watching West and me. I wave at him, and he gives me a shy wave back before turning his focus back down to the pages in his lap.

Then his dad hits me with, "This here is Coach Plain Face."

I snort and the girls finally blink.

"Really?" I ask, turning to West, who is wearing a mischievous, shit-eating grin. It's so bright it practically blinds me from beneath the brim of his hat. "You can all call me Sky. I'm just here to help."

The girls nod, but West isn't letting it go. "What? You've got a special name for me. It only seemed fair."

I have to think about it for a beat. A special name? Suddenly, it hits me.

Coach Thick Thighs.

He winks.

And I flush.

Every quippy joke I manage to get out around this guy turns into fodder for him to tease me with. He's fucking unflappable and it would annoy me if it weren't so damn endearing.

"Coach West," I say, enunciating each syllable with force.

"Yeah," one girl with raven black hair pipes up. "What else would we call you?"

West is still smiling when he straightens up and claps his hands. "Absolutely nothing, Lee. Now, are we ready? We're gonna hit 'em hard with our diamond formation and have some fun, right?"

"Yeah," a few of them shout, but several continue staring at me. I sense their parents staring from the sidelines too, but I try to ignore that feeling of being watched. The one that makes my scalp itchy.

"Okay, on three," West's voice booms from beside me, startling me.

They all push their hands into the middle of the circle, and I awkwardly do the same when West gives me another nudge.

"Three! Two! One!" Their sugary, little voices all shouting together makes a very real smile crack out over my face.

"Sparkly Turquoise Unicorns!" is their final shout before the girls spin and take off to their spots, some on the field and others on the sidelines. Emmy front and center.

I tilt my head in West's direction. "Sparkly Turquoise Unicorns?"

"Yes, ma'am. That's us," he responds as he crosses his arms and tips his chin out toward the field.

"Creative."

He snorts. "You should have heard the other options. We put it to a vote."

When I peek over at him, I realize the turquoise-colored cap he's wearing says *Sparkly Turquoise Unicorns*. Other than that, he's wearing a set of gym shorts, a simple black tee, and a pair of sneakers. But seeing him in full girl-dad mode makes my heart skip a beat.

I cross my arms and look out over the field as the opposing coach drops the ball on the grass. "Nice hat, Coach Thick Thighs."

He grins at me. "Thank you, fancy face. I got them for the entire team. Who doesn't love a sparkly turquoise unicorn, am I right?"

I laugh, shaking my head at him. Trying to wrap it

around someone so at ease in their own skin. What must that feel like?

"I'm going to go yell at them from the corners. You good to stay here and help with swapping pinnies when I do subs? And be ready to tie laces. Those fuckin' things might as well be designed to come undone."

I smile and salute him, then try not to gawk at his ass as he jogs down the sideline. Then I try not to stare at him as he "yells" at them. And I fail.

I fail over and over again.

Because West's version of yelling at kids is clapping and cheering and boisterously letting them know what a terrific job they're doing.

There's, "Get it, girls! Let's go!"

Followed by, "Beauty shot, Shelby! See you at the Olympics."

Beyond him, the goalie is doing a dance, not paying attention to the game at all. She gets an, "Eyes on the ball, Addie. Save the victory dance for after we win, you little clown!"

And then the real kicker, "Hell yeah, Emmy. That's my girl!"

That's my girl.

God, he just brims with pride watching his daughter and her friends play the most chaotic game of soccer in the world. It makes my chest ache, and for all my internal reminders, I don't stop myself from staring at him at all.

"Sheer! Stop eating shit outta the grass!" startles me back into reality.

One girl on the sideline is down on all fours, rifling through the grass like some sort of animal.

"But it's not shit!" the kid calls back, unruffled by West's gruff language. "Someone spilled Smarties here, Coach!"

When she pops some sort of colorful candy from the grass into her mouth, I jog in the girl's direction. "No, no, no, no, no." The word tumbles from my lips on repeat as if I might be able to make it not real. I wish I hadn't just watched a child eat god-knows-what out of the grass. "Spit it out."

Her eyes widen when she looks up at me.

"If you don't spit that out, I will write a song about the girl who ate old candy off the ground and record it, so everyone knows."

She blinks and I can tell she's thinking about it, but even that threat isn't a total deterrent. So, in a last-ditch effort, I try, "I also have Skittles in my bag that I'll share with you if you spit it out."

The tiny blond instantly spits the red candy out and lithely pops up to standing. Her hand shoots out, demanding payment from me for saving her from whatever illness would have come with finishing what was in her mouth.

Biting down on a grin, I reach inside my cross-body bag for one of the several packages of Skittles I like to keep on hand. I can't remember when that started, but there's something about the burst of sugar that can turn a difficult day around.

My hand lands on my phone and I recoil. I spent last night beating myself up and reading horribly cruel online comment sections about myself. No matter how bad it hurt, I couldn't seem to stop scrolling.

But the crinkle of the Skittles bag soothes me. With a tug, I pull it out and shake several out into my hand, then glance down at the little pebbles of candy before bending at the hips and holding them out to the girl. "Here, but you can't take the orange ones. Those are the only ones I like."

She wrinkles her nose. "Why?"

"I dunno. I'm just a fan of oranges, I guess? My favorite fruit. My favorite candy."

The girl shrugs, and I smile at her as she appraises my open palm like she's making a life-changing decision.

She goes for red. Just like the sweet I forced her to abandon.

Then a big hand with veins and tattoos swoops in and swipes almost all of them—including the orange ones.

"Thank you, Coach," West calls, jogging away backward with a twinkle in his eye. "Needed a pick-me-up."

"You didn't even ask. *And* you took orange ones."

His chin tips down as he looks at his hand. He pulls out an orange piece and holds it up between his thumb and forefinger. "Oh, like this?"

"Yes, like that."

He tosses it up in the air, leans his head back, centers himself, and catches the candy in his waiting mouth like an overgrown child playing with his food. He stares at me as he chews a few times and nods. "Oh yeah. The orange ones are good."

For a moment, I watch his throat work as he swallows.

I swallow, too.

Then I mouth *dick* in his direction, and all it does is

127

make him throw his head back and laugh. The most full, carefree laugh I've ever heard. In a world that's so manufactured, I'm not sure I've ever heard someone laugh as genuinely as West.

He's brimming with life.

He's like a magnet. And I get the sense I'm not the only one who's drawn to him. The kids hang on his every word. The parents shake his hand at the end of the game.

And a few of the moms smile just a little *too* brightly in his direction.

With a 12–5 victory under their belt, the girls are in high spirits as they make their way down the line of opposing team members. I'm grinning like a fool watching them because this was *fun*.

Good old-fashioned fun.

I shared Skittles in the sun, watched a bunch of girls work together to master a sport, and learned the cheer they have for the Sparkly Turquoise Unicorns.

Never saw myself here, but the world works in mysterious ways and all that.

It's when I turn to see West chatting with a fair-haired woman that the world seems extra mysterious. The woman is laughing, and Emmy has just launched herself into her arms with a loud "Mama."

My brow furrows as I hang back to watch. Emmy and Oliver seemed pretty open to talking about their mom and stepdad. But watching my parents attempt to rip each other into shreds these past months gets my back up about the whole thing.

It seems downright impossible that two people could divorce amicably. Yet here this man is, talking happily to his ex-wife as their daughter attempts to drag her away.

In my direction.

"Okay, Emmy. Okay. I'm coming," she says, laughing lightly as she allows her daughter to pull her toward me.

"Mom," Emmy announces. "This is *Skylar Stone*, and she's living in *our* bunkhouse."

The woman gives me a kind smile. She's all soft, feminine curves, with chocolate-brown eyes, freckles of a slightly lighter color dotting her pert nose. Her shoulder-length hair is golden like straw, and I can see the warmth of it lending that peachy tone to Emmy's. She's got that girl-next-door look down pat.

She's effortlessly beautiful.

"Hi, Skylar. I'm Mia," she says, with no squealing or slack-jawed staring. "It's a pleasure to meet you, and I am so sorry to hear about the bunkhouse." She sticks her hand out to shake mine.

My smile matches hers as I take her hand. "I'm crossing things off my bucket list I didn't even know existed, that's for sure."

"Hey now," West interrupts as he swaggers up to us. "You haven't lived until you've spent some nights in the bunkhouse. That's an internationally accepted fact."

Mia's eyes roll dramatically. "Your attachment to that place is one of the wonders of the world, Weston."

He nudges her with his elbow, and for a flash, I can see him doing that exact move as a child. I can imagine him as a little pest, ribbing everyone in sight. And for a flash, I also see the years of familiarity between the two of them. I imagine them together and it makes my stomach twist in a new way.

"Anytime you and Boring Brandon need a romantic getaway, it's yours. I won't even charge you."

She shakes her head at him and glances away to cover her smile. "Unbelievable." When she finally glances back at me, it's with a mocking type of seriousness. "Skylar, you're in luck because it's my week with the kids starting today. That means you'll only have to live on the same property with one child."

I chuckle. Mia gives off only good vibes. But I still turn my head away bashfully to cover my blush because the thought of being alone on the property with West has a thrill racing down my spine.

An entire week of avoiding him, so I don't throw myself at him again. And an entire week of being *friends* without his adorable kids as our buffer.

I'm biting my lip and staring at the ground when I see a flash of white from the corner of my eye. It draws my attention and I turn to look.

At a stray soccer ball.

One that hits me square in the face.

Just before my nose starts spraying blood.

CHAPTER 11

West

"You look fine."

"I do *not* look fine." She pats along both sides of her nose gingerly, as though she's making sure it hasn't sprung a leak.

"Okay, you look fabulous."

I get a scowl from beneath the brim of a spare Sparkly Turquoise Unicorns hat. "Nice try."

I lean back in the metal chair to get a better look at her from across the table. It's dimly lit on the floating dock at the Rose Hill Reach—the town's waterfront pub—but the patio lanterns strung around the perimeter reflect off the water and cast a cozy glow.

Still, the sky is a dark cobalt, and it matches the bruising that's cropping up on Skylar's fancy face just perfectly.

If you ask me, she looks downright beautiful. I don't tell her that, though.

"I have yet to meet a single person in the world who

doesn't look fabulous in a Sparkly Turquoise Unicorns hat," I say.

Her lips twitch, but she still doesn't break as she turns to gaze out over the inky water and back to the main bar, where she refused to have a drink because it was too well lit. There are other people at tables out here, but they don't spare us a second glance.

Did I force her to come out for a drink with me?

Maybe.

Is it better than her sitting in the bunkhouse, spiraling about whether her nose is broken?

Definitely.

And that's exactly what she was doing when I went to check on her.

Skylar reaches up again, trailing the pad of her finger down the bridge of her nose. "Well, at least now when the tabloids say I've had a good nose job, they'll be telling the truth."

"You don't need a nose job."

"You should write an article about that. Or maybe tweet it. People gobble up unsolicited opinions about me."

She says it like it's meant to be a joke, but I don't find it especially funny. "Why do you read that shit?"

She straightens, tipping her chin up. It's hard to see her eyes from beneath her hat, but I have no doubt they're flashing with defiance right now. She's not the soft-spoken media darling everyone has come to know. No, there's an edge to Skylar that someone's tried to disguise with pretty paint and curtains.

But I see it all the same. And I like it.

"It's part of my job to know how I'm perceived in the media."

I furrow my brow. "No, it's literally not. And who cares what they say about you? Are they right? Do they know you? Fuck 'em."

Her amber irises widen at that.

"I've known you for less than forty-eight hours, and you've mentioned tabloids twice. Stop. Looking. Fuck 'em."

"It's hard." Her voice is a whisper now. "It's like I know it's going to be made up and mean-spirited, but I check anyway, just so I know what's being said."

"Newsflash—people are going to say it whether or not you read it."

Teeth clamp down onto her pillowy bottom lip as she gives one terse nod.

"And you looking doesn't make it any truer. So what's the point?"

Skylar glances away again, but this time it's not to take in her surroundings. She's avoiding making eye contact with me. And I don't want to make her feel that way, so I drop it.

"Plus, your nose isn't broken. I can tell. No nose job necessary."

"Oh, are you a doctor now?" she snipes back.

I just laugh. I like her with her claws out. Seems more like the real Skylar to me.

"No, but I've had mine broken once and broke two others. Plus, I offered to take you to the ER and you said you didn't want to be recognized, so I'm as close as you're gonna get to an expert."

Her jaw drops open, and she flattens her palms on the metal table. "You've broken *two* people's noses?"

I cross my arms, grinning back at her. "That I know of. A couple of people ran away before I could find out for sure."

"*Why?*"

Now I scrub at my chin and turn to gaze out over the water. "Guess I had a bit of a rowdy streak growing up. Got a kick out of teaching lessons with my fists. I've outgrown it…mostly."

The brim of her hat shadows her face and I can tell she's about to say something, but our server walks up and interrupts.

"West, honey. How you doing tonight?" Doris props her tray against her hip and grins down at me with tobacco-stained teeth and permed hair that went out of style decades ago. The look she gives me is the same one she's been giving me since I'd sneak in here underage.

"Real good, Doris. How about you?"

"Knees are sore. Otherwise, can't complain. Got a roof over my head, food in my belly, and a husband with a big dick."

Skylar makes a shocked choking noise from across the table right as I bark out a laugh. Good ol' Doris. She never misses.

"On that note, what can I get ya?"

I wipe at my nose as I attempt to pull myself together. Usually, Doris's shit wouldn't land quite like that, but seeing the expression on Skylar's face made it that much funnier.

"Boy, you've got the giggles. Who is this?" She points at Skylar.

That's enough to make me straighten because gossip spreads like wildfire where locals are concerned, and I don't want a parade of people approaching Skylar tonight.

Not when I've finally got her to myself.

"This is a friend. I'll take a pint of Rose Hill Red and two cans of Buddyz Best. No glasses."

Doris scribbles on her notepad. She didn't use that when I was younger, but her memory isn't what it once was. "Right, another one of your friends. So help me, Weston, if I catch you shotgunning these cans out here…"

"Doris, my shotgunning days are over."

The woman hits me with a droll look and my head tips from side to side.

"Mostly."

She rolls her eyes and turns to Skylar. "Okay, *friend*. What can I get you?"

Skylar looks like a kid at the zoo for the first time—a little intimidated and a little excited. "Chardonnay?"

"That a question?"

Skylar snorts. "I'll have a chardonnay, *please*."

Doris's lips curve into a smile as she jots it down. Without looking at me, she mumbles, "This one's smarter than the others," before she stomps away on flat feet.

We watch her leave and turn back to face each other at the same time. Skylar's mouth opens like she's going to say something, but she closes it.

Then again. Open. And closed.

"Cat got your tongue, fancy face?"

"I…" Her head joggles as she searches for what to say. "She's amazing."

I agree with a solemn nod. "Indeed, she is. A town mainstay. She owns the place."

Skylar shifts her wide-eyed gaze back to the bar. "I need to channel her energy. Find my inner Doris."

"Okay, well, you've got a roof over your head at the bunkhouse. I'm about to buy you a plate of wings. And I have a big dick, but I can't marry you."

She smirks at me, and just when I think she's gonna give me hell about the bunkhouse barely constituting a roof, she surprises me by asking, "How big?"

I'm caught completely off guard. My face flushes red and my breath leaves me in a disbelieving huff. I stare at her slack-jawed for a few beats and then lick my lips as I regain my composure. "First, I am *scandalized* by that question. Second, I don't like to talk about it because then people start asking to see it and shit just gets weird."

She's grinning as she shakes her head. But I don't miss the way her eyes narrow. "Oh, do you not usually show your *friends* your dick?"

I bite down on my inner cheek and clench my biceps. "I have many friends. Of many sorts. I'm a friendly guy."

She quirks an eyebrow at me.

"Spit it out, fancy face. Ask away."

She shifts in her seat and links her fingers together on the table. "What did she mean when she called me *another one of your friends*?"

I look Skylar right in her bruised eyes. "It means she thinks I'm sleeping with you."

Silence settles over us. I swear I can hear her tongue as it swipes across her bottom lip. Even though with the hum of tables around us, that would be impossible.

"Do you sleep with all your friends?"

"No. Only a few."

Her eyes bug out comically now. "*A few?*"

"Not at once. But I'm not a monk, Skylar. I like to have some companionship, and I'm not set up for anything serious. Definitely not ready to add a relationship to the dynamic with my kids. I'm busy. Oliver has been improving slowly but surely, and I refuse to bring someone new into the fold and set him back. Especially since it took him so long to warm up to Brandon. So yes, since you're being snoopy, I have friends with benefits because that is the least complicated solution to remaining single as a thirty-three-year-old man."

She blinks. "Is it… Do you… Are you… You know what? Never mind."

Now she's flustered. She mirrors my position and crosses her arms, effectively shutting me out.

Since the silent drive over, our conversation has flowed easily, but it falls away. And I may not be in a relationship, but I'm not emotionally stunted either.

I'm not about to let her kill the ease between us.

"What's got you all pissed at me, Skylar?"

The muscle in her jaw pops, and I can tell she's grinding her teeth. "That stupid kiss," she hisses while glancing around like someone might hear us. "I shouldn't have done that. I feel like I kissed someone's boyfriend."

I bite back my chuckle, but it rumbles in my chest anyway. "Skylar, I am as single as they come."

Her gaze moves from my hand clasped around my arm up to my face, and her attention stops me in my tracks for a moment.

Fuck, she's pretty.

With a short shake of my head, I forge on. "And there was nothing stupid about that kiss. In fact—"

"Oh lordy, dropping and running. Pretend I was never here," Doris grumbles as she sets our drinks on the table and bolts.

Saving me from saying something I definitely shouldn't.

CHAPTER 12

Skylar

IN FACT.

In fact, what?

Never have two words in the English language infuriated me more.

Fucking Doris.

He was about to say something interesting. I could tell by the way his voice changed and his eyes heated. Even the warning about not doing serious relationships wasn't enough to scare me away. In fact, I leaned in closer, desperate for him to finish that sentence.

I know a casual hookup is the last thing I need.

But there's something about him.

Something that has my eyes lingering longer than they should, my body standing at attention, and my mind traveling down a path it shouldn't. Especially since I know it's not in the cards—he's made that much abundantly clear.

And yet, he doesn't push me away.

"Here." He slides a can with a sad-looking basset hound on it my way.

I eye it speculatively. "I don't know how to shotgun a beer."

West chuckles. "They aren't for shotgunning. No one should drink this swill." He reaches for the can, the cow skull tattooed on his finger stretching as it wraps around the can. Aluminum faintly crinkles as he picks it up before extending one corded arm across the small table and gently pressing the cold can to my cheekbone, just beside my nose.

I gasp and reach up, surprised by the contact. My fingers wrap around his forearm, drawing his gaze down for a bit before he's back to searching my eyes.

"It's for the swelling." With his opposite hand, he nudges the other can in my direction. "One for each side. Sips of chardonnay in between. Doctor's orders."

I nod because I don't know what to say. Internally, I beg myself not to leap across the flimsy table and kiss this man who is *as single as they come* again.

Because while I don't fancy myself a genius, I am not that colossally stupid. West is hot as hell, flirty as fuck, but he might as well have heartbreak tattooed on his forehead.

Above all, I have a fairly intact sense of self-preservation, so I pat his arm and draw back into the safety of my side of the table. He watches me as I take a deep, centering swig of white wine before I hold two cheap beer cans against my face.

I must look absolutely bizarre to anyone who's watching us. Silver lining, though—I also am not the least bit recognizable.

West sips his beer, but he's still staring at me with such intensity that I might launch myself into the lake just to get away from his gaze. It's too heavy. Too *much*.

Again, I'm struck by the feeling that he sees right through me. It's unnerving. And I want to throw him off just as much as he does me.

"Mia seems sweet," I blurt. It's easier to say it aloud because I'm essentially hiding behind the beer cans.

"She is."

"Seems like you get along pretty well."

"We do."

Annoyed by the fact West isn't the least bit put off by this conversation, I drop the cans on the table. "You're nice to her."

"Why wouldn't I be? She's my kids' mom. I'd be a royal dick if I wasn't."

I blink, instantly feeling like a total asshole for suggesting otherwise.

"So why did you split up?"

His head wobbles back and forth as he spins the pint glass between his hands and contemplates my question. "I think mostly because we weren't good friends."

I scoff and reach for my glass of wine. "Oh good, more friend talk."

"No, no. It's like…I think if you're going to be in a solid relationship with someone, you need to be friends on some level. Like…enjoy each other's company. You know? My parents are so solid that way. They bicker with each other, but at the end of the day, there's no one they'd rather bicker with.

ELSIE SILVER

Ford and Rosie are the same. Those two were peas in a pod before they even realized they were in the same pod."

That makes me smile. I could see their connection, and I barely know them.

West reaches up and scratches at the back of his neck. "Mia and I…we didn't enjoy each other's company. She wanted the full domestic experience. Wanted me to work nine-to-five, not doing night checks at 11 p.m. She wanted to be in bed by 8 p.m. so we could watch sitcoms together. And me? I dunno. I wanted every day to be different. I got bored too easily. And when I get bored, I get destructive."

I laugh. "That explains all the broken noses."

That gets me a grin, but he keeps going.

"She wanted boring. That's where the joke about Boring Brandon was born. And it is a joke—he's a great guy. Perfect for her. It's like we both knew we were incompatible, but we both liked kids. Making them. Raising them. Figured we'd try that again to see if it helped. But it turns out that babies don't fix what's already broken."

He chuckles and takes another swig of his beer before leaning back, resting his hands on the arms of the chair, and looking out over the water. "The upside is, she's a great mom and I respect the hell out of her. Not many people could co-parent the way we do. But dear god, please don't make me stay home and play Scrabble in my matching Christmas jammies beneath the sign on the mantel that says *Live Laugh Love.*"

An unladylike snort bursts from me at the visual he just gave me. Strong enough that it makes my eyes sting because my nose fucking *hurts.*

142

"Ow," I rasp as I reach for the cans again, sighing when their chill presses against my face. "Well, if you could share this wisdom with my parents, that would be great."

"Your parents?"

"Yeah, this is not public knowledge yet, but they're getting a divorce. A messy vicious one."

"I'm sorry, Skylar." And he means it. His voice—so often teasing—brims with sincerity.

I shrug. "It's about time. If your theory about friendship is right. It's been over for a long time—they can't stand each other. When I said I needed a breather and to get out of town, my mom announced she needed the same and took off to Aruba to 'decompress' or something. She really only communicates through her lawyer because she ends up throwing shit if she's in the same room as my dad. And my dad is fixated only on keeping as much money to himself as possible so he's no better."

"Then what's kept them together?"

"Me."

West nods. "Never understood the concept of staying together for the kids. I'd rather my kids see me happy alone than miserable with their mom."

My responding laugh is bitter. "That's sound logic. But it's not what I meant." I peek around the dock from beneath the brim of my sweet new hat to make sure no one is watching or listening to us. "If this is all over the news tomorrow, I'll know it was you."

West's cheek pops like he's irritated by my implication, but where I'm from, information is power. And I'm not sure I'm ready for this to break yet.

"What I meant was that they stuck together for me, as in…Skylar Stone Incorporated."

His brows draw together.

"Turns out all the money I made—and the rights I thought were mine from work I did as a minor—are held in a business that I only own a tiny percentage of. And most of it is tied up in divorce proceedings now, hence falling behind on the boyfriend payments."

I smile, but it's flat and feral. Like a wolf showing its teeth.

West gives me a blank stare. His jaw pops.

"Yeah, so I only have a fraction of what I thought was mine. I never looked carefully at my contracts. My dad would promise me he'd checked them over and that everything was as it should be. Then he'd say something like, 'This will be a great move for you, doll,' and I'd sign. Blissfully unaware."

I flinch at the memory before continuing. "I've spent my entire life working, missing out on so many things, and I have almost nothing to show for it. A fraction of what I should. I've been running myself ragged for the past decade to line their pockets. And now I get to watch them fight over the scraps like I'm an ATM instead of their daughter. So I've been grappling with that for weeks since I found out, trying to wrap my head around it. But my *boyfriend* being paid to date me was the straw that broke the camel's back."

My laugh is watery this time. I sniff and look out over the lake, shaking my head at how pathetic my story sounds, even to my own ears.

The boyfriend debacle may have been the final nudge

that pushed me over the edge. But the truth about what my parents have done is the real betrayal. The one that's so painful, so hard to face, I'd almost rather pretend it never happened.

"I bet you're wondering how I could be so gullible."

"That's not what I'm wondering."

I suck in such a deep breath that my shoulders draw up to my ears and then droop. I reach for my wine. It feels like I need it after sharing more personal information than I have with a single soul in an exceptionally long time.

Who am I? Put a little fresh mountain air in me and I'm spilling my guts to the local horse trainer? All my PR prep has gone to shit.

"What are you wondering, then?" I finally ask.

West's eyes flash for a second, and I suddenly don't doubt he's broken a few noses. His heavy gaze clears, and he covers with "Never mind."

The sigh I let out is ragged—tired. I don't have any fight left in me to push back. "Well, at any rate, I'm here to work with Ford because I need an album that's all mine. Even if I can't write the actual songs."

"You can write the songs."

West says it with a little shrug. With such unwavering certainty. I don't even have it in me to tell him he's wrong.

He's still staring at me. Analyzing. Eyes scanning. "Is this part of what's tripping you up in the media?"

I sag in my chair. Drink and nod.

My phone lights up on the table in front of me, drawing our attention.

It's a Google alert, the one I still have set for my name because, clearly, I really am a masochist. Without thinking, I swipe it off the table and open the notification.

In Nose vs. Soccer ball, Skylar Stone Loses Again!

A lovely photo of me doubled over in pain while my nose gushes blood accompanies the stupid headline. That part I remember quite clearly. But West crouched before me, hands gently cupping my elbows, tattoos on display, looks a lot more intimate than I remember.

Most of his face is concealed beneath the brim of his hat, but I can see the grim line of his mouth. I can hear him saying, "*Breathe through your mouth, Sky,*" and feel his thumb rubbing soothing circles on the inside of my arm.

"Lovely," I say before tossing my phone back on the table. The headline is far from the worst I've seen, but there's an underlying sense of glee in the wording. It's not funny or especially clever. It's smug. "Sorry, you're in the news now. Someone at the game today took a photo of my nose geyser." I gesture at the phone. "I swear people get some kind of sick thrill out of humiliating me. They know my name will get them clicks so they grasp at straws and nitpick every little thing I do. They all use me to make money without my consent. Thrive on knocking me down just so they can lift themselves up."

West picks it up, his hand practically swallowing it. His brows draw down low on his handsome face as he takes in the article.

The phone dings again, and I reach for it, but he moves it away from me. "I need to see that."

"No," he bites out. "You don't."

My heart rate accelerates, and my stomach takes that eternal plunge that has become a mainstay in my day-to-day life. Dread licks up my throat, and I swallow it down to keep the nausea at bay. My breathing goes ragged, and my vision goes a little blurry at the edges.

Oh god. Not now. Not in front of him.

"Sky."

With that one word, West reaches across the table and takes my hand in his.

He catches my eye as he squeezes and releases in a slow and steady rhythm.

Slow and steady. That's what this man represents. No chaos. No panic. He soothes me.

"It's okay. Here."

He hands me my phone, and I have a text from my dad. Or my manager, since that seems a more apt description for our relationship. After seeing West's parenting skills, I'm wondering if my dad has ever fulfilled a true parental role for me.

Dad: Saw the article. At least the media was polite enough to alert me to your actual whereabouts. You're going to need me if you plan to work with Ford Grant. You don't understand the business aspects of what you do. And don't worry about your nose. I know the best surgeon in town. No one will even be able to tell.

He doesn't ask how I am doing. His top priority is making sure I know he's disappointed in me and adding a flippant reminder that the way I look is what's most important to him.

"I'm starting to understand why Britney shaved her head," I blurt out in a tearful voice. "Being treated like you're just an object for people to behold is fucking demoralizing."

I keep my eyes on the phone because I can't bring myself to meet West's gaze. I just shared too much. And I don't want to share too much with anyone.

The pressure around my body builds anew, pressing in from every side, and my breathing goes shallow. A panic attack is wrapping itself around me, sinking its teeth into my flesh. Ripping away at me piece by piece.

It's always a runaway train I don't know how to exit.

Until I'm yanked right off of it.

West makes a deep, growling noise. It rumbles in his broad chest and vibrates through his hand where he's still gripping mine. He swipes the phone from my limp hand in one smooth movement and tosses it out into the inky expanse beside us.

For a solid three seconds, I watch in abject horror as what feels like my one lifeline sails through the air. The *plop* it makes when it slaps the water's surface echoes in my ears.

I stare, mouth agape. "What…what did you just do?"

"Something you should have done a long time ago."

I turn to West, and fury pours down the column of my spine as I yank my hand back violently. "How *dare* you?"

Obnoxiously, West looks casual as he crosses his arms

and glares back at me, not the least bit cowed by my venomous tone. "No, Skylar. How dare anyone—anyone at all—make you feel like an object. That man has failed you at every turn. He calls himself a father? He's supposed to love you."

"And what? You're with me for twenty-four hours, and you love me now?" I spit the words, ignoring the fact that being loved by someone like West feels like it might be impossible.

Someone like West would never love me.

He shrugs. "No. But I like *you*." He emphasizes the word and points across the table at me. "I might like you more than you like yourself. Like you enough to tell it like it is."

That line lands like an atomic bomb, obliterating every safety net I've strung up to protect me. Eradicating the carefully bricked-in corners of my consciousness.

At this moment, I hate Weston Belmont.

Because he's right.

My body vibrates with pure indignation as I lean in across the table to stare him down. "Fuck. You."

He doesn't even flinch. He just studies me. "That's better."

"What's better?" I bite, annoyed by my curiosity.

"Your eyes. This is the first time they don't look sad. Or blank. Or fake. You look like you're ready to light me on fire or shove me right off this dock."

"Nice. You throw my phone in the water and tell me I have crazy eyes. How fucking refreshing."

He smiles at me slowly, seductively. It's as if the

confrontational moment excites him. And the way he smol-ders at me has me vibrating with something far from fury.

"No, fancy face. Those"—he points at my face, finger flicking from side to side—"are wild eyes. The eyes of a woman who just chose fight over flight. Don't smother that. Keep 'em and you'll come out on top. Trust me."

I glance down, nostrils flaring as I breathe heavily. Annoying as it may be, I do trust him. But I also feel flayed open. Exposed. He has a way of seeing every vulnerable piece of the broken girl I am beneath the shiny veneer.

And I hate the feeling.

"You're buying me a new phone," I hiss through gritted teeth.

"One week."

"Come again?"

"One week with no phone." He gestures his chin at me and smirks this obnoxious, self-satisfied smirk. "I dare you."

"You dare me? The fucking nerve of you, Weston Belmont." Cursing feels good, uncouth. For once, I don't care what this person thinks of me.

"Yeah, bet you can't go a week without buying one yourself."

"Fuck you." I let the f-bombs fly, each one releasing a weight from my shoulders as it sails from my lips.

His full mouth twists in a wry smirk. "Yeah, you've men-tioned that."

I cross my arms and lean away. "It's a safety issue."

"So long as you don't try to pet a wolf next, you should be fine."

"There are wol—you know what, never mind. I have work to do."

"And you are staying within walking distance of where you plan to do that work. Private property to private property, so no paparazzi. I'm sure you have a laptop, so if you're really desperate for a fix, you'll get it. You're addicted. But I dare you to spend a week away from subjecting yourself to the opinions of random people who don't know you. See how you feel."

"Oh, right. Because you know me sooo fucking well now."

He shrugs one shoulder and looks me over with a gentleness that feels completely unfamiliar. My wrath doesn't scare him in the slightest. Doesn't even seem to leave a bad taste in his mouth. "I don't know you at all, but it feels like I do."

This time, I don't swear at him. Because that one sentence strikes me silent. He's smug and confident and…not wrong. It feels like he knows me.

And that is fucking terrifying.

We sip our drinks in peace after that. I silently take his bet, but I also don't want to give him any more pieces of myself. My foundation feels shaky.

And I refuse to crumble.

Once I'm alone…I crumble.

I leave West's truck without a word. Without looking back, I trudge woodenly through the trees. Unlock the front door of the shitty bunkhouse. Shut it and press myself flat against the wood. I kick my sandals across the room violently.

Then, where no one can see me, I fall apart in spectacular fashion.

I pace and laugh maniacally. I gasp for air that feels too thick to properly fill my lungs. I endure the pain in my throat that comes from forcing myself to stay quiet. To keep all my ugliest, most painful secrets tastefully tucked away. My heart races as though it wants to hammer its way out of my body and flop around on the floor like a fish out of water.

"Fuck…fuck…fuck…" I gasp the word while rubbing at my tight throat.

I feel like I want to get out of my own body. I don't like it here, and my tender nose has nothing to do with the feeling.

For once, I might cry. Really cry. Like the scream, wail, and break shit kind of cry. My fingers itch to rip and throw stuff.

I'm sad, and I'm scared, but god…I'm also so fucking angry.

I don't want to be an angry person—especially when I am so epically fortunate—but right now, I want to rage at the world.

"Fuck them." I growl the words, thumping my palm on my chest. "Fuck everyone."

"*Fuck everyone!*" Cherry wholeheartedly agrees.

The humor of her repeating this back to me pokes a little hole my indulgent, blanketed anger. I'm forced to suck in a breath to cover my surging manic laughter.

I spin on her and point. "Yes, Cherry. Fuck everyone. And fuck Coach Thick Thighs for throwing my phone in the lake."

"*Fuck Coach Thick Thighs!*" she squawks back.

I grit my teeth, not ready to stop seeing red, but also feeling my paralyzing level of anxiety recede. Who'd have thought a foul-mouthed parrot would become my emotional support animal? I may not have much, but at least I've got her.

I'm staring at her, still getting my breathing back under control, rubbing firm circles on my chest, when it happens.

Tiny, poky steps on my skin. I don't lose it right away—my synapses aren't firing at full capacity. Instead, I drop my chin, not immediately processing what I see.

It takes a few seconds.

Then I realize there is a small gray mouse making its way across the bare bridges of my feet.

And I scream.

CHAPTER 13

West

I CALL FORD AS SOON AS I JUMP OUT OF MY TRUCK. HE answers on the third ring as I stroll down toward the bunkhouse.

"Hello?"

"Hey, can you send me Skylar's email?"

Ford's gruff voice filters back through my receiver. "Why? Doesn't she live within spitting distance of you? Ask her yourself."

"I want it to be a surprise."

"This may come as a shock to you, but women don't actually like surprise dick pics."

"Get outta here. I have never sent a dick pic in my life."

He says nothing. But I can imagine the disbelieving scowl on Ford's face.

"Okay, fine. I have never sent an *unsolicited* dick pic in my life. It's not my fault people are constantly asking for them."

My best friend groans. "Jesus—"

But I stop listening partway through his response because I'm about halfway through the stand of pines when a scream pierces the soft night air. I freeze and take a quick inventory of what's around me.

"Just send the email," I bark before hanging up.

The scream stops.

But then it starts again.

It's coming from the bunkhouse, and I break into a sprint down the gentle slope toward Skylar.

I was on my way to apologize to her because I shouldn't have thrown her phone in the water. It was impulsive—something I'd have done as a teenager.

This is a girl who's used to having security and assistants with her, and I've left her without a way to call for help. Now she's screaming like a masked murderer has her cornered in the bunkhouse.

What the fuck was I thinking? My stomach swoops and feels like it falls right out of my body as my feet thump across the grass.

I blast through the door and come to a screeching halt.

Skylar is seated on the short counter, fingers gripping the edge so hard that her knuckles have turned white. She has her knees drawn up and her perfectly polished toes point down at the floor.

"What's wrong?" I turn on the spot, assessing the small space, before stomping past her and checking in the bathroom at the back. My heart thrashes against my rib cage as I check, half expecting an axe murderer to be hiding behind the door.

"It's…" she says from behind me.

When I turn to face her, Skylar's wide eyes are conflicted under the brim of her new hat. "It's what?"

"It's…nothing."

I take a few steps toward her, propping my hands on my hips and giving her my best *you have to be fucking kidding me* look that I practice on Emmy all the time. "Nothing?"

As I take another step in her direction, she draws my attention down by licking her lips. I don't want to crowd her when she's clearly worked up, but it's also hard to give her space in a place this small.

And I feel inexplicably drawn to her. To making sure she's okay.

"You expect me to believe that nothing is wrong when you were screaming like a banshee not ten seconds ago?"

Her knees drop at a snail's pace, and I watch as she examines the floor a little too carefully. Corner to corner. Like she lost one of her diamond earrings down there or something.

"No. But I can't tell you."

"Why not?"

Her tongue darts out again. And I'm weak, so I watch. *That fucking mouth.*

"Because I promised Rosie I wouldn't." She blows a loose strand of toffee-colored hair off her face. An almost exasperated action, like *I'm* inconveniencing *her* by coming to help. *Again.*

"My sister?"

She nods, top teeth pressing into her plush bottom lip

as though that will keep her from spilling whatever secret they share.

"We're all adults here. Just tell me so I can get whatever it is squared away."

She has the nerve to scowl at me, as if I'm the asshole for being concerned about a screaming woman on my property. "I made a promise. I do have some integrity, you know."

My brows drop down. "Stop assuming I'm always thinking the worst of you. I'm not—"

I stop because I see it. A flash of soft brown and the thin tail that trails behind as it scurries along below the cupboards.

"A mouse? I have traps."

That tendon in her jaw pops, and she removes her hands from the counter, crossing her arms and her legs. Back to the very image of composure. Prissy through and through. Screaming over a fucking mouse and then sitting there like a queen looking at *me* like *I'm* the idiot.

"His name is Scotty. He just surprised me. Pretend you don't know about him. If you set a trap, I will never forgive you."

"You and my sister want me to pretend I don't know there is a mouse named Scotty living in my bunkhouse?"

"Yes. I like her, and I won't let you kill her mouse. Walk away and pretend this never happened."

"You're talking an awfully big game for someone who's hiding on the counter to stay safe."

She scowls. "Erase it from your mind, West."

"Yeah? Just erase it?"

"Yes."

"Like the kiss?"

That tendon pulses before she bites out, "What kiss?"

I smile. Full and blinding. It's my panty-melting smile, and I'm not above pulling it out when needed. "That's how we're gonna play this, fancy face?"

She glares at me, defiance shining in her eyes. She hops down onto the floor bravely, though she can't keep her eyes from taking a quick scan around her. "Yup. You can go. I'm fine. Great even."

I cross my arms and widen my stance, ready for battle. "No fucking chance am I leaving you out here to sleep with my sister's weird pet mouse."

"Where are you expecting me to sleep? The barn?"

I shrug. "Won't stop ya if that's what tickles your fancy. But I have a spare room in my house. Queen-size bed, no mice. So that's where you'll sleep."

She thinks about my offer. I can see the flash of longing in her molten irises right before she smothers the idea. "Pass."

"You are beyond stubborn. Anyone ever told you that?"

"Nope." She pops the *p* with so much attitude, I have to bite down on a smile. "It's a new character trait for me. Sick of being told what to do."

I glance around the space, considering how I'd get a horse to quit fighting me on what we both know is best for them.

I'd take the pressure off.

"Your call. You know where to find me. I'll be doing night checks in a bit, and you can meet me at the barn. I promise to give you lots of space so you can work on that new character trait of yours."

"What about not wanting anyone around your kids?"

"My kids aren't here this week."

"And next week?"

I toss her a wink. "Maybe Scotty will be dead by then."

Her responding gasp sounds suspiciously like a laugh. "That's not funny."

"I didn't mean for it to be," I toss over my shoulder as I turn to leave.

It's right when I get to the door that Cherry pipes up with her filthy little beak. *"Fuck Coach Thick Thighs!"*

I pause before turning back to Skylar, who is struggling to keep her face blank. "You were talking to your bird about me?"

"No" comes out of her mouth just a little too quickly to be the truth, but I don't call her on it.

Instead, I leave smiling.

And later, when I see her walking through the barn doors, I smile even bigger.

CHAPTER 14

Skylar

I wake in an unfamiliar house. With unfamiliar bedding. And an unfamiliar throbbing on my face.

It takes me only a moment to figure out where I am, how I got here, and why my face hurts. The good news is…I slept.

In West's house, I slept better than I have in months.

It could be all the action and change and lack of sleep recently, but the minute I walked to the barn and he smiled at me, I felt a weight lift off my shoulders.

His smug smile insinuated he knew I couldn't resist a queen-size bed, but I didn't even mind.

I didn't mind when he offered to go back to the bunkhouse with me to get Cherry. I also didn't mind when he led me up the stairs to the first door on the right. Or when he told me to sleep tight and not let the bedbugs bite.

At first, I'd recoiled at the mention of bedbugs, but from what little I know of West, I assumed it was a joke. Or something he tells his kids. The sentiment was charming and fatherly and somehow made me feel safe.

As I slipped into cool, fresh sheets that smelled of laundry detergent, I truly let myself appreciate the type of person West is.

The type of man.

He wanted me to feel better for me, not for him. He wanted me safe under his roof, but he didn't force my hand. He let me make my own decision.

And that was refreshing.

Did I consider staying in the bunkhouse just to prove a point?

Fuck yes, I did.

But I didn't want to punish myself to win an argument in my head with a guy who'd be smirking at me the next morning anyway.

It felt good not to fight. Good enough that I slept until…I turn and glance at the nightstand where the small brass clock shows 10:45 a.m.

I blink a few times before sitting up and muttering, "That can't be right."

My fists press against my eye sockets, rotating gently to rub the sleep away. The pain reminds me of my face-to-face with a ball, though, so I stop and glance over at Cherry.

She quirks her head at me and blinks her black, bead-like eyes.

"Did you sleep as well as I did, Cherry?"

"*Feed me*" is the demand I get back. She's always bitchier when she's hungry.

"Okay, okay. Let's go find you something." I kick my feet

out of bed, place them flat on the hardwood floor, and reach around the bed, in search of my phone in the sheets. That's usually where it is because I spend my nights scrolling gossip sites until I fall asleep. Then I wake up and need to plug it in, followed by checking my name alerts.

Today, I don't find it.

What I find is a flash of annoyance, followed by a flood of relief.

I don't need to check…because I *can't*.

I sit with that knowledge for a minute, breathing it in and breathing it out. Next, I remove Cherry from her cage, let her climb up my arm to my shoulder, and make my way downstairs.

I don't even look at myself in the mirror on the way past. I already know I'm going to look very, very bruised. And I'm just vain enough to know I'd rather not see it.

Once downstairs, I take a peek around. "West? Hello? You here?"

"*Feed me. Feed me.*" The bird bobs and does a fake pecking motion on my cheek.

Cherry may be a snarky bitch, but she's never bitten me. Only other people.

Still, when the clock in the kitchen confirms that it is indeed almost 11 a.m., I opt not to take my chances. Deciding her pellets can wait, I head straight for the fruit bowl on the counter and peel a banana.

She practically lunges for it the moment it's open. While she eats, I hold it in place for her and stare at the spot where the glass broke the other day. Where West showed his true colors and made me confused enough to kiss him later like a colossal idiot.

The kiss he teases me about.

Because we're friends.

Friends.

My lip curls at the word, but I also rationalize that Weston Belmont might be an ideal starting point for a girl who doesn't have any. Even if I am a little perplexed by his steadiness and transparency. By how much he *cares*.

But then, perhaps that's the basis of normal friendships.

With that in mind, I go searching for him. Slipping my feet into my sandals, my hand clamps on the front doorknob, and I twist, only to open it to a woman standing right in front of me, fist up like she was about to knock and I ripped the door out from under her hand.

For a few beats, we stand and stare at each other.

Me in confusion.

Her with an air of hostility.

We size each other up. She's got icy-blue eyes and smooth chocolate-colored hair that frames her face in a silky sheet. Full brows and high cheekbones. The longer I stare at her flawless bone structure, the more I feel like a troll who just crawled out from under a bridge.

"Hi," I venture carefully. "I'm…not from here."

Way to go, Skylar, you awkward idiot.

"Are you…" I know the question even as she trails off. Her eyes race over me in shock.

With a full mouth, Cherry still gets out an enthusiastic, "*Go away!*" and I do my best not to cringe.

"Sorry, she's hangry," I offer lamely as Cherry rips another chunk out of the banana I'm holding up.

God. What must this woman be thinking right now? A bruised Skylar Stone answers the door with a rude parrot—who is dropping banana bits on my shirt as we speak.

"I'm just…" She shifts, peeking into the house. "I'm looking for West. Is he in?"

"Yeah, same. I'm also looking for him."

Her eyes narrow like she's wondering if I'm bullshitting her, and my cheeks heat as more explanations tumble from my lips. "I'm just at his house because we're friends. Not a clue where he is. I woke up, and he wasn't here."

Her mouth purses, and I realize how badly I'm blowing this. His explanation about *friends* last night drifts into my mind.

This. This is what I did not want.

"No. No. We're actual friends. Separate rooms type of friends."

The gorgeous woman seems to be at a loss for words. Probably because I sound like a bumbling idiot. And look like I've taken a header into a wall. I'm about to clarify—again—when West's deep baritone booms from the side of the wraparound deck.

"Bree."

I hate how familiar her name sounds on his lips. She spins so eagerly.

I've known this man for two days and I'm instantly jealous. It's ridiculous.

To cover, I put on a big smile. Based on the head

tilt West gives me, it must be a weird fucking smile. But whatever.

He smiles back at me, but she preens like it was meant for her. "I was worried about you after you canceled last night."

He holds both hands out wide as he approaches the front steps. All it does is show off his immense width. The veins that run the length of his thick arms. The bronzed skin peeking out from between the top of his jeans and the bottom of his shirt. "All in one piece."

The woman glances back at me and then at West. She's clearly trying to piece together what's going on.

I want nothing more than to escape. I know this type of drama, and I want no part in it.

They may need makeup sex, and as much as it turns my stomach, I decide to give them the space.

Because West and I are friends, not *friends*, and I don't want to be a cockblocker.

"Gonna go"—I point an awkward finger gun toward the bunkhouse—"feed Cherry."

"*Feed Cherry!*" she repeats, bobbing on my shoulder.

I edge past Bree, jog down the steps, step onto the grass, and flee toward safety.

But not before Cherry can skewer me on the way past West's rigid form. Her parting, "*Fuck Coach Thick Thighs!*" keeps me hustling forward with a beet-red face and a prayer for the ground to open up and swallow me whole.

I really need to have a heart-to-heart with my bird about boundaries.

Alone in the bunkhouse, I flip open my laptop. I figure since I have no phone, I might need to be more regular about checking my inbox.

There are emails from my agent, Jerry. Subject lines ranging from possible interviews and one particularly troubling one that says *List of possible dates*. Like I'm choosing a pair of shoes off a curated shelf.

It makes me sick.

But it's the email at the very top of my inbox that washes away any nausea. The sender is one Weston Belmont. And the subject line says, "BREAKING NEWS!"

Both curious and amused, I open the email.

BREAKING NEWS: Small town jerk is sorry for throwing Skylar Stone's phone in the lake.

I snort. That's all it says.

I consider writing him back but realize I don't know what to say. Instead, I just grin at the screen, basking in the glow of the world's most adorable apology.

A knock at the door startles me and I immediately move to answer it, secretly hoping it's West and that he's not spending time with Bree.

I yank the door open. And come face-to-face with his sister instead.

"I brought the sweatsuit!" Rosie cheerfully announces

from the front door of the bunkhouse. Followed by, "Oh my god, your nose."

I reach up to it self-consciously. "Is it that bad?"

"No," she says, shaking her head. "Just caught me by surprise. What happened? Did you try to pet another bear?" She deadpans the joke, but the twinkle in her eyes gives her away.

There's something so normal about getting ribbed like this. And yet, people don't generally tease me.

I decide I like it.

"Yeah. He booped me on the nose, stronger than I banked on."

She grins at my playful sarcasm as I reach forward and take the folded pile of pink cotton from her. "No, I helped West at Emmy's soccer game yesterday, and a kid accidentally kicked the ball straight into my face."

"Oh no." She steps closer, inspecting it from both sides. "Well, if it's any consolation, you're still hot as fuck."

A shocked choking noise lodges in my throat.

"No, I mean, really, I wish I looked like this with a bruised face." She leans back now, a smirk playing across her features. "Poor West."

Her comment leaves me confused, and I quirk my head. "Poor West?" She doesn't respond, so I venture, "Because I had to stay at his house last night?"

"You did?"

I swallow and rest my gaze on my feet for a few beats before admitting, "I met Scotty last night and…I freaked out. Screamed like a fucking baby. I tried to keep it a secret, but West found out about the mouse. He offered me a room at his place."

Rosie scoffs and waves a hand. "It's okay. I'll head up to his house and threaten him."

"Oh… On that, give him a bit."

It's Rosie's turn to tilt her head.

"There's a woman named Bree with him."

Understanding dawns on Rosie's face as she breathes out, "Ooooh." Then she shrugs and adds, "That's fine. Scotty's safety is more important to me than his privacy."

When she turns to leave, I'm struck by the casual power she exudes. Rosie has a certain quality that makes you want to follow her. A natural leader, an effortless sort of confidence.

That's why excitement surges through me when she turns back and says, "Oh! Drinks on Thursday? The guys have their bowling league, and my friend Tabby is free. You game? Or do you need more alone time?"

More alone time?

I don't know what my work schedule will look like yet. But the prospect of more time alone feels borderline stifling. And Rosie is so…chill. Which is why I immediately respond with, "Count me in."

CHAPTER 15

West

I'M ANTSY, SO I HEAD TO THE BARN AND START WORKING MY way through the horses. Grooming each one meticulously from head to toe. It's therapeutic, taking them from dusty to shiny. Dull hooves to richly oiled. Tangled mane to perfectly flowing.

My brain feels full, more so than usual, so I let it wander as I gently scrub circles on Copper's coat with a rubber curry comb—my first horse, the one that eventually kept me out of trouble. My parents' threat of selling him out from under me if they got one more visit from the cops changed my tune.

That's not to say I didn't find *any* trouble to get into. But I took a break from street racing and cutting class to hand out bags of pot to my classmates from behind the school dumpster.

That was a fucking dumb spot to start my illegal business, now that I think of it. Still makes me chuckle and shake my head.

My thoughts drift to Skylar, how angry she was when I tossed her phone. The immediate guilt I felt for having done it at all.

I think about Rosie and her fucking mouse. The way Skylar protected him simply because Rosie asked her to.

And I think about Bree. The accusation in her eyes followed by the loud growl of her engine as she peeled out of the property.

But most of all, I think about how flustered Skylar looked by her presence just before she ran away.

"Copper, old man. At least you've got my back," I murmur, running a palm over his swayback and watching his eyelids go heavy. He's old. Really old. I don't like to think about the day he'll eventually be gone, but at thirty-five, I know it's close. So I soak up these moments with him. Buffing his coat to a bronze shine that reminds me of Skylar's hair and making him bran mashes with a little too much molasses in them.

As I'm admiring him and what great condition he's in for his age, the air shifts behind me. It's a strange sensation, one I haven't felt before. It makes me turn slowly, and I'm not at all surprised when my eyes come to rest on Skylar Stone. Hair in wild waves around her face, eyes curious, body language a bit tentative.

"Am I interrupting?"

"My conversation with Copper? Yes. I find it to be rude, but he won't mind." I toss the brush into the bin near the alleyway edge, biting down a smile when she chuckles.

"Is Bree gone?" She steps forward, peering around as

though a woman I'm involved with might pop out of an empty stall half-naked and shout *Surprise!*

"She is."

"Okay" is all she says.

"I'm sorry I threw your phone in the lake," I finally confess.

"I got your email." She smirks at me as she walks my way.

"You love getting headlines. I figured I'd send you one that's actually true."

"Cute email. It really was kind of a dick move."

"And not the good kind," I concede, nodding.

"If that was your best move, the ladies would be disappointed. No matter how big it is."

Usually, I'd smile at that, but I drop her gaze and peek back up. "I'm sorry. I'll replace it."

She scoffs and waves me off. "No chance. You challenged me. Now I need to prove I can go without it for a week."

"You can. Might even like it."

Her head tilts. "Might even be good for me." She nibbles on her bottom lip as her eyes slice over to Copper. "What are you up to?"

I hike a thumb back over my shoulder. "Brushing my horse."

"What's his name?"

"Copper."

She eyes him speculatively before reaching forward to slide her hand down over his neck. "Is he what got you into this?" She looks around us, gesturing to the barn with her eyes.

"Yeah. My parents heard horses were good for keeping kids out of trouble. And it worked." My head wobbles. "Mostly."

Her fingers trail through his mane as she asks, "What do you mean mostly?"

"I mean, my new challenge was sticking the ride on the toughest, wildest horses I could find. Got my ass dumped in the dirt enough times that I learned I couldn't muscle a horse into being a willing partner. Started learning real training strategies to bring them around and got hooked. Went away and worked the odd cattle ranch. Performance horses. But ultimately, I wanted to be here and not on the road. I'm not interested in working cattle, and the allure of riding for show is lost on me. I like the simplicity of starting the young ones. Building that foundation. Seeing them flourish. It's something new and exciting every day, but it's good, honest work too. I love what I do."

She stares at me blankly for a few beats. Then, "That must feel incredible. To love what you do like that."

"You don't like what you do?"

"I think, like you, I love the simplicity of it. Of singing. Of figuring out a song and mastering it. The emotion that goes into taking words and making them into song. But more and more…the allure of singing for show is just…gone."

I nod along, unsure what to say to that. It's not for me to tell her how to handle it anyway. It just seems tragic to me that everyone around her has managed to ruin something that once brought her joy. "Wanna try?" I reach the brush out to her. "Horses are good for the soul."

172

Skylar hesitates. She's not an especially short woman, but she looks small right now.

"You don't have to. You can go do something else. I've just always found brushing horses to be kind of therapeutic. But you're welcome in the house, you know. Anywhere on the property."

Her head bobs slowly. "This is where I want to be."

"I thought you wanted to be alone."

She hits me with the softest smile before focusing on Copper. "I was for a few hours. It was… Well, it was a learning experience. Turns out I don't really know how to be alone. Being quiet with someone else sounds nice, though."

Her admission makes me sad. For both her and me. Because I know that feeling all too well.

Loneliness.

She takes the brush with a wobbly smile and steps past me toward Copper.

Wordlessly, I grab another brush and join her.

We spend the next few hours grooming every horse in the barn. We don't talk. She watches what I do with each type of brush and replicates my motions.

It's the kind of companionship I crave. It's intimate without even trying.

It's one of the most peaceful afternoons I've ever enjoyed.

After a week of having the fridge and pantry cleaned out by Emmy and Ollie, I decided it's time for a restock. I push my grocery cart up and down the aisles, restocking with all of their favorites so that I'm ready for their return. Head down to double check my list as I round the corner, I hear the clink of metal hitting metal.

"Shit, sorry," I mutter as I look up to find Skylar right in front of me, pushing a cart of her own, face partially hidden behind her Sparkly Turquoise Unicorns team hat.

Yesterday we brushed the horses together, but today I saw neither hide nor hair of her. I assume she went to Ford's to come up with a plan and get the lay of the land. But other than that, I have no idea what she's been up to. I know she slept in the house. She snuck in late to "not invade my space" as she called it, and I left early to work the horses before it got too hot.

"Are you stalking me? Should I be concerned?" she says with a smug smile on her face as she pops one hip out.

Fuck, she's hot.

I lick my lips, internally reminding myself again not to act starstruck around her. It would be easy enough to do, and it would shut her right down. She doesn't need another fan.

"Is it considered stalking if you like it?"

I get an amused eye roll and take a moment to peek at her cart. It's fully stocked. Which means when I asked if she wanted to stay for dinner last night and she told me she had a full fridge and would be fine, she was lying.

"Full cart you've got there, Sky. Didn't realize you had room in your full fridge for all those bags of salad."

She deflects by teasing me. "If you were any good at stalking, you'd know exactly how much room I have in my fridge."

I give her my best *give me a break* look.

"Listen, West. I like you. You're a good friend, considering I've known you for all of four days. But if I want to sit alone, eating the stale Pop-Tarts that were left in the bunkhouse with your sister's mouse, all while drinking an entire bottle of wine I found in the cupboard, that's what I'm gonna do. And I will not explain myself or apologize. And I don't need you to save me. *Again.* I needed to have a pity party and treat my body like a dumpster fire because I was never allowed to, and it felt freeing. Got it?"

"That sounds like a really tragic version of a bucket of ice cream and Hallmark movies."

"The only thing tragic about it was the way I felt this morning. Feeling free has consequences, it would seem."

"Hence the salad?"

She nods. "Hence the salad."

I gesture my chin at her. "How's the nose?"

Her hand moves up, fingers tapping gingerly along it. "Still a little tender. Felt fucking fabulous after a bottle of wine, though. I'll give the experience that much."

I maneuver around my shopping cart without even thinking. With only a few steps, I'm standing right in front of her, my fingers nudging the brim of her hat back so I can see her face. She doesn't flinch or move away. She only tips her head to stare up at me.

There's something heart-stopping about a woman who is so low on trust looking up at me the way she is right now. Fragile and fierce all at once.

I admire the hell out of her. But I don't say that. I settle for, "Let me see."

Her lips roll together and she nods slightly as I lift my hands to cup the back of her head. My gaze follows the path of my thumbs as they trace her cheekbones, the sides of her nose, and the top line of the bridge.

My tongue swipes out as I take a quick glance down at her mouth.

That fucking mouth.

"You look good, fancy face."

"Yeah?" she breathes, and I feel the rush of air against my damp lips.

I take the liberty of tracing the elegant swoop of her nose once more. "Perfect as ever."

It's too fucking far, saying that out loud. But the truth slipped out anyway. Her eyes widen on mine and my head inclines.

I don't know what the hell I'm doing. I meant to check her nose, and here I am, in the middle of the grocery store, admiring her openly.

Luckily, it's the loud clearing of a throat that startles us. We pull away from each other like two teenagers caught by their parents.

It's ridiculous. We're two single, consenting adults. If we want to kiss right here and now, we should.

Except we shouldn't.

A throat clears again, and we both turn to see Bree staring daggers at us. Skylar jumps away from me and begins nervously smoothing her hands over her clothes.

She clearly thinks there's something going on between Bree and me.

"Excuse me, *friends.* Just going to grab some Shreddies if you're done here."

Skylar winces before peeking back over her shoulder and abruptly steering her cart around the protruding end of mine.

She can't get away fast enough, and a part of me doesn't blame her.

I told her my life wasn't cut out for anything serious, and I meant it when I said it.

But for once, I find myself thinking something serious might not be so bad.

Skylar looks shocked when she swings the door open and finds me standing on the front landing of the bunkhouse, holding a pan of lasagna.

"I made this, and if you make me eat it alone, it will be tragic and possibly the lowest point of my life."

She doesn't open the door any wider, but she curves one brow at me. I haven't seen her since the grocery store yesterday, but I heard her tiptoe into the house last night.

"The very lowest?"

Now she scoffs. "Yeah, your metabolism seems like it's a huge problem."

"You're still thinking about me with my shirt off, aren't you? Regretting not taking a photo?"

"You're a shameless flirt, Weston Belmont."

I grin and hit her with a cocky wink. "Thank you."

Then we both get caught for a moment, staring at each other. And for one heartbeat, I'm back on that road with her body beneath me. I'm on a dark path behind the barn with her lips pressed to mine. I'm in a grocery store aisle, staring at her like nothing else exists.

I've always thought Skylar Stone was stunning. But Skylar Stone who lives next door is downright captivating. I feel like a child constantly caught gawking.

I want to talk to her.

I want to get to know her.

I want to eat with her.

From behind Skylar, Cherry coos, "*Go away!*" but we both ignore her.

It seems insane. I'm a grown-ass man. We've known each other for less than a week, yet I'm completely sucked into her orbit. And it's not just a physical attraction; it's not just a celebrity obsession... I—it feels like so much more.

I'm like a lost little boy. A fish out of water. So I settled on homemade lasagna to get her attention.

"I don't get the sense that Bree would love the idea of us sharing lasagna."

I glance down at the pan in my hand and let out a low whistle. "It *is* a pretty sexy lasagna."

A laugh lurches from her throat. "West, I'm serious."

"So am I. And I don't give a shit if she likes it or not."

Her nose wiggles as she mulls my response over in her

head. Still not opening the door any wider. "I don't want to be that girl."

"What girl?"

"The one who causes issues in another relationship."

"Skylar, there is no relationship."

Her eyes take a tour up near her brows. "Oh, sure. Your friend-with-benefits came over to your house to check on you because there is no relationship. *Right.*" Her head shakes like she's disappointed. "You're so damn likable, West. But that shit isn't."

"Whoa, whoa, whoa." I hold a hand up and turn to place the lasagna on the deck chair. "You think…" I step closer to her. "You think she came over to—"

"Benefit," she fills in, chin tipped up. "Which is great. I'm so thrilled for you." She nods vigorously, though her tone isn't as convincing as she may think. "I hope you are getting all the bene—"

"I broke it off with her."

Her verbal tangent comes to a screeching halt. "You what?"

"I ended the benefits. She may have been the one to end the friend part. We might be enemies-with-no-benefits now."

Skylar's eyes search my face. The makeup she's wearing today doesn't entirely cover the bruising, but it's better than it was. I hope she's been icing it. "When?"

"When what?"

"When did you end it?"

"After the pub. The night your phone met its end. I

called her from my truck. You sprinted away to the bunk-house like I had a contagious disease, so I called her. Then, when I was coming here to apologize about the phone, I heard you screaming."

Her brows draw together, and a look of concentration takes over her face. "Why?"

"Why what?"

"Why then? Why make the call then?"

I shift uncomfortably, weighing how I want to answer this question. Deciding how honest I want to be. Wondering if I've even completely figured it out myself.

Do I tell her I didn't like the way her face fell when I told her about my current relationship status? Do I tell her I want to be free in every way the next time she decides to kiss me? Do I tell her I want there to be a next time?

Or do I just say *fuck it* and kiss her myself?

I move incrementally closer.

But then stop.

I think about everything she's been through—everything that the people she trusted have taken from her. I don't want to be another person who takes more than she has to give. And I don't want to rush with her. Not when we're both still so clearly tangled up.

So I tell her something that's true.

"Because I had a good reason to."

A flush paints her cheeks and her gaze searches every corner of my face for some hint of a lie.

Then her voice comes out a bit wobbly as she lets me down easy.

"I'm going to pass on dinner…but save me a piece. I don't like the idea of today being the lowest point in your life." She steps back to shut the door. But not before adding, "And ruining a metabolism like *that* would be a damn shame."

CHAPTER 16

Skylar

BREAKING NEWS: Weston Belmont eats entire lasagna and ruins his metabolism. Sources say it's all Skylar Stone's fault.

I sit across from Ford on Monday morning, still chuckling over the fake headline West sent me this morning. We're on the leather couches that frame the open living space in the office. This corner of the office is lined with shelves that are full to the brim with a variety of vinyl records.

"Let's talk about the album."

I nod eagerly, leaning forward just a little. "Put me to work. I want to make this happen. And I want it to be fucking incredible."

Ford grins from where he lounges like a king in his castle. "Is this album payback?"

"Would it be off-putting for you if I said it was?"

"Absolutely not."

"Good. Because my parents have fucked me around my entire life, taken advantage of my work for financial gain. And I want them nowhere near this."

He rakes a hand through his mussed hair. "I will get you an ironclad contract."

"My dad and agent might try to contact you. To weasel their way in. They're going to want answers."

Ford just shrugs, looking suave and unaffected. "There's a pretty famous song about not always getting what you want."

I chuckle at that. "They are relentless."

The man across from me leans forward, eyes flashing. "Skylar, they are irrelevant to me. I don't owe them answers. I don't care about being liked. They can contact me all they want. I will happily delete their messages."

A relieved sigh rushes from me. It's like I didn't realize how badly I needed to hear that. "Thank you."

"You're welcome." Ford steeples his hands. "Now let's talk vibe. What are you after?"

Butterflies erupt in my stomach as I prepare to talk about my music. And it strikes me that I haven't felt this way about creating in a very long time. "Something stripped down. Something simple. Something…imperfect. Do you think that would be possible?"

"Definitely."

"I…" I grimace and press my lips into a flat line. "I have to be honest. My voice is good, but I'm no generational talent. Technology has been a huge help."

He just shrugs. "Plenty of excellent musicians haven't been the very best at their craft. I think it's more about what's in here." He taps at his chest, a chain with a small key is dangling there. "Have you got the heart to create something special, Skylar?"

My teeth gnash. "Yes."

And something about saying it out loud makes me believe myself.

"Good—"

"The only thing is…I don't write my own music. Or, well, I haven't."

His lips twitch as he mulls that over. "Okay. We can buy songs. But I'm going to need some time to get the right ones for us to look at. Then we can workshop them and see what fits with your vision. I'll call in some favors, see what I can do about musicians and hammering out recording timelines. How's the voice? Do you feel like you need coaching?"

I shake my head. "No. I'll practice this week. I'll be good." The truth is, I feel too raw to sing in front of anyone right now. I think if I sing, I'll cry.

"Okay." His hands slap his thighs. "We'll reconvene next Monday. And I'll bring my daughter, Cora. I promised her we'd work on this together. In fact, you were her pick. Is that all right?"

A watery smile touches my lips. How utterly, painfully sweet of him to do this with her. It makes my heart squeeze painfully to think of my own dad and our fucked-up relationship. I push past those feelings and tell him in the brightest voice I can muster, "Looking forward to meeting her. And I could use a breather. A week off will be wonderful."

My week off is miserable.

My plans to fill it with work and people and business goes up in smoke before my eyes. Instead, it's dark and sad and somehow deeply necessary. It makes me realize I've spent almost no time alone in my life. Just me, with my thoughts and feelings as my only company.

Okay, Cherry pipes up and calls me boring from time to time.

Still, there's something profound about those few days I spend on my own. They're fucking depressing because rather than sweeping away every uncomfortable thought that pops into my mind, I sit with it. Dig my fingers into all the tender spots and let myself feel the pain.

I practice singing in the shower. And it makes me cry.

In fact, a lot of innocuous things seem to make me cry. I cry, and no one comes to rub my back or tell me to pull it together.

And I like that.

I don't rush to do my hair and makeup in the morning "to look presentable," as my mom would say—as if I'm apparently repulsive when I haven't spent hours primping.

And I don't rush past the mirror either. I stop and stare at myself. My eyes. My nose. The light lines on my skin. The pores that I can never get quite small enough.

Each time, I'm less alarmed by the sight of myself. Each time, I like what I see just a little bit more.

I nap. At night, I sleep like the dead. I don't even hear West leave in the morning, and when I wake up late, I don't beat myself up about it. I never realized the extent of my exhaustion.

When the anger hits, I throw rocks into the lake and watch them crash down onto the silken surface.

After a couple of days, I don't even miss my phone. Instead, I read an old bodice-ripper romance I find on a shelf in West's living room within one day. When it's over, I feel happy and optimistic. Something about that guaranteed happy ending cheers me up. And I realize scrolling my phone *never* made me feel that way.

After four days of almost constant silence and nothing but my own company, I feel ready to face other humans.

Just maybe not West.

The two of us seem unable to quit bumping into each other. It's funny at this point. What makes it less funny is the way my body reacts to the mere sight of him, like it doesn't realize my brain is a fucking mess. Not to mention West has made it clear, he's not in a place for anything serious.

And I don't think I can do anything casual. Not with him. With him, I feel downright possessive.

Plus, my time here in Rose Hill is but a blip on the radar of my life, and I'll eventually have to leave.

I peer at myself in the mirror, popping my lips together to press my freshly applied lipstick evenly across them.

It's red. Bright red.

My parents would hate it and tell me it's not my brand. But with so many miles between us and all the shit I found out, my brand feels less important than ever.

As do they.

Sure, I see their emails when I check my inbox, but I feel no inclination to answer them beyond saying my phone was misplaced and I can only be reached via email. I told them I was taking a breather, and I am.

Their very own walking, talking paycheck has pulled her head out of the clouds, and I think they're a little scared of the view I've got now. A little worried about what I might find with my feet firmly planted on the ground.

I think what I'm finding is myself. And the knowledge that I won't let what they've done to me stand.

A quick glance at my watch tells me I should make my way to the main house. Rosie is picking me up at seven, and I've got five minutes to wander up there.

One last glance in the mirror brings a smile to my face. I'm wearing a black tank bodysuit to match the dainty black stiletto sandals that are wrapped around my ankles. They peek out from the frayed hemline of my skinny blue jeans that are so tight they look painted on.

I've flat-ironed my freshly washed hair into a silky curtain that falls midway down my back once I take all the curls out. The bruising on my face is all but gone, leaving a pale-yellow tone that was easily covered with makeup.

A few pieces of simple gold jewelry complete the outfit, and I reach for my leather jacket as I turn to leave.

I'm most likely overdone for a small mountain town, but I look sexy. Not cute and not sweet. And that feels new and somehow intrinsically me. Or at least the version of me I'm getting to know.

I walk gingerly to the main house, trying to keep the narrow heels from sinking into the porous ground beneath me, and breathe out a sigh of relief when I make it to the driveway. Rosie hasn't arrived yet, so I take a moment to gaze up at the farmhouse.

All the stray toys that were out when I first arrived have been tidied up or put away. I find myself missing that lived-in first impression. I'm barely acquainted with Emmy and Oliver, but the absence of their chaos saddens me. It makes me think of West asking me over for dinner.

A pang of guilt about turning him down hits me. It was an attempt at self-preservation, but now I'm wondering if I misunderstood. I wonder if the weeks they're gone are too quiet for a man so vivacious and bursting with energy.

As though I've summoned him with my thoughts, he strides out the front door, phone pressed between his ear and shoulder as he locks up.

The shirt he's wearing fits snugly around his broad shoulders. It's like a polo with buttons all the way down the front. On the back are the words "The Ball Busters," along with a logo displaying a bowling ball and pins.

I knew he was on a bowling team but seeing him all decked out makes me giggle.

He spins at the sound, eyes zeroing in on me.

"Yeah, be there in five," he says before hanging up. Then he looks me up and down.

Twice.

His teeth strum across his full bottom lip and a low groan rumbles in his chest.

My skin hums, my cheeks heat, and my stomach flips.

"You look at all your friends like that, Belmont?" I hike my purse up higher on my shoulder and cling to the strap to keep myself from walking up to him and petting him.

I've been attracted to men before. Or at least I thought I had been. I may have been wrong. Because even in a team shirt, color-blocked bowling shoes wedged between his arm and ribs, he's hotter than any man I've ever seen.

And I know it's his steady sweetness that has me down bad.

"Only you, fancy face."

Butterflies erupt in my chest as his eyes peruse my body. Again.

"Look. At. You." He smirks, softly shaking his head as he saunters toward me.

"Fan of the outfit?"

He's close enough now for me to catch his scent. He smells fresh. Like biting into a ripe pear. Like bergamot bodywash.

It makes me want to bite into him.

"Who wouldn't be?" His hand lifts, and his pointer finger shifts between my eyes. "But it's these eyes I'm the biggest fan of. You look good. Rested." His tongue makes a clucking noise. "You look ready to bring Rose Hill to its knees tonight."

Even though my makeup is perfect and my tits are pushed up, this man is going on about my eyes?

Suddenly, he's the only one I want to bring to their knees.

The crunching of tires on the driveway behind me shrivels that idea as quickly as it takes form.

I step up to West, watching his pupils dilate as I do. When he makes no attempt to move away, I flatten my palm on his chest. His heartbeat accelerates, and I can't help but lean in closer. Then I press a kiss to his cheek and murmur, "Good luck tonight," before turning and darting into Rosie's vehicle.

CHAPTER 17

West

"You have lipstick on your face," Ford deadpans from the driver's seat beside me.

I flip down the sun visor and slide the mirror open. Sure enough, there's a perfect red lip imprint of Skylar Stone's plush mouth on my cheek.

For a moment, I'm thrown back into the feel of her pressing up against me. The way her hand flattened against my chest tentatively.

When she kissed me behind the barn, it felt desperate. Like she was looking for something to make herself feel better, and I was the closest thing within reach.

But tonight, she stared me down. Feline eyes. Confident smirk. I tried not to be a creep and gawk at her, but it was hard to miss the swell of her breasts pushed up over the tight fucking outfit she was wearing.

But if she were a suspect in a crime, I'd never be able to give the cops any clothing details for a sketch.

I'd only be able to tell them about her eyes.

I flick the visor shut and settle back.

"You're not gonna wipe it off?"

I shrug and toss my best friend a wink as he maneuvers us out onto the highway to Rose Valley Alley, the old bowling alley outside of town. An absolute dive and one of the original businesses in this valley. A locals-only watering hole with a bowling alley set along the back wall.

A real relic.

"Who put it there?"

I shrug again. He'll work with Skylar, and I don't want to make anything weird for her by spilling things.

The smart motherfucker figures it out anyway.

"Ugh. Are you being a weird fanboy right now?"

"I'm not a weird fanboy. We're friends."

"You look like a teenage girl who got kissed by a Jonas brother. Are you going to swoon? Not wash your face for a week?"

"Get outta here." I glance out the window, trying not to laugh.

Ford is a mouthy prick, though. He doesn't let up. "You gonna touch your cheek and make out with your hand later?"

I punch him playfully this time, laughing while cussing him out. "Fuck you, man."

"I bet you'll actually use your hand to—"

"Choose your next words carefully." I give him a warning glare, and he just laughs.

"Oh *boy*."

"You oh boy." I volley back stupidly with a chuckle as I scrub at the mark. Secretly a little sad to part with proof of Skylar marching up and kissing me. It was far too easy to imagine that being the norm.

I am being a weird fanboy.

"Does she know you're obsessed with her?"

"I'm not obsessed with her."

Only a little bit.

"You're a fan. I told Rosie, you and little West would be too excited to handle her living on your property. I just can't make Bash build the guesthouse any faster when he's constantly called out to fires, or I'd stop torturing you."

Is it bad I'm wishing for more forest fires?

"I'm not a fan. Emmy is a fan, and I take an interest in all the things my daughter likes. And he's not little West. He's *big* West."

Ford's head turns to me at the red light, and he looks at me like I'm the biggest idiot he's ever seen. It's possible that I am. He's seen me do some dumb shit in our almost two decades of friendship.

"Does she know you have her episode of *SNL* saved as a favorite on YouTube?"

"It's a funny episode."

"What's your favorite skit?"

Silence descends because I don't fucking know. I don't watch the skits.

Ford bursts out laughing, and I can't contain myself

either. I cover my eyes with the heels of my hands. "Whatever. Just drop it. I'm trying to be cool, and you're not helping."

"Okay, next time I'll get Rosie to kiss my cheek with lipstick and we can show up matching."

"Gross, dude. That's my sister."

"I said my cheek, not my—"

"Just drive."

"Why do you suck so much tonight?" Bash grumbles from over the lip of his pint glass as I slither back to our seats from another gutter-ball performance.

He doesn't make eye contact with me, but disappointment wafts from him. That's nothing new for Bash, though. He always seems slightly disappointed—it's part of his grouchy persona.

"Because he can't see past the hearts in his eyes," Ford murmurs, sliding in next to me with a fresh beer in hand.

"Hey, I'm not as bad as Rhys." I point at the huge man beside him.

He's new to the team. Showed up a month ago and is only here intermittently.

When he is here, he doesn't say much about anything.

He and Bash side by side are like two of the seven dwarves—Grumpy and Broody.

"No one is as bad as Rhys," Bash comments as he rolls his eyes.

Rhys turns to give the older man a dry look. Bash isn't the least bit intimidated, though plenty of people would be. "You're lucky I show up at all, considering I don't actually live here."

"To be fair, you only show up occasionally," Ford points out, ever the stickler for details.

"Where *do* you live?" I ask, always snooping for more.

"Florida."

My head quirks. "Florida?"

Rhys shrugs. "Thinking of moving to town more permanently. So that might change."

We all stare at the man of few words, hoping he might share a few more. "What brought that about?"

Now it's my turn to get Rhys's signature dry look. "Like the bowling team."

"What did you say your kid's name is again?" I ask.

"I didn't."

The guy's a fucking enigma, so I try another strategy to get even a crumb of information. "Does Tabitha know you're moving here?"

We all know there's something up with him and Tabitha, the owner of the Bighorn Bistro—but not in a good way. In fact, they seem to despise each other. Not that he ever says anything about her.

He swallows and a muscle in his jaw pops. "Yep."

"Well, that should be entertaining at the very least," Bash mutters, sipping his beer again.

"But she hates you?" I prod.

Based on the way she marched him into Rose Hill Reach

mere weeks ago and shoved him at us like she was taking out the trash, I feel like I already know the answer.

"Seems to," he confirms.

"You ever gonna tell us what the deal is with you two?" I rock back on my feet, eager to know. Tabitha and Rosie played on the same volleyball team growing up, so I know her well enough to be concerned.

Rhys ignores me, then he unfolds his massive frame from his seat and announces, "My turn," before shoving past without addressing my question.

"You're a snoopy little bitch, you know that?" Ford mumbles, taking his turn to punch me on the shoulder.

"I thought you and your obsession with privacy was one of a kind, but that guy has you beat. I don't even know where he lives when he's in town. Crazy Clyde is crazy, but at least he had entertaining conspiracy theories to tell us."

Bash rolls his eyes. "Go visit him in the hospital like I do. He still has plenty of those."

"You guys need to leave Rhys alone," Ford cuts in. "Just let the man bowl."

We all look over, and Rhys has thrown the ball so hard that it seems like he's trying to knock out the entire back wall of the building. Instead, he throws such a bullet that it takes out the middle pin and nothing else.

That douchebag, Too Tall—our mortal bowling enemy—shoots me a mocking grin from his lane. I know him from high school but can't for the life of me remember his real name since he only introduces himself by his nickname now.

WILD EYES

I'm glad we're not playing him tonight because there's nothing worse than losing to Stretch—as Ford jokingly calls him. And although this league is supposed to be a fun dads' night out, I'm competitive enough to hate losing.

Still, Ford isn't entirely wrong.

My head is not in the game.

CHAPTER 18

Skylar

"OH BOY. HE'S GOT THE SMART ONE HANGING OUT WITH HIS sister now." Doris places a glass of wine in front of me before moving to the opposite side of our private corner booth.

"Thank you, Doris. It's so nice to see you again." I grin up at the woman and catch a twitch of her cheek when she meets my eye.

"The smart one?" Rosie asks, looking between us.

"You know that boy, always out gallivanting with someone new. They're all starry-eyed over him until they're teary-eyed over him. This one, though…she flipped the script on him. About time."

I blink because Doris is totally misreading West and me. He definitely isn't starry-eyed over me. I'm accustomed to starry-eyed, and he's treated me like nothing short of painfully normal since our first run-in.

"You've got a big fucking mouth, Doris," Tabitha

mumbles, giving her head a soft shake as she reaches for her glass of wine.

I don't know what I expected from Tabitha, but the woman we picked up from a small house in town is extremely petite, rail thin, and looks like she hasn't slept in weeks.

Doris must notice it too because, rather than snapping back, she pets her dark hair in a maternal way and says, "Drink your wine, Tabby. You need it."

"Is this—"

"The one you told me to bring in because…how did you put it? 'I'd rather drink a grape juice box than this swill'?"

With a soft smile, Tabitha peeks up at the older woman. "Sounds about right."

"Yep, this is the one." With that, she squeezes Tabitha's bony shoulder and leaves us.

Rosie lifts her glass in a cheers motion. "Thank you for your service, Tabby. This wine is far better than what we drank down by the lake as teenagers."

I toast to that too, feeling out of the loop. Lake parties were definitely not part of my life as a teenager.

Our glasses clink, and Tabby chuckles. "Anything is better than that garbage, Rosie."

We drink, and I realize that, much like on my night here with West, the wine is excellent for a small-town pub.

I glance over at Tabby, and she catches me, but she doesn't look away. Instead, she smiles and offers, "It's really nice to meet you, you know? I hope everyone has been on their best behavior. Let me know if anyone hasn't. I'll accidentally drop a ghost pepper in their dinner next time they're in."

She's been polite and didn't make a fuss over me, which had me letting out the world's biggest sigh of relief.

It's freeing to feel like I don't need to wear my usual mask around these women. And to be honest, people have looked a little wide-eyed at me in town, but they've been pretty chill. Except for whoever snapped that photo of me with a bleeding nose. But rather than being angry, I hope they at least got a good chunk of change for it. If the paps are too lazy to fly to Canada and drive three plus hours to find me, I hope they paid through the nose for that shot.

'Cause I sure did.

Ford offered me security this week when we met at his office, but I didn't feel the need. It's been nice not being followed around everywhere.

"Tabby owns the best restaurant in town, the Bighorn Bistro," Rosie says. "You and I can drop in sometime. I promise it's not just small-town good. It's better-than-big-city good."

Tabby scoffs. "That's my new slogan. *Better than big city good!*"

"It is! You grow your own herbs and vegetables. You bake your own croissants. You harvest your own roses for the tea. Oh, Skylar, you have to try the tea. I'll bring you some."

I watch these women. These normal women. Women who harvest their vegetables and offer to drop tea off for no good reason. I feel like I'm living in an alternate universe. One I actually like.

"Maybe I'll just swing by and grab some," I say. "I'd love to see your restaurant."

Tabby, with her elbow propped on the table and head against her open palm, brightens a tad, but her voice still comes out monotone when she replies, "I'd love that."

Rosie analyzes her friend. Eyes moving up, down, side to side. Head tilt. Brows down. "Tabby, my plan was to fill you with a bit more wine before starting my interrogation. But…what's going on?"

The woman's head turns slightly, still propped up by her hand. Like she's too tired to sit up straight. "If I tell you what's going on, you'll both think I'm the world's biggest downer and I'll ruin the night. I'll perk up, I promise."

I worry my bottom lip as I watch her. She looks…sad. She's got sad eyes.

I wonder absently if that's how I looked a week ago.

"My parents are getting a divorce and I found out I only own a small percentage of all the songs I've produced and all the contracts I've fulfilled. All the hours I've put in…I think they're more invested in the money than in me. Maybe they've always been. I'm officially *that* former child star," I blurt.

It's an overshare. So much so, Tabby sits up straight and stares at me head-on. "What assholes."

I sip and nod. "I know."

"Is that why you contacted Ford about doing an album?" Rosie pipes up.

"Yep."

"You think that has anything to do with how rough your interviews have been lately?" Tabby asks, her eyes brighter than they have been all night.

I shrug, not offended at all by her curiosity. In fact, I feel accepting of the question. It's one I've spent several days mulling over myself. "I guess. Probably." I take a drink of the French rosé.

They both stare at me, and it's almost comical.

"Yeah, actually. I'm positive it is. I don't know what to say when everything that comes out of my mouth is a lie. Lying, man…it catches up with you. Rots you from the inside out, I think."

"Facts." Rosie exhales the word as she flops back in her chair and takes a deep swig of her matching pink wine.

The vibe around the table seems more relaxed.

Like my honesty brightened the mood.

But it doesn't last because Tabitha's next bit of honesty darkens it.

"My sister died."

Rosie and I both freeze, staring at her. In the game of who has the saddest story, Tabitha just laid down a trump card.

"About a month ago."

Rosie's blue eyes bulge from their sockets, a glittering sheen covering them. "A *month*? Oh, Tabby, I'm so, so sorry."

Tabitha swipes a hand under her nose and slices her gaze away, avoiding eye contact. Rosie reaches across the table and clasps Tabitha's hand, still curled around the stem of her wineglass. "It's okay. It's fine. I always knew this day might come."

My heart cracks. I'm an only child and I don't know her, but I can feel the devastation rolling off the woman beside me. It's thick and bitter.

"I thought she was doing better," Rosie urges.

Tabitha sighs. "Same."

I watch in silence, feeling like an interloper, who is intruding on a private moment I shouldn't be privy to.

"And Milo?" Rosie's face is pinched.

"He's here. With me, for now. Almost three and running me ragged."

"For now?"

"It's complicated." Tabitha lets out a melancholy laugh. "Erika made it complicated. Because *of course* she did."

"Does it have to do with the big hunk of a man you donated to the bowling team?"

Tabitha's teeth clench. "Rhys? He's not a hunk. He's an overgrown pain in my ass. I'd sooner donate him to the local crematorium than have him in town."

Rosie whistles, and I stifle a laugh. It's not a funny moment, but I am entertained by Tabitha's creative insults.

"Tabby…a month? Why didn't you say something? I would have helped."

Her friend's eyes drop again. "You've been blissed out on billionaire dick, Rosie. I didn't want to burst that bubble. And you know Erika's reputation in town." Tabitha's voice cracks and her shoulders curl down ever so slightly as she wipes at her nose again.

"Sometimes it feels like I'm the only person in the world who really loved her in spite of how she struggled. I wanted to grieve without having to hear people tell me that drug addicts overdose, so it shouldn't really come as a surprise."

She says it like she's not grieving anymore, but her body language gives her away.

When her hand flops down on the table beside me, I eye it up carefully. And then I decide *fuck it*. I cover the top of her small hand with my palm. She shoots me a sweet smile and edges closer, as if being near people who aren't judging her is a comfort.

I can relate.

"I don't want to turn tonight into a big, lame public boo-hoo. I'm being a normal twenty-seven-year-old tonight. The restaurant is covered, and my parents have Milo for a sleepover. So let's turn our frowns upside down and drink too much rosé."

Rosie and I exchange glances and then lift our glasses for another toast.

And as the glasses clink, Tabby adds, "And shit-talk Rhys because he's the fuckin' worst."

I'm still holding Tabby's hand as I watch the gears turn in Rosie's head before an amused smirk forms on her lips.

"You know what we should do?"

Tabitha and I glance at each other and back at Rosie with a shrug.

"Drink this glass and then go shit-talk him in person."

My heart thunders in my chest because if I'm piecing this together correctly…Rhys is on the bowling team. Bowling is tonight. And going there means seeing West. With his friends. In his element. Not in a quiet barn or around his kids. Somewhere busy and public.

Nerves build, but so does my anticipation.

And I realize I always look forward to seeing him.

When we walk into the dingy bowling alley, the place is humming. Music. Chatter. The loud thump of balls followed by the noisy clatter of pins falling.

But when the door slams shut behind us and heads turn, the noise drops several decibels.

My body heats and my stomach drops. Too many eyes land on me, and all my limbs seize, freezing me in place. No one has asked me anything, so I can't make an ass of myself by struggling to speak my first language.

Instead, I'm reverting to my babyhood and feel like the ability to walk has fled me entirely.

Pretty challenging to be a performer with crippling anxiety. And just knowing that my life's work is spiraling because of this newfound anxiety amplifies every feeling of failure.

It makes it worse.

Tabby forges ahead, a tiny spitfire who doesn't give a shit what people think. She walks to the bar and pulls out a well-worn stool. I want so badly to follow her, but I feel like a deer in the headlights.

Frozen.

I look for a safe place. I look for West.

When I hear his laughter, the tension in my body eases a bit.

Rosie slings her arm around my shoulder and whispers, "Think of how good the wine *here* will be. Tabby is going to be in fine form."

I snort a very unladylike laugh and, just like that, my

body unlocks, and I let my new friend guide me forward. By the time we get to our seats, Tabby hasn't ordered wine—she's ordered tequila.

"Thanks, Frankie," she says with a radiant smile to the man behind the bar.

"Anything for my girl," he singsongs before turning away to another customer.

I settle on my stool and take in my surroundings. Our three stools are near the bottom of the U-shaped bar, right where a swinging gate divides the bowling alley section from the equally dated drinking area.

Neon signs illuminate the windows and old license plates decorate the walls, along with paper bills of various currencies and the occasional signed sports jersey. I only recognize one—Jasper Gervais, a famous hockey player.

The place has a run-down dive bar sort of charm. It feels totally different from the Reach, as the locals call it.

Rose Valley Alley feels exactly like the type of place Skylar Stone shouldn't be seen in. And that just makes me like it more.

Now that the chatter is back in full force, I no longer feel like the center of attention. In fact, now that I'm breathing evenly enough to take a proper look around, I'm wondering if the halt in activity was simply because women were standing in a bar full of men.

"Goddamn, this place is a sad little sausage fest," Tabby remarks from beneath a dark fringe of lashes before sipping on her tequila.

"Take that back, Tabby Cat. Those claws hurt," West

announces, popping up from behind us like a fucking jack-in-the-box. I start, but then the weight of his warm hand rests against my lower back and I instantly relax. "Plus, it's a big, happy sausage fest. And why are you sipping tequila like it's tea? That shit is meant for shooting."

"Because I don't want to be so drunk that I can't enjoy the hilarity of grown men dressing in matching outfits and playing games together."

"What are you doing here?" Ford saunters through the swinging gate, staring daggers at Rosie.

She grins maniacally. "Came to cheer you on."

Ford doesn't take the bait. In fact, he continues scowling at her. "You're not dressed like a cheerleader."

She shrugs. "I could be later."

"No. Please, god, no." West has his hands over his face, laughing. "I am so happy for you guys, but please do not have these conversations in front of me." When he drops his hands, the amusement is clear on his face. "The real question is, why are you ladies here on men's night?"

His sister's eyes narrow. "It's men's night"—she points over his shoulder—"over there. Behind the fence where you belong. Here, though? Here, it's just a regular night."

"This night is sacred," West says.

Tabby takes another sip of tequila, head shaking. "Listen, West. You're scared of women. *We get it.* Go throw your balls and pretend we're not here."

My head whips between everyone. I'm beyond amused. This level of camaraderie makes me feel like I'm living in a sitcom.

"I'm not afraid of women. I love women. I respect women." He leans toward her, propping a hand on her shoulder. "I just get a little nervous when they watch me throw my balls," he whispers.

Tabby smirks. "You're a child. That why you're such a commitment-phobe?"

"I'm not—"

"You're not the one who had to listen to Bree vent about you as she picked up her coffee. Do you know how shrill her voice is first thing in the morning? Who am I kidding? Of course you do." The more Tabby lays into West, the wider his mouth opens. "Anyway, you're definitely a commitment-phobe. And she kinda sucks, but my dude: boys' nights and friends-with-benefits… How old are you again?"

Ford has covered his lips with his palm, and Rosie is laughing so hard that she's making no noise at all.

My eyes lock with West's, and I get a soft wink from him. God, he's like Teflon—everything just rolls right off him. He's not offended, but I sense her ribbing smarts a bit. And I know he's reflective enough to consider what she's telling him.

"You are in fine form tonight, Tabby Cat. I'm not even mad. After all, it's you who inspired our team's name."

"What's your team's name?" I finally pipe up, taking a measured sip of the world's most toxic tequila.

"The Ball Busters," West announces, puffing his chest out a bit and giving Tabby's shoulder a one-finger poke.

She chuckles and rolls her eyes. "What an incredible honor. Thank you."

It's then that a tall, thin man waltzes up, leaning his elbows against the bar on the other side of the gate. He has a severe face, and gel saturates his hair to the point it looks almost wet.

"Oh joy, Stretch is here," Ford mumbles, not sounding remotely excited about the man's presence.

"Strikes me that if you wanted to name the team after Tabitha, you could have called it the Tongue Twisters. Can you still tie a knot in a cherry stem?"

Tabby stares back at the man, not a stitch of embarrassment on her face. In fact, it's more like she oozes pity. "Still dreaming about the only blow job you ever got, Terence? Was that tenth grade? Shame that you peaked so young."

My attention volleys to Rosie. She rolls her eyes but doesn't miss a beat. She's so comfortable in this setting.

The man flushes right as Ford turns to Rosie and mouths *Terence*?

"You know—"

He doesn't get to finish because a man so tall, so broad that he looms like a mountain over Terence approaches from behind. He is beautiful and terrifying all at once. Built like a warrior, scowling like a predator.

He doesn't hesitate to rest an oversized palm on the back of the skinny guy's neck. It could be a friendly gesture—but it's not.

"You know what I could tie a knot in? This long fucking neck. And then no one would have to tolerate your presence here. Anyone have any objections?" His voice is so deep that it shouldn't be possible to make it out over the social hum of the bar.

And yet, it feels like everyone hears him.

Except Tabby, who has taken a sudden interest in the water-stained foam tiles on the ceiling.

This must be the infamous Rhys.

His obsidian eyes land on each of us but rest longer on Tabitha. A flicker of something passes there, and I find myself invested in whatever is going on with them. It seems to me like she may have glossed over some key details where this man is concerned.

"Wow, not a single objection. Imagine that, Terry," Ford says with dry amusement. And when the man jerks himself free and hustles away with his tail between his legs, he adds, "I fucking hate that guy."

Tabby takes another drink and stares at Mr. Dark and Foreboding. "Everyone hates that guy," she says simply.

His jaw twitches as he watches her keenly. If I didn't know any better, I'd say he looked downright green with jealousy.

But he says nothing, just turns to leave.

West claps his hands, always on a constant mission to lighten the mood. "Okay, fine. You guys can stay."

Now it's my turn to roll my eyes. And this time, rather than sipping my tequila, I toss it straight back. It burns, making me feel alive. "No one asked for your permission, West," I say as I slam the shot glass down on the bar top. "Now beat it. This is girls' night out."

"Hear, hear!" Rosie echoes before following suit. "Drink up, Tabby. You've got a real embarrassing blow job to explain."

Tabitha glosses over the jab with an eye roll, zeroing

straight back in on West. "Never thought I'd see the day that Skylar Stone walked you like a dog, but here we are." She tosses her drink back with a thoroughly amused twist to her mouth.

West doesn't have time to respond because another man pops up from their lane farther back. Thick brows, threads of silver in his sideburns, and a bored scowl grace his masculine face. "Let's go, you fucking clowns," he calls out. "This isn't high school. Leave the girls alone."

"Coming, Dad," West shouts back, garnering himself a chorus of laughs from around the bar. The man shakes his head like he's disappointed before turning and flopping back down onto their bench.

West and Ford make their way to the guy, giggling like schoolgirls the entire way. They exchange a few shoulder punches, and I grin like a fool at their boyish interaction. It's wholesome.

"Oh shit," Rosie whispers from beside me. She's close enough that I can smell the tequila on her breath.

"What?"

She flashes me a conspiratorial smile and I know she busted me staring at her brother with stars in my eyes. "Nothing."

Relieved she doesn't call me on it, I casually change the subject. "How long have they known each other?"

She shrugs. "A couple of decades."

"Ford might be the only non-blood relative West has committed to," Tabby says.

Rosie slings a soft hand at Tabby. "Quit picking on him.

He'll leave Neverland when the time is right. Plus, we need to talk about you more than him."

She gets up and slides onto the stool on the other side of her friend, so we make a little Tabby sandwich.

"I'm not fun. I thought we were here to shit-talk Rhys."

"What are we going to say to him?" I ask, trying to contain my laughter. "Your physique is too much like Jason Momoa, Rhys," I mock-shout with a hand cupped by my mouth.

Rosie laughs.

Tabby does not.

Then Rosie follows suit. "The way you fill out those jeans is criminal, Rhys."

Then me. "Your hands don't need to be that big, Rhys."

Then Rosie. "How dare you defend Tabby's honor, Rhys? You piece of shit."

Tabitha drops her head into her hands, rolling her head against her palms. "You guys are not helping. We hate him, remember?"

Rosie blinks her baby blues. "Why do we hate him again? Visually, I can think of no reason at all to hate the man. I mean, I know you were avoiding so much as glancing in his direction, but have you *seen* him?"

"It's complicated."

"Didn't you sign him up for the bowling team yourself?" Rosie prods.

"I needed him out of the house."

We both stare at Tabby now, and I don't know why my voice comes out as a whisper when I ask, "He's living with you?"

Tabby groans and slaps a hand against the bar. "Frankie. I need more tequila."

"Comin' right up, babe," the man with the belly calls back from his leaning position on the bar.

We watch silently as Rhys walks up to take his turn. He's rigid and uncomfortable, and I get the sense he knows we're watching him.

Perhaps it's the pressure, but he throws the ball so hard and so crooked that it fires straight into the gutter. He does it with such force that I wonder if that's where he meant to send it.

Rosie stands up on the rung of her barstool, pressing her palms onto the bar top. "Hey, Rhys," she shouts across the small space. "You're supposed to aim for the pins. Get this man some bumpers, Frankie."

He turns his head and glares at her over his shoulder. While several of the men chuckle, he does not. His response only makes Rosie tip her head back and laugh, blond hair streaming down her back.

When she sits back down, Tabby smiles into the freshly filled shot glass. "Okay," she murmurs. "Now I'm having fun."

We then proceed to have a little *too* much of it.

CHAPTER 19

West

"I can't believe Rosie had the staff bring those bumpers out for Rhys." Skylar laughs the words from where she's sitting a little crooked in the passenger seat beside me.

I handle the wheel carefully and bite down on my smile. "I can. Rosie takes her shit-talk seriously. You should have seen her and Ford when we were kids. Out to kill each other with their jabs."

"Turns out they just wanted to fuck each other."

I bark out a laugh. Tipsy Skylar has zero filter, and I love it.

"They're a cute couple," she adds, a wistful note in her voice.

"They are."

"They're good friends, aren't they?"

I peek over at her as we hit the last stoplight on the road that leads us back to the farm. "They are."

"They genuinely enjoy each other's company."

I nod. "Yeah, they do."

Skylar hums, lips working as though she is chewing on those words. I wonder if she's thinking about what I told her about Mia and me.

"That must be nice."

My palms twist on the wheel as her words hit unexpectedly hard for drunken mumblings. "Mm-hmm," I manage to get out, but then we fall into silence as we cover the final stretch back home.

Home.

An ache cracks my chest. During the weeks I don't have the kids, it doesn't feel much like home. I thrive in social situations, surrounded by friends and family. The horses are great companions, but they're often not enough.

When Ford moved back, I looked forward to having my best friend around, but our dynamic has changed. And I don't begrudge him one bit.

But some days I meander around the property, searching for things to do. Wondering if no matter how fun and likable I am, there's something about me that isn't enough to keep people around.

People who enjoy my company and don't just want to tie me down. Lately, I'm not sure if that's better or worse than being on my own.

With this in mind, I pull up in front of the house and proclaim, "You shouldn't go to sleep yet. You've had too much tequila."

She directs her amber eyes to me as I turn the truck off. "You don't have to take care of me. I've been drunk before."

"I know," I say before I hop out of my seat and round the truck to her side. I tug open the door and look up at her.

She turns, pointy heels catching on the side runner of my truck. Her eyes cascade over me as though she's sizing me up. "Can we do night check, then?"

I perk up, a grin stretching my lips. "I'll grab you a bottle of water."

Without even thinking, I reach for her. My hands wrap around her rib cage, and I lower her to the ground, purposely ignoring how the flats of her palms feel against my pecs. The way her pinky moves in a stuttering path, out and back in.

The motion draws both our eyes for a beat, but she clears her throat and steps away.

"Helping me out of cars now, huh? Thought you knew you don't need to take care of me."

My throat feels hot and so do my cheeks as I turn away. I need to go get her a bottle of water before I do something stupid like shove her up against my truck and kiss her.

So I stride toward the old farmhouse, but not without glancing over my shoulder and calling back to her, "I know I don't need to. Doesn't stop me from wanting to, though."

When Skylar asked if *we* could do night check, she meant she was going to talk my ear off while *I* did night check.

She's giving me big Emmy vibes, and that is such a stark

change for her in a matter of a week that I'm not even mad about doing all the work.

One hand has her heels hooked on her fingers, while the other hand holds an open water bottle.

"…and honestly, I'm not sure why she hates him. She wasn't exactly forthcoming. Rosie seemed shocked by the news of her sister's passing."

That last bit brings me up short and I stop, dropping the wheelbarrow down on the concrete. "Erika is dead?"

Skylar's features turn downwards, like it hurts her to confirm it. "Yeah."

"When?"

"About a month ago."

"Jesus." I comb my fingers through my hair, absorbing the death of a woman far too young to die. Seems like just yesterday I saw her at school. Except it wasn't yesterday. We're not in high school anymore, and it feels like it went by in a blink.

I think about Ollie and Emmy and how fast they'll grow up.

Then I think of how it would feel to lose one of them.

It's fucking unbearable.

"Is that why Rhys is here? That guy doesn't tell us shit."

"I don't know. She didn't tell us shit about him either. My only real takeaway is that she hates him."

I swallow. It does seem that way.

"Gonna have to pay her family a visit. Check on Tabby," I choke out before turning away to hang my utility knife on its hook.

"You're a good man, West."

I nod, but my throat feels too thick to talk. Poor Erika. What a sad fucking story. I swipe a hand beneath my nose and turn back to Skylar's wide eyes and glossy lips.

I scramble for something to say that will lighten the mood and pull my head out of that depressing news. I settle on, "I can't believe you're walking around the barn in bare feet."

We both glance down. Her cute toes wiggle on the dusty concrete floor.

Skylar seems unbothered, though. She shrugs it off. "It feels good."

That makes me smile. But as her words settle, they reroute my brain. Suddenly I'm thinking about Skylar. And feeling good.

"Is that your new motto? *If it feels good, do it?*"

Her eyes flare and her teeth strum over her bottom lip. Once. Twice.

God, the way this girl looks at me. Her eyes are like an open book. An instruction manual.

"Guess so."

An almost nervous swipe of her tongue over those plush lips as her eyes rake over my body and I'm practically panting.

"So what are you going to do now?"

Her cheeks flush, and we both know that even though she said she's scrubbed that kiss from her brain—she's thinking about it.

And so am I.

But she's also gun shy and doesn't fully trust me—or herself—because she drops my stare. "Go to bed."

My head tilts. "That always feels good."

She huffs out a laugh and peers up at the bank lighting above us. "Why does everything you say sound sexual?"

My cheeks hitch and I toss her a wink when she finally peeks over at me. "You and your tequila brain might be employing a little wishful thinking. I'm just talking about going to bed. I didn't say together."

"Wishful thinking?" Her jaw drops.

"Hey, I'm just calling it how I see it. I'm not sure if you remember, but *you* kissed *me*."

Her feet pad across the floor as she approaches me. Her shoulder bumps into mine on the way past. She must be heading for the door behind me.

Going to bed. All alone.

But then she stops and looks me in the eye. "Yeah, yeah, yeah. But you know what, Weston?" Her voice is low, so I bend slightly to listen. She stands on her tip-toes and hits me with a salacious smirk right as she whispers, "You've been dreaming about kissing me back. And I'm thinking that if I kissed you again, right here…you wouldn't pull away."

Her warm breath grazes the shell of my ear and my tongue darts out as though I could taste her. An electric shock skitters across my skin when she reaches out and runs her pinky finger along the side of my hand that hangs limply at my side.

The touch is subtle, but there's no doubt in my mind

that Skylar Stone is flirting with me. And she's doing a bang-up job.

My fist clenches, grasping at air. Because she's already gone. Marching straight out of my barn and into the dark night.

Leaving me to go to bed all by myself.

CHAPTER 20

Skylar

My hangover and I check my email the next morning after my girls' night out and find missives from both my dad and Jerry asking about when they should come out to Rose Hill to help with a new album. I don't respond. I don't want them here, and I don't feel like facing the fallout of telling them as much.

If Ford can ignore them, so can I.

What I don't ignore is another fake news headline from West. I'm grinning before I even open it.

BREAKING NEWS: Style experts say wearing red lipstick every day is so in this season.

I hope he never stops sending me these. And I may need to stock up on that lipstick now.

I peek around the corner and see West prepping a bale for night check.

I knew he'd be here.

It's been twenty-four hours since we stood in this exact spot. I don't know where he went today or what he did, but I found myself checking on the house. Peeking up at the barn. Strolling past to see if he was around.

Last night, I secretly hoped he'd follow me. Blast through the door to the guest bedroom, shove me against the wall, and kiss me senseless.

And against all my better judgment, I would've let him. I wanted him to. Until he didn't.

Lying in bed, I heard him moving about the house, turning off all the lights, and making sure all doors and windows were shut. My body was strung tight, like it might snap when he marched past my bedroom door.

I wanted him to turn the handle. Crawl into my bed. He'd have found me naked between the sheets, and I'd have reveled in the feel of his strong body over mine.

But he didn't. And I slept naked, waking once or twice to the sensation of the bed spinning. This morning, I pushed away all my drunken, horny thoughts and blamed them on the tequila.

I popped an Advil and pulled myself together. Sat Cherry on my shoulder for a brisk walk around the property to try and burn some of the tequila calories. And then met with Ford and Rosie to hammer out a recording schedule. Having a plan written down on paper put me at an instant sort of ease. This place and what I'm about to do here felt instantly real and not just like a pipe dream.

It was with this newfound sense of peace that I took another walk. This one was longer and more meandering, and I didn't think about calories at all. I just soaked in my surroundings. It led me out to the road and down the main driveway to West's farm.

The sign from the road said *Wild West Ranch.* The logo depicted a saddle in a rope frame, but as I drew nearer, I saw a piece of paper tacked to the bottom with duct tape.

On it, and clearly drawn by a child, a similar logo with a unicorn inside the frame. The title that curved around the bottom said *Sparkly Turquoise Unicorn Ranch.*

It made me laugh as I stood there staring at it. Although I barely know Emmy and Oliver, I could tell she drew it, and her big brother wrote the words for her. I reached into my big boho purse to search for my phone, wanting to take a picture of it. Something to look at and remember this place by when I'm gone.

But of course, my phone wasn't there.

So I settled for running my fingers over it and doing my best to commit it to memory. The endearing simplicity of it. The charming lack of pageantry.

Rose Hill has proven to be all those things. And I love that about this place.

About West.

I watch his strong hands tug the orange twine from the bale, and I sigh before forcing my feet to move into the barn.

"Can I help?" I ask.

His shoulders jump in surprise as he turns to face me.

I swallow as I take him in. God. He really is all man. Head to toe.

He makes my mouth go dry.

"Sure," he replies, eyes softening as he gazes at me.

We start off working in a quiet rhythm.

"Didn't see you around today," I eventually say.

"Were you looking for me, fancy face?"

I smile and shake my head down at the wheelbarrow. It seems safest not to answer that question, so I carry on checking the horses on my side of the barn and filing their feeders with the sweet-smelling dried grass.

"Since you're avoiding the question, I started early to beat the heat. Then I picked up a new training horse first thing. Surprised you didn't hear his angry whinnies and heavy hooves all afternoon."

Now that he mentions it, I did. His voice comes out a little flat and a lot unlike him. So I press, hoping to get him talking about something he loves.

"Are most of the horses here not yours?"

"A few," he says, turning away to his next stall. "Mostly they come and go. Someone hires me. Their horse spends a couple months here, which sets them on the right path for their next job. Sometimes I buy one I like, train it myself, and then sell it at a profit. Other times I get too attached to sell them at all. And now and then I get a"— his hands lift in air quotes—"problem horse that needs fixing."

My brows furrow. "How does a horse become a problem horse?"

He shrugs, hands back in the hay. "Usually someone who doesn't know what they're doing has messed with their heads. Mistreated them. Problem horses aren't born. They're made."

I find myself blinking rapidly, relating just a little too closely to this conversation about horses. So I switch gears as I turn to check on the next horse. "Fascinating. What else did you get up to?"

West doesn't respond right away. In fact, his silence has me turning to glance at him. The tendon in his jaw flexes, and he gives his head a subtle shake.

"I went to visit Tabby. Then her parents. And then my own. Never know when it might be the last time."

I swallow, not wanting to think about the terms I'm on with my parents. They may be awful, but sometimes I can convince myself they aren't. It has to be a coping mechanism.

Even drunk, I could tell from his reaction last night that the news of Erika's death had winded him.

"That was kind of you." It doesn't seem like enough, but it's all I can think to say.

His head joggles as he steps out the rear door and onto the dirt path that leads to the back paddocks. "Maybe."

"Not maybe."

"I never got into hard drugs the way Erika did, but I did my fair share of dumb shit when I was younger. Constantly in trouble for something. Sneaking out. Getting in fights. Crashing my car. Put my parents through the wringer in that regard. It struck me last night that it could easily have been me instead."

He tosses a flake over the fence. "So maybe it was kind. And maybe it was out of guilt. Either way, it's terrible. Her little boy—" He doesn't finish the sentence, just clicks his tongue and forges ahead with his work.

We finish the rest of the night check quietly. I get the sense West is secluded in his head tonight, and after the week I've had, I've realized that sometimes—as uncomfortable as it is—that's exactly where we need to spend some time.

After we close up, we walk back to the house without saying a word. Just his boots thumping on the grass, my flip-flops making a slapping noise against my heels.

Though I sleep in the house nightly, I've made a point of not making myself at home. I spend my days at the bunkhouse, and West and I have been like ships passing in the night when it comes to spending time together inside.

He made it clear he wants to keep this space sacred for him and his kids. And I respect that.

I don't want to make him feel uncomfortable, so when he hits the front steps, I break the silence. "I know Oliver and Emmy will be back tomorrow. I'll move back to the bunkhouse in the morning."

I don't look up at him, but I can feel his eyes on me all the same.

"You're welcome in the house. You don't need to do that."

"I do."

"What about the mouse?"

I smile, finally braving a glance up at his handsome face. "I've seen him a few times now. He's growing on me. I'll be fine. It's like exposure therapy."

His responding chuckle is soft and warm, and I can hear the bristles of his stubble as he scrubs a hand over his chin. "Wherever you're most comfortable."

I nod and watch him turn and head toward the lake.

"Night, Skylar."

"Where are you going?"

He stops, broad back to me as he stares off into the distance, like he can see the sparkling water through the stand of trees. The fabric of his pale-green T-shirt stretches across his broad shoulders.

And don't even get me started on the gray wash jeans.

"I'm gonna take the canoe out."

My brows drop. "In the dark?"

"Do it all the time when the kids are with Mia. It doesn't feel that dark once your eyes adjust."

The thought of West canoeing on a dark lake by himself tugs on my heartstrings. "Can I come?"

He turns to me, his expression betraying his surprise. "You wanna come canoeing in the dark with me?"

I don't know why he seems surprised by the fact that I enjoy his company. I'm not. In fact, I'm at the point where I'm seeking it and not talking myself out of it.

I offer a simple nod and set off toward him. "I do. Is that okay?"

His throat works on a heavy swallow. "I'd love that."

"There's a song about this, you know." I trail my fingertips in the water. It feels like they're skating over the cold surface. It's a still night, the only ripples coming from the oars that slice through the water with a reassuring regularity.

Steady and even.

Just like the man handling them.

"Fancy face, we aren't fishing." His voice is hushed. Even though no one is around, we're almost whispering.

I tip my head back and forth, considering. "We could be."

The swish of his rowing fills the peaceful atmosphere. "Do you even know how to fish?"

I shrug and pull my hand from the water. "No, but you could teach me."

"You gonna do a lot of fishing when you head back to Los Angeles? Or Nashville? Where is your home base anyway?"

Home. Neither of those places feel much like home. "I have houses in both."

A disbelieving huff passes through his lips. The notion of owning properties in two cities must seem absurd to him. Excessive.

And truthfully, after only a week spent in Rose Hill, it seems that way to me too. I've just never known any different.

"Which one do you like better?"

Images of the two lavish homes flash in my mind. One all sleek, modern glass facing the Pacific. The other, a country estate. Both have so many bedrooms and bathrooms that I opt to leave several doors closed.

A flash of the bunkhouse follows. West's cozy, white farmhouse with its red tin roof. Children's toys scattered across the lawn.

That's the house that makes my heart beat faster.

"I'm not especially attached to either. I spend a lot of time on the road."

"Do you like being on the road?"

I turn my head to peek around us. The outdoor lights of the lakefront homes glow. We aren't that far from the shore, yet it's so peaceful. So quiet.

"No. I hate it."

His arms still, and he studies me as we float on the dark water. His attention is too heavy, so I tip my head back and pretend to be especially interested in the milky blanket of stars overhead.

I breathe in.

I breathe out.

I try to escape that creeping sense of dread that fills me anytime I let myself think about going back on the road. Performing. Doing interviews. I think I liked it once. I know I loved to sing. When it wasn't all about money and fame and the next album. It got old fast. And now I'm burned out.

"What are you most afraid of?" I ask.

"Me?"

My chin drops only so I can give him a droll look. "No, the fish we should be catching."

That gets me an eye roll, but I can tell he's pondering my question.

"My kids dying."

"That's an obvious one. I think any parent fears that happening. Even my shitty ones."

I get a growl for that reference, and he throws the question back at me. "What are *you* afraid of?"

I figure if he's going to skirt the question, I will too. "People finding out my tits are fake."

He coughs, thumping a fist on his chest to clear his airway. I'm not sure what he's choking on. Hopefully, the words *Can I see them?*

"Out of everything, that's what you're afraid of?"

I smile and press my shoulder blades together to push my breasts out. The moonlight highlights the rounded top of each globe in the low boatneck T-shirt I'm wearing.

I can feel his eyes on me. On *them.* Gooseflesh pebbles my skin and I tell myself it's because it's colder on the water.

"Paid a lot of money for these babies. Enough that no one could ever truly tell. Hard to be the buxom country bombshell when you're flat as a board. How terrible does that make me sound?"

"Do you like them?"

My eyes flick to him. "What?"

"Your boobs." He swallows audibly. "Forget about everyone else. Do they make you happy? Do they make you feel good?"

I look back down at my breasts, considering his question. A slow smile curves across my lips. "I fucking love them."

West barks out a laugh from his bench, a short distance from me. We sit facing each other, but his bare foot pushes forward, almost toe to toe with mine. He's rolled his jeans up, and his feet are *big*.

"Then who gives a fuck what anyone else thinks, Skylar?

Who cares if anyone finds out? You love them. They make you happy. No shame in that."

"What about you?"

"I mean, listen, I'm not gonna lie. They make me pretty happy too."

My cheeks flare with heat, and I grin so wide that they ache. My hands press in on either side of my face like that will cool me down.

I feel like a giddy schoolgirl because this rugged country boy—no, man—said my boobs make him happy.

But a few beats later, it hits me that he's covering the question with humor. I blink at him a few times, and I can think of no reason not to spill my guts to this man who's proven to be nothing short of trustworthy.

"I think what I'm really afraid of is being irrelevant. You know?" The lighthearted expression on his face morphs to a serious one, and I continue. "That everyone figures out the public image of me they've been spoon-fed isn't real. That they'll turn their nose up at what's left. A girl with crippling anxiety and fake boobs who tries to pet grizzly bears and doesn't write her own music or play an instrument. I started off in pageants as a kid, and I'm just an overgrown version of that now. No friends, no special skills, just…plastic."

My breathing feels labored by the time I get everything out. But I also feel lighter. Freer.

Until I look at West. The darkness makes it difficult to fully read his expression, but it's tinged with sadness.

When he speaks, his voice is all gravel. "Well, I've been here to see you try to pet a bear. I've seen you with a bruised face. I've seen you get anxious. And Skylar? I like all those versions of you. You have me. You'll always be relevant to me."

My eyes sting as I nod and let out a shaky breath.

"I'm afraid of being alone."

His words freeze me.

"It's not just my kids dying. It's the impermanence of *everything*." He clicks his tongue and looks away, like he can't meet my eyes as he spills his secrets. "I'm lonely. I'm especially lonely during the weeks Emmy and Ollie are with Mia. Those are the weeks I struggle with…purpose. I work, sleep, and live in my head. And in my head, I'm a guy who already failed once at a committed relationship—to the detriment of my kids, most likely. And that feels like a heavy burden to carry on with. I don't want to fail them again."

"What about the people who work at the barn? I know you train the horses, but I've seen other people around."

A dry chuckle crests his lips, and he finally meets my eyes. "Those are staff. Not friends. And the ones who could be have their own dynamics outside of the ranch. Everyone around me is creating a life, and I'm just stuck here. Alone. When the kids are at their mom's house, it becomes abundantly clear that if I don't go to people, no one seeks me out."

I hum, thinking about what he's just said, really chewing on his confession. I remember turning him away that night with the lasagna, and a pit forms in my stomach.

He came to me. He was lonely. And I sent him away.

The moment aches with intimacy and a sort of sorrow. West is the happy, wild guy, and he just shared his most painful inner worries with heartbreaking honesty.

I've never felt closer to another human than I do to West right now.

"You and I, we're not so different."

All I get back is a rough grumble and dropped eye contact. His shoulders slump as his elbows rest on his knees, his fingers weaving together. Then he bows his head, and it's inherently *wrong* for this beautiful, deeply *good* man to look so beaten down.

I want to prop him back up tall. Lift his spirits. Make him feel better.

My body moves toward him on instinct. Taking care not to tip the boat, I drop to my bare knees on the base of the canoe and delicately crawl across the few feet that separates us.

At first, he doesn't react, but when my hands land on his knees, the muscles in his quads go tense beneath my fingertips.

His warm exhale fans against the tops of my breasts, the gooseflesh more apparent than ever.

"What are you doing, Skylar?"

I move closer, ignoring the warning in his voice. My knees press against the arches of his feet as I position myself between his legs and languidly slide my palms up his thighs. The boat rocks with the motion. We both sway in time.

I tilt my head just a fraction, angling my lips up toward his. "Seeking you out."

He doesn't respond, but that doesn't deter me. My fingers clamp onto his jeans, and I squeeze his legs the way I've dreamed of doing since I first laid eyes on him.

I press my lips to his knuckles, still braided together before me. Place a kiss on each of the four tattoos that adorn them. This time, when I glance back up at him, I find his eyes tracking my every movement with rapt attention. They dive into mine right as his hands unlatch and move to cradle my head.

When he holds me, I let loose a breath I didn't realize I'd been holding.

"And when you leave?" he asks, eyes bouncing between mine like he might be able to will the answer he wants from me. But we both know I'll leave. We both know this place is a stepping stone. Real life is somewhere else. Doing something else. I can't throw away a life's work to make promises to a man I barely know.

Still, my chest aches. My heart throbs uncomfortably. I've known West for what feels like a blink of an eye and a lifetime all at once.

People write songs about this feeling.

He calls to me the same way I call to him. Desperately. Thoroughly. Without even meaning to.

Which is why I look him in the eye and whisper the painful truth of it. "I will miss you terribly."

The flash of pain in his dark blue depths is more than I can bear. I kiss him to cover it. Kiss him to apologize because this will feel good until it doesn't.

One week to the day, I kiss Weston Belmont for the second time with everything I have, even though I know it's going to hurt later.

This time, he kisses me back.

My hands on his thighs, his thumbs on my cheekbones—our hungry lips press together.

We kiss.

And we kiss.

And we *kiss*.

I can barely breathe as he stakes his claim. His teeth grazing over my bottom lip. The way his tongue tangles with mine. The soft lapping of water beneath us. The cozy cover of darkness above us.

All I want is to be closer.

I reach for him, slide my hands beneath his shirt. Warm skin, hard lines, and a light dusting of hair beneath my fingertips.

"You're so beautiful," I murmur between passionate kisses.

He chuckles against my lips, and a shiver racks my body. That sound. It's a shot straight to my core. The twisting sensation behind my hip bones is unbearable.

Another shiver.

"Get up here," he growls against my mouth, and I swallow the words, not wanting him to stop.

I fucking cling to him.

But he doesn't draw away like last time. His hands move lower, and he lifts me, pulling me closer. Placing me right on his lap. My knees land on either side of his body, my pussy lined up with the massive bulge in his jeans. His hands rove over my rib cage. Under my shirt. Fingers slipping *just* under the strap of my bra.

He pulls back and lifts his hand to trail his fingers over the edges of my lips. "This fucking mouth, Skylar."

"You like it?" I dart my tongue out, egging him on.

"If I told you all the things I've dreamed about doing to this mouth, you'd turn the prettiest shade of pink."

I nip at the lower line of his jaw and grind down on his cock. "Then you better tell me in broad daylight, so you can be sure I do."

His fingers flick at my back, and my bra gapes open between my shoulders. My hips swivel. The feel of him overwhelms me, the pressure of grinding myself on him through our clothes has every nerve ending dancing. I feel him swell even thicker and longer beneath me and gasp at the feel.

"Guess I'll have to settle for feeling my way around tonight and fuck your mouth tomorrow then." West's voice scrapes over my skin, hands pushing up to cup my breasts. They fit so perfectly in his big hands. They may have been made for me, but it *feels* like they were made for him.

"Fuck," I mutter as his head drops and his stubbled face drags over my collarbones, lips exploring, teeth dragging, tongue swirling. He tastes my skin like I'm his favorite treat, and I want him to never stop.

His thumbs flick at my already pointed nipples before he plucks at them, teasing me. I tip my head back, eyes closed, letting him play.

"Gonna fuck these too, fancy face."

"Yeah?" My pelvis clenches and I rock against him eagerly, listening to his breathing go ragged.

The boat's motion only adds to the friction, and I'm so eager for his touch. I arch my back, offering myself to him. His palms are so big and rough and warm. I want so badly to see how they look on me right now. To watch him explore. Never has such a simple touch set me so alight.

"Fuck yeah. But first…" He shifts, turning us. "I'm—"

But as we turn, so does the boat.

It feels as though it happens in slow motion. He throws his weight to correct it. I lose my balance.

And rather than letting me go and saving himself from the cold water…

He comes with me.

CHAPTER 21

West

I don't let go of Skylar. My brain rushes a mile a minute. For a beat, I'm stressed. If this girl doesn't know how to make a bed, does she know how to swim?

Within seconds, we surface together, under the cover of the canoe. Her legs kick just as steady as mine. She's just as thoroughly soaked as I am.

"Are you—" Right as I'm about to ask her if she's okay, she bursts out laughing.

It's a deep belly laugh, magnified by the wooden dome overhead. It's too dark for me to make her out, but I can feel her arms moving.

I'm struck for a moment. Struck by the fact that I don't think I've heard her laugh—not like this. It's different. Without a shred of self-consciousness. Here, in this dark, private bubble, she seems a little more herself than she is outside of it.

I feel as though I know her better than I have any right to after tonight. And that has nothing to do with having had my hands on her body and her legs around my waist.

There's no point in denying it.

I enjoy Skylar's company.

"Only us," she wheezes, treading water. "This would only happen to us."

"If you hadn't been grinding on my dick like an eager little—"

"You're the one who picked me up and ruined my grinding."

I can't help but laugh now. "It was hot as hell while it lasted, though, wasn't it?"

She agrees without hesitation. "It was hot as hell."

"I'm glad you can swim."

She scoffs at me. "I'm glad *you* can swim. Can you imagine if I had to drag your heavy ass to shore? Let's get outta here."

With that, she takes a deep breath and drops out from under the canoe. I follow her, and when we resurface, the night around us feels downright bright compared to the blacked-out cover we came from.

"I got the boat. You just get to shore."

Another scoff. She swims to the other side of the canoe. "It'll be easier if we do it together."

I swallow, doing my best not to overthink that sentence. I do a lot alone, and I try not to let myself think too much about how nice it would be to have someone around. Instead, I focus on the complications that would come with it.

With Skylar, the complications don't feel so complicated.

We don't talk as we flip the canoe back over; we work in unison without even trying. Swimming it back to shore, wet clothes drape heavily from our limbs.

Based on the heavy silence that takes over, I may have mauled Skylar Stone for the first and last time tonight. I had my hands all over her and now she's struggling to do her bra clasp back up.

"Here, let me." I step around the canoe on the shore and gesture for her to face away from me.

Her wide eyes catch on mine and she slowly turns away, using both hands to gather her hair over one shoulder. I slide one hand up her back, starting at the waist of her jean shorts, fingers pushing beneath the heavy cotton of her tee.

A shiver wracks her body as my fingers slide up the column of her spine. But we both know it's not cold out. "You don't have to do this."

She goes to step away, but my free hand juts out, gripping her hip to keep her close. "I undid it, only seems fair I put it back where I found it."

All I get in return is a nod. My second hand joins the first under her shirt and I make quick work of the clasp. Still, I find myself out of breath by the time I finish.

"Thanks," she whispers, glancing at me over her shoulder with a million questions swimming in her eyes.

"Of course. This way." I nudge my chin to the left along the shoreline as we lift the canoe in tandem, leading us back over the rough sand in bare feet. Luckily, we spent more time floating than rowing and didn't make it too far from my property.

We move at an unhurried pace, picking our way around large rocks and logs. Both lost to our own thoughts, we don't talk. She hisses a couple of times when the going gets rough on bare feet. But it's followed by a quick, "I'm fine!" or "Just keep going."

So I do. And when we get back to the tree where Ollie likes to sit, I stop for a beat to stare at it, to let us catch our breath. And yet, my chest tightens.

Just like she seems to have done every moment until now, Skylar sees straight through the break. "It'll be nice to have him back tomorrow."

I suck in a sharp breath, caught off guard by the way she plucked the thought from my head. Over my shoulder, I peek back at her. The silvery moonlight highlights the bow at the top of her lips as they curve into a soft smile.

The mention of tomorrow makes me realize we need to talk. Especially after what just happened on the boat. The things we did. The things I said.

So I tip my head, gesturing that we put the canoe down here. It'll be fine wedged up against the embankment for the night, and it'll give me a good reason to take the kids out fishing tomorrow afternoon. Spend some quality time out on the water with them.

God knows after that intense, sudden pang of missing them, I'll probably do anything they want.

With the boat stashed, we shove our feet back into our shoes where we left them on the shore, and I lead Skylar to the short path up to the sloping lawn.

I count to ten before I decide to say something. I don't

often struggle to find words—it's usually more about struggling to shut up—but this woman has me off-kilter in the most unfamiliar way.

Then, all at once, we both speak.

"So, about tomorr—"

"I think we should—"

We both bite down on our lips before glancing at each other. Humor etches her features, and I drop her gaze, staring down at my uncomfortable, wet jeans and her toned legs as we continue our march up the hill.

"You go," she says.

I shake my head. "Ladies first." She didn't mean anything by telling me to go first, but it's so her. It's proof of the way they trained her to behave. Like her opinion doesn't matter as much. Like she should hold back her thoughts and feelings until everyone else has had a go.

And who knows? Maybe we both want to say the same thing.

"Okay, first, I won't be erasing *that* from my memory."

I chuckle, watching the grass between my feet turn to dry dirt and pine needles as we pass closer to the house. "Thank fuck, because it's burned into mine."

She makes this sweet little humming noise, and it reminds me of her moaning into my mouth while my hands roamed. My dick feels uncomfortable against the wet denim.

"Second, we need to take a breath. I start working with Ford next week. I'm feeling invigorated about making something all on my own, rather than terrified about it, and I want to keep feeling that way. I also know your kids are coming back. You've made it clear that you want to protect their space"—she huffs out a breath—"and, god, do I respect you for it."

The house comes closer and closer, and at the bottom of the stairs, she turns to face me. "You're a great dad, West. I may not know you that well yet, but I know you love your kids in a way that I wish every kid got to experience. So, let's…" A wry laugh escapes her lips. "Let's back it up a bit. I'm going to start sleeping in the bunkhouse again tomorrow. We can take a breather for the week. I'm complicated, and I don't want that to spill over into your family time. Plus, we're good at being friends, yeah?"

She's looking at me with such expectancy, such candor sparkling in her eyes. She's being so mature and responsible.

Two traits I love.

But right now, I fucking hate them.

And all I want to do is blow up the mature and responsible parts of my brain and disagree with her. But I've learned to harness those urges over the years, so I nod and force a smile to my mouth.

"Yeah," I say, because we are good at being friends. Something tells me we'd be good at more too.

But I give her the win.

Trying to ignore the way my spine tingles as she follows me into the house. Trying to ignore the way my fingers itch to reach for her as we go our separate ways down the silent hallway.

I thought she and I might say the same thing tonight, but I was wrong.

She went with being responsible. And I was going to say *Fuck what I said. I want you.*

As I shower and crawl into bed, the more I think about it, the more I think I would have scared her if I had said it.

So I settle on showing her. I've got an entire week with the world's biggest cockblockers in the house to show Skylar that with us…something is different.

CHAPTER 22

West

"WHY ARE THERE GIRL CLOTHES IN THE DRYER?" OLLIE shouts at me from the laundry room.

I freeze right as I'm about to flip the grilled cheese sandwich in the pan before me. I'm a grown-ass man, and I feel like I'm in trouble with an eight-year-old. Like I'm sneaking around somehow.

I consider making something up, but why?

"Those are Skylar's, bud," I call back.

He walks into the living room with a basket of Skylar's dry clothes and plunks them on the table. The world's most helpful kid, I swear. His sister is probably upstairs destroying something after losing her soccer game this morning, and he's here, putting his favorite clothes through the wash after a week at his mom's house.

"Gotcha" is all he says as he drops the basket on the living room table.

I steal a glance at him, but he casually makes his way to the table for lunch. He doesn't ask why her clothes are in the wash, and I don't know why I'm expecting him to interrogate me or look at me accusingly.

"Was thinking we could go out fishing after lunch."

"Cool," Ollie says as he pulls out a chair for himself. "Can we invite Skylar?"

I almost drop the sandwich on the floor as I go to transfer it to the plate. "Fishing?"

He shrugs, and his lips tug up. "Yeah. She must be lonely in the bunkhouse."

"I doubt she has a license." My heart thuds like I'm a teenager about to get busted for street racing all over again.

"I can fill out an application for her. It's easy."

Emmy stomps down the stairs into the kitchen, her temper somewhat subdued. "I wanna be the one who clubs the fish when we catch it. I need to hit something," she grumbles as she approaches the table—a monster drawn out of her lair by the smell of food.

"You scare me" is all I say, plating the food and setting it in front of them.

While we eat, I work up the courage to go knock on Skylar's door to ask if she wants to come fishing with us.

An hour later, my misfits and I roll up to the bunkhouse and find Skylar sitting on the front porch. It seems cleaner, like she swept and wiped things down. She looks bright and well rested, her hair falling in wild waves around her face.

"*Coach Thick Thighs!*" The evil bird announces me from her shoulder, and it makes Skylar's cheeks turn pink. Her eyes flick to the side as though the parrot will pick up on the accusation in her expression.

"What does that me—"

"Wanna come fishing?" I cut Emmy off with our invite, lifting the tackle box in my hand.

Skylar's eyes go wide as they flit to mine. "In what?"

"Our canoe," Emmy provides, her eyes sparkling with excitement.

The pink glow of Skylar's cheeks creeps down her throat and over her chest as her eyes meet mine.

"Please?" Ollie asks quietly, and I try not to double take. The kid who never talks to someone new is out here showing off with one-word sentences.

I don't miss the way Skylar's body softens as she watches him.

He keeps his eyes trained on the ground and kicks at a rock as he adds a mumbled, "I got you a license and everything."

Cherry bobs eagerly on Skylar's shoulder, as though the motion could urge her up out of her seat.

"I didn't know you needed a license to fish," she ventures carefully.

Emmy lets out a little scoff before turning to me dramatically. "It's amateur hour over here."

I ignore Emmy. "Yeah, fishing, hunting...bear petting. All licensed activities."

"Bear petting?" the kids ask at once.

Skylar narrows her eyes at me. "He's joking. But yes, sure. I'll come."

I watch my children's body language change. Oliver straightens his lips, tipping them up in a shy smile. Emmy is less subdued, letting out a loud whoop and shooting her fist up in the air as though this win makes up for the morning's loss.

They're both already heading down to the water when Skylar asks, "Is there room on the canoe for all of us?"

"We can—"

"If there's not, you can always sit on my dad's lap," Emmy cuts me off, shouting back.

All traces of pink on Skylar's skin blaze red now. I doubt I'm any better. I feel like a fucking kid blushing over his crush.

Still, I cover a laugh and meet Skylar's stunned gaze. "Kids, man" is all I offer with a shrug as I turn away. I wave my hand over my shoulder, urging her to follow.

I take a few steps, just to be sure Emmy and Ollie are far enough ahead to be out of earshot. "I know it's one of your favorite pastimes, but quit staring at my ass, fancy face. Put your bitchy bird away. Let's go."

"Are you flirting with me?" Her voice is all music and amusement.

I grin at the water and don't turn back when I say, "Absolutely."

"You screamed." Emmy jabs her fork at Skylar, and I wince. Her enthusiasm is borderline violent sometimes.

Skylar rolls her eyes from where she's seated across from me. From where they are *all* seated across from me.

Both kids wanted to sit beside her at dinner, so their three chairs are wedged in tight on one side of the table. Leaving me alone on the other.

I feel like I'm at the world's most ridiculous interrogation.

"I did not scream."

"Yeah," Ollie adds, rushing to Skylar's defense. She turns a conspiratorial smile his way, but a little too soon. "It was more like a squeal."

Her mouth pops open, and I watch my shy son grin up at her.

"I did not squeal. Pigs squeal. I was just surprised by the fish flopping everywhere."

The truth is that she was so startled by it, I thought she was going to dive out of the boat to get away from it.

Emmy laughs. "You almost tipped the whole canoe. And that thing never tips."

I cough into a fist, pretending that it's food down the wrong tube rather than laughter. Because if Emmy only knew.

Skylar presses her lips together and gives me a scolding look. As though the kids are going to magically guess that she and I did, in fact, tip it while dry humping the hell out of each other.

"Well, thank you for humoring me and putting it back," Skylar says while taking a bite of her barbecue chicken.

Now it's Emmy's turn to roll her eyes. Skylar didn't want

to kill the fish—in fact, she looked downright devastated over the prospect.

I'm not sure where she thinks her food comes from, but then again, this is a woman who brought her purse fishing with us as though she could use her black Amex out on the water.

Emmy pats Skylar's arm and smiles up at her, like she's the adult placating the child. "It's okay. I forgive you. You'll get used to it eventually. Before you know it, you'll be reaching for the bat and putting those sorry suckers out of their misery yourself."

My daughter goes back to eating as if she didn't just speak words like a grizzled old fisherman, implying that Skylar will be around to go fishing with us all the time.

I scrub at my stubble, shaking my head.

Emmy is a wild child, but instead of being horrified by her bluntness, Skylar's expression is full of endearment. "Never change, Emmy," she says, looking my daughter in the eyes. "Never, not for anyone."

Emmy's head tilts as she stares back at her, but then she nods. Something passes between them. Some sort of understanding. Some sort of promise.

Watching them together makes my heart pump faster, my chest puff up with pride.

With longing.

"Your clothes are here, Skylar," Ollie tosses out, making both of us freeze.

"Oh...thanks," she replies, attempting to act casual as she spears a watermelon ball into her mouth.

Emmy mimics Skylar and, daintily forks a melon ball

and then proceeds to talk with an open mouth as she chews. "Why are your clothes here?"

"Because I wanted to do some laundry, and your dad said I didn't need to go to the laundrom—"

"Because Skylar stayed at the house while you guys were away," I blurt out. Never been big on sugarcoating shit for my kids, so why start now? I didn't break any laws by letting her stay in the guest room.

Two sets of blue eyes that match my own stare at me from across the table. I don't know why I feel like I'm in trouble, but I do.

It's quiet for a beat, then Emmy shrugs and goes back to her plate of food. "Fair. I wouldn't want to sleep in the bunkhouse either. Auntie Rosie's mouse lives there."

Skylar and I lock eyes.

"You knew about Auntie Rosie's mouse?"

Emmy freezes, turning big baby blues up at me. "Oh no. I wasn't supposed to tell you that."

Skylar tries and fails to bite down on a giggle.

I'm about to express all the ways I'm going to get back at Rosie for playing house with a goddamn rodent on my property when Skylar cuts me off. "It's okay. Scotty and I will become friends this week."

Ollie's brow furrows. "Wait. You're going back out there?"

"Yep." Skylar shrugs.

"Why?"

She smiles a practiced smile, one I recognize from the glossy pages of magazines in the grocery store checkout line.

Not the one she gives me when we're alone. "Because you guys have a lot going on here. I don't want to intrude."

My son turns to look at her. "You're not intruding. We like having you here."

She blinks down at him, a sheen in her eyes.

"You should just stay. There's a room for you and everything." He turns to me. "Right, Dad?"

I watch them across the table, both wedged in beside her like they want to be close to her too. Like they're just as inexplicably attached as I am.

It's new and foreign and…right.

That's why I stare straight into her amber irises and say, "Stay."

CHAPTER 23

Skylar

I woke up nervous about today's meeting. But the headline sitting in my inbox really turned my day around. It read:

> **BREAKING NEWS:** Sources say Skylar Stone lives in fear of being attacked by lake trout.

I really had freaked out. And the kids had laughed so hard that it was worth coming across as the ultimate city girl. The memory will always make me smile. It's one I'll cherish forever.

So now I sit across from Ford and his daughter, Cora, in the cozy living room area set up at the back of their office feeling more confident than ever. It's a charming atmosphere with a wood-burning stove in the corner and a wall covered in shelves and records behind them.

On the coffee table between us, sheets of paper are spread out.

"No." Cora shakes her head as she tosses sheets down one by one. "No. Nope. Hell no."

She continues flicking through them, and I can't keep the amusement off my face as I watch Ford stare at her with a furrowed brow. I've been observing them together for an hour now, and they are a marvel.

Both so similar. Both so dry. I could watch them all day.

"Where did you find these songs, Ford? Teenyboppers R Us?" She doesn't look at him as she says it, just groans and discards another sheet with such force that my lips twitch.

"These are from well-respected songwriters."

She rolls her eyes from beneath her heavy, black bangs. "Well, they don't have my respect."

When Ford told me his daughter was the driving force behind working with me and that she wanted to be involved in producing the record, it surprised me. But somehow, even at only thirteen years old, she has a vision. An idea.

As someone who's been told over and over again that she doesn't need to have her own ideas, I respect the hell out of Ford for including her. I already liked him, but watching him now makes me understand him. This album is a special project for me. But it's a special project for the father and daughter across from me too.

She points at the sheets. "These are all boring, sappy love songs."

Ford shrugs. "People like love songs."

She turns to me. "Are love songs what you want to sing?"

I blink a few times, searching her petite face. "I…I don't know. I'm in a period of discovery, I guess."

Cora sighs down at the discarded pages. "What you need are *fuck you* songs. Songs that hurt. No more Auto-Tune. Your voice is sweet enough already. You could tell someone to go die, and they'd say thank you."

"Cora." Ford groans and drops his head into his hands.

I laugh. "No, it's okay. I get what she's saying. I wish I could write my own songs."

Cora glances up at me. "Who said you can't?"

My mouth opens to say *everyone*, but that might come across as more self-pity than is necessary. Ultimately, I'm responsible for my life and my actions.

"Just haven't tried to do it. Like instruments. I'm a one-trick pony."

Cora tosses the last of the sheets onto the table and flops back, looking every bit the teenager she is. "Your voice is your instrument. You don't need to be good at everything, but I bet you've got something to say. You should say it."

My lips quirk. She's so matter-of-fact. She's excited—eager, even—but not manic. Cora's fucking cool—and judging by the way Ford is smirking at her, he must think so too.

"Maybe I should."

Their matching eyes slice up at me. "Yeah?" Ford asks. "This is your album. Your call. I know when we talked last week, you didn't seem keen on it. I'm not going to force you to do anything you're not on board with."

That sentiment strikes a heavy blow. No producer has *ever* said that to me before.

I watch them, shimmying my shoulders as I straighten. I feel more in control of my destiny every day.

This is my album.

This is my career.

This is my call.

I nod once and steeple my hands as I gaze down at the discarded songs on the table. The ones that mean nothing to me. Written to top charts and nothing more.

There's nothing wrong with them, per se. They represent the old me—pretty and polished and curated for mass consumption.

The woman I'm becoming, though? She's not.

"Yeah," I say. "I'm going to try."

And as I say it out loud, I feel more sure of myself than ever.

Nestled between the tree roots, I sit on the log with a coil-bound notebook laid across my lap and a pen in my hand. For three days, I've been trying to write something. *Anything.*

For three days, I have written nothing.

I'm not sure how long I've been sitting here, only that it seems like an eternity and the page remains blank. Which makes me feel remarkably stupid for ever thinking I could just sit down and write a song.

With a heavy sigh, I lay the pen down on the lined sheet and close my eyes. I listen to the birds trill, the water ripple, the light rustle of leaves. It's more overcast than sunny today.

Moodier than the bluebird skies and bright yellow sun that has graced the valley for the past ten days.

I breathe in, and I breathe out.

I realize that the week without a phone has passed. Won that bet. But I smile because I'm not inclined to replace it.

I feel better than I have in my entire adult life.

It's as I'm mentally running through the current state of everything that I hear soft footsteps. I'm certain that a week ago, I wouldn't have been present enough to notice. But everything around me feels a little brighter these days. A little more in focus.

I don't open my eyes, but I sense a small body folding down onto the log beside me.

"Got this for you." Oliver's voice is tentative as a weight is added to my lap.

My eyes snap open, and when I look down, I see a book. It appears to be a bird encyclopedia.

I run my fingers over the glossy cover. "Like, from the house?"

I've spent an inordinate amount of time browsing the bookshelves in West's home, as if that might provide me with a window into his soul, some deeper understanding of a man who comes off so casual and carefree but is, in fact, lonely.

I've found everything from historical romances to biographies to Scandinavian murder mysteries. But no bird books.

"No. Bought it with my allowance. We just got back from the bookstore. It's a gift."

I blink at the blue-eyed boy. And then back down at the

book in my lap. People have given me gifts my entire life. Expensive gifts. Over-the-top gifts. But this…

"This is my favorite gift I've ever received," I tell him, my voice thick.

His chin drops and he smiles shyly into his lap. He's got a brand-new graphic novel in his hand and a flush on his cheeks.

I nudge his shoulder, not trusting myself to speak.

He nudges me back.

Then we both fall into a companionable silence. Me, looking through my bird book and discovering what I saw last week was an osprey. Him, raptly flipping the pages of his graphic novel, top teeth strumming his bottom lip, as though he could inhale the story.

Eventually, I pull my notebook back out and stare out over the rough water. I tap my pen against the open page, deciding what I want to say.

Who I want to be.

"What are you doing?" Ollie asks.

I sigh and lean back into the roots behind us. "Trying to write a song. But I've never written one before. I don't know where to start."

"I love reading and writing. Feels a bit like talking to someone."

I blink a few times, mulling over the greater meaning of what he's just told me. This boy of few words who happily offers me his.

"Talking to people is hard sometimes. Scary. You know?"

I hum and dip my chin in recognition. "I know."

"I worry about what to say. And how people will take it."

"Highly relatable."

I see a soft smile touch his lips. "But when I write, I can say whatever I want. And it doesn't really matter what people think of it."

My throat feels thick again as I choke out my response. "That's very wise, Ollie."

"Sometimes it feels like I have so many things to say. But I just can't get them out. Or I can't choose where to start."

I sniff and gently press against him. He's killing me. His sugary, little voice, speaking with such brave honesty. "I love talking to you. No matter what you say, I will always listen."

"I love talking to you too, Skylar."

His body presses back against mine so that we lean together. When I glance at him, I can see his eyes roving my blank page. Then he reaches for the notebook and the pen, his small hand gripping it as it moves across the page.

When he hands it back, he's written the first line of a song.

It all started on a backroad.

When I peek over at him, he's grinning—a tight-lipped grin that's keeping him from laughing, though I can tell he wants to.

"Your dad told you about the bear, huh?"

A soft chortle escapes him as he nods. "Emmy is at an outdoor survival camp this week. Bet she'll have advice for you."

"*Really funny*, Ollie." I bump him again with my shoulder, and this time he does laugh. It's so light, so childlike.

It's fucking music to my ears.

I look down at the first line he's written…

And it seems as good a place as any to start.

A soft knock at the guest room door has me tearing my attention from my bird book. I've been flipping through it, savoring every page. The art is beautiful.

I showed Cherry a blue jay, and she said, "*Ugly bird,*" but I'm sure she's just jealous because she's mostly gray.

"I need to talk to you," a voice whispers urgently. My heart pounds hard for a few beats, thinking it might be West knocking. But it's not him.

It's Emmy. And she comes in before I even have a chance to answer. A quick glance at the clock on the bedside table tells me it's eleven o'clock at night.

Well past her bedtime.

And also, the time we all know West goes out to do a night check.

Night check that I haven't been accompanying him on because that feels like a slippery slope. Put us in a quiet barn together and one of three things happens:

I spill my deepest, darkest secrets.

I kiss him.

We stand in silence, eye fucking the hell out of each other.

The only place more dangerous for us is, apparently, a canoe.

She shuts the door with the utmost care and tiptoes across the guest room. Then, without asking, she crawls up onto my bed and kneels beside me with wide eyes.

"Skylar, we need to talk about bear safety," she says somberly.

I clamp my lips together, desperately trying to hold in my laughter as I nod back at her. *Very* seriously.

"Our dad told us about how you guys met today."

I'm definitely going to kill West.

"*Boooring*," Cherry taunts, and I slice her a glare. Based on Emmy's giggles, she seems amused by my parrot's sarcasm.

"He did, did he?"

She nods, now serious again from head to toe. "You're lucky to be alive. Bears are unpredictable apex predators."

After a day of learning about wilderness survival, she spent dinner talking about different ways to start a fire and how to use a compass, but not bears.

"You wanted to tell me this now?"

"I didn't want to embarrass you at dinner."

That makes me smile. She may be wild, but she is thoughtful. Just like her dad.

Her dad, who has taken me into his house. Included me in their dinners. Shared meaningful conversation with me— like he cares about what I have to say.

And over the past few days, he hasn't even made fun of me when I ogle him while he works his training horses in the arena behind the barn. I've been sitting on the bleachers, attempting to find the words to express what I want to say. Turns out writing songs is about as hard as trying not to peek back up at West in his jeans as he talks in soft tones to the horse beneath him. His hands are gentle, and his patience knows no bounds.

I try so hard not to stare, but he usually catches me and tosses me a wink. Followed by a knowing smirk.

Still, West and his kids have made me feel more at home in their house than I have anywhere else in the world.

"That's very considerate of you, Emmy. Thank you," I say, rubbing her pajama-clad knee.

She reaches behind her back for a plastic bag and holds it out to me. "I got this for you."

"You and Ollie *both* getting me gifts? What have I done to deserve this?"

She glances around the room before oh-so-casually dropping, "We like you. And you make our dad happy."

That strikes me silent for a moment. The plastic crinkles beneath my fingers and breathing feels just a bit harder after that offhanded comment. "I think your dad is just a happy kind of guy."

She shrugs. "Yeah. But he's happier with you here. Like when we came back this week. I can tell. Sometimes I think he's lonely without us. Mom has Brandon, so I feel bad for leaving my dad."

From the mouths of babes.

I stare at the girl. She thinks she's just having a regular conversation, but she's thrown me right off with her level of empathy.

She shoves her chin at the bag in my hand. "Open it."

So I do. And what I find inside is... "You bought me a knife?"

"It's a pocketknife. In case you run into another bear. I didn't have enough money to buy it. My dad told me I need to be more responsible with my allowance and wouldn't give me any extra, so Ollie lent me some. He says I'm in his debt now, whatever that means."

"You think I'm going to stab a bear?"

She rolls her eyes like my aversion to violence is childish. "I'll teach you how. You go for the eyes or mouth."

"I don't think I'm equipped to fight off a bear. I'd just let him eat me."

"Skylar, that's quitter talk. Plus, my dad would be really sad if his favorite singer died."

I laugh now, holding the cool wooden handle against my palm. "I'm not his favorite singer."

The expression on Emmy's face is pure confusion. "Of course you are."

"I highly doubt—"

"I'll prove it. Be right back." With that, she leaps off the bed and tears out of the room. All pretense of sneaking around has completely disappeared.

When she returns, she's wearing the world's widest grin and holding up a T-shirt.

My T-shirt.

Except it's West's T-shirt.

But it has a faded black-and-white photo of me in a spotlight, holding a mic with my signature bandana tied around it, and wearing a pair of cut offs so short that the pocket liners peek out.

"He usually wears it but hasn't lately."

Probably because my eyes would have rolled out of my head like they are now.

"Huh," I say dumbly. Because I don't know what else to say. This man has done nothing but treat me like I'm the most normal person he's ever met.

No one treats me like that.

Least of all people who are fans.

"Yeah, told you so. Anyway…" She tosses the shirt, and I watch it land in a heap on the floor on the far side of the bed. I have an urge to pick it up, but I'm not sure I want to touch it.

I'm not mad West didn't tell me. In fact, I appreciate it. And yet…it feels a little like he withheld something from me. Something integral to how he sees me, how we interact. I'd heard him singing my song that first night, but I assumed it had just been stuck in his head.

I brush the nagging sensation aside and focus back on his daughter, who has now crawled under the covers, so she's leaned back against the headboard at my side.

"Okay, Skylar. Your bear lesson begins *now*…"

She starts to talk.

She talks, and she talks, and she talks. Eventually she switches over to talking about nature in more general terms. She explains photosynthesis. She tells me all about how plants turn light and water and all these things from their immediate surroundings into energy—into life. And as I lie there with my eyes closed, the process strikes me as both remarkably simple and remarkably special.

I don't know when the talking stops; all I know is that I'm not awake to experience it.

CHAPTER 24

West

I WAKE UP TO THE SMELL OF BACON AND THE SUBTLE THUMP of bass on a song I'd know anywhere.

I know it because it's one of Skylar's.

Skylar, who slept down the hall from me last night, with my daughter starfished beside her—or kind of on top.

When I peeked in after night check, the door was open, light spilling from inside.

I had the crazy idea that I'd check on her, only to find her passed out with my kid. A sight that made my heart skip a few beats. Rather than wake them, I just flicked off the bedside lamp and left, only slightly disappointed she hadn't been alone.

I'm making any excuse to spend time around her at this point. We have dinner together daily. Grocery shop at the same time, because why take two cars to the same place? Also, charging a Tesla out here is a fucking nightmare. We bump into each other at the coffeepot in the kitchen when I take a midmorning break. After that, she follows me back to the barn, conversation flowing between us easily. She sits on the bleachers at ringside, writing while I ride.

I catch her staring at me sometimes. She blushes every time I do, but then she focuses so hard on the notepad in her lap that I get free rein to stare at her openly.

The lack of dark circles beneath her eyes. The subtle glow on her skin from time spent outdoors. The relaxed set to her plush mouth.

She's always looked good to me.

But after weeks spent in Rose Hill, she looks *better*.

I rub my hands over my face and stretch. That's when I hear voices coming from downstairs. But they aren't talking.

They're singing along.

I grin and give my head a shake, marveling at the way my kids have taken to her.

When I exchanged them with Mia at soccer last weekend, she poked me and said, "You fucking one-upper. All they talked about this week was Skylar Stone. I'll never be the cool parent at this rate."

"Boring Brandon isn't hard to beat," I responded, and that time, she punched me.

"You never change," she said before walking away, laughing.

But I have changed—or am changing. I can't put my finger on it, but something feels different.

With that in mind and knowing I have to get the kids to

camp before getting started on the horses, I roll out of bed and toss on sweats and a tee.

Thank god for my morning staff.

I jog down the creaky, old stairs but freeze when I hit the kitchen.

Emmy stands on the countertop singing into a spatula as though it's a microphone, while Ollie stands on a step stool, flipping bacon. He's wearing my This Guy Rubs His Own Meat apron, which makes me cringe.

All of this takes place as Skylar stirs a bowlful of batter, still in her Calvin Klein sleep shorts. The ones with the thick elastic waistband that are just short enough to distract me and make me jump when Emmy shouts, "Daddy," over the music.

But the true distraction comes when Skylar turns around, making me see double.

Because tucked into that thick elastic waistband is my shirt.

My Skylar Stone shirt.

And just above the image of her is the real her.

Smirking at me.

My stomach somersaults. After days of making Skylar blush, she has flipped the switch on me because I am positive I've turned the brightest shade of red.

"Good morning, Weston," Skylar says smoothly, quirking an eyebrow at me. "Do you like my shirt?"

I swallow, mind racing. I feel like a kid who just got caught with his hand down his pants. "It looks better on you than it does on me."

Now I'm not the only one blushing.

I make my way into the kitchen and pull out a stool at the counter. "What's going on in here?" I ask, redirecting the conversation.

"I'm doing a concert for Skylar while she and Ollie make bacon and pancakes." My daughter, with messy bedhead and flushed cheeks, smiles down at me, still clad in her unicorn pajamas. "We had a sleepover." She huffs, eyes twinkling. "How many people can say they've had a sleepover with Skylar Stone?"

Skylar groans and I hold back a laugh. "Probably not many, Emmy baby."

Emmy hops down into the seat beside me and plants a breathless kiss on my cheek. "Good morning, Daddy."

She talks my ear off about bear safety as I watch Skylar and Oliver make breakfast together. They speak in short, muted sentences, and there's a sort of harmony in the moment. It would be a hell of a lot more peaceful if I weren't still internally cringing over the T-shirt.

Soon, Ollie sets cutlery up on the table, and Emmy and I make our way over to our spots.

She's gabbing about cougars when Skylar slides my plate in front of me. "This one's for you, Coach," she whispers against my ear while patting my shoulder.

And when I glance down, one massive pancake takes up my entire plate.

One massive pancake with *NUMBER 1 FAN* written across the top in chocolate chips.

I bark out a laugh and Skylar grins from ear to ear, hip

cocked out, amusement flashing in her golden eyes. "Enjoy," she murmurs before giving my earlobe a slight tug.

And when she turns to walk away, I have to focus on not reaching for her. Her hip. Her waist. Her ass.

I can still feel her on top of me. Smell her. Taste her.

I look back at the taunting pancake and dig in while listening to the kids talk about their week. Ollie's coding camp sounds a lot less unhinged than Emmy's nature camp. But they both speak with equal excitement about what they're learning.

It's hard to get a word in edgewise. Eventually, we finish breakfast, and I send them off to get dressed.

Then it's just Skylar and me, staring at each other from across the kitchen table.

"I'll get this cleaned up," she announces before pushing to stand, taking her plate with her to the counter.

I watch her round ass move with every step, and my control snaps. I'm up and across the kitchen, pressed close to her in a matter of seconds.

I lean my front against her back because I just can't help myself. My arms cage her in on both sides. "Skylar, what are you playing at?"

My lips dust across the shell of her ear, and she shivers before placing the plate on the counter and spinning on me.

Skylar places her palms against my chest and gives me an uninspired shove. "I could ask you the same thing." Her eyes flash, and a hint of betrayal resides there. Sure, she's teased me all morning, but I can read those hazel irises clear as day. They're the window into her soul—her mind—and I know what she's thinking.

That I wasn't honest with her.

And maybe I wasn't, but goddamn it, I've known this woman for the blink of an eye. I've shared more with her than I have with anyone.

I wrap my fingers around her waist and lift her easily up onto the counter, stepping in close to stand between her open legs.

Our eyes lock as we face off. The energy between us is electric. And definitely not *friendly*.

"Are you a fan, West?" her velvety voice taunts.

I chuckle, spreading my palms on her bare thighs. My hands slide up, fingertips toying with the bottom hem of her shorts, and she lets out a breathy little gasp. I groan at the sound, at the sight of my hands on her. In a flash, I'm back in that canoe. Possessing her.

"Were you ever planning on coming clean?"

Clean. It's as though she thinks she's a dirty secret. That I'd be embarrassed for liking her.

But I'm not.

"There's nothing dirty about being your number-one fan, Skylar. And mark my words, I am. I'm fan enough to be the only person who gives you what you really need—space, friendship—no matter how much it's killing me."

She sucks in a sharp breath.

"What I really want to tell you is that I'm a fan of you in my shirt," I breathe out against her damp lips. Restraint shot, I nip at her jawline. "I'm a fan of you in my house." My lips travel to her neck.

Her head tilts and her legs widen further, offering me better access.

"I'm a fan of you in my lap." My hands glide under the fabric, and I squeeze the sides of her bare ass as I bite down on the crook of her neck. "And once we have this place to ourselves," I murmur against her skin, "I'm gonna be a big fan of you in my bed."

"Fuck." The single word escapes her on a breath, and I drag my mouth over her collarbones.

"And then I'll be a big fan here." I tug her closer, kneading her ass as her legs wrap around my waist. "On the kitchen counter."

Her fingers trail up the back of my neck, slipping through my close-cut hair. Tipping my head up as her mouth angles over mine.

"I'll make such a fucking mess of you that I'll have to be a fan in the shower too."

"West…I thought we were taking a breather."

"Right, but the week is almost up." I drop my lips closer to hers, watching her eyes heat as I do. "Then this fucking breather is over. You can go ahead and breathe through your nose because this mouth will be busy."

She flushes, teeth pressing down on her lip. "That's not really what I meant by a breather."

"Breathing is overrated. I'd rather be drowning in you."

Her hands tug me closer, and our lips press together. Hard. Fast. Desperate. It doesn't last. It can't, not with the kids stomping around upstairs. But she pours herself into it all the same. We kiss until we're breathless.

When she pulls back, our noses touch, and she whispers, "Yeah, definitely overrated."

I kiss her once more, taking liberties I shouldn't, but everything about her is a green light right now. So why the fuck not? She tastes like pancakes. Syrup and chocolate chips. And mine.

It pains me to take a step back, but I can't keep going the way I want to. Not here and not now. So I settle on memorizing the sight of her freshly kissed. Freshly mussed.

Shorts wedged high. Nipples pressing against the thin cotton of *my* shirt. Wild eyes latched onto *me*.

I bite my lip and wave a finger over her form. "Big fan of you looking like this too."

If she weren't already flushed, I bet she'd go pink.

She stares at me. I can tell her mind is going a mile a minute because she only turns away when we hear heavy footsteps bounding down the stairs. Those footsteps send me back over to the table, where I can pretend I'm dutifully cleaning up after breakfast.

"Dad, I need to borrow some money."

"Why?" I ask Emmy without looking up. From the corner of my eye, I see Skylar hop off the counter and busy herself at the sink.

"I bet Ollie you'd go for the most money at the fair on Saturday. He says there's no way you make it three years in a row."

I grimace as Skylar's gaze narrows in on Emmy. "The fair?"

"Yes," she squeals with excitement. "You have to come. There's a hypnotist and rides, and they auction off all the men for dates."

"You make it sound like some kind of illegal trade, Emmy," I say to calm her down a bit, noting the tension in Skylar's shoulders. "It's a bachelor auction for the food bank—*for charity*."

"Oh," Skylar says in a hushed tone before pressing her lips together and going back to cleaning. And refusing to look my way.

"You guys sure it's tomorrow?" Fuck. *Fuck.*

I walk over to the calendar, where I try—and fail—to keep my life organized. Sure enough, I've scribbled *Town Fair* on Saturday. It's just for fun, but getting auctioned off to the women in town when I just said those things to Skylar makes me feel guilty.

"I told Doris she could put me in to help raise money," I explain.

"I love how charitable you are," she says with a brittle smile as she fills the sink with soap and water. She tries really hard not to make eye contact with me, but when she takes a peek from beneath her lashes, my guilt only intensifies.

I may not be well-versed in relationships, but I am well-versed in people looking at me like they're disappointed.

And seeing it on Skylar's face, when I can still feel her in my hands and taste her on my lips makes me despise that look more than ever.

CHAPTER 25

Skylar

BREAKING NEWS: Skylar Stone's number-one fan has been unmasked by tiny traitors.

BEING ANNOYED WITH WEST WHEN HE CONTINUES TO SEND me adorable emails is almost impossible. And being irritated at him for volunteering to raise money for the food bank is beneath me.

But here I am, slumming it in the gutter.

I'd rather be drowning in you.

I play that one sentence on repeat in my head as I walk to the shore. After breakfast, I helped clean up and put on a happy face. I'm good at putting on a happy face, even when it doesn't match what's inside. Now, West is taking the kids to soccer, and I'm going to sit by the water in the wake of whatever I'm feeling.

And I'm pretty sure what I'm feeling is jealousy. A white-hot, turn-your-stomach kind of jealousy.

I'm acutely aware of it being irrational, and that makes no difference.

It's not a feeling I'm familiar with. In past relationships, the prospect of other women never bothered me. And not because I trusted my partner not to step out. I just didn't think about it. Possibly because I didn't care enough to be bothered.

And I've never been jealous of my peers in my career. I love seeing other women top the charts or go home with awards.

So it's fucking bizarre that West is not my boyfriend and yet I feel sick about another woman "winning" him.

My chest feels tight and temper flashes as my teeth grind. My emotions are out of control. If my parents saw me right now, they'd tell me to pull it together. To stay in character.

They've always wanted me to fake it until I made it.

But for the first time in my life, I've let go of worrying about how my feelings make me appear to other people. For the first time in my life, I feel childish and irrational and… like I have something to say.

So I sit down on a log, and I write.

An impressed whistle draws my head up as I walk down the stairs in West's house.

"Hell. Yes. Girl." Rosie looks me up and down from the entryway with approval. "That dress was made for you."

I blink. "It actually was," I blurt out honestly.

Rosie laughs as she takes in the dress. It's one of my favorites. The white fabric has a dense print of tiny, repeating oranges, a small stem leading to a pop of green where the leaf fans out. Straps tie at the crest of each shoulder, and I've paired it with a simple pair of white sneakers and my new favorite red lipstick. Because it's so 'in' this season and all.

"Of course it was. Where's West?" Rosie snags a banana from the fruit bowl and peels it, hip propped against the counter. She's wearing a flowy pink romper with a pair of strappy, nude wedge sandals for our dreaded trip to the fair.

"Took the kids to soccer."

"Oh, right, back to Mia this week. Is he heading straight to the fundraiser after?"

I swallow and glance away. I've been avoiding West for the past day, afraid of saying something unhinged. Like demanding he not take part in some stupid archaic man auction. I could donate and spare him the embarrassment.

But I didn't tell him that. He's a grown-ass man. Besides, I have no claim on him. I've only known him a short time, and I don't want to be a stage-ten clinger.

And the truth is, the entire process of bidding on a person—well-meaning as it might be—is borderline triggering for me. In a world where I feel constantly whittled down to how I look or act being the basis for my value, the entire thing feels wrong.

So I've settled on being aloof, and that's been simple

enough because he's been busy with new horses arriving and others departing. Turns out Ford's office is a great place to hang out, even though I'm sure Rosie and I chattering away isn't great for productivity.

"Not sure."

She eyes me with an air of suspicion. "Is something going on with you two?"

"We're friends," I reply, swiping an orange from the same bowl.

"Right, but West doesn't bring women around his kids—it's a whole thing with him. And you're staying here. And Ollie and Emmy have been here all week."

I shrug, moving toward the door as though I can outrun this conversation. "Yeah, he told me about that rule, but we're just friends, so it's different. Plus, I enjoy hanging out with the kids. It'll be weird next week without them."

"I heard Ollie talks to you."

I smile, waving Rosie along and out the door. As I lock up, I think of our daily meetups down by the lake once he's finished camp for the day. Where he reads and I write. When I get stuck, I hand my scribbler over and he adds a line in without saying a single word to me. "He does. A bit."

When I turn to her, she's staring at me rather seriously. "I hope you understand how special that is."

I nod, matching the tone. She's in protective-auntie mode right now, and I respect that about her. She's fierce. I wish I had family members like this who would have gone to bat for me when I was forced to go on stage sick—or tolerate creepy, wandering hands to seal a deal.

My eyes lock with hers. "I promise you, I do."

"West too."

My brows jump in surprise. "What?"

"He might seem like a big, dumb, happy-go-lucky kind of guy, but it's all an act. He's cautious, short on trust, and a hell of a lot more sensitive than he seems. Please don't hurt him if you can help it."

I blow out a slow breath, as though I can feel the physical weight of what she just said to me. But words escape me. I settle on a nod, one she returns before spinning on her heel and marching away.

"But actually—"

Keys in her hand, she waves at me over her shoulder. "Don't bother denying it. He's had a hard-on for you for years, dumped his hookup the minute you got to town, and has you living under his roof. I know my brother."

When she puts it like that, I feel clueless.

And a little sick for avoiding him.

But even more sick over attending an event where I have to watch other women ogle him when I've done nothing but push him away.

"Where's Ford?"

Rosie smirks. "This isn't his scene, and I know better than to drag him here. Poor guy would be miserable, but he'd do it for me." She smiles wistfully, staring over at the sparkling water. "I suspect he's reading by the lake or swimming laps obsessively. He'll write Doris an anonymous check or something equally billionaire-hermit-like."

My chest constricts at the pure affection in her voice, so I pivot, asking someone a little less in love about where her roommate might be.

"Is Rhys in the auction?" I ask Tabitha, who is nursing a beer in a plastic cup beside me.

She scoffs. "No. He's away for work. *Again*. And I don't want to auction him off for a day. I want to auction him off forever. To a serial killer."

"Dark," Rosie snorts.

"What does he do for work?"

"I don't know. I try not to talk to him. Something in the entertainment industry."

Huh. That's the most information she's ever given about the guy, so I press further. "What are you guys to—"

I practically watch a gate clamp down over her eyes. "Oh, look"—she points with her beer in hand—"they're starting."

Rosie and I exchange worried glances, but I don't ask anything else. As much as my curiosity is killing me, I know how it feels to endure unwanted prying. And I may not know Tabby well, but she seems too fragile for that right now.

With our attention back on the stage, I focus on sipping my cider to cover for my nerves. *Local apples,* they told me, though I'm not sure I taste it at all. We've taken a walk around the grounds. There's a chili competition, various food and drink trucks set up, and sparse rides. It's not big by any means, but it is bustling. It smells like popcorn and cotton candy, and the sounds of squealing children bring a smile to my face.

Everyone is so busy enjoying themselves that they don't bother staring at me, and I feel almost normal, wandering a fair with a couple of friends. If I wasn't stressed about West and what we are or what we are not, I'd be enjoying myself.

Instead, I'm thinking about all the places he told me he was going to fuck me and wondering who is going to win a day with him and when they'll cash it in. In my effort to fly under the radar, I've decided to be a spectator only. The last thing I want is for West to be splashed on some headline because my green-eyed monster came out to play.

Doris takes the stage, set up in the open, grassy space next to her pub, and my stomach flips. She stomps across it like she's irritated by the mere presence of people here. She yanks the mic down, a loud rustling noise coming from the speakers. I clamp my lips together to cover the smile.

"Right, well. Thanks for coming. Again. Every year you all show up to help me fundraise for the food bank, and as irritated as I may seem by your presence, I appreciate it. As many of you know, I grew up relying on the food bank. And in small towns, sometimes those stores run dry. I'm fortunate to have ended up where I am, but your support today will keep cans of food in the storehouse and provide breakfast and lunch grab bags for the local schools. Our kids shouldn't be hungry at school, I'm sure we can all agree."

She swallows, looking out over the crowd. Her eyes shine with more emotion than I expected from the woman. And suddenly I feel it too, a stinging at the bridge of my nose as I blink rapidly to keep my tears at bay. I may have been through the wringer, but I never went hungry. At least not by necessity.

Doris clears her throat and swipes a hand under her nose. "And, well, after years of living in a world run by the patriarchy, I feel like men could use a little objectification."

That earns her a chorus of groans and barked laughter. "So bid carelessly and enjoy the show."

She literally drops the mic, its loud bang echoing through the outdoor space, and stomps back off the stage while I laugh silently behind my hand.

Beyond the stage, fair sounds rage on, and behind us is the stillness of the pub. Farther back is a parking lot and… well, forest. One I feel I'd like to run and hide in right now.

But as an older man takes the stage and everyone presses closer, I'm caught in the crowd, wondering why the hell I'm doing this to myself.

To prove I don't care. To keep my image in check.

The man picks up the mic and talks about the rules and what you get if you win and where to make your donation. And then the event starts.

Seeing it in practice isn't as dehumanizing as I imagined. The guys all look happy and amused, cracking jokes to crowd-wide laughter. And they are all ages and all body types. Each man raises a couple hundred dollars, and I beat myself up for putting a kinky Hollywood spin on what is a charming little fundraiser for a worthy cause.

When West comes out, the hooting and hollering gets louder. Each decibel makes my stomach drop lower, carving out a pit just behind my ribs.

I press both my hands there and Rosie's eyes follow the motion.

"You can bid, you know," she whispers.

I scrunch my face and shake my head. I'm an interloper here, and I don't need to be territorial over a man I barely know. He can go on a date with someone.

I'll be *fine*.

"We've got the town's favorite eternal bachelor up now," the announcer says. "Weston Belmont. He's here for a good time, not a long time, ladies."

West props his hands on his hips and drops his head, body shaking with laughter. He looks fucking edible. Brown leather lace-up boots, done up loosely so the tongue hangs down. Light wash jeans. Thick thighs. A plain white T-shirt. So simple, but on his tanned skin, it pops. He glows.

The older man nudges him. "He loves getting into trouble. You can often find him on the back of a horse. Buck as much as you want, he'll stick the ride."

"Good lord, man," West chuckles as he scrubs a hand over his stubble, cheeks flushing pink above the neatly trimmed line of his beard.

My shoulders heave under a labored sigh. His gaze finds mine across the sea of people and we're caught in each other's eyes for a moment. West's body tenses, and I'm pretty sure I can see all his muscles through his shirt.

My fingers burn with the memory of touching him freely.

I itch to do it now. March up there and show everyone how fucking blistering the heat between us is. They can take him on a date, but they'll never have *that*. I know because that kind of chemistry doesn't come around every day. Or even every lifetime.

"Let's start the bidding at one hundred dollars because I know y'all love to spend on this hometown boy."

Hands fly up.

My heart drops. I turn my head away to stare at the lake, pretending I'm bored even though I am anything but unaffected.

Two hundred.

Three hundred.

Four hundred.

Then a voice I recognize has my head whipping to my right. "Five hundred," Bree shouts with a smirk on her lips. The women around her pat her shoulder like she's done something impressive and not just forced a guy who ended things to spend time with her. Which he will because he's a man of his word.

I cringe.

Six hundred.

Seven hundred.

"Eight hundred," she calls, shiny red nails glinting in the sun as her hand shoots up.

I seethe.

Nine hundred.

"A thousand," she screams. Her hand does this swirl of a flourish, and the crowd goes *aww* as though there's something adorable about her and West.

Based on the tight set of his jaw, there's nothing

adorable about this. His baby blues latch on to me and I glance down quickly to avoid showing him the insecurity I'm feeling.

"Seems like we have a new record, folks. Do I see eleven hundred?"

The man peers out over the crowd, and I stare at him. I refuse to look at West, though I swear I can feel his gaze on me.

"Going once…"

I peek over at Bree. She's fucking preening—arms crossed, so sure of herself—and a part of me can't blame her. West is special.

But he's also mine.

In a world of things that have never been my own, it feels like he is. And I'm fucking sick of sharing. With my parents. With my record labels. With Bree.

"Going twice…"

"Ten thousand dollars!" I yell, and my hand shoots up before I can think better of it.

A wave of gasps breaks out around me.

From the corner of my eye, I see Bree's furious gaze slice my way. I can sense the blatant shock rolling off Rosie and Tabby beside me.

"Oh shit," Rosie murmurs right as the man on the stage shakes off his own shock.

"Well, now *that* is a new record, and I suspect one that might never be broken." The host chuckles, and the crowd follows suit.

When I finally let my gaze travel back to West, he's

staring at me. I can't place the expression. Anger? Hunger? Something intense. Something that makes it impossible for me to hold his gaze.

I find myself peering down at my perfectly white sneakers, wondering why I went and did that.

Because you needed to.

My inner voice isn't the least bit horrified. It's only my anxiety-riddled brain that beats me up.

The announcer counts down again, though I know I won't be outbid.

When I peek up at Rosie, her eyebrows waggle, and I roll my eyes.

"What? It's for a good cause" is all I say as I turn and walk away. Heading straight to the bar, where I'll be giving my credit card a good workout.

For a good cause.

CHAPTER 26

West

I jog down the steps that lead off the temporary stage. When Skylar walked away, I was stuck in place, waiting through the next auctions, cursing Doris under my breath. I wanted to chase after Skylar but refused to fuck up a fundraiser by making a scene.

But now I'm coming for her.

My feet hit the grass, and I make a beeline for the bar—but Bree steps into my path. She places a hand on my chest, and I flinch.

"West, I…" she says, but I'm not listening. I'm fixated on the fucking nerve of her.

Trying to win a date when I made my feelings clear. Touching me like she has the right. The only hands I want on me are Skylar's.

"Bree. We've covered this," I bite out, trying to keep it cordial but also relaying my agitation with her. "Respectfully… Back. Off."

She rears back like I've slapped her, and I don't miss the looks her friends exchange behind her.

But I don't care. I'm polite, and I'm kind. And I have been nothing but honest and upfront with her.

Right now, I just want to find Skylar, so I shove past, not having anything else to say. With long strides, I push through the crowd. I feel their eyes on me and hear the announcer's voice ringing through the speakers.

When I get past the throngs of people, I head for the bar, knowing Skylar has to pay inside. I charge through the doors, heart beating fast when I don't see her anywhere. My eyes land on Doris, standing at her till and counting cash with a pleased smirk on her face.

"Where is she?"

"Mind your manners, caveman."

"Doris, I like your snark, but not today."

Her eyes narrow on me. "The feeling is mutual." She looks me over like she finds me lacking. "I like that girl. See a lot of myself in her, ready to run at any moment."

I nip back a joke about hoping there isn't too much Doris in Skylar.

"She needs a home, not more bullshit. Don't be the reason she runs."

My throat constricts at the mention of her running. I've always known she wouldn't stay here, but it still hits me like a wrecking ball.

"Doris, please tell me where she is."

"I knew you'd find your manners," she mutters, going back to counting the bills in her hands. "She left out the side door toward the woods. You should go rescue her."

My teeth grind as I toss her a nod before blazing out the side door after Skylar. I look right at the parking lot, not sure why she'd go there. I look left, beyond the lilac tree and toward the lake. She loves being by the lake, but I can see the tops of a few heads down there, and I suspect she'd go somewhere to be alone right now. Whatever she's feeling, she wouldn't want an audience. And when she's overwhelmed, I know she likes to be alone.

So I look ahead into the trees and let my feet carry me toward them. The scent of earth and pine swirls up around me as my boots crunch on dry needles and twigs. I don't know how long I search for her. Through the trees, back up along the shoreline. I search long enough that my brain has a grand ol' time coming up with all the terrible things that could have happened to Skylar.

A bear.

A cougar.

A stalker.

A serial killer.

My heart pounds so hard, I hear it in my ears—it feels like it's rattling against my shirt. I take my phone out to call her and realize I'm the asshole who threw hers into the lake. Seemed good for her mental health. Hadn't really considered mine.

When I wind up back at the parking lot, I turn in a circle and comb my fingers through my hair, tugging at the ends. "Fuck," I grit out.

WILD EYES

This reminds me of the time Emmy wandered away in the grocery store and we kept missing each other between aisles. Except this area is massive and people are milling about everywhere. The whirring noise of rides and the happy squeals of children drift through the air. I call her name a few times but feel cautious about causing a scene.

I told her not to worry about the press or the headlines, but so help me, if I see another one making her out to be some sort of idiot, I'm going to hop on a plane to Los Angeles and let fists fly.

It wouldn't be the first time.

"Fuck." My eyes scan again and again as I try to think of where Skylar would go. Where would she run?

Home.

I almost shake the idea away, somehow doubting she'd feel much of an attachment to my place. But it's all I can come up with, so that's where I head.

The feeling of uneasiness doesn't recede at all as I jump into my truck, and it only worsens as I head down the back-road toward my house. It's a short drive, but it feels impossibly long. If she's not there, I don't know what I'll do.

Start tearing this entire town apart, probably.

I pass the sign with Emmy's unicorn taped below. I speed onto the property, knowing that if I caught anyone driving like this onto my land, I'd lose my shit on them.

Agitation lines every limb as I make the final turn around the side of the house.

And she's there.

Sitting on the old tree swing. *Swinging.*

There's something childlike about the way she looks right now. Summer dress draped over extended legs, fingers gripping the worn ropes, face tipped up to the sun, with wisps of hair trailing behind her.

Ignoring me. Though she'd have to be deaf not to have heard me come roaring in here.

I yank the door open and drop from my truck, boots heavy on the gravel.

She still doesn't give me her attention.

I'm keeping my cool, but my voice shakes when I call across the space to her. "You've been ignoring me for twenty-four hours. Then you drop ten grand on me. And now you're going to continue to ignore me?"

"I don't want my date right now." She swings again.

"Skylar, I have been searching high and low for you for the past thirty minutes, and so help me, if you don't turn around and address me—"

She leaps from the swing and spins on me, eyes blazing as her voice bounces off the tall pines surrounding us. "What? If I don't pay attention to you, you're gonna what?"

I swallow, happy to take her anger over her indifference.

"I've had it up to here"—her hand slices through the air above her head as she shouts—"with people demanding my attention. And I'm not ignoring you. I went for a fucking walk."

Good god, she walked back?

"I'm trying to keep it together so I don't make a total fool of myself. Again," she adds quietly.

The heat from the front grill of my truck pushes against

my back, making me want to move in closer, but I don't. I'm too concerned about scaring her off. Startling her. Doris's words about her looking ready to run echo through my head.

"Not once have you made a fool of yourself."

Her scoff floats across the warm summer air between us. "Oh, let's see. I freeze up on camera. I try to pet wild bears—"

"That's an exaggeration, and you know it."

She takes assertive steps in my direction, staring me down as she continues to list all her perceived failings. "I take a soccer ball to the face. I kiss a guy who tells me he only wants to be friends. I kiss that guy again and then *I* tell him we're better off as friends. And then I…I…I throw a jealous fit and buy him at some small-town man auction. And now I'm sitting here trying to train my brain into thinking I did that because it was for a good cause."

A foot of grass separates us now. She's close enough now that I can smell her. Her skin. Her lotion. Coconuts and pineapple. Perfectly applied makeup and those red fucking lips.

I bite my tongue, inclining my head to take her in as she rakes her hands through her hair and averts her eyes. Like she hates what she just admitted.

She doesn't even realize how she's blossomed since that first night. "First of all," I bite out, clenching my fists to keep from grabbing her, "you should be fucking proud of yourself. You are strong and you are capable, and you've done nothing but prove that to yourself and everyone around you for the past several weeks."

She starts, eyes widening as her hands fall limp at her sides.

"Second of all, I'm buying you a phone because not knowing where you were made me fucking *sick*."

A flush streaks up her cheeks, and I see the apology in her eyes.

"And third of all, the only foolish thing you've done is continue to refer to us as *friends*." I spit the word. "That word makes me want to break something."

"Well, great. Thank you for that—"

Her eyes roll, and I snap.

I step up to her and grip her chin, the defiance in her eyes a match for my own. "Don't you fucking get it, Skylar? How much clearer can I be? I moved you into my house. I've included you in my family. I cleared any other complication without a second thought. I spend almost every waking moment with you. I fist my cock every night thinking about you. You see any other *friends* of mine hanging around?"

I turn, peering around dramatically. "'Cause I sure as shit don't."

"That's not funny." I feel her rough swallow against my palm, and when she draws away, I slide my hand to the back of her neck. Forcing her to stay, to see me. To hear me.

"Good, because I wasn't fucking joking."

My right hand snakes around her, and I lift, turning and dropping her on the hood of my truck. I step between her knees, dress draping between them, and slide my hands beneath the fabric. "I'm done pretending that being your friend is enough." I grip her thighs. "Now spread your legs."

"West—" My name ends on a gasp as my palms move higher, but she does as she's told, and I explore until I reach the lace underwear wedged against her hips.

"I want these off." My fingers hook and my arms jerk back, tugging the flimsy fabric down her shaking thighs. Soon, nude lace stretches between her spread knees and my cock jumps at the sight. "They're in my way." I yank again and the delicate fabric rips.

"Those were expensive," she hisses, nails digging into my shoulder, temper flaring as I toss the expensive scraps onto the dirt and rocks at my feet.

I pull her to the edge of the hood and press my palm to her sternum, pushing her back so she lands on her elbows.

Not a single thread of resistance in her body, mad as she might be.

"Then stop wasting your money on them, fancy face. They only get in my way."

She lets out a low, frustrated growl, but she stays splayed out before me. I reach up and release the end of each shoulder tie from her dress. Soft fabric tumbles off her shoulders. And one tug at the front leaves her breasts exposed to the fresh air and bright sun.

Fucking perfect.

Her lips pop open, and gooseflesh covers her skin as my eyes rake over her heaving chest.

"That fucking mouth, Skylar. The things I want to do to it."

"Then do them." The pink tip of her tongue darts out over her bottom lip, and I groan, my jeans becoming downright painful. "You're the only one who's never treated me like porcelain. Don't start now. Do. Them."

I palm her breasts, watching raptly as her lashes flutter shut and her back arches up into my touch. My gaze follows the path of my hands as they move lower. Exploring every curve.

Hips.

Thighs.

Down to her knees, where I draw a slow circle with the tip of my index finger. She squirms, hips pressing toward me. And I get off on it.

"What are you asking me for, Skylar?"

I peek up at her—damp lips, glazed eyes, pretty fucking tits. A tendon in her jaw flexes, and I can tell she's still agitated.

Hot and agitated.

"I want…"

My hands glide back up. "What do you want, baby? Let me hear it."

"I want you to fuck me."

The words come out soft and low, and I smirk at her. "I know you do. I can tell. Practically begging for it."

She finds her voice and corrects me. "No, I am demanding you fuck me."

My head tilts as I hold her gaze and press her thighs farther open, her dress nothing more than bunched fabric around her waist. One flick of my eyes has me seeing everything I didn't that night in the dark.

"You're fucking soaked, Sky. Is this all for me?"

She huffs out a breath and glances away.

I pinch her clit, and it draws a gasp and glare.

"Eyes on me when I'm touching you."

"Then get to touching me, West. You're doing an awful lot of staring—"

I bite down on my bottom lip as my thumb strums over her clit. Once. Twice. Three times. That movement shuts her up, has her squirming and arching toward me. "Don't rush me," I mutter, watching my index finger disappear inside her as she clamps down on me. "I'm enjoying the view."

"Fuck, West."

I add a second finger on the next stroke in and twist, gliding into her so easily. She whimpers as I fill her, slow and steady.

"Atta girl. Make a mess on my hand. I fucking love it," I grit out, draping one of her knees over my shoulder as I continue working her cunt. "How many times should I make you come today? Tell me."

Her eyes snap to mine, body rocking gently against the hood of the truck. "Sometimes I'm slow. Like, it can take a while. So don't worry if I don't—"

"Oh, fuck yeah." I grin, adding my thumb to her clit. "I love a challenge."

Then I drop my head between her legs and get to work on orgasm number one.

CHAPTER 27

Skylar

WEST PUTS HIS MOUTH ON ME, AND I MELT INTO NOTHING. My hands fly into his hair, my legs wrap around his shoulders.

My mind goes blank, and my bones disintegrate in my body.

All at once, he's everywhere and everything, and I am just eager moans and desperate pants and lost in his touch.

"Oh my god…" I shimmy closer and pull him tighter, trying to smother him without remorse.

Two fingers fuck my pussy. Harsh and hard.

But his tongue. His fucking mouth. Firm yet soft. Hungry yet steady.

"West. West," I pant his name.

I chant his name like it's a hymn, and I'm worshipping at his altar.

He is mind-bending.

Has been since day one. But this… "This is unlike anything I've ever—"

"That's because you've been too busy fucking clueless pretty boys, fancy face," he mutters, nipping firmly at my inner thigh.

I try not to cringe over the fact that I swapped from an internal monologue to an external one. I cover by pulling his head back to my core, spreading my legs, and dropping my knees as wide as they can go on the truck's warm hood.

"Look at you." He licks his lips, eyes dragging over my body so languidly that I swear my skin burns in their path. "Fucking delicious."

I almost combust on the spot.

It's public and primal and thrilling. Us, right here, right now, where anyone could see. The petty, little bitch inside me wishes Bree would pull up now and see firsthand the way West glows for me. The way he couldn't even wait to get inside before devouring me.

The flash of jealousy makes me grind on West's hand, his thumb darting over my clit in response. "More."

His brow quirks before he stares down between my legs. The way he looks at me, like he's memorizing everything, makes me want to hide and beg for more, all at once. "Of the best pussy I've ever tasted?" Another swipe to my clit. "What a fucking treat, Skylar. Might just keep you like this all week."

"On your truck?" I joke.

"No, on your back with your legs spread for me."

"Fuck," I hiss.

He drops his head, and I feel his rough chuckle against my wetness. "And screaming my name while you come."

With that, his mouth suctions onto my clit, and his fingers curl inside my body. What usually takes a fair amount of coaxing is bearing down on me in a hot, bright flash. The telltale full-body flush, the tingling pressure coiling behind my hip bones. Followed by the blistering shock of my body breaking apart, cracking and shattering as I scream his name.

Every muscle. Every nerve ending. Every brittle wall built around my heart.

Weston obliterates them all with a world-class orgasm.

His touches soften. His lips kiss my inner thighs. His fingers spread my wetness all over my pussy like he's an artist putting the finishing touches on his favorite piece.

My mind races, my body still recovering, as he pulls me down off the truck and kisses me. I taste myself on his lips, on his tongue, when he presses it into my mouth. His hand cups the back of my head as he kisses me.

Soft, but not too soft.

I don't want soft from him right now.

And he must know it because his fingers curl into a fist, gripping my hair and tilting my head back. "How many are we at? I wanna hear you say it."

I smirk. "Only one."

"Only? You think I'm done here?" He grins, playful and predatory. "Turn around. Hands flat on the hood."

"Thought you wanted to do things to my mouth, big talker." I follow his instructions, palms sliding over the sparkling silver paint as his fingers work at my dress. Tugging it up to expose my bare ass as I take in the remaining wetness in front of me. One booted foot lands between my sneakers, kicking my feet apart as he chuckles.

My body complies without hesitation, and I follow his lead almost desperately.

"If you need something to do with your mouth, you can use it to clean up the mess you left on my truck while I fuck you."

I flush and bite down on my lip to cover the immediate moan that lurches from my throat.

The soft breeze tickles my bare skin as anticipation zings through me. No one has ever made me feel like this—filthy and powerful. It's a fucking high.

I'll never get over it.

The rip of a condom wrapper crinkles behind me, and a shiver races down my spine. It's like a countdown, and in mere seconds, I know he'll be—

My forehead drops to the hood as he runs the thick, blunt head of his cock through my dripping slit. Looking down and back, all I can see is West's big, rough hand—tattoos and all—gripping my hip and his booted feet with fallen jeans positioned between mine.

I'm at his mercy and it's a thrill.

"Hard or soft?"

I pant and lick my lips. Nervous. Hungry. Eager. It's hard to say. With him, I want it all.

"Hard—" I barely get the words out before he plunges into me on a heavy groan.

"Fuuuck," he rasps as my body struggles to adjust to his size. His width fills me so completely.

We pause, both panting. Both feeling each other. His thumb rubs circles on my lower back. Punishing and soothing.

Always soothing. Always anticipating my needs and looking out for me.

All without smothering me. Unfamiliar feelings squirm and writhe in my chest. Ones that make me feel warm and a little ill at the same time.

Then he draws back out. My fingers curl against the hood of the truck, and one of his hands palms the cheek of my ass. I know he's watching me. Watching us. I can always feel his eyes on me—right now is no different.

I whimper, forehead rolling again on the warm metal. A fire burns in my body. I want to tell him how good he feels, but only a desperate moan spills from my lips as he shoves his cock back into my aching pussy.

"I know, baby, I know," he murmurs as he reaches up to stroke my hair while he pumps in and out slowly. He's gentle at first, but soon he gives my locks a firm tug, turning my head to him so our eyes meet. "Who's gonna play with your clit? You or me?"

God. Just the mere question makes me flush. I'm by no means virginal, but the things that come out of this man's mouth are—

"Too slow, Skylar." His hand moves down behind my knee, and he lifts my leg. With my foot propped on the front bumper, his arm slides down the inner length of my thigh and his fingers find my clit as he drives into me.

I can see the question in his eyes. Asking if this is okay, if this feels good. Since day one, we've connected on a plane beyond words. It's all always been in his eyes.

"West…*yes*."

His jaw pops and a sheen of sweat dots his forehead, but he never looks away.

He fucks me like I'm his. His dream. His obsession.

He fucks me like he's my biggest fan, and I finally understand what he meant.

And it has nothing to do with fame or music.

The thrusts come harder, and my hands go slick against the silver paint as I struggle to keep my bearings.

"You take it so well, Sky." His finger moves in steady, firm circles and his cock presses so deep inside me, I know I'll be feeling it for days. "Eyes on me. Pretty, little pussy leaking down your thigh. Fucking love it, don't you?"

Fuck. My teeth bear down on my bottom lip as I give him an eager nod. "Yes. Yes." I gasp out the words as he fucks me harder, my body shaking with the force. "I fucking love it."

He smirks at me.

He smirks at me while he's fucking me. Confident and sure and pleased. It sets me off, and the friction of him against my walls becomes nothing more than sensuous torture. The heavy wall of his body at my back, deeply protective. And the strum of his fingers on my clit, my undoing.

"West, I'm gonna… *Fuck*, West."

My body spasms as my orgasm hits me like a train. Dropping my body to the truck is the only thing that keeps me from melting to the ground. My breasts ache against the hood, and even that warm pressure feels amazing. My back seizes, hips pushing back, as though my body wants to feel him deeper. I'm quite sure my nails leave marks in the paint. My vision goes white and hazy before my lashes fall down.

His fingers strum again on my oversensitive clit and my whole body shakes.

"Fucking beautiful" filters in as he draws his hand away, hiking my leg up higher and spreading me where I'm collapsed to give himself a better angle.

And I don't resist. I soak up the feel of his body inside of mine. The closeness. The affection in every touch, every thrust—no matter how rough.

His thighs slap against my bare ass as he takes me, fast and frantic and unforgiving. It's delicious in every way. His hands. The noises he makes.

I might may be the one prone and bent over, but I know he's the one on his knees for me. Bringing him to this point—making him feel this pleasure—it's rewarding in a way I've never known.

"Sky, fuck. You should see how good we look together."

I clench and moan as his thrusts turn slow but demanding. Primal. He stiffens around me, and his fingers grip my hips hard enough to leave bruises as he bottoms out and erupts.

His cock pulses inside me in the same rhythm as his fingers against my skin. I find myself wishing there was no barrier between us. That I could feel *him*. His cum dripping down my leg along with my own. I've never had that, but I want it with him.

It hits me all at once that I inexplicably want so much with him.

A shiver races down my spine as his hard, warm body collapses over mine under the blue sky. A shield—a comfort blanket—just like the first day we met.

Our breathing comes out ragged, and we say nothing as we both catch our breath. His hand massages the thigh of the leg he's now returned to vertical, like he knows I'll be sore from that position.

West nuzzles his nose against my sweat-slicked neck, and his mouth paints a line of soft kisses down my spine. His stubble rasps and gooseflesh dots my body even in the wake of the most mind-blowing sex I've ever had.

"How many, Skylar?"

"Two," I breathe, amusement weaving its way into my tone. "I've never had two in a row."

"You're fucking perfect, you know that?" The words dance out across my damp skin and make me smile. "Best sex of my life."

"I just laid here. You did all the work."

His deep, comforting laugh rumbles against my back. "It's okay. I'll make you get on top for number three. I wanna suck on those perfect tits while you ride my cock."

Much to my surprise, my body perks up at the idea. "Okay," I exclaim with an excessive amount of enthusiasm.

"Now who is who's biggest fan?" He nips at my earlobe, and I let loose a giddy giggle before blushing. I internally admonish myself for being down this bad already.

Air rushes between us as he draws away, and when he slides out of me, I feel empty. Like I want him back.

I turn to watch him roll the condom from his length. He catches me staring, and with a smug look, he takes the rubber and tosses it on top of my ripped panties.

His cum oozes onto the fabric and my jaw drops. "Rude."

All I get back from him is an amused laugh as he buckles his jeans back up. "Then why are you glaring at your underwear like you're jealous of them?"

I shrug and bite down on the smile that still breaks through. "Maybe I am."

"Fuck, Sky." His eyes fall to my still-exposed breasts. "You shouldn't put ideas like that in my head."

I reach for the ties on my dress, attempting—and failing—to retie them with post-orgasm shaky hands.

"Don't bother," he grumbles, batting my hand away gently. "I'm gonna come on those next."

Then West hefts me into his arms. He lifts me with remarkable ease, and I squeal when I leave the ground. His boots eat up the ground as he carries me to the front door like an eager caveman. And I tell him as much. I'm laughing when he crosses the threshold into his house.

He stops only to kiss me. Soundly. Mouth hard on mine. Like we're sealing whatever this is with a promise.

And I've never felt more cherished.

CHAPTER 28

West

"How many, Skylar?" I huff against her ear, feeling all at once more accomplished and more exhausted than I ever have.

She mumbles something from beneath where her arm is slung over her face. But we both know that was number five.

She's naked and splayed across my kitchen counter like a fucking smorgasbord. And I've enjoyed every inch.

"Please feed me. I might die if you make me come again," she pants, chest heaving. There are hickeys all over her tits, and her legs are trembling where they're propped against the stone. Her pussy is wet and puffy, and if she didn't look so fucking good like this, I'd feel bad.

We've put each other through our paces, and there's not a single regret in sight.

"Feed you this?" I lift my cock—hardened from taking

in how thoroughly fucked she looks right now—and run it through her tender center.

She laughs at first, but gasps when she feels my bare flesh against hers.

"God, it would feel so good to fuck you bare. Blow in this tight, little cunt and watch it drip out."

Her body shakes with a chuckle as I swipe through once more, groaning and torturing myself. "You're all talk, Weston Belmont."

"Okay, little miss *I'm slow to finish* who's been coming on my cock for the past couple of hours."

"You should do it."

I freeze. "Pardon me?"

She peeks at me from between her fingers now. "I'd like that, I think. Bare. I've never not used a condom. I need to get back on the pill."

"Fuck, Sky." I look down at us, already touching. I could shove myself in so easily. "Don't tempt me."

She spreads her legs and wraps them around my lower back with a knowing grin on her face.

"Easy, crazy fan." I slip two fingers into her and make her gasp in shock. "I'm being safe with you. I'm always careful, but let me see the doc this week. You get your pills, then we'll talk."

Her legs go limp, and she sighs. She knows I'm right, even though she huffs out, "Buzzkill."

My fingers pull out and I press a quick kiss to her clit, feeling her knees snap up on either side of my head.

"Okay, one more," she whines, holding me in place.

"Not a chance." My hands land on her knees, prying her viselike grip off my head before reaching for my boxers. "You told me you'd die if I made you come again." Dressed enough, I round the island and head toward the fridge. "And I'd hate for you to die on an empty stomach."

Her laughter filters toward me. "Death by dick. What a way to go."

I'm smiling as I reach for the butter and a block of ched-dar. "Grilled cheese?"

"Hell yes," she responds, hopping off the counter. She leaves the kitchen as I work on slicing the cheese and build-ing the sandwich, and when she comes back, she's wearing my shirt.

My shirt. Her face. Whatever.

She's also wearing a teasing smile on her lips as she saun-ters toward me, hair mussed, eyes soft. She glides across the floor, and there's something familiar about it.

Bare feet and an oversized shirt. Sun streaming through the windows in the middle of the afternoon. Just the two of us. Her arms wrap around me from behind and she rests her head against my back.

We're in a hazy, happy bubble, and I never want to leave.

She doesn't let me go until I start to fry the sandwiches, and I'd be a fucking liar if I said I didn't want her back here, clinging to me.

Instead, she's propped a shoulder against the fridge while watching me make the most basic meal in the world like I'm a fucking Michelin-starred chef.

"Don't look so impressed. This isn't foie gras, Sky."

She smiles. "It's better. I don't think anyone has ever made me a grilled cheese sandwich."

My eyes dart to her. She's fixated on the pan. My fall-back feast that I make for the kids in a pinch—a few slices of cucumber on the side and we call it a square meal.

"Even as a kid?"

She shrugs. "We had a chef. My mom was always trying out different diets. None of which included butter and melted cheese. I just ate what they ate."

"That's a crime. You can make grilled cheese in so many fun ways. Different cheeses. Pickles. Onions. Meat. The options are endless."

"Perfect. You can just fuck me and feed me grilled cheese for the rest of the weekend."

It's my turn to grin now. "Not gonna lie, fancy face. That sounds damn good to me."

We end up sitting on the kitchen floor facing each other, too bone-tired to even make it to the table—my back against the oven, hers against the island, our feet tangled in the space that separates us as we eat our grilled cheese with a side of cucumber slices.

Somehow, this is better. Cozier. The counters provide walls around us, and I feel like I'm in a private little hideaway with her.

"Tell me about the tattoos." She gestures to my hand. "You don't have any others—I can now confirm," she adds with a saucy wink.

I turn my hand over as I shake my head at her and stare at the spaces between each knuckle marked with a symbol.

"A cow skull on the thumb because the time I took working on a cattle ranch after high school set me straight. Hard to get into trouble when you're so tired, you can barely drag your ass to bed at night. Learned a lot, but it was like bootcamp." I smile at the memory. "A pine tree on the pointer finger because Ollie's middle name is Forest. A fleur-de-lis on the middle finger because Lily is Emmy's middle name and also because that finger just suits her whole vibe."

We both laugh and a familiar pang zips through my chest when I realize I won't see them until next week. I glance back down now, tracing the bare ring finger. "Left this one blank, for obvious reasons." I peek at Skylar, who nods and chews thoughtfully. "And a sun on the pinky, because, well, I guess I'm an optimist. There's always a bright side."

She looks me dead in the eye when she says, "I love that about you."

I swallow.

"It's infectious. You make me feel like everything will be okay."

"It will be."

Her expression turns serious. "Even us?"

Us. Neither of us knows what this is, but we know it's not a connection you walk away from. It's… With her, it's different.

"Especially us."

"How can you know that?"

I shrug. "I don't know anything, but I believe it. And for me, that's enough."

She smiles but it wobbles. Silence settles in for a moment, but she doesn't look away.

"Hey, Sky?"

"Yeah?"

"You good if I treat you like porcelain, just for a little bit?"

She blinks, then stares down at the plate resting on her legs, our feet where they lean together. "Yeah, I'd like that."

I put our plates on the counter and reach down to give her my hand. She lets me lead her through the house, light softening as the day drifts toward evening. When we hit the glass encasement of the en suite shower, I turn, picking up a piece of her hair. One of the strands that trends a bit blonder, toward the front.

Gold skin, bronze hair—everything about her shimmers. I want to remember this. This day. This moment. This spot of brightness.

I pull her to me and press a kiss to her forehead as I reach into the shower and twist the knob, setting the spray to the right temperature before going back to Skylar. Her eyes are downcast, and she seems anxious.

My palm glides over the back of her head. "You good?"

She laughs. "Is it weird that this feels more intimate than fucking?"

"No," I reply simply, lifting the oversized shirt over her head and letting it fall to the floor. She looks at me now, gaze searching as I step out of my boxers. "Let's go. In the shower."

Her eyes brighten. "More sex?"

My jaw drops. "You're a fiend. You have an…a-dick-tion."

I wink, and she bursts out laughing as she turns away from me.

"That is the daddest dad joke of all dad jokes."

In turn, I reach forward and land a playful slap on her ass. "Get your fine ass in there, fancy face."

When the warm spray hits, I'd be lying if I said I didn't think about more sex, but I contain myself because something tells me that's not what she needs.

With the door shut behind us, steam fills the space, and I draw her close. We let the warm water pour over us, breathing each other in for a few beats.

Then I reach for the soap and wash her. Her arms. Her breasts. *Fuuuck. Her breasts.* I force my hands down to her stomach.

"What are you doing?" Her brows furrow.

"Washing you."

Her head tilts.

"Haven't you ever showered with someone before?"

"Yeah, but not where we wash each other." A vision of her doing this with someone else in this moment flashes behind my eyes. "Usually, it's just straight se—"

"You know what?" I cut her off. "Forget I asked. I don't want to hear about that."

I reach behind her and soap her back. Her ass.

"Are you jealous, Weston?" She has a playful gleam in her eye.

I chuckle at that. "If I had ten grand to spend on fucking your exes over, I would."

"They wouldn't bid."

She says it so matter-of-factly. I hate it. I hate that for her.

"I would bid on you every time," I say, crouching down and pressing a kiss to her stomach before soaping her legs. Her ankles. I swipe a hand over her pussy, and she hisses.

"Sore?" I ask, pushing up to standing.

"Well, yeah. I've been taking your massive pole for the last couple of hours."

"Massive pole," I muse, soaping myself. "That has a very lyrical ring to it. You should put it in a song."

"Yeah, yeah. Take your victory lap."

"I'm sorry. Would you prefer I pull out an acoustic guitar and serenade you? I could cry a little at the beauty of what we shared on the hood of my truck?"

She's full-on laughing now. "I've actually had both those things happen to me."

I reach for the shampoo, shaking my head with a grin on my face as it pours out of the bottle. The scent of rosemary and mint fills the shower. "Those assholes should have been washing your hair and treating you like a princess, not crying with their instruments." With my empty hand, I twirl my finger in a spinning motion. "Now turn."

She blinks a few times, like she can't process this pampering. "You know, I was jealous of that horse the first day I saw you washing her."

I bark out a laugh at that. *This woman.* "Well, today is your lucky day, then. You get the full training package."

I see the tail end of a smile as she turns in place. But she lets me wash her hair. Condition it too. We stay in the shower, quiet and contemplative, until the warm water runs cool. And when we step out, I slather her in lotion, walk her to my king-size bed, and watch her eyes drift shut in a matter of minutes.

I watch her sleep for I don't know how long. I think, and I think, and I overthink. I sneak out only to do the night check, and then I come back to her. Naked. In my bed. It seems surreal. It seems too good to be true. So I decide to soak it up for as long as I've got it.

My hands reach for her under the covers, and hers reach back for me. We spend the night naked and tangled up in each other.

Clinging to one another.

And I don't know how it happened so quickly, so out of the blue, but Skylar feels integral to me. It's inexplicable—cellular.

All I know is that she and I were meant to meet on that road.

CHAPTER 29

Skylar

BREAKING NEWS: Skylar Stone declares that Weston
Belmont has a "massive pole."

"CAN YOU GRAB THAT?" WEST CALLS TO ME FROM THE
kitchen as I make my way down the stairs, trying for what
feels like the hundredth time to get my hair into a passable
ponytail. Between the showers and the bed and all the fucking, it feels like a rat's nest.

"On it." I grin as I hit the main floor and take him in.
He's shirtless in the kitchen, making what he referred to as
to as "breakfast grilled cheese." He brought me coffee in bed,
though it's no longer hot since bringing me coffee turned
into bringing me another orgasm.

With my lukewarm coffee in hand and West's shirt of me over a pair of sleep shorts, I answer the front door.

And come face-to-face with an older woman I don't know, but who is staring at me like she recognizes me just fine.

"Oh, look at you." She claps her hands together and smiles. "You even have the same shirt as West. How lovely."

Leaning against the car behind her, a lean man with hair thinning at his crown shakes his head and stares up at the sky. He has a no-nonsense, tough-love vibe about him. "They don't have the same shirt, Greta. That *is* the same shirt."

"We shouldn't be presumptuous, Andy. It's a nice shirt. Lots of people probably have it."

"Ask me how I know that's the same shirt," he grumbles, while Greta blinks back at me, wearing an apologetic smile.

And me?

I want to dig my own grave right at my feet, crawl in, and cover myself with dirt. Because I'm positive these are West's parents.

My lips pop open, then close. I don't know how many times I try—and fail—to find any words to say to these people.

Andy is right—it's pretty obvious what they've walked in on.

I settle on "Hi, I'm Skylar." I extend a hand, and the woman takes it.

Her enthusiasm is genuine when she responds with "I'm West's mom, Greta. It's such a pleasure to meet you." Then she drops her voice to a stage whisper. "That's his dad, Andy.

I'm sorry about him." She hikes a thumb over her shoulder. "All bark, no bite. He's grumpy because I'm keeping us from our pickleball time slot." She shifts to peek around me. "Is West home?"

"Oh, yup." I nod rapidly, eager for him to come bail me out. "West," I call into the house.

Within moments, he saunters to the front door.

And tosses an arm right over my shoulder.

All casual.

Like we do this all the time.

"Hey, Ma." He leans forward and presses a kiss to her cheek. "How ya doin'? I see you guys met Skylar."

"We did, and we're good." She grins at him, reaching out to rub a hand over his arm. "Just wanted to check in on you."

"She's snoopin'," Andy calls out, scowling at his wife.

"I am not." She spins on him. "People were talking after the fair yesterday, and I wanted to make sure he was okay."

"Woman, we pulled up to underwear and a condom on the driveway. We both knew he was just fine. Now let's go. I didn't get you that fake ID for nothing."

I go rigid and wonder if it's possible to bury myself alive twice.

West?

West laughs. "You're both snoopin'. Call before you stop by next time. I have a phone. And what's this about a fake ID? I thought that was my move."

"Still have three of them in a box at home, ya fuckin' shit disturber," his dad mutters.

"Your dad got me a fake ID."

West blinks, and I'm grateful we've all just brushed over the panties and condom. "Why?"

"Because the only good pickleball time slots at the rec center are for fifty-five plus. And I'm only fifty-three, which means we can't go together, so he paid a tourist who looked similar to me for hers."

"I don't enjoy spending time with other people, and you keep telling me I need to exercise," Andy grumbles. Although he seems irritated, there's something incredibly sweet about the sentiment.

My hand finds its way up over my mouth to cover my amusement. After all, my ripped underwear are mere feet away—I have nothing to be smug about.

West looks between them in total shock. "But everyone knows who you are."

"It was enough to shut them up." Andy holds his hand out to his wife from where he stands on the gravel driveway. "Can we go now? We're gonna be late."

She smiles at him before turning back to wink at us. "Nice to meet you, Skylar. You two come up to the house for dinner sometime. We'd like that."

"I would too," I add softly, feeling West's fingertips strum soothingly on my shoulder.

She pivots to leave, jogging away down the front steps, and West straightens beside me. "Wait, why'd you really come over?"

She's already getting into the car while Andy holds the door for her, but she glances up and calls back, "Oh, I really was just snooping. And, Weston, clean the driveway."

She drops into her seat and Andy closes her door with another shake of his head. When they pull away, his mom waves with excitement while his dad continues shaking his head.

We watch them disappear down the road, standing side by side in stunned silence.

"Well, that was something," West says. "One day, we'll look back on this and laugh about the day you met my parents."

An awkward giggle erupts from me. Partly because that was one of the most embarrassing experiences of my life. And partly because when West talks about us—the future—like it's such a sure thing, it makes me downright giddy.

"Why did you have three fake IDs?" I blurt, my mind tripping up on that tidbit.

West presses a rough kiss to my temple and grins. "Kept getting a new one because Dad kept taking them away. He only got three. I had more."

"You weren't kidding about being a handful."

He laughs, all warm and deep. The vibration rolls through my body, and I press closer just to be near him. I want to soak him in as much as I can. To bask in this rosy, happy bubble.

"My mom always said she had to hug me a little longer just in case it was the last one. I used to laugh about that, play it off like she was being ridiculous. Now? As a parent?" He scrubs a hand over his beard and shakes his head but never answers his question. I can guess what he's thinking.

Just in case it's the last one.

The sentiment of his mom's saying hits me hard, and I hug him tighter, nuzzling into his side.

He kisses my hair and murmurs, "How about we eat and go get you a phone, so I don't tear this town apart the next time I can't find you?"

All I can muster is a nod because the thought of being separated from West hits sharp and fast and leaves me at a loss for words.

By Wednesday, I've given up pretending that I don't gawk at West while he sits on the back of a horse. Sure, my notepad is in my lap, but I enjoy the stillness, the simplicity of just sitting and watching him. The sun on my skin, the birds overhead.

Shit, I've even come to enjoy the smell of the barn.

Most days I lose count of how many horses he rides. It seems like it varies each time I watch. But he infrequently leaves the arena. A groom or a farmhand brings him his next horse and even I can tell that they leave the ring better than they came in.

More calm.

More accepting.

More sure of themselves.

And I can relate. I've spent the last four nights in West's bed—his arms around me, his lips on my skin—and I feel all of those things too.

"This one's spicy," the man I've come to know as Conor

calls as he leads out a horse I don't recognize. She trots side-ways, showing the whites of her eyes. "She's been pissed since the moment she arrived this morning."

West nods while he walks the bay gelding that he just hopped off to the fence and loops the reins over the post. His broad palm swipes over the horse's face, and its eyes flutter shut when he says, "Good man," to it.

He tosses me a wink as I lean back on the bleachers. During this time of day, the sun hits them directly, and I'm enjoying getting a tan that doesn't rub off on my sheets at night. This may give me wrinkles when I'm older, but I'll love each one as memories of this blissful little stop in my life.

West approaches Conor and takes the filly's reins. She's a dark dapple gray. Her coat is incredible, giving her a silver-spotted appearance. West murmurs to her, ignoring every spin and prance. He goes about his work with all the patience in the world as Conor slides over to grab the one West left near the post.

"Skylar." He offers me a professional nod and I return it with a quick wave.

"Conor."

He's a no-nonsense kind of guy. Works hard and goes home to his family. I tried making conversation with him once and it fell flat, so I stick to polite greetings now.

Soon he's gone, and it's just me and West and the flashy horse in the ring. I don't know how long I watch them, but West never stops talking to her as he follows her lead around the ring. The muscles in his arms flex as he grips the reins, and as she spins in circles and dances around him, he remains unruffled. Her eyes and her closest ear flick in his direction a little more frequently, as though she's deciding if he's really so bad.

After a while, she turns her entire head toward him and sniffs, taking him in like it's the first deep breath she's allowed herself.

"There you go, sweetheart," he says in a gentle voice, and I bite down on my bottom lip.

Watching him with the horses has become a favorite daily treat. First, he looks fucking killer in jeans and a T-shirt. Second, he says things like *that*. Third, he's amazing at this. I know little about horses, but I don't need to know much to see it. The way he talks to them, touches them. He respects them.

He's incredibly capable. And fuck, that's hot.

I cross my legs as I watch him lead the filly around the ring, explaining the farm to her in dulcet tones as though she were a human. "Just over there is my house."

He points at it as he walks her into the corner and lets her sniff every inch of the place. The step stool. The poles stacked near the end.

I can see the anxiety loosen around her. She's still tense, but she's warming up to West. When she sniffs the scuffed end of his boot, her lips wiggle against it softly. He runs his hand over her neck, over her shoulder, and back up.

"There she goes, huh? All right, pretty girl. You did good today."

He turns to lead her out of the ring, and I can't keep myself from asking as he walks past, "That's it? You're not going to ride her?"

West's eyes flash up to mine, then back to the filly. "Nah, she's not ready. Doesn't trust me." He grins at me. "But she will. And I'm in no rush."

He leaves me sitting here, slack-jawed. I know we were talking about the horse, but I can't help but feel a kinship with her somehow. I was a nervous wreck when I got here too. And West soothed me. Never pushed me too far. Always made me feel better about myself, never worse.

God, he's treated me with such love.

It makes my heart race.

It makes my heart ache.

It makes my heart a little more his than it already was.

CHAPTER 30

West

IT'S BECOME PART OF OUR RHYTHM OVER THE LAST FEW DAYS to do night check together. We work in tandem, her humming an unfamiliar tune softly as she stands on her tippy toes to peek into every stall and me trying not to track her every motion like a man obsessed.

Because I am.

But I'm not sure I want to be. Falling for someone who's only going to be here for what amounts to a blink of an eye seems like a reckless thing to do.

We both know it. And yet, we don't acknowledge it. Hell, I even told her I believe everything will be okay. But over the past few days, a sense of dread has set in. Like I can say that all I want, but it doesn't change the reality of our situation. I can't manifest everything into existence.

We play house with our blinders firmly in place. I can't decide if what I'm doing feels like a leap of faith or if I'm just setting myself up for heartbreak down the line.

She'll record here, and then she'll be gone. She'll tour, and she'll be carted around, appearing on daytime television first thing in the morning before attending high-brow promotional events at night.

And I'll be here. Breaking horses and looking after my kids. Mia and I agreed we'd never leave while the kids were still small. That we wanted a simple life for them here.

And I still think that's best. But the weight of knowing we're not set up to make it is heavy because I'll be the one who ends up alone again.

It agitates me to feel like I have found someone who fits me so perfectly and to know I can't keep her—not really. Not the way I want.

I stew on it as we complete the chores. After I flick the lights off and pull the sliding barn doors shut, she slips her hand into mine.

It's as we walk past the arena that she unlinks her fingers and moves toward the sand ring. Instead of stopping at the fence line, she dips between the boards and steps onto the other side. Overhead lights cast a gentle glow, and I watch her body sway as she marches into the middle.

"Where you headed, fancy face?" I ask, trailing behind her. I'm on edge, and I want to get home. I want to sink into bed with her. Get lost in her.

"To see what the view is like from in here," she muses as she spins slowly in place. "I like watching you ride."

At the fence, I prop my elbows on the top board and observe her. Cut-off shorts, toned legs, and loose crew neck draping off one shoulder.

I swallow when I realize there's no bra strap in sight. Then my teeth clamp because I don't want to talk about my work. I want to be home. In bed. Naked with her.

"I thought you were writing songs." I'd have to be blind to not to notice her watching me. Sometimes I swear I can feel her gaze roving my skin without so much as glancing her way.

"Trying to."

I rake my fingers through my hair and let out a frustrated sigh as I turn and peer over my shoulder toward the main house. "Sky, let's g—"

"But I usually end up eye fucking you instead. You should see how good your arms look when you're on a horse."

"I thought you were a fan of my thighs?" I grit out as I turn back to her.

"Your dick too," she murmurs as she casually pulls a tube of lipstick out of her pocket. *The* lipstick. The red lipstick she wears when she's out. She stares at the gold tube like she can't remember how it got there, then shrugs and applies it. I watch her raptly, the fullness of her lips giving way under the pressure of each swipe, eyes zeroing in on mine.

Just watching her is giving me far too many ideas.

"The mouth on you, girl."

The things she says. The way she smiles. Those fucking lips.

"What about it?"

The air crackles between us, and I care a lot less about getting back to the house.

Suddenly, right here will do.

I duck through the boards and saunter toward her. She pockets the lipstick, and her chest rises as she sucks in a breath. Skylar isn't short by any stretch of the imagination, but I'm still tall enough to glare down at her. To tower over her when I get close enough, forcing her head back to make eye contact just by being bigger than her.

"Your mouth?" I dip my head to whisper roughly in her ear. "Filthy."

Her breath stutters and her eyes flash with heat. Even though I'm towering over her, she's not the least bit intimidated by me. The fragile woman who showed up here all those weeks ago is nothing more than a memory. My chest swells with pride.

But I also realize I've loved every iteration of this woman. The terrified one on the highway. The frantic one in the bunkhouse. The introspective one at the beach. The jealous one at the fair.

And the one who's looking at me right now like she wants to eat me alive.

I reach up and swipe a thumb over her lips, dragging them to the side just enough to smudge her lipstick. Getting off on the way her breathing quickens as her eyes darken.

My thumb comes away a bit red. "This goddamn lipstick." I shake my head as I stare down at it. "Been thinking about fucking it right off your fancy face since the first day you wore it."

A small moan catches in her throat, and I peek up to catch her tongue darting out over her soft lips. Still plenty of red painted across them as they curve up into a smirk.

"All talk, no action makes West a dull b—"

I cut off her taunt by wrapping my hand around her delicate throat. "Skylar, get on your knees."

My fingers tighten, but she lowers herself with excitement in her eyes, dropping to the sand at my feet as my hand slips from her neck to her hair.

"Now what?" Her palms brace on my thighs and she stares up at me like she's waiting for direction. "You can't just talk a big game like that and then go quiet on—"

"You're really full of opinions tonight, huh?" My fingers clench in her hair, my boots shifting in the sand. "Quit fucking around. Undo my pants, Sky. Pull my cock out. Put that smart mouth to use."

She smirks at me but follows my directions. Her fingers nimbly undo my belt, button, and zipper. Skylar makes quick work of my jeans and boxers and a rush of cool air caresses my bare cock as it springs free between us.

Her eyes flare as I go to grip the base, but she knocks my hand away, placing hers there instead. She gives me her eyes and licks her lips like she's starving.

"You want my cock, baby?"

She huffs out a labored breath, eyes twinkling under the dark sky as she nods. Her other hand wraps around me as she gives a couple eager tugs.

I decide to get out of her way, keep my hands on her hair. "Spit on it, Sky."

"Fuck," she mutters, gaze locked on my dick. Her cheeks hollow out as her tongue works for a few moments. She gazes up at me. "All that talk about putting my smart mouth to use made it go dry."

My fingers soften in her silky hair, and I tip her head up gently this time. "I can help with that."

I bend and start with a light kiss before slipping my tongue into her mouth to explore. She softens in my hands, her tongue meeting mine as she whimpers into my mouth. After a few seconds, I ease away and grip her jaw.

With my thumb on her chin, I pop her mouth open. Hover over her lips. And spit.

"You're welcome," I rasp before straightening and place my fingers over hers where they're holding my cock. "Try again." Her hazel eyes darken in the low light and her back arches at the sight of my cock in my hand. "Spit on it."

And this time, she does. We both pause for a second, staring at my cock. Our spit. Our hands. All of it is so fucking hot.

But not nearly as hot as her lips wrapping around me as she dives forward and sucks me into her mouth. My fingers tangle in her hair as she takes me to the back of her throat like she can't get enough.

I don't need to do anything. My hands are just along for the ride, and she's fully taken charge.

The hollow of her cheeks dip with shadow as she sucks. Her tongue swirls. Her lips clamp. She moans, and the vibration travels all the way up my spine.

One hand trails up, cupping my balls firmly, and I buck against her face. "Fuck, Sky. Fuck."

She keeps working her magic, and my head tips back. The stars blur above me. And I can hear Skylar sucking below me. Hottest blow job of my life.

When I glance back down at her, she's got her eyes trained on me. She slow blinks once and smiles around my length like the tease she is.

"You love this, don't you? Knees in the dirt. My cock in your mouth."

Her head bobs, even with my dick shoved so far to the back of her throat that her eyes look damp.

"Put your fingers in your pussy. Show me."

She doesn't hesitate to remove a hand from my thigh and push it down the front of her shorts. Her eyelids flutter heavily when she gets there. I know because it's the same expression she makes when I slide inside her.

"You're wet, aren't you?"

She slides her hand away from my dick to the back of my thigh and her mouth pops off me as she murmurs, "Soaked."

I slap my dick on her mouth. "Good. Come on your fingers while I fuck your face."

"Yes." She grins up at me, forearm flexing as she fingers herself. "And don't be gentle. I won't break."

"*God*" is the last word I get out before I grab her head and shove myself back between her waiting lips. "Such a hot little mouth, Sky." I thrust in hard and her nose flares as she works to breathe around me. Her shirt slips farther down her shoulder, her right breast bare to me now, bouncing with every stroke. "Tight, little cunt. I bet it feels so good."

Her gaze stays latched on mine while we each chase our own release. Soon, my strokes gentle and slow until she's lapping at my dick like it's a popsicle. I'm getting off just by watching her.

I can see it coming. The languid blinks. The flush on her cheeks that seems darker in the night.

"Used to think you looked pretty onstage, but that's just because I hadn't seen you on your knees for me."

"West," she breathes out against my swollen head as her knees slip farther apart in the sand. "I'm gonna—" She cuts herself off, taking me in again as she writhes at my feet. Her hips grind. Her arm freezes. Her tongue is soft against me as she evens out.

It's not the feel of her mouth that pushes me over the edge. It's watching her fall apart. It's seeing the pleasure on her face. Hearing the way her breathing hitches when she explodes.

Watching Skylar Stone come is my undoing.

My fingers form a fist in her hair, and I pull out. "Mouth open," I bite out harshly before fisting my cock with the opposite hand.

I jerk once before blowing on her face. Shot after shot. Her waiting tongue. Her cherry lips. Her cheeks.

I paint her—mark her.

And I feel no remorse, especially not when her tongue darts out for a taste.

"Fucking hot, Sky," I breathe, stroking her hair. I can't tear my gaze from the captivating woman on her knees. Her smirk. Her little humming noise as she tastes me.

She nods, teeth pressing into her bottom lip. "So hot. I'm going to be coming down to the arena a lot more often."

"So I can make a mess of your fancy face?"

She wipes her finger over her cheek and sticks it in her mouth before proclaiming, "Definitely."

I shake my head. "Filthy mind to match your filthy mouth," I mutter as I reach back to tug my shirt off.

"You love it," she quips.

I don't laugh at the joke. Instead, I drop to my knees and come face-to-face with her. "I do."

Our gazes clash. Unspoken truths linger in the air between us, but neither of us says a thing. We remain silent as I use the shirt to carefully wipe up the mess I made before tossing her over my shoulder and carrying her back to the house to make another.

I may not have her forever, but I'm going to enjoy the hell out of her while I do.

CHAPTER 31

West

THE CHANGES WITH SKYLAR start slowly.

She hums as she tosses a flake of hay into a stall. She doesn't even look horrified by the dust on her shirt.

"What are you humming?"

Skylar stops, confusion touching her features. "Was I?"

"Yeah. Didn't recognize it." The beat alone felt different from anything I've ever heard her perform.

Her head tilts. "Huh, I'm not sure."

We smile at each other and go back to doing night check in a companionable silence. Soon, she begins to hum the same tune. I don't ask about it this time, but after a couple minutes, she turns to me. "Can I borrow your phone?"

Brow furrowed, I pull it out of my back pocket and hand it to her without question.

"What's the password?"

With a sheepish look, I confess, "It's 1-2-3-4. I should

change it since Emmy has it figured out now, but I just haven't gotten around to it."

All I get back is a wide grin and a quiet, "Thanks." Then I watch her hold the phone to her mouth as she walks the alleyway back and forth. Humming the same tune that she has been with a little added flourish. When she finishes, she peeks up at me, "Mind if I send this to Ford?"

I'm speechless for a moment. I feel like I'm here, watching her come back to life.

"Of course not."

"I can't believe you like red grapes better than green grapes." We hop into my truck after leaving the grocery store, and Skylar is shaking her head over my grape preference.

"We got the green ones, didn't we? Don't kick a guy while he's down."

She beams back at me. "We could have gotten both."

I wave her off. "Nah, I'll learn to love the green ones."

I hear the sound of her seat belt buckle in, and then see the flash of an arm that reaches forward to open the glove box. She's rifling through, and I'm confused.

"What are you doing?"

"I need a piece of paper and a pen."

"Why?"

"A lyric just came to mind. If I don't write it down, I'll forget it."

She seems borderline frantic, and I know she won't find

what she's searching for in there. So I open the center console and pull out a receipt I never needed in the first place and a pen with barely any ink left.

"My hero," she sighs without even looking up. Then I sit and watch the ink spill from the pen across the crumpled piece of paper.

I found home in a broken glass
I found home in the words that he gave me

She peeks up, catching me watching her. But she doesn't hide the words. She just grins.

"Careful Weston. Your number-one fan is showing."

I laugh it off and start the truck. Pulling out of the driveway to the sound of more pen strokes. It feels special sitting next to her right now.

The girl who told me she couldn't write a song.

Writing a song.

I feel like I haven't seen Skylar in days. She's been leaving at the crack of dawn and crawling into bed late—but never without waking me up for some attention. Attention I happily give.

But aside from that, she's been living at the recording studio with Ford. Working. She's got the bug and it's inspiring to see. A little part of me wants to see this moment unfold in person. To watch her in her element and just…admire.

Which is why I'm here, sneaking into the studio.

Ford is on one side of the glass with Cora and some other guy, all of them are wearing headphones and watching raptly. In the actual studio, I can see Skylar, and a guy on the keyboard, and…Ford's dad, holding his guitar. The three of them are talking animatedly. Skylar's eyes are bright and her cheeks are pink.

My jaw drops. Ford Grant Senior. My best friend really called in the big guns.

"Fucking cool, right?"

I'm so busy gawking that I don't hear Rosie sneak up from beside me. "Super fucking cool. Did it kill Ford to ask his dad?"

Rosie bites down on a smile. "It will be worth it, and he knows it. He brought his friend to play the keyboard. They're keeping it super simple. But it sounds amazing."

I'm so happy for my girl that I could burst.

"You gonna head in? Say hi?"

I glance down at my sister with a grin. "Nah. I just want to watch her for a bit."

The look I get back is both amused and knowing. But she doesn't rib me about it. Instead, she walks away shaking her head and leaving me to watch in peace.

So I do. And it's fucking incredible.

CHAPTER 32

Skylar

BREAKING NEWS: Skylar Stone is a stone-cold badass who completed her own album and released a banger of a single that everyone loves almost as much Weston Belmont, her number one fan.

I WAKE WITH A START TO A PITCH-BLACK ROOM, LIGHT FILtering in from the door that leads to the hall.

"Dad? Skylar?" Emmy's sugary voice filters in from the bedroom door and I freeze.

West and I have been sleeping together for several weeks now, but it's not something we've advertised to the kids. I must have passed out after sneaking in here.

We've been making up for lost time since I became a

woman obsessed with getting him naked. Everything is hot and filthy between us, and I've never felt freer or safer to experiment with sex in my life.

He's my new addiction.

The kids are back to school. The album is recorded. We released the first single almost immediately, and it was an instant fan favorite.

Once the words started flowing, they poured out of me like a faucet. The minute the studio was ready, Ford and I got busy making music. He brought in musicians. I brought the words. We worked like mad. It feels like we put our heads down to see what we could come up with and got so obsessed that by the time we looked up, we had an entire album.

Inspiration has never felt so consuming.

"Emmy?" I whisper back, hearing her feet pad across the floor as she approaches the bed.

He hasn't said it to my face, but I know why he hasn't outright told them. He told me once that he wasn't going to bring someone into their life who was impermanent.

I know he thinks I'll leave. Leave them all behind for the city lights. With my album recorded, it feels like we're barreling toward that moment. But the longer I spend here, the more impossible it feels to leave.

Emmy's small hand wraps around mine, and her voice cracks when she tells me, "I had a bad dream."

"Hey, hey. That's okay." I push up on an elbow and reach forward to swipe a hand over her hair. "We all have bad dreams sometimes."

What I don't tell her is that my recurring one is about

having to leave Rose Hill and going back to my old life. The one I dread. The one I'm more and more happy to leave behind.

"Can I come in with you?" I hesitate at that, and not because we haven't been affectionate. Hell, she's crashed in my room on more than one occasion. But with both West and myself in the bed, it feels infinitely more…family-like? And I don't know if I fit into that.

All the same, she doesn't seem alarmed to find me here.

"Of course. I'll go back to my room so you can get in."

West stirs and throws an arm over me as I lift the covers.

"Oh, no." Emmy's small hand lands on my forearm. "You probably had a bad dream too. You should stay." Then she crawls up onto the bed, rolling herself over my body to wedge herself between West and me.

"I had a bad dream?" I whisper as she hunkers down.

"Yeah. You had a bad dream and came to my dad. He's the best at making you feel all warm and happy inside."

West's deep chuckle rumbles across the sheets, and I can hear the smile in it.

And Emmy is right.

I feel warm and happy inside.

"Go to sleep, girls. No bad dreams allowed here," West rasps sleepily as he edges back to make more room.

I feel like an interloper. Entirely out of place. Whenever I had a nightmare, my parents sent me back to bed, and the next day, I'd have to hear about how annoying it was that I woke them up. There were no 3 a.m. snuggles in the Stone household.

"I should go."

West's arm reaches across Emmy and his big, calloused palm rubs over my shoulder.

"Stay."

This is the second time he's asked me to stay.

And so, I do.

With watery eyes and warm, happy insides, I stay in bed, listening to them breathe in unison. And the significance of the invite isn't lost on me.

I stare at the screen before me and feel all the blood drain from my face. Feels like it might be spilling out around me onto the floor. My coffee is forgotten as my hands shake.

A Billboard Music Award nomination for the new single.

A nomination for something all my own. Something made with joy. And we haven't even released the entire album. This is just the first song of many. The most special one.

It's no Grammy, but I've never expected a Grammy. I don't actually know what I've expected or what my goals have been.

It dawns on me as I sit staring at the email that I've been punching the clock and doing what it takes to make the paycheck. The paychecks I've practically signed away to my parents.

Until now. Until this.

Ford and I released the first single last month, and it blew up. It's swampy and stripped down. "Dolly Parton vibes" is what Cora keeps calling it.

It's not danceable. It's me. Sitting on a stool, mic in hand, sharing my secrets. And it's the first song I've ever released that I love. From top to bottom, I love it. Ford made sure of it.

I made sure of it.

A tear slips down my cheek, but it's not a sad one. It's brimming with pride.

I am so proud of myself, I could burst, and I can genuinely admit this is a new experience for me.

The creak of the back door doesn't draw my attention away. I keep reading the email over and over again.

"*We are thrilled to announce…*"

"What's wrong?" West's voice is downright glacial from across the kitchen, and when I look up at him, his eyes trace the tears on my cheeks like they offend them. "Who made you cry? I'll fucking—"

I hold a hand up and give him a watery smile. "Happy tears" is all I choke out before waving him forward.

He stalks across the room with a furrowed brow, and I can't help but feel so loved in the way he rushes to defend me.

It never gets old. Him. The way he is—it's helped me heal.

West rounds the stool and props a hand on the counter, towering over my shoulder. His breath rushes out when the words hit home.

"Fuck…" His head shakes and I know he must be reading it over again. "Fuck yeah, Sky. That's my girl."

He says it with such heartrending affection. Such awe-struck admiration.

More tears fall as I turn to him and smile softly. His eyes brim with wonder as his arms snake around my body. He lifts me off the stool and before I know it, he's spinning me. Hugging me. Pressing excited kisses all over my cheeks.

I squeal and give back everything I'm getting. I bask in his praise.

"That's my fucking girl," he whoops, and I squeeze him harder.

My number-one fan.

When he finally puts me back down, he holds me at arm's length and asks, "How do you feel?"

"Incredible" is my breathless response.

His fingers trail over my cheekbone and tenderly comb loose strands of hair back behind my ear. "That's how you should always feel. God, I'm so proud of you, Sky."

He kisses me, and I melt. For him. Into him. I melt so completely that I hope I'm stuck to him forever.

We haven't really talked about forever. Me, too afraid to insert myself into his life. Him, too afraid to ask me to stay. Both of us too shit-scared to mess up something that feels so vital.

He hugs me to his chest, and I can hear his heartbeat against the shell of my ear. Steady and sure. His arms encase me like the warmest blanket and the toughest shield.

"I've been putting off meeting with my agent, and I really should…I don't know, do something about this nomination. The other emails are all interview requests. And I finally feel up to talking about my music. So I'm going to need to go back to LA soon to prepare. This award show is only a few weeks away."

"I know." His chin rests on my head so I can feel him nod.

"I'll come back though, okay?"

His arms clamp down on me tighter. "You fucking better."

"I promise."

He nods again, his voice more tentative now. "I can't leave, Skylar. Not for any real amount of time. My kids—"

"I know." He doesn't need to tell me, I *know*.

"But I also don't want you stuck here. This is incredible. You've worked so hard, and you deserve to soak up every moment. To go after every dream. I want us, but I want that for you more."

Now my tears are sad. *Go after every dream.* The words clog in my throat, and I don't want to turn into a weepy mess, so I skirt the truth.

The truth is, my dreams have changed.

"I promised that I'll be back, and I meant it."

This time, when he nods, he doesn't say anything. He just holds me. For a long, long time.

Photosynthesis by Skylar Stone

Backroads
Are never paved by a girl like me
Can't be seen

WILD EYES

No emerald
But the leaving I've seen
Still lies right before me

I'm a spoonful of polish
Just blind trust turned faithless

But my world doesn't matter here
And my porcelain life is behind me
I found peace in these clashin' chairs
Never knew such a small life could free me

In the pines, by the water
In the arms of another
Little hands with big hearts find me
And I find peace

My life
Is tailored to fit just so
Never chosen

Then you came
Set fire to the lies I honed
Now I'm hoping

The future is perfect,
Strip me down to human

But my world doesn't matter here

And my porcelain life is behind me
I found peace in the calmer air
In the simplicity of a new dream

In the pines, by the water
In the arms of a lover
Little hands with big hearts find me
And I find peace

Breathing in until my lungs cry
It's like I'm forced here, trapped in two lives
Oh, the peace I've found
Or my old doll house

Breathing out the love you've shown me
Got a bird's eye view of healing
Found in innocence
Photosynthesis

'Cause my world doesn't matter here
I left that version of me in the city
I found home in a broken glass
I found home in the words that he gave me

In the pines, by the water
In the arms of a lover
Little hands with big hearts find me
And I find peace

CHAPTER 33

West

"So, when is Skylar back?" Ford asks as he finishes tying his bowling shoes. Big nerd finally got sick of wearing the disease-riddled rentals and invested in his own pair. I've never been more satisfied by anything in my life.

"Tomorrow." I rip open a bag of Skittles and pop a green one in my mouth as we wait for Rhys and Bash to show up to the lanes.

"Oh, that's not bad."

I shrug. It's fucking awful, is what it is. She left a week ago, and I've been moping ever since. I know her promise to come back is not a hollow one, but I miss her so much, it hurts.

I also know she's worked hard to achieve her status. Sure, Rose Hill could be home base, but for how long? Or for how many days a year? And could I settle for having only snippets of time with her?

Yes.

The word pops up in my head, and I know I'd take any sliver of time I can get with her. I've fallen in love with her. And I live in fear of not being enough. It's a heavy burden in some ways to know I could be the thing that makes her change the course of her career.

Deep down, I'm not sure I'm worthy of someone changing their entire life to accommodate me. The pressure of it—of thinking I could let them down and become the source of their regret—that's what keeps me up at night.

"Are you addicted to Skittles?" Ford snaps me out of my spiral by eyeing me judgmentally as I pop a few sugar bombs into my mouth.

I ignore him and offer the bag. "Want some?"

His superior look fades as he reaches for the bag.

"No orange ones."

"What? Why?" His brows furrow as he takes the candy.

"I know you're accustomed to getting everything you want, but no orange ones."

I catch the end of an eye roll right as Bash stomps in with a deadly scowl on his face. He's got Crazy Clyde in tow.

"Clyde," I announce, reaching forward to give him a shoulder slap. He was a long-time member of the team but hasn't left the hospital much lately. "Good to see ya, man. We've missed you."

He snorts as he steps gingerly around me to take a seat. Truth be told, he looks terrible. Puffy and pale where he's always been sinewy and tanned from hours spent in the sun fishing, hunting, and meandering through the woods. Bash is the only one who really knows him, and Bash is a man of few words, so none of us know Clyde that well. Only that he's the hermit who lives on the other side of the mountain and believes a lot of wild conspiracy theories.

"You haven't missed me. That's just the 5G radiation fuckin' with your brain."

"Programmed by the government?" Ford guesses.

My head tilts. "I thought it gave you cancer?"

Clyde grumbles at us before snapping his finger at Bash. "Grab me a beer while you're up there, will ya?"

Bash glares at him, jaw popping. "Are you fuckin' kidding me? A beer right now?"

Clyde scoffs. "No better time, wouldn't you say?"

My eyes narrow as I watch them, trying to figure out the friction. "What's going o—"

"Sorry I'm late." Rhys towers over us as he ambles to our table, mouth set in a grim line despite his flushed cheeks and bright eyes. "Was working on something."

My head tilts as I regard him. "Working on something? Does this mean you're finally going to tell us something about yourself? Because right now, I'm pretty sure you're a secret porn star."

Rhys's cheek twitches, and he huffs out a dry laugh. "I am not a porn star. Though I am flattered by the guess."

"I thought he was a porn star too," Bash says as he ties his shoes.

"I'm not—" Rhys cuts off, raking an agitated hand through his hair. "Listen, I'm planning a wedding. Wondering if you guys would like to come to it?"

"Who's getting married?" I ask, now confused. "Wait, are you saying you're a wedding planner?"

"No. I'm getting married."

We all stare at him with blank faces. I can only speak for myself, but I have no doubt the other guys are just as stunned as me. Rhys is a mystery. He comes and goes from town with no explanation, and he makes no attempt to share that information with us. Hell, I didn't even know he was living with Tabby until Skylar told me. I guess that's why I have a hard time imagining him being in a relationship.

The man is an island.

"To who?" I ask.

He tilts his head to both sides, as though he's cracking his neck, before looking over my head like he's found something interesting on the wall across the room. I fall for it and turn to check. But there's nothing, just a wood-paneled wall with pin holes in it from old posters.

We all watch with bated breath as he lifts his hand to squeeze the back of his neck before he finally answers.

"Tabitha."

If I thought I was stunned before, it's got nothing on how I feel now.

"Like Tabby? Chef Tabby? Bighorn Bistro Tabby? Wants-to-kill-you Tabby?"

"Yep." Rhys nods firmly and gets to putting his massive bowling shoes on while we all stare at him in fascination.

"I thought you guys hated each other?" Ford sounds suspicious.

"Feelings change," he mutters as he laces his shoes.

"Well, I, for one, am happy for ya. Hate sex is some of the best sex, as far as I'm concerned," Clyde says, eliciting groans from Ford and me and a glare from Bash.

Rhys ignores the offhanded comment, though. Instead, he pushes to stand and glares down his nose at us all. "Looks like I'll be here for the long haul. So we should try not to suck so much. I hate losing."

And with that, he marches over to the screen to input our names for the game.

We go on to lose, but not as badly as usual.

After bowling, Ford drops me off at my empty house, and I try not to let that niggling sensation of loneliness creep in after what was a fun night. When I cross the front door, the light over the stove is on, but there's no sound. No laughter.

"*Fuck you!*"

There's just Cherry.

Skylar was nervous as hell to leave her behind, but I promised her that if I could take care of a barn full of other people's horses, I could take care of one mouthy parrot.

"That's fuckin' rude, Cherry," I say back as I toe off my shoes.

"*Fuckin' rude. Fuckin' rude.*"

I chuckle as I walk across the floor toward the cage and flick open the door. "You like that one, huh?"

"*Like it. Like it,*" she repeats to me as she steps gingerly onto my hand. I pull her out and feel my lips twitch as she edges her way up to my shoulder. "*Feed the horses!*"

Yes. My nightly routine with Skylar has now become my nightly routine with Cherry.

"Yep, feed the horses." I move toward the back door and head outside to the barn. Cherry bobs the entire way there and squawks with glee as I toss flakes of hay into every stall. And it's not until I'm on my way back to the house that I quietly admit, "You aren't so bad, Cherry. Like, for a bird."

"*Fuck you.*"

I peek at her, secretly satisfied that she didn't yell it at me like normal. She used a kinder voice, I swear.

Once I've filled her food and water, I finally take a shower and head to my computer wearing only the boxers I plan to sleep in. Skylar was on a morning show today, and I missed it because I had to work. I'm hoping they have video clips up now.

I find it easily. She's on a stage, in the prettiest green dress, sitting at a table and talking with a bunch of women. Beaming. Glowing. *Thriving*.

God, I'm so in love with her.

It hits my chest hard, hollows me out. I press a hand against my sternum to rub the ache. And like I willed her into existence, my phone lights up with her name. I'm thankful we got her a phone before she left, even if she insisted on the lowest-tech one she could find. Though the texting and internet capabilities on the flip phone leave something to be desired, we talk every day. My hand darts out to answer it before the second ring can even sound.

"Sky." I breathe her name like I need it to survive.

"Hi." Her simple, breathless greeting feels much the same.

"Hi."

"I miss you."

"Fuck, girl. Me too. What are you up to?"

"Just got back to my old place after dinner with my agent."

My old place. In my head, that sounds an awful lot like my house is her new place.

"How about you?" she continues.

I scratch my hand across my beard and consider skewing the truth, so I don't come off as lovesick as I am. Then I decide I don't want to hide the truth from her. "Watching the clip of you from this morning."

"Oh." I can hear the smile in her voice.

"If you needed proof of how much I miss you, there it is. Number-one fan and all that."

She sighs on the other end of the line. "One more sleep. I booked a car service from the airport. No more Tesla. Coming straight to you as soon as I land."

"And then you'll be coming again when you get here."

She laughs. "Speaking of coming, I was calling to tell you to check your email."

My brows shoot up. "Oh, yeah?"

"Yeah. In case you were wondering what I wore under that dress this morning."

My dick thickens as I click open a new browser window. And sure enough, I have an email from Skylar.

I lick my lips. "I should open it now?"

Her laugh is soft and low. "That's the idea, yeah."

I click and my skin hums with anticipation.

Then it flushes with heat.

"Fuck."

My finger rolls along the mouse, taking me through the series of photos.

Skylar.

Naked in front of a mirror, perfect tits on full display, hand demurely covering her pussy. Hand pulled away. Another with black lacy underwear, curls cascading around her bare breasts. Then with a bra. Then with nylons and fucking garters. Then with heels.

I groan and adjust my cock as I make it to the last few. A dress. A coat. And then an adorable toe kick while she blows the mirror a kiss.

It's like an R-rated flip book of my girl getting dressed.

"Do you like them? The camera on my laptop isn't all bad."

"Do I like them? Skylar, I'm going to jerk off to them the minute I get off the phone with you. Probably frame them when I'm done. Your laptop is really out here doing the Lord's work."

"Why wait until you're off the phone?" Her voice is sultry.

"Oh, is that what you were after?" I push my boxers down.

"I miss the way you say my name when you come. I want to hear it. Tide me over until tomorrow."

She doesn't need to ask twice. I put the phone on speaker and set it beside my computer.

"My palm is wrapped around my cock. Tight like your pussy. You gonna join me?"

I can hear rustling as her breathing grows heavier. "Yes. Yes. Okay, I'm getting on my bed."

"What are you wearing?"

"The same set as in the pictures."

"Hell yeah." I pump my hand, base to tip, and watch a pearl of precum form as I do.

"Where are you?"

"At my desk. The one I never use. I'll fuck you on it tomorrow."

"You can fuck me anywhere."

I chuckle, but it's dark, labored, as I fuck my hand and pretend it's Skylar. "That's a dangerous thing to offer, Sky."

"It's true."

I swipe my thumb over the top of my cock, spreading that drop of cum over the head as my breathing goes ragged. "You got your legs spread? Fingers stuffed in that pretty little cunt?"

"Yes," she breathes, drawing out the word.

"How many? How many fingers are getting soaked in there, baby?"

"Three."

"Fucking desperate for my cock, aren't you?"

"So desperate," she whimpers. "I need your cock so bad."

"You look so good, Sky. God, I miss you."

I jerk myself faster—my eyes on her photos, her voice in my ears—over and over again to her sexy sounds. Moaning my name. Breathing. Cursing.

It's fucking hot. With her, everything is like that.

"West. I'm gonna come."

"Me too, baby. Me too."

My dick swells. I don't let up. Twisting. Rubbing. Imagining it's her hot mouth. Her tight pussy. She cries out my name and I follow suit as I lean back and blow on my stomach. Each shot of cum surging in time with her moans. "Skylar, fuck. Fuuuck."

When I finally catch my breath, I take a Kleenex from the box on my desk and wipe myself up before flopping back in the chair.

"I should have bought a phone with video calling, so I could watch. I knew that was going to piss me off."

I laugh and run a hand through my hair, still gathering myself after that experience with her. "It's okay. I'll show you up close tomorrow."

We end the night talking in bed until we both fall asleep. And when I wake up in the morning and reach for her, she isn't there. But my screen shows the call is still active four hours later.

CHAPTER 34

Skylar

NOT-SO-BREAKING NEWS: I miss you.

I CAN BARELY SIT STILL ON THE RIDE BACK TO ROSE HILL. I woke up earlier than expected this morning, considering I stayed up late into the night talking to West on the phone. I'm fairly certain I fell asleep that way.

Waking up with my phone in my bed rather than him was enough to spur me into action. My bags were already packed, so I tried my hand at getting an earlier flight. And it worked.

Now I'm just enduring the three-hour drive back to Rose Hill. Which feels like its own special brand of torture. I want to snap my fingers and be in his arms.

The trip back to Los Angeles hadn't been as bad as I expected. I managed to keep my cool while being interviewed. Talking about a song or an album that I actually feel passionate about had words rolling off my tongue.

Nothing I said was a lie, nothing I did was for show. There's something freeing about loving your work so much that you don't give a flying fuck if anyone else does. And that's this album—*Photosynthesis*. And from the moment I heard the playback—just me and Ford Grant Senior on his acoustic guitar—I knew I loved it enough that no one could pop my bubble.

I wouldn't let them. Even my dad milling around walking on egg shells bothered me less than I thought it would. Knowing he couldn't touch this project gave me peace. He wasn't worth the fight, and so I chose to ignore him.

I felt secure in myself for the first time. Because, for once in my life, I knew where I belonged—what I was going home to.

And West was man enough to let me go do what I needed to do. He didn't cling to me or make me feel guilty for leaving. He didn't gaslight me or make it about him. And after a lifetime spent around self-centered men who treat me like I can't do anything myself, there's a comfort in knowing West believes in me so thoroughly that he doesn't try to overstep.

There's a man who will do everything for you.

And then there's a man who is secure enough to realize there are things you need to do for yourself—who steps back and revels in watching you soar.

That's the man who's your biggest fan.

That's West.

My throat aches as we turn down the backroad that brings me closer to him. "That sign, right there." I point to the Sparkly Turquoise Unicorn Ranch sign that still dangles from the official one and smile with watery eyes. It's more sun-bleached than it used to be.

It's more perfect than ever.

When the tires hit the gravel driveway, I sigh and melt back into the town car's leather seat.

Home.

Sure, I stayed at a house I own in Los Angeles, but this? This is home.

The sun hangs low in the sky, and I can feel that nip in the air as we barrel toward fall. Some leaves here in the valley already look suspiciously yellow. I close my eyes and let myself imagine this place in the winter. Bluebird skies. Pine-covered mountains turned to snow-covered mountains. Skating on the lake. Tobogganing with Emmy and Ollie. Hot chocolate. Morning snuggles.

Excitement surges in my veins, and a sense of peace wraps itself around me at the prospect.

Yes. This is where I want to be.

When the car pulls to a stop, I leap from the back like an excited child. I don't bother going for my suitcase. I don't even close the door. Instead, I jog up the front steps to the farmhouse, flashes of my first day here flitting through my mind. The kids' tea set. Bikes. West in his ridiculous apron.

I fling the door open. "West?"

"Sky?" He sounds surprised, and I grin as I kick my shoes off and go searching for him.

"Sky?" His footsteps thud as he jogs down the creaky stairs. "You back early?"

"*Missed you!*"

"Aw, Cherry, I missed you too." They hit the landing and my heart stops in my chest. It's only been a week, and I missed him. I've never truly missed a person.

It's fucking gut-wrenching. I hate it.

"Hi," I breathe as I take them in. Cherry is perched comfortably on West's shoulder. Both of them look so happy to see me.

Suddenly, I feel a little uncertain about what I should do next. Throwing myself at his feet and sucking his dick seems a little extreme, considering the driver is probably about to bring my bags into the house. And Cherry might pick up some new colorful language if she heard the mouth on West.

I settle on smiling at them, wide and relieved and unencumbered.

"*Love you!*" Cherry adds, right before…flying to me.

My parrot, who hasn't spread her wings in years, swoops across the space between us and lands on my shoulder. Stunning me.

I stare wide-eyed at West as she nuzzles her head against my cheek. "*Love you! Love you!*"

"Did she just? Did you—are you a parrot trainer now?"

He scoffs, and I realize he seems just as alarmed as me. "We spent a lot of time together this week, but she has not done *that*."

Cherry's body flexes as she takes off again. Back to West. When she lands, she pecks at his tightly cut fade. "*Like you! Like you!*"

I tear up watching this bird, who was treated so badly, finally feel safe enough to fly.

Cherry and I have been in this thing together for a long time, and watching her take a chance has tears spilling over my lashes.

She never likes anyone. But she likes West.

Again, she flies. Back to me, where she nuzzles and tells me she loves me. "*Feed the horses?*" She says it like a question.

"Feed the horses?" I stare at West, who is still staring at me.

His tongue darts out over his lips as his gaze rakes over me. "Yeah. Doing night check alone was depressing, so I made Cherry my assistant."

I nod, lips pinched together, and look back and forth between the bird I love and the man I love.

Because I do. How could I not? Did I ever stand a chance? It wasn't even a choice. It just is.

"Ma'am, I'll leave your bags here at the door. Is that okay?"

I turn to the portly man who drove me all this way. "Of course. Thank you so much."

Then he's gone, and West's eyes bore into mine.

"Get over here, fancy face." He holds one arm out, and within seconds, I close the distance between us. My head on his chest, my arms clamped around his ribs. He grips me, holding me tight against his hard body, and I feel it again.

Home.

"I never want to leave again."

His broad palm smooths over the back of my head and he chuckles. "That seems excessive. How will we take vacations?"

A watery laugh spills from my lips as I nuzzle against his sternum and let the sound of his heartbeat soothe me. "You know what I mean."

"Then you don't have to leave. Literally, whatever you want. It's yours. Me. This place. The future. Just tell me what you want, and I will do everything in my power to give it to you."

I sigh as his words sink in. *The future.* I very much want that with him.

"I want to go to bed and be naked with you all night long and only stop to have you feed me bizarre variations of grilled cheese sandwiches."

"*Want to be naked!*"

West's body shakes with laughter. "This bird is one of my new favorite people."

"She needs to go to bed now, or she's gonna develop an even worse mouth than she already has."

He lets me go and steps back. "Off you go, Cherry." When he holds his hand out, she takes a little jump onto his waiting arm. Without complaint. And without shit-talk.

I watch West put her back in her cage, murmuring to her about how he promises to take her back out for night check.

I'm not sure I've ever wanted to fuck him more.

Which is why I don't wait. I don't talk, fearing it might

slow us down. Instead, I take his outstretched hand and let him lead me up the stairs onto the second level of the sun-drenched farmhouse. In the master bedroom, it's clear that he has been preparing for my return. The cracked windows allow the linen drapes to flutter across the hardwood floor. The bed is impeccable, as if he agonized over smoothing out every wrinkle on the blue-and-white patterned duvet. It's so fresh that I can smell the laundry soap on the soft breeze.

My eyes flutter shut, and I inhale his signature smell, the soap, the light pine scent that always permeates the air here in Rose Hill.

Home.

He turns on me and my gaze lands on his baby blues, flashing with need. With *love*.

"Strip."

I bite down on my lip and quirk an eyebrow at him. "The pictures weren't enough?"

"It's never enough with you. I'm greedy with you. I always want more, more, more." He steps closer, thumbing the bottom hem of my shirt like he's considering whether he should remove it gently or rip the fabric from my body. "It felt like I couldn't breathe when you were gone."

He focuses on his fingers, still tugging at my shirt. "I've never felt like that before. It feels like that sometimes when the kids are gone. But you too? It was…"

"It's almost like you're my number-one fan." I reach out and caress his forearm to comfort him. West's an actions kind of guy, so I'm not oblivious to this being a vulnerable moment for him.

"No, Skylar." His eyes snap up to mine. "It's almost like I love you."

I hiss in a harsh inhale. He couldn't breathe while I was gone, and I can't breathe right now.

"Almost?" My voice shakes.

"There's no almost. No question, no doubt in my mind. I love you, Skylar Stone. I think I fell that day on a backroad. The first moment I laid eyes on you."

I blink. And I think. And I try to wrap my head around what he's telling me. I'm not sure anyone has ever loved me like that. With such surety. With no qualifiers.

I never have.

Until now.

My palms land on his pecs, and I slide them up over his chest until my arms link around his neck. "Well, thank god for that. Because I'd hate to love you the way I do and not have you do the same."

Then I kiss him.

I pour myself into it. Into him. Us.

Everything feels right in the world. It's not. But somehow knowing West loves me makes me feel like things that are wrong aren't so insurmountable. My parents. My royalties. My anxiety.

In his arms, everything feels better.

We undress each other with torturous care. Every graze of his hand over my bare skin sends a wave of gooseflesh out in its wake.

Every touch is reverent. Every word is tender. Every look holds promise.

West and I have done our fair share of fucking, but this is not that.

I have the sinking suspicion—cheesy as it sounds—that I'm about to make love for the first time in my life.

Stripped naked, our clothes splayed across the floor, we take a minute to admire each other. Full light and not a shred of shyness between us.

His body is roughly hewn, hard and masculine and *big*. There's nothing refined about West, and that's what I first found so damn appealing about him.

That was before I got to know his heart. His mind. He's so much more than meets the eye.

His big hands cup my head, and he kisses me as he walks me back toward the bed. We tumble onto the soft, fresh sheets, still warm from the sun. They feel almost as delicious as the weight of him on top of me.

One gentle hand trails down my body, exploratory and expert. I arch into him when he gets to my breast, first palming and squeezing, then plucking at my nipple. He moves down, his mouth finding my opposite nipple.

He sucks, he licks, he nips. He makes me see stars. And then he moves to the other and does the same.

"West, West…" I'm breathlessly moaning his name on repeat as he works my body. God, he hasn't even gotten inside me, hasn't even touched my clit, and I could come. He's got me keyed up in a way I have never experienced.

"Yes, fancy face?" He drags his lips across the valley between my breasts.

"I feel like…I feel like…"

One of his fingers swirls over my inner thigh, and I lose my train of thought.

"You feel like you're gonna come?" he asks as he sinks two fingers into me without preamble.

When I look down, my tits glisten with his saliva, nipples stiffened to hard points. His bright blue eyes glow in my direction while his fingers twist inside me.

"Yeah, I can tell."

"How can you tell?" I breathe the words, my hips bucking against his hand.

"Hmm… Because I get off on watching you. And you get this pretty pink flush that starts on your cheeks."

He's there, hovering over my face. He kisses my cheeks in turn.

"Then it creeps down your throat, here."

His mouth grazes over the exact spot. His stubble makes me shiver.

"And then your chest."

This time his lips drag over my collarbones, his fingers still working my pussy at a painfully slow pace.

"And then these tits. I love them almost as much as you." He chuckles and sucks a nipple into his mouth. My body shoots straight back up to attention. "Pretty sure if I tried, I could make you come just by playing with them."

His fingers thrust harder now, and he presses his thumb down on my clit, almost clamping me in place. My head falls back on a sharp gasp.

"But it would be a shame to ignore this"—his fingers

slam in hard—"seeing as how you're making a mess all over your thighs already."

"Yes. Yes."

"Whatever you want, baby. Just like I told you, whatever you want." His head drops and he does this *thing*. I don't know what it is, but between the heavenly suction of his mouth, the fullness of his fingers, and the heavy weight of his thumb…

I fall.

I fall in love.

I fall apart.

He plays me like an expert. Like I was made for him.

"West!" I cry out and comb my nails over his scalp as my body seizes beneath his. And he doesn't let up. He rides the wave until I'm putty in his hands.

I'm borderline delirious when he pushes up to his knees and nudges my legs apart, spreading me. He looks fucking incredible. Bronze skin. Huge cock. Flushed cheeks. His broad chest, lightly dusted in hair, heaves as he stares down at me like I'm his last meal.

He fists his cock and runs his tongue over his lips. "I sure hope that birth control is working, Sky." He swipes his swollen head through my core. "Because I have every intention of filling this pretty little cunt with my cum today."

"Fuck." I hiss the word. "Yes. Do it."

That's all the invitation he needs before he's feeding me his cock. Inch by delicious inch. My head flips from side to side. After only a week apart, the fit feels even tighter. He fills every bit of space. Like I was made to fit him.

Bare skin on skin just feels…incredible. *Addictive*.

He grips my thighs, lifting my legs as he draws out and pushes back in. "Fuck, we look so good together. You take me so well, Sky," he rasps as he seats himself inside me with intensity and attention. And when he's in to the hilt, he collapses over me, his elbows bracketing either side of my face.

He rocks his hips, and his eyes search mine as I wrap myself around him. My legs around his waist, my arms around his shoulders.

Then we kiss, and we roll, and our skin is hot and given to sensation with every touch and every damp slide. I've never felt more whole than I do in this moment.

"It's too much," I whisper. And I don't mean physically.

His hips hit me harder. "You can take it, Sky."

"God." My eyes flutter shut. "Yes. Again."

"Again? I'm trying to be gentle."

My eyes flash to his. "You have been. Now fuck me."

A sultry smirk hits his lips as he draws away. "I told you whatever you want, didn't I?"

I nod, licking my lips as he considers. And this time, when he takes my thighs, he pushes them up, practically folding me in half.

"Hell yeah. Fuckin' look at you. Perfect from head to toe," he grits out before slamming in hard. Hitting me deeper than before. My moan is louder this time.

He fucks me in earnest now. Perspiration dots his brow as his fingers grip my legs harder. He's hypnotized by the sight of his cock inside me.

With every thrust, I cry out. I don't even know what I'm

saying. It's mostly wordless, just noise to go with his pants and the sound of his balls slapping my ass as he unleashes.

"Pinch that clit, baby. Let me watch you."

My shaking hand jumps to obey. "Oh, fuck."

"Again. Do it until you come on my cock."

I do it again, and again, while he rails me. And before I know it, I'm screaming his name. I've never been loud in bed, but with West I feel safe enough to let go. And I do. I explode. I see literal stars.

"Oh, fuck yeah." His strokes turn from short and quick to long and punishing. My body shakes on every downstroke.

And true to his word, watching me come is his undoing.

I feel him. Every pulse, every twitch, as he empties himself inside me. His entire body tenses.

Fuck. It's so hot.

Almost as hot as when he pulls out to inspect his handiwork.

"That's what I love to see," he murmurs as he trails his fingers over my swollen pussy. His touch makes me shiver even though I'm hot all over.

"How do I look?" I tease, breathless as I stare up at the ceiling, mind blown by the simplest and hottest sex of my life.

"You look an awful lot like you belong to me." I can feel his seed leaking out. But not for long because he catches it, pushing it back into me with one gentle finger. "So fucking pretty like this."

"Yes," I whimper as my legs shake. I arch into him.

"So eager for more. Never enough, is it?"

"With you? No."

He adds a second finger, pumping into our wetness.

"Oh god…" My nerves surge to life under his touch—under his gaze.

"I think I'll watch you come like this too."

And he does. All afternoon. All night. And the only breaks we take from being wrapped up in each other are to eat grilled cheese sandwiches with pickles inside.

CHAPTER 35

West

I'VE GOT THE KIDS IN THE BACK AND SKYLAR AT MY SIDE AS we drive home from soccer. We're all wearing Sparkly Turquoise Unicorn hats. Skylar is laughing at one of Emmy's dramatic game recaps, and I can see Oliver staring down at his book with a soft smile on his face through the rearview mirror.

And my life has never felt more complete.

All of us under one roof is going to feel the best. I'm itching to get home and make a big, over-the-top weekend breakfast— pancakes, hash browns, bacon, sausage, eggs. I should throw in some fruit, considering Skylar and I have been living on a diet of cheese and bread.

"So do you know when the wedding is?" Skylar asks. I told her the news about Rhys and Tabby earlier, and she keeps coming back to it like she can't quite believe it's true.

"No. But I think they might kill each other before they make it down the aisle."

"My money is on Tabby."

I snort at that. She's probably not wrong. "Would be a shame. I was kind of looking forward to taking you as my date."

Her cheek twitches. "No. *I* will take *you* as my date. My ten-thousand-dollar date."

When Ford's name pops up on my truck's Bluetooth screen, I don't think twice about answering on speakerphone. My best friend calling me on the world's best Saturday morning? Maybe he and Cora and Rosie will want to meet for dinner.

"Hey, man. What's up?"

I expect a casual tone in response, but his words turn the air in the truck glacial with their urgency.

"West, are you with Skylar? I'm trying to track her down. Her phone is going straight to voicemail."

The motion of Skylar's head whipping in my direction draws my attention to her. We both know she turned it off last night and hasn't turned it back on. In fact, she's so unattached to it now that I expect she left it somewhere at home.

"I'm here, Ford," Skylar says, her voice taking on a detached sort of faraway tone.

"Yeah, you're on speakerphone. She and the kids are in the car."

Ford lets out a heavy breath. "Hey, Skylar. Are you guys heading back to the house? I'll meet you there."

My stomach constricts, and I'm sure Skylar is feeling much the same based on the way her teeth are now digging into her bottom lip. "Ford, is everything okay? Cora? Rosie?"

He waits a couple of beats as though weighing his next words. "Cora and Rosie are both totally fine. Everyone is safe. I'll see you soon."

Without another word, he hangs up, and all I hear is my heart thundering in my ears. An uncomfortable silence fills the cab, and I reach across the console to take Skylar's cool, damp hand. Then I turn the music up and focus on the five-minute drive that takes us back to the house.

Ford is sitting on the front porch when we arrive, and I don't miss the nervous look Skylar slides my way. We hop out, and so do the kids.

"Hey, Uncle Ford," Emmy calls out and runs to him for a hug. He crouches a little to hug her back before offering Ollie a fist bump on his way past. Where Emmy seems oblivious to the tension in the air, Ollie is not. His shoulders are held taut, and I can see the tense set to his jaw.

"West. Skylar." Ford nods in our direction. "Skylar, you got a sec?"

Her lips press together, and she nods. "Mm-hmm."

When I tilt my head at Ford, he shakes his. He's telling me to back off, and as much as my anxiety is off the charts right now, I decide to be respectful of that. "Okay, kiddos. Let's go get breakfast started."

I kiss Skylar's cheek and whisper, "I love you," into her ear before ushering my kids inside.

I sit them at the kitchen counter, where their backs are to the front window, so I can watch Skylar and Ford talk outside like the fucking rubbernecker I am.

He gestures for her to sit down, but she waves him off and shakes her head. I watch my best friend almost wince as he rakes his hands through his hair. He always does that when he's agitated. Then his lips move and I watch every fleck of color drain from Skylar's face.

My heart lurches and my stomach twists. I'm dying to know what's going on, but clearly Ford felt whatever this news is, it was best delivered one-on-one.

She looks my way through the glass, but her expression gives nothing away. When she turns back to Ford, her arms cross over her chest, and she shimmies her shoulders to make herself as tall as possible.

I mix the pancake batter for far too long as I watch them. Ollie is staring at his book, and Emmy is chattering away, but I don't hear anything she says.

My heart is out on the porch with the woman I love, watching her throat work as she swallows and takes Ford's phone from his hand.

She scrolls.

And she blinks.

Her tongue presses out into the side of her cheek.

Then she hands it back.

Ford is talking again now, but Skylar is standing stock-still. She looks like she's in shock, and I fight the urge to rush out there. The only thing keeping me from acting unhinged over this woman right now is that my kids are sitting right in front of me, and if something is seriously wrong, I want to be able to prepare them.

But all my control flies out the window when I watch

a sob rack Skylar's body and her hands fly up over her face. I drop the whisk and jog past my kids, out the front door.

When Ford turns to face me, his mouth is set in a grim line. His usually keen eyes are downright tortured.

"What the fuck is going on out here?"

My friend gives me a stern headshake as he rubs a soothing palm over Skylar's back.

I stalk toward them, glaring at Ford. "What did you do to her—"

"West, now isn't the moment for you to blow up." He knows me well enough to know how I get when someone I care about is hurting. "I'm gonna go. If either of you needs anything, let me know. And, Skylar? I'm sparing no expense in figuring this out."

Skylar nods and presses the heels of her hands into her eye sockets even harder. "Thank you, Ford."

Ford shoots her a heartbroken glance before turning to leave, and I immediately pull Skylar into my arms. Her entire body shakes, and no matter how much I stroke her back or tell her it's going to be okay, her breathing grows more and more frantic.

"I…I can't breathe. I can't breathe." Her feet shift frantically beneath her.

"Sky, you can. I know you can. Sky, baby, I'm gonna need you to take a long, slow breath in."

Her head rolls against my chest, where she is still hiding behind her hands, and her breathing becomes more panicked.

"Okay. Okay," I murmur as I lift her into my arms and

carry her over to the porch swing. Holding her against me like I would a child, I gently rock us as a knot takes up residence in my stomach. "In for three…" I suck in a breath. "One…two…three…"

She gasps.

"And out for three. One. Two. Three."

I repeat the steps for I don't know how long. Eventually, her breathing slows, and even her uncontrollable trembling eases.

I'm not sure how long we sit together. Me holding her while she crumbles. Trying so desperately not to ask her what's going on. When I peek over my shoulder into the house, both kids have turned to watch us. They look stressed too, and I try to give them a reassuring smile, but it comes out as an anxiety-riddled grimace.

Eventually, Skylar lets out an exhausted sigh. I turn back to her, stroking her hair.

And then she talks.

"Those naked photos I sent to you? They're all over the internet."

Her voice breaks on the word *internet*.

And my heart shatters for her in that instant.

CHAPTER 36

Skylar

As much as I want to pull myself together and sit through breakfast with the kids, I can't. Even though I'm calmer, I still feel like I can't catch my breath. Every exhale hurts. Every inhale feels too shallow to keep me upright.

I step out of West's arms and press a hand to his chest, almost pushing him away. "I just wanna sit. I don't know… by the lake. You go be with your kids."

West scoffs before tugging my hand off and linking his fingers through mine. "I'm not leaving you," he grits out before popping his head into the house. "You guys good with cereal? Ollie, can I get you to help your sister? Let's pivot. I'll make breakfast for dinner."

"Yup" and "Okay!" filter back out to us, and their little voices put another sharp dent in my armor. I can't look at them. West leads me down to the water, and it hits me…

They're going to find out.

His kids are going to find out. His nice, normal parents. The friends, the acquaintances I've made here. They're going to see the most personal parts of me and there's not a fucking thing I can do about it.

Shame pelts me from every direction. It's heavy on my chest, on my shoulders, in my gut. I have no idea how they got out. All I know is that everyone will see them. Everyone will share them. They will never be truly scrubbed from the internet. Photos I took for fun and intended with love have been sullied.

And I feel dirty.

It feels like the safety of the bubble I've created here is—*poof*—gone in an instant. I felt different in Rose Hill, reborn. Like I could be a new version of myself and the world would keep turning.

But this is proof that I can be a new version of myself, but I'll never really escape the old version. That Skylar, and everything she comes with, will poison the water, no matter how far I swim.

Before I know it, we're at the log where Ollie and I like to sit together.

Ollie.

"Fuck," I whisper, feeling my heart crack from corner to corner. A fat tear rolls down my cheek.

How will he see me now? How will he see me five years from now? How will I look him in the eye? And Emmy? What am I supposed to tell her about the world? About fame? About being a woman in this day and age?

"Fuck, fuck, fuck," I breathe out, dread and panic setting in.

I'm right back where I started when I got to this town—paralyzed by knowing I don't belong to myself. Nothing is mine; everything I do is for mass consumption.

Even when I don't want it to be.

West's palms land on my shoulders, and he gently presses, seating me on the log. I feel wooden, like a Barbie whose legs you can bend.

He stays close but doesn't invade my space.

From the corner of my eye, I see West, elbows propped on his thick fucking thighs, tattooed fingers linked, tossing nervous glances my way. I keep my gaze fixed on the water. Facing him feels like too much.

"What can I do?"

"There's nothing you can do."

I hear the low rumble in his throat and watch his fingers tense and flex like he's imagining hitting someone. But that's the thing about this situation—he can't fight me out of this mess. The man whose inclination has been to protect me from the beginning can't protect me from this.

I'm sure it's killing him. But the worst part is...

"I did this to myself."

I can hear his teeth grind as he shakes his head. He reaches for me, drags me into his lap, and holds me close. "Skylar, don't say that. You didn't share them on the internet."

"If I'd been thinking straight, I'd have considered the possibility that this could happen. Things like this happen to people like me."

"Doesn't make it your fault."

I roll my lips together. It sure feels like my fault. The guilt is almost as crushing as the embarrassment.

"What did Ford say?"

My laugh is tearful. Poor, sweet Ford. His big, bleeding heart was not cut out for delivering news like this. He sounded choked up at first, and then...venomous. "He said he was going to spare no expense scrubbing the internet and finding where they came from."

West nods now. "Don't doubt it. He's the type who would."

"It won't make a difference, West."

He sighs, but there's a pained moan in it. A little peek of heavy emotion that's pushed its way through. Then he holds me tighter. "I'm so fucking sorry someone did this to you."

I smile sadly, still staring at the water. Too humiliated to even face the man I love.

"Me too."

In an attempt to prove to myself that everything is fine, I decide to leave the property on Monday morning to get Cherry a restock on her dwindling birdseed. West left me—hesitantly—to go to work. And I'm not about to make him run my errands on top of everything else that he's already done.

I'm not that pathetic.

In fact, I tell myself I'm wearing the Sparkly Turquoise Unicorns hat because I'm a fan of the team and not because

I'm hoping to hide under the brim. And the aviator sunglasses? They are just because it's sunny.

Downtown Rose Hill is quiet right now and I convince myself everything will be fine. I haven't looked at my phone. I did briefly check my inbox, but all I saw were requests for comments and emails from my dad and my agent explaining how we can use this publicity in a positive way. I closed it pretty quickly after reading that.

I tug the door to the pet food store open and stride inside, dropping my head as the bell above jingles. I definitely don't need to be announced by a bell right now. That's too much for me, even in this moment of bravery.

My eyes scan the shelves and land on the brand Cherry likes best. Every other type has caused her to dump the feed all over the bottom of her cage before shouting, "*Hate it!*"

"There it is," I mumble to myself in relief as I slide it off the shelf. I'm feeling more at ease about my foray out into the world as I turn at the end of the aisle to head back to the front till.

But the foray turns to shit when I come face-to-face with Bree in the cat food section.

I offer her a muted smile and hustle past, but her words bring me to a screeching halt.

"I love him, you know."

I turn, shoulders tense, arms wrapped tightly around the bag of seed. "Oh-kay." I enunciate the word carefully.

Bree sighs, and when I chance a look at her face, I see no trace of venom, just a brow crinkled by concern.

"I know I must be the villain in your story, but I'm not

trying to be. I just love him. I've always loved him. And I had a shot. Until you."

It's tough to cover my wince. I know what it's like to love West, and a part of me is sad for her. To love him and lose him would be…unthinkable.

"I'm sorry."

"Do you love him?" she presses, her pretty, dark eyes so earnest.

It feels like an incredibly personal question, but I answer anyway. "I do."

Hurt flashes across her features, and her eyes fall for a moment before lifting back to mine. "You're going to hurt him, and you probably won't even mean to do it. His kids? His family? That's sacred to him. He protects his family at all costs. And as sorry as I am for what's happened to you this week, you have to know it's not only going to blow back on you. It's going to blow back on *him*."

My breathing stops as Bree digs a finger into a worry I hadn't made sense of myself. I've spent forty-eight hours reeling. My anxiety spiral has only just gotten started.

"It's going to blow back on those kids."

Bam. A bullet right to the heart. *Him and his kids.*

I lick my lips, eyes flicking away. I don't know what to say. *You're right* is on the tip of my tongue, but I don't want to give her that type of satisfaction.

"I'm not trying to be…" She runs a hand through her hair and shifts like she's finally realized how fucking bizarre this conversation is. "Ha, you know. It doesn't matter. I wouldn't like me either if I were you. I'm just looking out for them. And if you love him enough to let him go, I could still make him happy. He could be happy."

I gaze into her shrink-wrapped eyes. Yes, I should hate her, but mostly I hate how right she is. How she's given a voice to one of my deepest fears.

And I especially hate that my chest is so tight that I can't breathe in enough air to say something cutting or eloquent.

All I do is nod, pay for my birdseed, and walk out the front door.

Right into the waiting lenses of several paparazzi.

CHAPTER 37

Skylar

AFTER MY RUN-IN WITH BREE AND THE PAPS, I DON'T LEAVE the property. In the town where I finally felt free to roam and make genuine connections, I feel trapped. I know on West's property, I'm safe from the cameras. And I'm safe from the prying eyes of everyone in town.

And yet, I feel more vulnerable than I ever have.

Telling the kids there might be stories and pictures about me when they go back to school was a conversation I wish I could scrub from my brain. But West and I knew they needed to hear it from us first before they heard it at school.

It fucking sucked. Sugarcoating it and spinning it in a way that was palatable for a child. It was a long, harrowing conversation riddled with Emmy's curious questions. I remember the expressions on their faces as they absorbed the news. Their innocent eyes. Their bright red cheeks.

Their hugs.

It was their hugs that made me bawl. In fact, I believe I may be defying science with how much I've cried. After years of not crying, it seems I'm now unable to turn the tears off.

I'm gutted, and I'm furious, and I'm terrible company.

The thought of facing anyone makes my skin crawl. And the worst part is knowing I'll have to put on a happy face and strut around events and concerts like nothing happened. I'll have to answer probing questions about the scandal.

So I sit and stew by the lake.

I don't even leave to watch West ride. I haven't told him about my run-in with Bree because I don't want to add one more mark in the *Feel Bad for Skylar* column. Plus, I know he'll march out there and try to fix it. And I don't want to add to his burden. But it makes things strained between us. There's a distance that I can't figure out how to bridge.

I don't mean to be punishing him. His hugs, his gentle touches, and his reassuring words, they…they don't match the way I'm talking to myself on the inside. And I'm back to feeling like there's a part of me that believes I don't deserve his brand of kindness. His brand of unwavering love.

I've avoided intimacy since the bombshell, and he hasn't pushed. He's a gentleman, so he spends all night holding me instead of fucking me.

He has a beautiful life here, and I can't stop thinking about why he'd want me here when I bring shit like this to his front doorstep. Deep down, I know these thoughts are just popping up because of the headspace I'm in. And I know they may not be totally accurate. But anxiety works in mysterious ways, and I find their sentiment following me all the same.

They're hard to shake.

I feel like he should be angry with me—disappointed with me—and he's just not. He's steadfast in his love and affection, and I'm convincing myself it's a front. It's pity.

You're going to hurt him, and you probably won't even mean to do it.

That's the sentiment that haunts me. Because I'm realizing I would endure any level of pain to keep West and those kids from hurting. The burden is cumbersome.

I want to go to sleep and wake up to realize this was all a terrible dream.

"You're gonna grow right into that log if you keep sitting here."

My head pivots as Rosie saunters down the narrow path to the lakeside. She's dressed casually in jeans and a crewneck. Socks and Birkenstocks—which I try to overlook.

When she gets to me, she brushes her hands together and stares out over the lake before plopping down on the log beside me.

"How are you, Skylar?"

"Ha!" I bark out a laugh. "Oh, you know, just fucking peachy, Rosie."

"Yeah, being violated is just a walk in the park, right?" From her biting tone, I get the sense she's got her own story too. We all do, I guess. But still I sigh, feeling a little more at ease around her.

"How bad is it?"

Her head joggles, and I can tell she's considering her next words. "Ya know, I'm not going to lie to you. It's pretty bad."

My stomach drops like I'm on an awful carnival ride. "Cool. Love that for me."

"I would have come sooner, but West is acting like a fucking wolf protecting his den. He told me you wanted to be alone, and he hasn't allowed me over."

"I did tell him that."

She snorts. "Well, he's taken the duty seriously. The way he's working his horses is by patrolling the property fence lines."

Tears spring up in my eyes. What a good man. What a good fucking man. And what an inconvenience to have to patrol your own home like that.

"I should hire security."

"Ford already did."

My lips clamp down to hold back a sob.

"Can I ask you something?"

I nod swiftly, not trusting myself to talk.

"Do you like being famous?"

"Not right now."

"Have you ever?"

I scoff now. "Of course I have. I…must have…"

"Like, what parts?"

Rosie's gaze wanders my face as I rack my brain to remember the parts of my life I can honestly say I've enjoyed. "I like singing."

"You can sing at church, Skylar. What is it that makes you want to go out there and perform? Sell the music? Do the interviews? See and be seen?"

"I…" My mouth opens and closes as I scramble,

searching for the answer. It shouldn't be this hard to find. In fact, I'm so well media-trained that I can recite all the answers people want to hear.

I love my fans.

It's a thrill every time.

I have the best job in the world.

But none of them ring true.

"I…I guess…I guess I just always have. I was told to as a child. It started with pageants and modeling and snowballed from there."

Rosie nods along, bent over her legs as her fingers flick through the different pebbles at her feet. "Has anyone ever told you that you don't have to? You don't have to keep doing this job if it doesn't bring you joy."

It makes me miserable. It makes me sick.

I whisper, "No. No one has ever told me that."

Rosie sits up and looks me in the eye. "Skylar, you have done more in your young life than most people accomplish before they die. How much money do you need to live comfortably? Happily?"

"I…" I shake my head. "It's not about that."

"Then what is it about?"

I don't answer her because I don't know. No one has ever asked me what I want when it comes to my work.

She takes my hands in hers and squeezes as she orients in my direction. "You are allowed to quit."

I suck in a breath.

"I know you don't need my permission. But it's okay to turn over a new leaf. It's okay to sing. Hell, it's okay to record and release songs for absolutely no one but yourself. So what if they don't top charts? You don't have to feed the machine for the rest of your life. Especially not when it's clearly killing you. You could be *here* and *healthy*."

Silent tears roll down my face as I squeeze her hands back.

I wish it were that simple.

Maybe it would be healthy for me to stay here, but what about everyone else?

CHAPTER 38

West

WHEN I HEAR THE FRONT DOOR OPEN AND CLOSE, I GRIMACE. And then I glance back at my son, who I picked up from school sporting a split lip and a black eye.

His gaze slices to mine and back down. Emmy is sitting at the kitchen counter beside him, glaring at me, holding his hand like she'll be the one to protect him from getting in trouble.

"Hey, kiddos. Are you home?" Skylar's voice filters in, but it's not brimming with excitement for life like I've come to expect. It's flat with a little warble.

She sounds like she did when she first showed up on my doorstep. Like she's going through the paces of life. Like the night Emmy shattered that glass all over the floor.

When she turns into the kitchen, she draws up short. Her eyes go wide, and then, "Ollie." She pushes past me where I'm leaning against the stove, rounding the island to get to him. She reaches for him and her gentle fingers trail over the blue swelling on his cheek and the cut on his lip. "What happened?"

My son looks over at me and back at Skylar. "Nothing. Got in a bit of a scuffle."

The silence in the room is awkward. Even Emmy doesn't add to his explanation. They both want to protect her, and I'd be lying if I said it wasn't killing me.

"Over what? I'll kill them." She tilts his head to inspect his cheekbone more carefully. Nothing is broken, I already know. But I don't tell her that. There's something about seeing her dote on him that feels profoundly special.

I've watched her and my kids form a bond. Organic from the start. Like they chose each other.

"It's fine, Skylar."

Her hands fall away, and her flat voice takes on a hint of anger. "This is not fine. What happened, West? You need to get down to the school. There needs to be consequences."

I nod. "There will be. Trust me."

"I do. But this… Why won't you tell me what—"

It's like a lightbulb flickers to life in her head without me even telling her. It's painful to watch.

"Is this about me?"

Ollie stares at her, unflinching.

"Don't worry, Skylar," Emmy says. "Ollie taught him a lesson. You should see the other guy. He looks even worse. Dad taught us both how to make fists with thumbs on the outside." Emmy winks at her like keeping your thumb on the outside is a special secret trick.

From the side, I watch Skylar's face fall. "Oh, buddy." Her voice breaks as she leans over and wraps her arms around him. He hugs her back. Hard. And without hesitation. "Oh, buddy. Oh, buddy. I'm so sorry."

My eyes sting and my throat aches. I blink furiously as I turn my head away.

"I'm not. He got what he deserved." Ollie sounds older than he is, and he also sounds furious.

"What did he say? You shouldn't…you can't start fighting my battles." She pulls away, holding him by the shoulders as though waiting for an answer.

"It doesn't matter."

I watch her jaw flex as her eyes search his face. I thought she'd crumble, but instead, I watch as an eerie sort of armor clicks into place. "I love you, Ollie. I hope you know that. And, Emmy? I love you too. Never change. Either of you. You have both made my time here better than I could ever have imagined. I'm the luckiest girl in the world to have gotten to know you."

Then she wraps an arm around each of them and pulls them into a desperate hug. She keeps her head dropped, and they both cling to her. I'm pretty sure I hear murmurs of *I love you too*. Which is my undoing. I walk away to the bathroom to catch my breath and give them a moment of privacy.

The moment is too sensitive even for me to endure.

But what really has me choked up is that Skylar's words sounded an awful lot like goodbye.

"I'm going to kill that little prick," Mia whispers to me as the kids charge into her house to get settled for the week.

"Maybe we can kill him together?"

"And the administration." She got the same call I did yesterday, but I went to the school to get Ollie and updated her after we got home. Knowing Mia, they haven't heard the last of this from us. They're about to be really tired of us, that's for sure. "And his parents. What kind of clown are the Matthews raising?"

"He still won't tell me what the kid said, so I imagine it was pretty bad."

Mia nods, and I can hear Brandon talking to the kids from inside the house. "I'm kind of proud of him, you know? Quiet little Ollie throwing fists to defend a woman's honor. Maybe he's got some of you in him after all." She punches my shoulder, and I laugh. "How is Skylar?"

I scrunch my nose and look away. "Surviving."

Seems about as close to the truth as I can get without telling my ex too much. I've never told her outright about us, but she knows all the same. She's a smart cookie that way.

"She makes you happy, huh? I can tell. And I know the kids love her."

I smile, trying not to give away the sinking feeling of dread that has taken over since Skylar saw Ollie yesterday. Something has shifted, and I'm trying not to think too hard about what it might mean. I don't want to go there. It hurts too much. All I give back is a casual, "Yeah."

"Good. You deserve that. Give her a hug for me, okay? Once I finish up at the school, I'd be happy to kill whoever did this to her too."

"Yeah, Mia, you're gonna have to get in line for that one."

She laughs as I turn to leave. "Don't get arrested" is what she jokingly calls back to me. But we both know there's a little truth in that joke.

There's a part of me that hopes Ford never finds out who did this because I hate to think what I'd do to them.

Skylar and I spend the night making love. We sleep for a few hours and then one of us will wake the other. Her crawling on top of me. Me disappearing beneath the sheets. There's a softness between us. Few words are exchanged. We say enough with every touch.

But not enough, because when I wake up in the morning, she's sitting on the edge of the bed, fully dressed in acid-wash jeans and a black tube top. Makeup perfectly applied. Hair perfectly straightened.

Alarm bells sound in my head. "What's wrong?"

Her lips are pressed in a tight line and her eyes have taken on that bland, removed look they constantly sported when she first showed up here.

"I'm going to head back to Los Angeles."

Adrenaline races through my veins as I get my bearings and push to sitting. "Why?"

"The award show is in a week. I need to get ready."

"So you'll be back after?" I can hear the desperation in my voice. *I knew this would happen.*

"I'm sure I will come back to record with Ford from time to time, but I'll need to go on tour with this album."

I'm sure my jaw hangs open. "And you decided to tell me like this? Who decided you *need* to go on tour?" God, I hate myself for even asking that. I knew she was here for a short time, and I'm the one who went dreaming of more. I told her I'd never stand between her and her career, and I meant it.

But I still hate it.

"I don't think there is a good way to tell someone this." Her voice is perfectly even. Perfectly checked out. "Sometimes things don't turn out the way we want them to."

"Whoa. Whoa. Whoa. Nah." I shake a hand at her as I kick my legs out of bed and come to stand. "I have sat by your side and given you space for the past week while you worked through this in the way you wanted to. I haven't made a single demand of you. But you need to explain this to me in a way that makes sense."

Her eyes turn pleading now as she stares up at me. "We're a love song, West. Tragic and true all at once. I thought I could be both versions of myself. Starlet Skylar *and* Rose Hill Skylar. But I'm only going to ruin what you have here. I won't mean to, but I will. That's the nature of my beast. Please don't be another person telling me what to do with my life."

I blink at her, lost for words. She stands and faces me, her features pained. I'm stunned and not at all shocked. I've been able to feel her pulling away all week.

"I love you, West. I love you enough not to ruin what you've built here. The looks. The whispers. The paparazzi.

Your children being teased. Getting hurt"—she thrusts a hard finger at her chest—"because of me?"

A sad laugh slips from her lips as her head shakes. "I can't live with that, and you shouldn't have to settle for it. I know what growing up in the press is like. I know what gets spit out on the other side, and trust me, you don't want that for your kids."

"I—"

She holds up a hand to cut me off. "I know what you're going to say. That I'm worth it. That we'll make it work. I love your eternal optimism, and I hope I can take some of that with me when I go, but make no mistake, I am going. And you might hate me for it right now, but one day you'll look back and know it was the right call. My life has never really been my own, but yours is."

I just stare at her, frozen in place, as she continues.

"This place is sacred. Don't let me sully it. I've traveled the entire world and seen nowhere more beautiful. I want it to stay that way. You and Rose Hill, exactly the way I imagine them—fucking perfect." Her voice cracks on the final whispered words.

I hate what she's saying. I hate it with every fiber of my being. But that deeply rooted insecurity of mine rears its ugly head and keeps me from begging her to change her mind.

I'm not enough to keep her here, and I need to hold on to a few threads of my dignity if I plan to survive her walking away. So what I say is, "I love you enough to want you to do what's best for yourself."

Her nose wiggles, and we can't hold each other's gazes. This all feels wrong.

"My car will be here soon."

A shot in the chest.

Knowing she planned this kills me, but I refuse to crumble until I'm alone. "Let me get dressed. I'll help you with your bags."

I feel her eyes on me as I step into my most comfortable pair of jeans and toss on a dark gray tee, then I scoop up her bags and head downstairs. She follows me silently. Being mature and gentlemanly has never felt so fucking awful. Young West is raging inside me, telling me to do something crazy, but that's an impulse I've learned to ignore.

I don't bother putting on shoes. I carry her bags, one in each hand, out to the driveway where Cherry's blanket-covered cage is already waiting. I'm even going to miss that fucking bird.

My throat constricts as I stare out at my land, at what I've built here. It feels a lot less special knowing she won't be here, and for a guy who mostly keeps his feelings locked up tight, I'm sure drowning in them right now.

The sound of the screen door closing behind me signals that Skylar is headed my way, but I'm too wounded to look. Too mad at the world and afraid of what I might say.

She doesn't hesitate to plant herself right in front of me, though. Her eyes are glassy, and her fingers are fiddling with a manilla envelope. "You'll need these papers. Those diamond earrings? I sold them when I was back in Los Angeles.

I put the money from each one into an education savings account for Ollie and Emmy. Ollie is so smart—"

Her voice cracks, and she reaches for her throat. "I just know he's going to do amazing things with that big brain and soft heart. And Emmy is so passionate. I'm pretty sure she's going to take over the world. I'll always be cheering them on."

She presses the envelope to my chest. "There's also the credit for the song that Ollie helped me write. There were only a few lines, but I wouldn't have written my first song if it wasn't for him. It hasn't been released yet, but when it is, he'll get royalties for the rest of his life."

"Skylar, this is..." I look down at the envelope. Too much.

"Please take it. And please, no matter how angry you are with me, promise you'll only tell them good things about my time here."

The kids. Fuck. They're going to be as gutted as I am. Not that we ever told them about our relationship, but they're used to her being here with us. This is what I never wanted for them. Coming and going. Instability. And here I am, putting them through it.

Guilt hits hard and tangles itself up with the shock and dread already coursing through my system.

The manilla envelope falls to the ground as Skylar steps in close, one hand on my chest, one hand on my rib cage. "Can you please remember only the good things too? I don't know if I can stand the idea of you hating me."

"Sky..." I shake my head slowly, staring down into her

glossy hazel irises. My voice is thick with emotion, so I take a break from trying to talk. I pinch a piece of her hair and watch the bronze strands slip across the pads of my fingers. Memories of that same hair falling like a curtain around me when she climbed on top pummel me in flashes. That same hair on my pillow. That same hair looped through the back of a turquoise hat. "Don't you get it? I could never hate you. Only miss you terribly."

Then I kiss her. In the soft morning light, we cling to each other and share the most agonizing kiss. It's soft and desperate and fucking tragic. She whimpers and splays her hands against me.

The sound of wheels crunching on the driveway makes my heart free-fall into my stomach. I pull her closer as though I can kiss her hard enough to make her change her mind or will that town car out of existence.

Maybe I could be enough to keep her here.

But none of it works.

She leaves.

And I crawl into a bed that still smells like her and fall apart.

CHAPTER 39

Skylar

I'M A MANNEQUIN PROPPED ON A STAGE. I'M SITTING DELI-
cately on a stool talking to the two hosts of the talk show, facing
the studio audience and a legion of cameras, a reminder that
this interview is live. My legs beneath the hem of my miniskirt
shimmer unnaturally with the amount of product that's been
slathered on, and as much as I love doing my makeup, the
amount that is caked onto my face right now makes it feel
heavy. It kills my ability to make any facial expressions.

Or maybe that's just because I feel empty inside. For
days, I have felt empty inside.

I haven't cried since I left Rose Hill. Instead, it's like I
plucked my soul right out of my body and replaced her with
a robot just to make it through.

I feel nothing.

"You look amazing," one of the hosts says, and I can't
help but wonder if she's blind or just willfully oblivious.

I checked myself over in the mirror before I waltzed out here and thought to myself that West would take one look at me and know that I'm a bone-deep level of miserable.

Does no one else see me at all?

"Thank you," I say demurely, smoothing my skirt down while hoping there's no up-skirt camera angle.

My agent's words echo in my head.

All press is good press. This kind of exposure only makes you even bigger.

The problem is, I don't think I want to be bigger.

"Especially on the heels of what's been an eventful time for you."

My head tilts and my eyes zero in on the woman. I gave my dad and agent a list of questions I wouldn't be answering, but I'm sensing they're going to get asked anyway. "Well, I am thrilled about the nomination. I could not be prouder of this album or this song."

"But there's also been the scandal. That's been the talk of the town. Do you want to explain?" She uses this obnoxious news broadcaster voice like she's performing some sort of hard-hitting journalism.

I look at her and wonder where she gets off and how she decided this would be the first question of our interview. Then I glance to the side of the stage. My dad and agent are here watching. I didn't want them to be, but they're a package deal at this point, and they scheduled the interview. And I'm too numb to care about their presence. Kicking them out would involve talking to them, so I continue to ignore them instead.

All I have to do is remind myself that Ford has these recordings locked down legally, so I know there's nothing they can touch. And, quite frankly, I've grown accustomed to them loitering around me like leeches.

The devil you know and all that.

Plus, my dad has never felt like a parent—I know that now that I've seen a great one in action—so my expectations for him are low. Still, agitation flares when he rolls his hand at me, urging me to say something. He'll berate me for freezing up when we get behind closed doors, telling me my image should always be intact. But his reaction begs the question: Did he relay my no-go questions at all?

It was too easy to think I could just fall back into my old role. From the minute I landed, it's all been out of whack. It feels like forcing my feet into a pair of shoes that are too small.

Like a wrecking ball, it hits me that it's bizarre to allow them here. To allow them access to me at all. To roll over and show them my belly like a beaten-down girl who came slinking back when her trial run at independence didn't work.

I may not have West, but I still have my wits. I still own all that growing I did out in Rose Hill, and it kicks in all at once.

"Skylar?" the other host asks in a gentle voice. "Are you—"

I know he's about to reference me freezing up, so I cut him off. "Am I horrified that you'd invite me here, then ask me to explain myself on national television as though I've done something wrong? I am not a scandal. I'm a victim of a despicable breach of my privacy. *I've* been violated, and you want me to *explain* myself?"

A manic laugh bubbles up in my throat as I straighten to turn and face the pink-faced talk show hosts. "This"—I point between them—"this is what the media does, to women especially. It's not my job to take accountability for someone else's shitty behavior. I don't owe anyone an explanation. I don't owe anyone insight into my private life or consensual love life—least of all vultures like you. Asking about it? Searching for it? You're just as guilty as whoever leaked those photos for perpetuating it."

"Skylar…" The man tries to placate me while the woman turns the most satisfying shade of dark red. Like my favorite fucking lipstick. The one my agent told me was "too vixen" for this interview.

Fuck them all.

I can see my dad's ruddy face and my agent rapidly shaking his head, but I don't care. I feel like Cherry that day she flew between West and me.

It's impossible to forget how flying feels.

"No." I reach back and yank the cord off my back. The mic unit crashes to the floor with a single angry tug. "I'm done here. Want to boost your ratings?" I can see the camera people and producers gesturing wildly. They won't capture this next part quite as loudly, but it won't stop it from spreading like wildfire on the internet. And I won't ask Ford to lift a single finger to stop it. "You can quote this. Go. Fuck. Yourselves."

With that, I spin on my three-inch heels and strut off

the stage, straight toward my dad and agent. One sickly white, the other red like a rage-infused tomato. I hold up a hand to cut them both off. "Don't waste your words on me." I face my agent. "You're fired." Then I turn to my sperm donor. "You're fired and cut off. I never want to see you again."

His jaw works as he struggles to swallow his rage. "Skylar, you're having a nervous breakdown."

I snort. There's the gaslighting. I see it now for what it is. I see him for who he is.

And I see myself for who I've become.

My own woman.

"No, *Dad*. I'm having an awakening. I already had the nervous breakdown, and it was really fucking low. This is my rebirth. And you're not my daddy anymore. You're not my manager. You are nothing without me, and that's exactly what you deserve. Expect to hear from my lawyers." I add the last bit with extra flourish. I don't have my own lawyers yet, but I'm marching out of here to get them.

I leave the studio with only my purse and my pride. I skip the town car and duck into a cab. When it pulls away, I sigh and pull out my ridiculous flip phone. The first person I call is Ford Grant.

He answers on the first ring with, "Fuck yeah, Skylar," and I instantly know he was watching the show. Ford has never told me what to do, only empowered me to do it. I'm not sure how I'll ever thank him for taking a chance on me.

"I need a favor."

"Anything."

"Numbers for the absolute meanest lawyers money can buy."

"I'll have Belinda call you."

I smile. Of course Ford has a shark of a lawyer. He doesn't take any shit.

And neither do I. Not anymore.

"There's something else I need to tell you," he says. "And it's going to suck."

"Ford, nothing can suck more than the past couple of weeks. Out with it."

"My investigator got back to me. They traced the hack and the leak back to your agent."

I suck in a breath. We don't say it, but we both know that means my dad too. Those two are thick as fucking thieves.

"Well, it's a good thing I just fired them both."

I hear him sigh. "What else can I do?"

"You've done enough. Just get me Belinda and all the proof. Let's see what she can do. I've been paralyzed by this for too long. I'm ready for a fight."

"This could be a violation of your old contracts too, you know."

And now I smile. "Photosynthesis, Ford. Gonna take all this garbage and convert it into a win."

"Good…" He trails off and I know there's another question on his tongue. "Can I tell West?"

My heart hurts instantly. Just hearing his name sucks the air from my lungs. "Sure. How is he?"

"Fucking terrible, but this will help."

If I wasn't so sad, I'd laugh. Ford is not one to mince

words. "Okay," I say before hanging up with an aching heaviness in my chest.

Then I watch the city pass by in a blur, making plans for how to fix the mistakes I've made. To take back control, to ask myself what I really want out of this life. Before long, a sense of optimism creeps in. It reminds me of West.

A sense of empowerment settles over me. And I wonder if this is how Cherry felt that day she spread her wings.

Because it's fucking fantastic.

And I'm only getting started.

CHAPTER 40

West

"NICE HORSE," FORD ANNOUNCES AS HE SLIDES ONTO THE same bench Skylar always sat on. I have to bite down on my tongue to keep from snapping at him to get off of it.

That would be entirely unhinged of me.

Maybe it's the lack of sleep or the lack of food, but without the kids here this week, I have treated myself like shit.

I miss Skylar so badly that I feel like I have the flu. My bones ache with it. All that optimism she likes about me is nowhere to be found.

I'm floundering.

Only the horses make me feel better.

"Yeah? What makes it a nice horse, Ford?" I call back from the back of the horse Skylar watched me start only a few weeks ago. She's gotten a little better every day and spending time doting on her has made me feel a little less stricken. I can't truly make myself feel better but watching her come around to handling has been a small victory over a bleak few days.

"Uh…" Ford fumbles around, head tilting back and forth. He doesn't know shit about horses, and he's not a big talk-about-our-feelings kind of guy. I remember him telling me about Rosie and him getting together. He ripped that Band-Aid off with little tact and a lot of awkward body language.

This feels similar.

"It's got…nice hair?"

"Her coat? You like her coat?" I ask with a chuckle that feels unfamiliar in my throat.

"Yeah, sure. Whatever. I'm trying to be nice and normal and shit."

I urge the mare forward, bringing her to a halt and facing Ford at the fence of the arena. "You're not doing very well."

"Yeah, I know. I'm a dick and kind of weird, but I tried."

I laugh now. "Ford, we've been friends for over twenty years. Why are you trying to be something you're not?"

He swallows and pins me with his green eyes. "Because I've never seen you like this, and I don't know what to do."

I lick my lips and glance away, then force my shoulders up into an unaffected shrug. "It's fine. I'll survive. I always do."

He leans back on the bleachers, looking casual and disheveled as he props his elbows on the board behind himself. "No, I don't mean survive. I've seen you sad before. What I haven't seen is you giving up so fucking easily. It's pathetic."

I start. Then my spine straightens, and my voice turns icy. "Come again?"

He kicks a foot and curls his lip, trying to get horseshit off the bottom of his expensive boot. "You'll *survive*? What is that? That's fucking quitter talk. Where's the fight, West? Where's the guy who was ready to throw hands when someone so much as looked at his little sister the wrong way?"

"Come on. We both know I'm not like that anymore."

"Why, though? There's a time and a place for that kind of passion. And this? This, West?" He points at the ground in front of my horse. "This is the fucking time. You're always so busy fighting for everyone else. Your kids, your sister,—hell, even me. But how about yourself?"

I blink. "You're really leaning into that whole dick character trait right now, huh?"

"Someone has to. Everyone else is so busy feeling bad for you that they're scared to tell you the truth."

My teeth grind. I hate this. I hate everything Ford is saying to me right now.

I hate it because it's true.

I hate it because it makes me hate myself a little more than I already do.

"Best friends don't sit by and watch each other fuck up their lives. Consider this your intervention. You know I'm a private person. And that's what keeps me from ever asking too many questions about your personal life. So I don't know a lot about your relationship with Skylar, but I know what it's like to spend years pining after someone. I know what it's like to watch them leave and start a new life. And it's fucking miserable."

Dread. Dread sinks in and all I can think is…

What have I done?

"I fucked up." My voice cracks, and I scrub a hand over my face. "I was so certain she'd leave. And then she did. She told me to let her go. She was so confident about it. And it's like…I did this to myself. I should have known better."

"You're new to long-term relationships that you actually want to be in, but let me tell you something I know for sure: You don't love someone only when it's convenient or easy. You love them when it's fucking awful and the world is falling apart around you."

"Is that from one of your emo poetry books?"

Ford rolls his eyes at me as I cover my overflowing emotion with a jab about his reading preferences as a kid. "Skylar has spent her entire life expecting people to let her down. She's so used to it that she's not even offended by it. But I am. She deserves better. And, West? So. Do. You."

The knowledge that Skylar is accepting of people letting her down guts me. And Ford's words land like shrapnel in my chest. Like he just *knows* the things that will get to me. Like he's privy to the things I tell myself when no one is around.

You don't deserve her. She was always out of your league. This will get easier.

But that last one is a lie for sure. Skylar is my person. My life could never be better without her in it. I've sentenced myself to a lifetime of misery to respect her wishes.

"I know you. And you are the hardest working, toughest motherfucker I know. So quit moping and start acting like it. Go fight for her." With that, he pushes to stand, wipes his hands over his pants like just being near the barn has made him dirty, and then turns to walk away.

But not before calling back over his shoulder, "Oh, by the way, her dad and agent hacked her email and distributed the photos. She burned the world down on morning television today. Fired everyone. She's trending on every social media outlet. I'm pretty sure she's going to win that award this weekend too."

What?

"Why didn't you lead with that?"

"Wanted to be a dick first."

My mind spins. I want to kill her dad. I want to give her the biggest high five. I want to watch her win that award.

I want *her*.

I don't think twice before calling out to Ford's retreating form, "Can I borrow your private jet?"

And I can only imagine the smug smirk of on his dickish face as he responds, "It's fueled up and ready when you are."

CHAPTER 41

Skylar

BREAKING NEWS: Skylar Stone is going to win tonight.

    I already know it.

I BREATHE IN THROUGH MY NOSE FOR THREE, OUT THROUGH my mouth for three. But the butterflies crashing against my rib cage don't seem to care.

This isn't my first award show, but it is the first one where I've felt truly invested in the outcome. I want to win. I want to win so badly it hurts.

Not for the clout and not for what it could do for my career going forward.

I want to win solely to prove to myself that I can. That, all on my own, I can create something worthy of an award.

With my own words on a page, a small production studio, and a lot of passion, I am worthy of my career.

That not every bit of it was fake.

That's what I need to finish my story. To prove that—not for lack of trying—I cannot be defeated.

My limo progresses through the red-carpet line, and I take out the compact in my purse to check my red lipstick one last time.

I'm not fucking around. I'm in full vixen mode and I don't care how I look to anyone else.

The car ahead moves into the unloading spot and I give myself a quiet, "You got this, Skylar. You're a fucking badass."

No one else is here to tell me, so I might as well tell myself.

Ford will meet me at the entrance, since he's attending with his dad, whose band will be performing tonight, so at least I won't have to walk the red carpet alone.

I'm sure my ex-parents and ex-agent will be here too, acting like all is well in the Skylar Stone world. But the joke will be on them when Belinda rakes them over the coals for failing to work in the best interests of the asset.

Then I'll sit back, sip champagne, and watch them all sink.

The divider drops. "Ma'am, we're next. I'll get out to open the door for you. Security is already in place."

I nod to my driver in the rearview mirror. "Thank you." Then I wipe my damp palms over my red Oscar de la Renta dress. It's structured, classy, and powerful. My parents didn't choose it and neither did my agent. There's no "image" I'm going for—I just plain liked it.

"Here we are." His kind eyes flash to mine. "You ready?"

I smile back. "Hell yeah."

"Good luck, Miss Stone. I'll be rooting for ya."

I nod to him in thanks, grateful for that final vote of confidence, and step out into the chaos. The sun is bright, but the camera flashes are brighter.

My shoulders stiffen, and I steel myself to carry on.

I hate this.

And then…relief. Relief that I can finally admit I hate this circus. This show. This life.

I blink once and step up the gently sloped ramp with a natural smile on my face. It doesn't hurt my cheeks, and I'm not faking it.

I intend to fully enjoy this walk down the red carpet.

After all, I intend for it to be my last.

"Skylar!"

"Miss Stone!"

"Skylar!"

People call my name from every direction, and I tune them out. What I hear in my head is the soft lapping of waves on a lakeshore and the call of a loon as it floats across the water. It centers me, but I start when a hand lands on my back.

I turn, expecting it to be Ford.

"Oh, there you—"

I stop short when my gaze lands on baby blues I'd know anywhere.

"West," I breathe as I soak in the sight of him as though he might be some sort of cruel mirage.

He's here.

He looks fucking edible in a tuxedo. Hair styled. Stubble the perfect length so that he doesn't look too put together.

He's here.

He's a sight for sore eyes. And yet…I can find no words to say to him.

He's really here.

I'm shocked.

His hand wraps around my hip possessively as his head dips close to my ear. "Surprise?"

I can't stop the shiver that races down my spine, and I don't hesitate at all as my body turns in toward his. I want nothing more than to be close to him. To touch him.

"You're here" are the only words my addled brain can string together.

His smile. It's warm. It's safe. It's all for me. "I'm here."

"What are you doing here?"

One cheek tugs up, a dimple forming in its wake. "Didn't really think your number-one fan would miss his girl winning tonight, did you?"

"I haven't won."

His eyes work their way over my face. He doesn't rush. He soaks me in, like I'm water after he's been stranded in the desert. "You will."

The way West believes in me will never fail to take my breath away.

I step closer, seeking his heat despite the warm weather.

"I—" My voice cracks, and I blink faster to cover the emotion. I refuse to cry on the red carpet for everyone to see. "I've missed you."

His head shakes softly from side to side, his eyes brighter than usual. "Me too, fancy face. Me too." He pulls me against him—with cameras and fans and people screaming my name—and hugs me like I'm his.

Because I am.

And neither of us cares who sees it.

"I'm so fucking sorry. So sorry I let you walk out that door." His words rasp over my scalp, tangling in the loose waves that cascade down my shoulders. "I froze. And I should have fought harder. I was busy licking my wounds when what I should have told you is that it doesn't matter how hard the road is. Bears. Paparazzi. The lowest lows. You and me? We do this thing together. You're my person. Nothing will change that."

I gulp to swallow the tears. "You're my person too. I'm fucking miserable without you."

He breathes me in, and I nuzzle him, knowing I'm getting makeup on his lapels but finding that I don't especially care. "What about the kids? They—"

He holds me out now, gripping my shoulders and bending his knees so he can look me in the eye. "Will be fine. We'll make sure they are. It's better when we do it together, yeah?"

My molars grit as I nod back at this man. This big, beautiful man who I get to call my own. At this moment, I can't help but hate myself for walking away from him.

He got to me first.

But my plan for tonight was always to make my way back to him.

And now he gets to be here to see me do it.

"Always better when we're together," I say, smiling as I repeat the words back to him. Then I step in close and kiss him squarely on the mouth.

Cameras flash as they capture the moment.

And for once, it doesn't bother me.

"The nominees for song of the year are…"

The screen filters through snippets of songs and music videos, but when it gets to mine, they pan to me. Sitting next to West, in what was supposed to be Ford's seat.

Earlier, after Ford checked to make sure West and I found each other, he mumbled, "Good. Now I can leave. I fucking hate these things. I'll watch you win from the hotel."

Turns out he wasn't accompanying his dad at all.

He was playing matchmaker.

West squeezes my hand and grins down at me. I smile and dip my head, a hint of shyness creeping in. My cheeks flush and the voice from the stage carries on with the other nominees.

"Don't be nervous. You're going to win."

"How do you know?" I whisper to West.

He shrugs. "I just do."

I don't know what to say to that, so I settle for resting

my head on his broad shoulder while squeezing the hell out of his hand.

Eventually, the moment comes.

"All right, here we go." The ripping of an envelope filters over the speakers. "And the award goes to…Skylar Stone for 'Photosynthesis'!"

I literally feel like I can't move. The only thing that gets me up out of my seat is West shooting up to cheer with abandon and pulling me into the strongest, happiest hug. "You did it. You fucking did it. I'm so proud of you," he shouts in my ear over the thunderous applause surrounding us.

We both turn when there's a boisterous, "That's my girl," shouted from several rows back.

My fucking dad.

West's muscles tense as he glares back, and I tap him with my hand. "Don't give him the satisfaction. He's pathetic, and everyone is about to know it."

With that, I kiss my man, hold my head up high, and make my way to the stage.

Hugs and thank-yous are exchanged as I take the trophy in my hand. The applause stops when I finally let out a heavy sigh at the podium.

"Wow, this…" I look around the auditorium, soaking in this moment. Wanting to commit it to memory. Hoping I'll remember it clearly enough to tell West's and my children one day. "This is an incredible honor. This has been a dream of mine since I was a little girl. And I don't mean just winning an award because I've done that in the past. I mean winning an award for something I am incredibly proud of because I have *not* done that in the past."

The theater is quiet save for the odd murmur.

"As some of you may know, I've been at this for a long time. So long that I can't remember a time when I wasn't performing. Even my personal life has mostly been a performance. And it's recently dawned on me I am very, very tired of performing. And this new album…is not a performance. It's a labor of love. It's pride. It's joy. It's heartbreak."

My eyes find West's across the rows of attendees.

"I was raised in a household where nothing I did was good enough, where any misstep was met with abuse and condescension."

Gasps echo to the stage, but I don't stop. I expect music to start playing to cut me off. But it never comes.

"But I've recently sought shelter in a household where all my anxieties and all my missteps are met with unconditional love and support. It's taken me a long time to accept that I deserve that kind of happiness. That what the media says about me isn't actually who I am. I've only recently felt empowered enough to write my music and produce an album—shout-out to Ford Grant and his daughter, Cora, both of whom are endlessly kind and talented—that I am proud of from start to finish. It's with this sense of pride that I have finally come to realize what I will and will not stand for in my life. Ford, you have given me a gift that is invaluable and yet integral to the woman who stands here on this stage."

Someone whistles their support, and I flash a smile in their general direction.

"I've also recently met two small children whose strength and good nature make me want to be in their company always. I've met a man who loves me at my lowest of lows, who is my number-one fan. West, I *love* you."

I hold the award up in West's direction and his cheeks are bright red but he still blows me a kiss back. Cheers and hoots ring out and all the words I planned to say flow from my lips.

"This album, and this title track in particular, is about growing and changing and evolving and the process of taking energy and turning it into life. This album is my permission to do the same. After years of faking it, I'm going to be real. I'm taking this life, the one I do not enjoy at all, and I'm turning it into one that I do."

West whoops from his seat and tears spring up in my eyes.

"I will be forever grateful for this career and the privileges it has afforded me. And this award? This award is proof that I can do hard things. That I can rise above even the cruelest attempts to tear me down. I can turn a heaping pile of shit into a win. And it's the perfect place to hang my hat. Thank you for the award. Thank you for the years of inclusion in this industry. I hope you all love the rest of the album too, because it will be my last. You may see me around, or you may not."

I shrug and scan the audience over watery lashes. "I'll be busy living my best life in a small Canadian mountain town that feels like the safe haven I've always dreamed of. Ollie? Emmy?" I hold the award up to the camera in front of me. "This one's for you. See you at home."

A smattering of applause builds. It builds and builds until I can barely hear myself think. I grin a real, wide grin as I lift my dress in one hand and make my way down the stairs.

Peers congratulate me on my way past. They shake my hand. They hug me. But it's all a blur, a holdup. I don't care about schmoozing. All I want to do is get to West.

I can see him. Standing. Clapping. Smiling.

So close and so far away.

When I finally get to our row, he steps out to hug me again. "Was that always part of the plan?"

I smile into his neck and breathe him in. "Once I realized I couldn't live without you and I'd be miserable for the rest of my life if I tried? Yes. But I'm glad you were here to hear it in person. My flight out is tonight. I was coming straight back to you."

"Home."

I pull back, one hand on each of his cheeks. "Home."

Then I kiss him again. Hard. I can't get enough. He smiles against my mouth, and it makes me melt against his hard body.

"Remember how I don't do things I don't want to anymore?"

He chuckles, as an usher hustles toward us, likely rushing to tell us to sit down. "Yeah?"

"I don't want to stay for the rest of this show. Get me the fuck out of here, Coach Thick Thighs."

West smiles down at me. "With pleasure."

"We're going, we're going," I politely assure the usher as West takes my hand to lead me out of the building.

"Yeah, we're going." West holds up his index finger to the scrawny kid. "I just have one thing I need to do."

My brow furrows as he leads me several rows up the aisle.

Right to where my parents and agent are seated. My dad is red-faced. Again. Clearly not a fan of my acceptance speech. But he still has the gall to stand up and reach around West to shake my hand.

Which is when West strikes.

His fist flies hard and fast. The blood that sails from my father's mouth, though? I follow its arc in fascinated slow motion.

There are gasps. Shouts.

West takes my dad by his collar and sits him back in his seat like he's a rag doll. "You want to talk to *my* girl, asshole? You go through me. And I'm not letting you anywhere near her ever again. Understand?"

I blink and step in close to West, leaning on him for safety like I have since day one. Not because I need to but because I trust him to protect me.

He towers over my dad, whose face is in his hands, and points at my agent next. "The same goes for you. You see her walk past? I want you both to look the other way."

I shouldn't feel as satisfied as I do by this spectacle. But my dad is certainly having exactly the type of day he deserves. And I find myself loving West even more for this wild protective streak of his.

When he straightens, he tugs at his lapels to smooth his jacket and then takes my hand.

"Skylar, let's blow this popsicle stand."

And we do.

I can't take my eyes off him as he leads me out of that auditorium. The powerful way he carries himself takes my breath away. And the twitch of his lips has me tilting my head in with a whispered question. "What's so funny?"

His eyes slice over to me and his fingers pulse around mine. "Three."

"Three what?"

Now he grins.

"Noses."

I bark out a laugh as we step into the sun. "It's okay, I heard he knows a great surgeon."

CHAPTER 42

Skylar

I EYE UP THE CANADA GOOSE. ITS BLACK, BEADY EYES MEET mine. I've been back in Rose Hill for several weeks and have been dying to get close to one.

"Skylar." I can hear the warning tone in West's voice and it just makes me smile. "That goose is not your friend."

"Then why is he friend-shaped?"

West scoffs and the kids giggle. We came down to the lake for a picnic and I was immediately taken by the bird. His dinosaur-like feet. His long, graceful neck. I swiped a cracker from the old wicker picnic basket and approached him immediately.

"Skylar, I'm serious. I'm more scared of that goose than I am of a grizzly bear."

I glance over my shoulder and glare at him. "Don't be ridiculous."

"Only sixty percent of Americans think they could beat a goose unarmed. It's in the article. Look it up."

My eyes roll now. "That's pathetic. Why would I fight him? I just want to feed him." My voice goes all gooey. "Don't I, fella? I just wanna give you a cracker."

"I'm going to tell Cherry you cheated on her."

I snort at that but ignore him as I step closer slowly.

"Tomorrow I'm going to send you a headline that says 'Breaking news: Skylar Stone is tragically murdered by the world's meanest animal.'"

I almost laugh but decide I don't want to scare the goose and bite down on it. My back says turned to him. For some reason, I need to do this. It's inexplicable.

"Hi, friend. Are you hungry?"

"Yeah, for blood."

Fucking West.

My lips twitch as I reach forward. The goose's neck arches and his head moves in my direction. Before I know it his beak darts out and he violently rips the cracker from my hand.

I squeal and leap back in surprise, which only makes everyone burst out laughing. The goose makes a huge mess, crackers crumbling everywhere, and I turn back to West and the kids with a know-it-all smile plastered on my face.

"I did it!" I raise my fists in the air like I've won a race. But the motion is so exaggerated that the goose startles and takes off, skimming onto the water just to get away from me.

"See? I'm country now. A friend of wild geese. Protector of mice."

"As long as you're not a feeder of bears," West quips, reaching for me and pressing a brusque kiss to my temple.

My head tips from side to side. "I still think they're cute."

I turn, kissing his cheek chastely, and when my palm lands on his chest I can feel his heart beating, hard. Like maybe he really is afraid of the goose.

Then I step away, eyeing Ollie, who is sitting in our spot—the spot where we read and where the first lines of my first song were ever written. This spot? It's magic.

So I trudge over there and snuggle up beside him under one of the blankets he brought down from the house. Minutes pass as we watch West and Emmy lay out the picnic they packed. A blanket, a couple low-slung chairs. The two of them bicker about the layout of the meal and I peek over to see Ollie roll his eyes.

I can't help but giggle.

"Are you just going to sit there?" West teases as he pulls out a thermos of apple cider.

I lean back into the roots of the tree behind me, throw an arm over Ollie's shoulders, and let out a deep and dramatic sigh. "I think I will. Paid good money for this date."

West's eyes narrow. "I can't believe you paid for a date with me *and* the kids."

My cheeks pinch together as I bite down on another smile. He's not going to let me live that one down. But the truth is, in the weeks I've been back, we've gotten plenty of time alone. And I get so much attention from him that I would never need to cash that date in anyway. This just seemed like the perfect crisp fall afternoon to relax by the lake with the kids.

And I'm tired.

Body tired from the horseback riding lesson he gave me earlier. And brain tired from the session with my therapist after that. Heart full because now that I've started writing music, I can't seem to stop. I don't know where this new craving will take me, but I'm excited to have rediscovered my passion for music.

My anxiety has improved with my exit from the public eye.

Both my parents have slunk off to their respective snake pits, finally having realized that their meal ticket is no longer valid. I can't be sure I'll get back what they took from me. But the more time I spend away from them, the less I even care.

Even the press seems less and less interested in me. What I do now doesn't sell gossip magazines at the grocery checkout. And even if it did, I'm getting better every day at handling the moments when those self-doubting thoughts start to pummel me. I've learned to identify that voice as "just my anxiety" and tend not to believe her when she tells me things that make my chest feel tight.

Instead, right now, my chest feels tight for entirely different reasons.

Reasons like my eyes catching on a large mason jar that West just pulled from the picnic basket. My heart stutters as I take it in. And when I glance back up, West is watching me. He's propped on his knees and grinning at me, looking so utterly proud of himself.

"What is that?"

"Why it's a jar of Skittles, fancy face."

My eyes scan again. There's no rainbow to be tasted in that jar.

"They're all orange," I say, making the most obvious observation.

"Of course. Orange is your favorite."

A watery laugh falls from my lips as I shake my head in disbelief. "What did you do with all the other ones?"

He smirks as he twists the lid open and holds the jar out me. "Ate them. Can't you tell? They went straight to my thighs."

Our eyes lock, and in his baby blues, I see the sparkle and devotion I've come to revel in. The kind of sparkles that keeps me laughing every damn day. And the kind of devotion that has had him snacking on all the most disgusting flavors of Skittles for who knows how long just to save me an entire jar of my favorites.

"This is…" I trail off, reaching in for a few pieces of candy. And then I grin as I turn my palm over and see them there. The gift is ridiculous and significant all at once. "Too much."

"Uncle Ford agrees," Emmy pipes up. "He told me you overpaid for this date with our dad."

Ollie laughs and West just grins.

"You can tell your uncle Ford that I wholeheartedly disagree." Then I toss a wink at West. "Plus, it was for a very good cause."

EPILOGUE

West

THE FOLLOWING YEAR…

I'M SEATED IN THE FRONT ROW. I'VE BEEN HERE SINCE DORIS started setting up in the school gymnasium. She and Skylar started a charity that brings arts education to underprivileged children, and today is the fundraising talent show.

Guests begin to filter in. My parents take seats beside me. Ford and Rosie on the other side. Cora flits around onstage and backstage, wearing her signature black from head to toe and getting everything set up.

She recently told Ford she wants to be a roadie, traveling with bands, and he looked like he wanted to die.

It was the best.

Before long, people from town pack the entire gym. The same people who've accepted Skylar since her retirement—protected Skylar since her retirement. In the beginning, a few paparazzi tried snooping for a shot, but they soon discovered the hotels were full and the restaurants were fresh out of food and drinks.

They didn't last long. And now, we live peacefully on the farm together. Or at least as peacefully as Emmy will allow now that she's dead set on learning to play the guitar.

Ollie, though still quiet, has started to stretch his wings and talk to new people. A slow, steady evolution. He told me once he wanted to be just as brave as Skylar.

To me, he's always been brave. But watching him flourish has been one of life's greatest gifts.

As I reflect on how incredible the last year has been—how my life feels full to the point of overflowing while also feeling like it's just getting started—the lights dim and Doris takes the stage.

"Right, well, good of you all to come out and bring your wallets. I'll be honest, some of these performances are worth the ticket price and some just aren't. But you have to clap anyway. All right?"

Laughter echoes through the gym. The acoustics are terrible, but it doesn't matter. Everyone is here for a good cause. A small community coming together. I've always loved living in Rose Hill, but I'm not sure I fully appreciated it until I got to see it through Skylar's eyes.

"But," Doris continues, "this first group is pretty damn good. Apparently, one member is well-known in some circles. In others, she'll always be the girl with the broken nose who decided to stick around."

I'm laughing when I hold my hands up on either side of my mouth and call out, "It wasn't broken!"

"Weston, sit your ass down and enjoy the show. Everyone else too."

And with that, Doris stomps off the stage.

Within moments, Skylar walks out, wearing that pretty summer dress with oranges on it. Emmy and Ollie tag along on either side of her. She helps them get situated. Ollie at the piano and Emmy in the open space beside the mic.

"Ready?" she whispers to them.

Emmy grins almost maniacally and whisper-shouts back, "Yes!"

Ollie blushes and nods his head while looking down at the piano keys.

I'm choked up watching them prepare to play the song she and Oliver wrote. And they haven't even started yet.

Skylar tosses me a wink and they start.

Ollie plays.

Emmy dances.

Skylar sings.

And I fall in love with her all over again.

Wild Eyes by Skylar Stone

It all started on a backroad
When I didn't need saving
Just a new road for me to take

ELSIE SILVER

I'm a soul with no home
No place that I belong
Until you chased my clouds away

City lights don't shine
As bright as the window
Where I watch your life at bay
I'd give up every bit of fame
For moonlights by the water
And the way you whisper my name

Your arms keep me from falling
Your heart's held my own,
Since the start
And I need you to know
My dreams have all come true
Since all I dream of is you

You're all the orange skittles
Every lyric in a love song
A safe place to rest my weary bones
A shelter from the storm,
I have never flown this high
And my smile has a truthful tone

Everything's easier with you
Everything now

Until you, it felt so wrong

WILD EYES

All my life, traveling alone
My love got lost in the crossroads
I was a long, long way from home

I can't stop the fighting now,
No more lonely nights in hopeless towns,
No more empty promises or lies
Just the way you love my wild eyes

It's the only thing that matters
Only home I need to know
If we're better together

Take my hand, let's end the show

I'm finally home,
You're my forever home.
We're finally home,
It's a forever home.

"Where are we going?" Skylar bounces on the spot as she looks out the window of my truck.

My fingers twist on the steering wheel as we navigate the winding backroad that heads out of Rose Hill. "I can't tell you."

"Whatever it is, it's too bad the kids couldn't come. It's such a nice day."

I nod. It *is* a nice day. The sun is shining. The roads are quiet and…

"Do you know what today is, Skylar?" I ask as we round a rocky corner.

"Saturday," she replies, grinning proudly.

I scoff. "You know that's not what I meant."

Then I pull the truck over onto the side of the road, put it in park, and turn in my seat to face her.

"Oh, is this a road-head thing? I could do it while you drive."

I groan and scrub a hand over my face. "Listen, I might take you up on that later. But right now…" I open my door and jog around the truck to open hers.

"Is hitchhiking on your bucket list or something?"

My eyes roll as I reach my hand up to hers. "That fucking mouth, Sky. Hop out."

She does, with a laugh that sounds like music to my ears.

"Do you know where we were one year ago today?"

She stops, fingers slipping from mine as she turns in a slow circle to take in her surroundings. "I… We… Is this the spot we met?"

I clamp down on my grin, feeling pretty damn excited to be here all over again a year later. "Yes."

Her eyes widen and a softness takes over her features. Eyes tracing the path we took. Where she parked. Where I parked. Where I walked.

"How did you remember?" she murmurs as I walk her toward the spot where I threw myself over her.

"I put it on my calendar."

Her steps falter. "What? Why?"

I shrug. "I'm not entirely sure why I did it then. I just did. Something about the moment felt important."

We walk a few more paces, until we're right on the spot.

And then I turn. Pulling the velvet box from my back pocket as I drop to one knee.

"Now I know I did it because it was the day I met the woman I'd marry."

Her hands fly up over her mouth, a squeal echoing behind them. "West!"

"Skylar Stone. I met you in this exact spot one year ago. I knew it then, and I know it now: You are my person. Everything is better when we do it together. You're home to me. Would you do me the incredible honor of being my wife?"

"Yes!" She practically knocks me over with her enthusiasm.

"After this, I'm taking you to the Calgary Zoo, where I will take all that social media footage of you with bears that I promised you one year ago—"

She cuts me off when she drops to her knees to kiss me. Right here on the warm asphalt, we make a promise to be in this together. Always.

And just like that day…

Everything works out the way it was meant to.

READ ON FOR A SNEAK PEEK AT THE NEXT BOOK IN THE ROSE HILL SERIES, *WILD SIDE*

Rhys

I hear the doorbell. And I ignore it. I don't want whatever they're selling.

So I continue surfing through the options of TV shows to watch next. But nothing appeals. *Ted Lasso* left me in a slump. And being too injured to work out has me bored.

Now there are three strong knocks at the door. And I still don't want to answer it. I come to this place to be left alone. So I pretend I don't hear it. Door-to-door people always go away eventually.

But not this person. Now they knock *five* times.

Agitated, I push to stand and ignore the twinge in my knee as I march across the open living space.

"Whatever it is, I'm not interested—" I grumble as I yank the front door open. But I come eye-to-eye with absolutely no one. Just a clear view of the front street.

"Hi. I'm Tabitha." The firm voice comes from below me, and I drop my chin to follow the sound. "Rhys, right?"

There's a woman standing on my front doorstep. She has dark hair, nearly black. The onyx slashes of her eyebrows frame narrowed chocolate eyes that are ringed with a thick fringe of lashes. She's short—next to me, most people are—but there's something about the way she carries herself that *feels* tall.

She has a presence.

I say nothing, but she sticks her hand out to shake mine anyway. I stare at it, not wanting to be rude, but also wondering what the hell she wants. This place is my haven. When I'm in Emerald Lake, no one bugs me.

No one knows me in Canada.

And that's how I like it.

"Hi? Hello?" She bobs her hand again, calling me out on the fact that I've stood here glaring at her and not made a single move. "If English isn't your first language, I have some passable French. Otherwise, I'll pull my phone out to translate."

My lips flatten and I reach forward to wrap my hand around her small one. "I speak English," I mutter as I meet her eyes once more. "I just wasn't expecting anyone."

I can feel the callouses on her palms as she grips my hand. Hard. It's a real, proper, honest handshake. "Who doesn't love a surprise, am I right?"

"Me. I don't love surprises." Her eyes don't leave mine and I get the sense she's sizing me up. Judging my worthiness. For what, I have no clue.

We continue staring and shaking hands tightly, even

though at this point the custom has dragged on for longer than necessary.

"Well, surprise! I'm your new tenant's sister and I'm currently helping her move in. I need to have a chat with you while she's out."

I drop her hand and blink. Her tone makes me feel like I'm in trouble. All I wanted was someone unobtrusive to live next door and maintain the place during my stretches away. Now I have some tiny terror on my front step, looking like she's ready to interrogate me.

"Invite me in. We'll cover our bases, and I'll be on my merry way." She smiles now.

And it's fucking blinding. It's not demure or shy. It's a weapon, and she knows exactly what she's doing by pulling it out on me.

Before I was quiet because I'm always suspicious of people who randomly show up at my door. Now I'm quiet because my brain is short circuiting, and my eyes are wandering. Wandering over shiny strands of dark hair, tan skin, and the feminine flare of her hips.

Yeah. Tabitha, sister of my new tenant, is hot, looks like she thinks I might have bodies buried in my basement, *and* has a mean handshake.

Strangely, I'm into it.

So I step aside and gesture her in.

For a flash, she softens. Her smile is relieved as she wipes her palms against her acid wash jeans, suggesting she's a bit nervous. Then her chin dips as she steps into the foyer with a muted, "Thanks."

I muster a nod before closing the door and gesturing her through to the kitchen. The windows on this side of the A-frame directly face the lake. It's a stunning view, and I can't blame her for stopping to take it in.

"Beautiful," she says.

I watch her for a beat. Shoulders carried tall, plush lips just slightly parted. "It is."

A sly grin twists those lips now as she turns to me with a quirked brow. "A man of few words, huh?"

"Guess so," I respond, giving her my back as I open the fridge. "Drink?"

"Nah. I won't be that long." I can hear the amusement in her voice as she tugs out a stool at the island.

I take out a can of soda water and crack it, leaning against the counter behind me to face her. She's folded her hands, fingers woven together, and her lips are pressed in a tight line.

"So…" The word trails off and I wait.

And I wait.

I take a casual sip of my bubbly water and prop it on the counter beside me.

She continues staring at me, and I'm not oblivious to the way her eyes have shifted, following my arms as I cross them in front of me and take her in.

Busted.

"So," I say back, with a small twitch of my lips.

She sniffs and straightens, eyes flitting to the side and back. "I'm just going to come out with it. Erika has not had an easy go of it. Her stories are not mine to share. I just need to know that her and her son Milo will be safe here."

I shift slightly. "Okay. My home base is out of the country, and I'm only here now and then. There's an alarm system though."

"That's not the kind of safe I mean." Her teeth strum at her bottom lip and she sighs. "Listen, I know I'm overstepping. She's just finally in a good place and I don't know what she would or wouldn't…ugh." The woman runs an agitated hand through her hair. "I hate myself for asking this, and she'd fucking kill me, but…if you have any drugs stronger than Tylenol, can you please put them somewhere that no one would suspect?"

My brows drop and I lean forward. "What?"

"Prescription drugs. I want to make sure she won't have access to them."

"She'll be living next door. Not with me."

Tabitha shrugs, wrinkles her nose, and looks away again. "She's charming and beautiful and finally back on track. Never say never."

This woman must not understand how deep my trust issues go if she thinks I have designs on my new tenant. "I'm not planning on pursuing your sister."

She flinches but doesn't hesitate to look me dead in the eye when she says, "Well, that plan might be one-sided."

"Are you…" I trail off, not sure what to say. I have never had a more bizarre conversation with a perfect stranger in my life.

"I am being a snoopy, overprotective sister who has listened to her gush about you for two days. Just nod if you understand me and we can never talk about this again."

I have spent all of about thirty minutes around Erika. She seemed accommodating about managing the yard and gardens. She was nice. Okay, really nice.

Maybe too nice?

And her kid was cute.

But my head definitely didn't go there.

Still, I nod.

Tabitha's palm slaps against the granite countertop, and a triumphant grin emerges on her face. "Excellent. Great. Good talk." She slides off the stool, but not before taking one longing glance back over the space. "It's a nice kitchen. Nothing better than cooking with a view."

"You like to cook?"

A soft smile touches her lips now. "You could say that."

I move past the island, padding across the hardwood floors, drawn to her chaos and unpredictability. But she's already walking toward the door.

Blowing out the way she blew in. Confident and direct, but also…tentative.

You could say that.

It makes me wonder what's written between the lines of that response. This entire encounter also makes me wonder what the story with her sister is.

"Should I be worried about her? Your sister. As a tenant?"

After toeing on her sandals, she straightens and faces me once more. The evening sun filters in from the windows surrounding the front door, illuminating her features in a warm glow. Her cheeks have a pink tint, like she's just a little bit embarrassed for barging in here and oversharing. For interfering.

"She's a girl who got injured playing volleyball in high school and was prescribed something she shouldn't have been. She's been low. Really low. But she's healthy now. She's gotten help. I swear. She's a good mom. And she'll be a good tenant. I promise."

"Okay." I dip my chin and shove my hands into the pockets of my gray sweats. We've all hit rough patches. Far be it from me to hold that over the head of a woman I barely know.

"But…"

I glance back up slowly, not liking the sound of that *but*.

"If—and this is a big if—she ever falls behind on rent, can you please call me? Day, night, whenever. I want her somewhere safe. I want a roof over her head. I want Milo happy and safe. I will pay if it comes to it."

She slips a business card from her back pocket and holds it out to me. I reach for it—probably a little too eagerly. My fingers pinch the card stock, and I can see *The Bighorn Bistro* printed on it, but when I go to pull, she doesn't let go.

My eyes snap to hers, and I can see the ferocity burning in them. She holds her opposite hand up, pinky finger extended. "Pinky swear."

"Pinky swear?"

This encounter just keeps getting stranger.

"Yes. Pinky swear to me that you will call me if there's a problem."

I hold my pinky up with a deep chuckle. "You know these aren't legally binding, right?"

Her finger curls around mine as her eyes point like

arrows in my direction. "I know, but only a total asshole breaks a pinky promise."

The woman is dead serious. And I'm too off-kilter to deny her.

"I pinky promise," I reply gruffly.

She watches me for a beat, as though judging the truthfulness of my promise. Then she nods and draws away. Without another word, she pulls the front door open and saunters out of my house. And I just stand there, arm propped on the doorframe, trying to wrap my head around that conversation.

That woman.

The one who, further down the front walkway, turns and peeks back over her shoulder.

And I catch her looking. Or she catches me looking. To be honest, I don't really care which one it is.

I just know that usually I go out of my way to hide from too much attention.

But I don't mind the way she looks at me.

CHAPTER 1

Tabitha

TWO YEARS LATER

THE YELLOW DOOR BEFORE ME IS ALTOGETHER TOO CHEER-ful for a day like today.

Scuffs near the keyhole tell a story of full hands and rushed attempts to open the door. There's a pink splatter over the canary gold at the bottom. Likely the only evidence of a grape-juice-box-meets-the-ground type of crime scene.

Milo loves grape juice.

His mom does too.

Did.

Erika *loved*—past tense—grape juice.

Heat builds behind my lashes, and I blink away the tears. Crying isn't going to see me through this job. Everyone around me has been crying. I can't start too.

If I start, I worry I won't know how to stop. Then shit won't get done. And that's my job right now.

Take care of her little boy. Navigate my parents' grief. Run my restaurant.

Get shit done.

Numb is preferable. So, I push aside the urge to cry and roll from toe to heel a few times, as though I might be able to rock myself forward. Into motion.

Toward my dead sister's abandoned townhome to collect her belongings.

I both need to go in there and dread going in there. My lips twist in a sardonic smirk. Erika would have gotten a real kick out of this. Me wringing my hands on her front step too chicken-shit to even face what she left behind. I suspect she's somewhere watching me with a grin on her face right now. She'd say something like, "You just identified my body. Vampirism takes more than twenty minutes to take effect."

I chuckle at my own made-up joke.

She wasn't perfect—hell, I'm not either—but her dark sense of humor was spot on.

"Okay, Erika, I'm going. I'm going," I mutter in an amused tone, digging out the spare key I've been holding onto for two years.

I had it made when I helped her move in here and haven't needed to use it until now. Mostly because I thought she was doing okay. I've always known that addiction is a lifelong battle. I just thought she was holding the line.

I thought wrong.

The key clicks when I slide it in, and the door gives way

when I grip the handle and press my thumb onto the lever. Sucking in a deep breath, I wait to see if any strong smells register. Nothing comes.

Judgmental little bitch.

I can hear Erika taunting me, clear as day. Somehow, this entirely imaginary interaction brings me a sense of comfort. As a kid, she'd have killed me for going into her room. Borrowing her clothes or makeup always ended in a cat fight.

But we also always made up.

I chuckle darkly and shake my head. "Okay, sissy." My arm straightens as I push the door open. "I'm going to take your jewelry and there's nothing you can do about it this time."

Milo will want her things one day. I want him to have memories of her. Good ones.

With that in my head, my foot finally leaves the ground and I move to step into the house.

But a deep, foreboding voice brings me up short, and I freeze. "What the fuck do you think you're doing?"

My heart rate accelerates as I slowly turn away from the door. And then my eyes land on *him*.

Rhys. Her landlord. The one who evicted her without a second fucking thought.

In an instant, my urge to cry evaporates. Instead, I feel the urge to rage on the hulking man standing on the front lawn, staring daggers at me.

If Milo didn't need me, I'd kill this big fucker with my bare hands and march myself to prison, convinced that I'd fulfilled my life's purpose.

For now, I opt to clench my molars and glare back as I bite out as few words as possible. "I won't take long." I have three days to pack up all of my big sister's worldly possessions and then I never have to set foot in this godforsaken town again.

The man's head tilts, and a loose piece of dark hair flops over his forehead. It's too long, and he's used a touch too much product, making it appear almost wet. I focus on how unappealing that one piece of hair is so that my eyes don't look at the rest of him.

The impossibly wide shoulders, the towering height, the dangerously dark eyes. Everything about this man screams *sex*.

I already know that he's physically appealing.

But now I also know that he's indirectly responsible for Erika's overdose. And I hate him for it.

"You can't go in there." His tone hedges no room for debate.

"Legally, I *can* go in there."

He crosses his arms, which, with the size of his biceps, looks borderline uncomfortable. "Your name isn't on the lease, and I never gave you a key. I doubt Erika did either." A tendon pulses in his jaw, and the disdain in his gaze intensifies my anger.

"You doubt Erika did?" I repeat the words and almost laugh as they leave my lips. "You've got a lot of nerve acting like you speak for her."

"Says the woman who just announced she was going in to take jewelry. We both know she wouldn't want you in there."

My mouth pops open. How dare he pretend he knows what terms my sister and I were on. "Are you fucking kidding me right now?"

He stands taller, like a sentinel guarding a castle. It infuriates me. Where was this sense of contractual integrity when he booted her without honoring the pinky promise we made?

That agreement may have been childish, but it meant something to me.

The asshole's facial expression gives nothing away. His delivery is perfectly even. "Not a joke in sight. If you want to enter the unit, you'll need Erika's permission."

I bark out a loud, disbelieving laugh and shake my head at him. "Right, well, since you're the Erika expert now, I'll just wait here while you head down to the morgue and ask her permission."

The mountain of a man flinches as though I slapped him, but then he takes a stuttered step forward, eyes searching. "Come again?"

"My sister is dead."

God, saying it out loud is a shot to the heart. My voice cracks, but I forge ahead.

"My emotional bandwidth is shot, and my desire to talk to you is non-existent. I'm next of kin, so if you want to call the cops and have me removed from the property"—I wave a dramatic hand over the front lawn as if welcoming a crowd to a show—"please be my guest."

With that, I spin and barge into the house. I'm about to slam the door in his face with a flourish when he's suddenly *there*. Crowding me, towering over me, one massive hand gripping the door and keeping it from hitting him in the face. I can feel the heat of his body, sense the threat in his stance, and smell the cinnamon of his hair product.

"And Milo?" His voice is all gravel, and I swear there's a threat in his rough tone. One I don't fucking appreciate.

But I also recognize his concern over the small boy because I feel it too. *Acutely*.

I let my eyes crash against his, both confused and agitated by his distress.

What I see in his dark irises is an apocalypse of storms. Fire and brimstone. And I'm certain mine are no better. As his gaze traces my face, I let my hatred take center stage on every feature. Wanting to show him I'm not standing down, no matter how much he stomps around like he's the fucking man of the house or whatever this territorial show is.

I decide on as little information as possible, but enough to get him to leave. "Milo is happy and safe."

A brief flash of relief touches the man's features as he retreats incrementally.

A soft moment.

A perfect spot for me to strike.

"I *pinky promise*," I add cynically.

And then I slam the door in his face.

ACKNOWLEDGMENTS

Wild Eyes is a story that will live in my head—and my heart—for a very long time. Not only because Skylar and West possess that cosmic sort of soul mate vibe I love so much, but also because I poured so much of myself and my own insecurities into this book. Writing is an incredibly vulnerable profession. Putting your stories out to the public is always nerve-wracking and anxiety inducing. And publishing a book is ever easy, but learning to love my words and my characters in an unshakable way makes it easier.

It's being able to say: I hope you loved this book as much as me…but actually that would be impossible because I will forever love it the most.

But of course, a lot of other people have loved it along the way. A book—like a child—takes a village to grow into something that is ready for readers. Luckily, I have one of the very best villages a girl could ask for. So, I really need to thank everyone who helped me make this story what is today.

First, the biggest songwriting shoutout to Alyssa Brigiotta for writing *Photosythesis* and to both Alyssa and Leticia Teixeira for collaborating on writing *Wild Eyes*! You ladies are INCREDIBLE. You are both so talented and generous. I am beyond grateful to have your support and beyond proud to have your songs in my books. Thank you for sharing your words with the world.

My husband, my constant source of book boyfriend inspiration and most supportive cheerleader. I can't imagine my life without you.

My son, my sunshine. My happy boy who makes even the worst days feel so much better. I love you to the moon and back.

My assistant, Krista. As of writing this we've worked together for two whole years, and I just know there are many more to come. Thank you for keeping me organized and sane.

My friend, Catherine Cowles. The person I write with pretty much every day. I'll never stop thanking the universe for bringing us together. I don't have a sister, but you feel like one.

My girls, Lena Hendrix and Kandi Steiner. The cheer squad, the safe space, two of the most incredibly talented and kindhearted women I know. This job would be a hell of a lot lonelier without you. Love you big.

My editor, Paula Dawn. This is our ELEVENTH book together. I doubt I can write one without you and your brain.

Retirement is when I say so. Thank you for all the notes in the margins.

My sensitivity reader and clinical therapist, Jill, who shared so many expert opinions to make sure these characters were represented correctly. Thank you especially for helping me see Skylar through her journey.

My beta reader/proofreader, Leticia, and my beta reader Júlia. The time you ladies spent on this book with me helped make it what it is. The voice memos, the suggestions, the constant hair-petting—you're stuck with me.

Aimee Ashcraft, your feedback was utterly invaluable. No doubt in my mind that this book would not be as good as it is without having had your hands on it. Thank you.

My agent, Kimberly Brower. The woman, the myth, the legend. Lol. Jk. Kinda? But honestly, it's such an honor to work with you. Your dedication is unparalleled and I'm so fortunate to have you on my side. But also, please never take me for tea.

My editor, Christa Désir, and the entire team at Bloom Books. You all worked so hard on this book and I am forever grateful. Thank you from the bottom of my heart for taking a chance on me. I literally pinch myself every time I see my books in stores.

My editor, Rebekah West, and the entire team at Piatkus and Hachette. Thank you, thank you for believing in me and for sharing my books with the world. Seeing them in the hands of readers from so many places is such a thrill.

Finally, to my readers. You blow me away every day. Your love. Your support. Your excitement. I'm so lucky to have every last one of you. Thank you for trusting me and following me to Rose Hill. I hope you love it here as much as I do.

I've said it before, and I'll say it again: Elsie readers are the best readers.

xo,
Elsie

ABOUT THE AUTHOR

Elsie Silver is a *New York Times* bestselling Canadian author of sassy, sexy, small-town romance who loves good book boyfriends and the strong heroines who bring them to their knees. She lives just outside Vancouver, British Columbia, with her husband, son, and three dogs and has been voraciously reading romance books since before she was probably supposed to.

She loves cooking and trying new foods, traveling, and spending time with her boys—especially outdoors. Elsie has also become a big fan of her quiet 5:00 a.m. mornings, which is when most of her writing happens. It's during this time that she can sip a cup of hot coffee and dream up a fictional world full of romantic stories to share with her readers.

Website: elsiesilver.com
Facebook: authorelsiesilver
Instagram: @authorelsiesilver